SMALL IRONIES

a novel

J. Peter Bergman

authorHOUSE®

AuthorHouse™
1663 Liberty Drive
Bloomington, IN 47403
www.authorhouse.com
Phone: 1-800-839-8640

First published by AuthorHouse   2/24/2011

ISBN: 978-1-4567-2316-3 (sc)
ISBN: 978-1-4567-2314-9 (hc)
ISBN: 978-1-4567-2315-6 (e)

Library of Congress Control Number: 2011901199

Printed in the United States of America

Acknowledgments

When, in 2002, I received an award from the New York Chapter of the Friends of Charles Dickens for my collection of short fiction, *Counterpoints*, I was inspired to try my hand at serial fiction, ala Dickens. On my website, BerkshireBrightFocus.com, I began a series of short stories geared to the number of Sundays in a given month and wrote these tales in four or five segments. Dickens had written many of his best novels and novellas for newspaper publication in much the same fashion and I finally felt compelled to try a novel. I predicted it in fifty-two chapters, decided on a prologue and epilogue and armed with a theme and a goal for that theme, embarked on *Small Ironies* in 2008. The book, in three parts, took sixty weeks to complete. There was no outline and only a vague list of characters when I began writing.

The story developed a following of readers who often e-mailed questions, suggestions and comments. A few have begged for a sequel, but there are no plans for such a book at this time. Instead, at the request of several folks who seemed to love Max and Freddy and their trials and woes, this book has been prepared. Special thanks go to Johnna Murray for her insights and her willingness to share, in depth, her reactions.

Many changes have taken place in the narrative. Chapters have been re-ordered. Events have been illuminated. Relationships have been re-examined and the result of this eight months of rewrites, I think, has been a better book than the original version. The story is still the same, in case you are worried about that.

With thanks to those who responded to the novel on line and to the various members of the Lee (MA) Fiction Writers who often listened to me reading sections and whose comments are always of great importance and implicit use, here is the novel in its final form.

This book is dedicated to the memory of Ruth Percival Bergman.

Chapters in Max's voice open with items quoted from the April, 1946 edition, Volume 48, No 288 of Reader's Digest, published by The Reader's Digest Association, Inc., Pleasantville, NY.

Chapters in Freddy's voice open with items quoted from The Dictionary of Phrase & Fable by E. Cobham Brewer, published 1978 by Avenal Books, distributed by Crown Publishers, Inc., NY.

Chapters in Vinnie's voice open with items quoted from The International Thesaurus of Quotations, compiled by Eugene Ehrlich and Marshall De Bruehl, published 1996 by Harper Perennial, a division of HarperCollins, NY.

Chapter's in Paul's voice open with items quoted from Theatre Language by William Parker Bowman and Robert Hamilton Ball, published 1961 by Theatre Arts Books, NY.

In Chapter Nine: Edna St. Vincent Millay quote from Make Bright the Arrows (1940); in Chapter Forty-Four: quote from Keen, from The Harp Weaver and Other Poems (1928); in Chapter Forty-Four, Dirge from Second April (1922), used with permission from the Edna St. Vincent Millay Society, Elizabeth Barnett, Literary Executor.

In Chapter Ten: Lyrics to "S'Wonderful" by Ira Gershwin, published 1927

"SMALL IRONIES"
a novel
by J. Peter Bergman

PROLOGUE: April, 1946

From The Reader's Digest, April, 1946:

From Spotlight on Today: "The manager of a midtown
New York hotel quit his job the other day. He now
works as a waiter there. He has fewer headaches & and
makes more money!"
Dorothy Kilgallen, King Features

Small ironies erupt around my birth. My father, the manager of a midtown
New York hotel quits his job. The stress has caused him to live with a
twitch that never leaves his face, it seems. His left hand has developed a
tremor all its own and he cannot hold me in his arms. We need money to
live, my mother, I'm told, keeps saying this over and over, and my father
has taken the only job he can find, working as a waiter in the same hotel
he ruled for eleven years. He only takes orders now, works a sane schedule
and makes a bundle in tips. In part this is the result of his former job in
the building. He knows which rooms are available and can advise his
customers in the small bar in the hotel as to where they can adjourn for
an hour to make love, make whatever perverted sort of passion come to
life. For this knowledge, more than for his memory of who ordered which

1

cocktail, he is rewarded with cash. My mother is satisfied. We live well. My father, whose conscience never allowed him to indulge clients of the hotel in this way when he managed the place, now has no conscience at all, it would appear. He lives for the money. He holds himself completely free of the cares that would otherwise bind him to report malfeasance, to avoid corruption. He serves drinks. He sells information. He, himself, is not corrupt. He is feeding his family.

My older sister, eleven years older to be exact, has decided this April to become a prostitute when she is old enough. She has confided this fact to only one person, our grandmother. Granny Elainie is pleased to know that her grandchild has elected the old family profession without even prior knowledge of Elainie's own outrageous youth. Briana - my sister - it turns out, doesn't know what a prostitute does; she only knows that there is good money to be made and you don't have to work in the daytime. She loves the daylight hours. Her passion is to sleep late, breakfast at noon and go to bed about eleven o'clock. Somewhere she has learned that prostitutes work in the evening. That suits her timetable perfectly. When she tells Granny Elainie about her decision she honestly believes that prostitutes are nothing more or less than women who go to dinner with gentlemen and then dance with them. That is her belief at age eleven. Granny won't fill her in on the finer details for another two years when Briana suddenly develops breasts. Remarkably Briana is not discouraged by the full disclosure.

I, on the other hand, know very little two years later. In April, 1948 I am still the perfect innocent. I don't know about my father, mother, my grandmother or my sister. I know them, of course, but not about them. That takes longer. But I am already a prostitute; I am one who "sells himself for an unworthy purpose." I am a baby model. My face and hands and body are up for grabs. I sell inferior baby products: food, clothing, toys. My joyous expressions convince millions of mothers and fathers, doting aunts and uncles, gullible grandparents to purchase products which, in the long run, may indeed prove to be harmful to the children who relish these gifts.

The family profession, it seems, goes forward. Small ironies.

CHAPTER ONE

From Reader's Digest, April, 1946"

From Hollywood Spot Light: "Edna Ferber was invited to a studio to see a film that had been made from one of her manuscripts.

'It's a good picture,' she said afterward, 'but it isn't my story. I wonder if you'll let me buy my story back'"

The movie magnates finally agreed to sell it back. 'But,' they said, 'you've got to give us an option on the movie rights.'"

Walter Winchell

The hotel where my father worked, the year I was born, was the Excelsior Grand on West 38th Street. It was a reasonably fashionable place, especially for the opera singers at the Metropolitan - that's the old Met, not the new one, of course - because they could get back and forth easily, the stage door being only a block and a half away. My father knew many of them well. In fact, according to Briana, he knew two of them extremely well, close and well. It makes me laugh to think about that, because he knew nothing about their music, didn't even like it very much. There was a period of time, I was about twenty, when they had a subscription series at the Met - that's the new Met, not the old ne - and he always complained about going, literally begged me to take her. But it was the singers, not the songs, that held him in thrall in the 1940s.

"Helga says she can't stand the new line," he told my mother once when I was still an infant. It's a sentence I remember hearing, obviously not understanding, but hearing it anyway. What caught my ear in that first year of my life and stayed with me was the oddness of it, I suppose. I could recognize words, even grasp their meaning sometimes, but not restate them in any coherent fashion, a not unusual situation I suppose for a child of less than one year old. "Helga says she can't stand the new line." What could that mean? Even today I don't truly grasp the nuance, the hidden revelation.

Helga, it turned out, was the Wagnerian soprano my father had befriended at his hotel: Helga Meerstadt. And the "new line," what the hell was that? Clothing? Music? I never knew for sure. Now, now that I'm older and I fully understand the family history, the family profession, I wonder if that was a code, a buzz-word for some sexual by-play, something too outside the limits for Frau Meerstadt to indulge in during those idle hours in a room upstairs at the Excelsior Grand.

My father's other operatic companion was the American basso Paul Donner. He was from California. He was tall, elegant, with dark flashing eyes and bright, overly white teeth. Donner had a rich, lush voice and even when he spoke there was a clarity and a strength that made your blood boil over, your skin tingle. I think he was the sexiest male singer in the classical music world of his day. He made three movies. I've seen them all. In them he overacts and his hammy gestures and his speaking voice don't seem connected. In real life, and I saw him quite a lot up until I was about ten, he was just plain dynamic, just plain sexy. You couldn't avoid the animal side of this man and when he opened his mouth and sang, that voice ran over you like molten silver. It heated up everyone in the room, female, male, it made no difference. Any room where he sang became an intimate space. Carnegie Hall, the Met, our living room, it didn?t matter. He lassoed you with that dark sound and reeled you in like a heifer at a rodeo.

They were both married in 1946, Donner and Meerstadt, though not to one another. His wife lived on their ranch in California and raised chickens and artichokes. Her husband lived outside of Vienna and analyzed sex-starved women and sex-crazed men. I met them each just once. But in 1946, the year I was born, and the year my father was a waiter and not the manager of the Excelsior Grand, Donner and Meerstadt were lovers and my father arranged for the room. He was their connection. He was, for all intents and purposes, their pimp. They each paid him handsomely for his friendship and his services. His "tips, " going out and coming in, were proof that his pudding had gelled nicely.

My father had a successful career going and he had an eleven year old daughter and a newborn son, a wife and a mother-in-law, my Granny, and he had his parents as well. He had a rich existence. He was content, well reasonably content, I suppose. He also had a brother and sister-in-law, my Uncle Frank, my Aunt Gussie.

Frank and Gussie were older than my parents. They had been married for seventeen years at that point in time and they were still childless, a situation my mother loved to bring up every time Frank or Gussie got the slightest bit judgmental about my father and his "career."

This conversation I am about to relate is not one I remember. I don't recall a single word of it personally, but I heard my mother repeat it and repeat it incessantly during the years I spent listening to her every word, worshiping the family stories she liked to tell. This is how she related the incident that I don't remember.

It was over dinner at our apartment. Only family was present. The main course had been consumed and dessert was underway. Granny Elainie was in the kitchen dishing out the Apple Brown Betty when the argument began, so she only heard part of it, only participated in the final moments.

"I think it's disgusting," Aunt Gussie apparently said, starting the fight.

"Gussie, don't go on," Uncle Frank added quickly.

"And there are children," she said before he had even finished admonishing her.

"Gussie, mind your own business," my mother said firmly.

"You shut up!" Gussie responded. "You have no right to...."

"No right? In my own house, no right?"

"Come on, ladies...Gussie, please," my father said.

"Don't you call her a lady, Jimmy. Any real lady is offended by that!" Gussie retorted, heaving her breasts upward, her arms crossed firmly, supporting them.

"She is my wife!" my father said, slamming his large, flat hand down on the table and making the glassware ring.

"Your choice, not mine," Gussie shouted.

"Gussie, please, keep your voice down, the children..." Uncle Frank hissed at her.

"The children? The children? The children should know who their mother is," my aunt spat back at him.

"My children know their mother, know who she is, what and how she is," my mother said. "Don't you babies?"

Briana, eleven years old, said quickly, "I hate you Aunt Gussie. Your twat is dead. No babies for you."

"Don't say those words, Briana," my father shouted at her, although apparently he was smiling when he said it.

"Did you hear her? Did you hear her language? How can she say such a thing to me?" Aunt Gussie cried.

"You brought in on yourself, Gussie," Uncle Frank told her.

"Dried up old man," Briana continued, pointing her finger at Uncle Frank. "Dried up gizzum. No babies for you."

"Where does she learn this language?" Aunt Gussie shrieked.

"From me, you hideous hag." Granny Elainie had come in from the kitchen and overheard this last part, I guess. "You prune, you pissant, you heinous heartless half-a-harlot. You don't even have the good sense to sell what no one can disturb."

"Elainie! You shock me," Aunt Gussie sounded like she was whimpering when she said this, my mother always told us.

"Do I? Good. Your system could take a few shocks. Might be the best thing for it."

"Mama, please," my father said, but she waved him off with a flaccid gesture.

"You owe these people, your generous hosts, an apology, Gussie. You owe them an apology so big *you* should hit the streets and work the men until you can repay them for this vile humiliation with dirty dollars you earn on your knees in back alleys."

According to my mother, Aunt Gussie fainted dead away at this concept and had to be taken home in a taxi. Two weeks later, by the time of the next family dinner, all of this had been set aside, put away somewhere in a drawer with a lilac cachet to cover its stench. Everyone was nice to everyone and nothing was said. I don't know, to this day, if in between those two get-togethers something was said, or done, to put this all right. But somehow the family came together and nothing was said. It was supposedly a pleasant time, but I don't remember that either. That's just what I was told.

My immediate family. Now you know about them. I should tell more about me, for this is my story, not theirs, but without them there would be no me. There's a small irony buried in that statement. It's obvious that without my parents there would not have been a me. But the others you've met, Gussie and Frank, Granny Elainie and my sister Briana, had as much to do with forming me, creating me, as my own parents ever did when they were still alive.

When I was ten I read Charles Dickens's novel David Copperfield. Are you familiar with it? "I am born," he wrote. "I am born." Well, I was born, too, and I led a life that so mirrors young Davey's it sometimes confounds and confuses me, especially on those long nights in winter when memories flood the room where I sit with a brandy in a snifter on a table in front of a roaring fire. Music plays in this room, usually old opera recordings, mostly Paul Donner. His voice gets inside my body and swells it up, fills it with emotions and desires and even a tinge of sorrow. "I am born." I was raised. Some are raised up. I, oddly, was raised down.

CHAPTER TWO

Quoted in The Reader's Digest, April, 1946:

"A friend is a present you give yourself

-- Robert Louis Stevenson"

I had a friend when I was about five years old. We vowed to be best friends forever and he suggested we should be blood brothers. He was almost a whole year older, you see, and knew about these things.

His name, curiously was Robert Louis Stevenson, but he wasn't the same one. His parents had an apartment near ours, in the next building actually. We met one day when I was sitting on the front stoop watching traffic, something I seemingly adored at that age. At any rate, he came up the stairs and sat down next to me and imitated my pose, chin on cupped hands, elbows on knees, and he watched with me. We never spoke that day. When I'd had enough of this, I stood up and went into our building. He, I believe, stood up and went home to his own. I don't know for sure, because I didn't look around to see what he was doing.

A few days later we met on the street and he nodded solemnly to me and I returned the nod. As I moved a few steps past him, I heard him giggle and I laughed in return. Suddenly we had a secret. I don't think my mother realized what had happened that day. I don't know about his.

When we met for the third time he introduced himself and I was forced to do the same thing.

"I'm Robert Louis Stevenson," he said, extending his right hand, open and flat, palm up. "How do you do?"

"I do fine," I said. "Thanks."

"And who are you?"

I hesitated a moment. "I am...I am Maxwell Draper.

"I have three names."

"So do I!" I snapped that back at him. "Max. Well. Draper."

"Oh, okay," he said sweetly enough, "then I'll just call you Max. And you can call me Louie."

We shook hands, like the grownups always did when they came to an agreement. I knew right then that Louie would be my best friend and that I could tell him anything.

We saw a lot of each other that spring and summer. New York City was an easy place for children in 1951. It was safe for us to run around the block and play in the alleys behind our buildings. There were women on the steps of almost every building , hanging out of windows, shopping in the local stores. It seemed that there was always someone nearby who knew Louie or me or our parents or my sister. We were protected by the neighborhood, safe in our world. Cars didn't speed then. Or at least they never seemed to do so. Garbage cans were our fortresses. Fire escape ladders were our circus tents' center rings. We jumped, flew, hid and ran. We weren't angels, but we weren't devils either. We were two kids playing and two people developing personalities along the way. Louie, being slightly older, developed quickly, but I was keeping up with him most of the time.

It was late in August. We had been playing cops and robbers for hours and I was tired of the game. I dashed up the stairs of Louie's building and got myself a perfect top step seat on the stoop. The iron railing of his front stairs included wide bands of textured metal, painted black and at that particular point I could squeeze myself tiny behind three of them and be almost completely out of sight while maintaining a perfect view of the street below. I was in place when he came hightailing it out of the alley next door. He stopped at the curb and looked up and down the street for me, but he didn't see me. I saw his shoulders drop a bit and his neck bend forward so that his head could droop a bit. He looked tired to me. Then I heard him sob once. It hurt me to hear that. I didn't understand it.

Without hesitation I called out his name and stood up so he could see me behind the metal bars. He threw back his head and laughed and came quickly up the nine steps of his stoop, throwing himself down on top of me. It was a roughhouse sort of thing, a way of playing and we wrestled around a bit. Winded, he stopped suddenly and pulled back and stared at me.

"We should be blood brothers," he said. I nodded, not knowing what he was talking about. "Alvin told me about it. You don't know him. He lives in Brooklyn. He's my cousin."

"Okay," I said rather absently. That was all I said; I didn't understand a word of it.

"You don't know what that is, do you?" Louie asked me.

"No. What is it?"

"Well, it's like this," he said, "you make a cut in your wrist and I make a cut in mine and when we're bleeding good and hard we put our wrists together and our bloods mix and you get mine in you and I get yours in mine and we're blood brothers, forever and always."

"I'd have to cut my wrist?" I asked him.

"Sure. All guys do it."

"I don't know about that."

"Indians do it, too."

"I'm not an Indian," I told him.

"Well, they do it and we can do it. We're as good as any damn Indian."

"Better," I said. "My sister knows an Indian and she doesn't like him, but she likes you."

"How does your sister know an Indian?"

"She knows him at work," I said. Briana was fourteen now and she had a part time job in the drug store making sodas at the fountain. An Indian who worked on the bridges liked to come in and drink an egg cream every afternoon and she had talked to him.

"Golly gee," Louie said. "That sounds like something big."

"Yeah," I said, sorry I'd said it because my father always told me not to say 'yeah.'

"Well, we have to be blood brothers, Max. That's all there is to it."

I agreed and we decided to meet the next day and cut ourselves and become really best friend blood brothers forever and always. The truth was I didn't want to do it, but I knew I had to do it and that was that.

At dinner that night I didn't tell anyone about the plans that Louie and I had made that day. I was already afraid of what my mother might do but I had some questions about the bleeding and I had to ask someone something, so I brought up the subject after dinner. My father had gone back to the hotel to work a partial night shift and Briana wanted to listen to some dance music on the radio. So this would be a perfect opportunity to talk to mother.

"I have a question," I said to her.

"Is it about modeling, Maxie? I know you love to do it."

I did, but that wasn't my goal, as I told you, so I shook my head emphatically.

"Oh, all right then, what's on your mind?"

"Its about the bleeding," I started to say, but she grabbed me and put her hand over my mouth.

"It happens to me every month, darling, and it's nothing for you to worry about."

"You do it every month?" I asked her, not believing what I was hearing.

"Yes, all women do."

I stared at her not believing what I was hearing.

"You must have a lot of best friends," I said.

"Yes, I do, darling, why?"

"If you do it every month."

"I'm sorry?"

"I love you so much, and now I think you're terrific," I said and I hugged her very hard. She hugged me back and held me close to her heart. I could smell her perfume and her sweat all mixed together. Then she relaxed her grip.

"Maxie, I think it was very sweet of you to be so concerned about the bleeding, but there's nothing to worry about. I have these nice large pads to absorb the blood and in a few days I'm fine."

I knew the pads she meant. I'd seen them in her dresser drawer. It was an immediate decision that followed: I would take one and bring it with me for the bleeding ceremony. That would make things all right.

As soon as I could the next morning I stole into my parents room and took one of her absorbing pads and hid it in my pants. Right after lunch I went out to play and found Louie already waiting on my stoop.

"I found the perfect place to do it," he said. "Follow me."

I rushed off after him, entering the basement door of a building around the corner from the block on which we lived. It was dark in this basement hallway and I could barely see Louie who was still ahead of me. Then he pushed open a heavy metal door and stepped inside a lighted room. I followed him in. It was a laundry room. All of the machines were going and that made it both noisy and hot. I felt perspiration on my brow and I wiped it off with the back of my hand.

"I brought something," I said, "for the extra blood." I pulled out my mother's pad and showed it to him.

"You won't need that," Louie replied. "After we mix our blood, if there's any left, we can just put our arms in the washing machines."

That was clever. I would never have thought of that. I stuffed the pad back down my pants. I knew what we had to do, and this was the time to do it.

"Hold out your arm, Max," he said, and I did, shutting my eyes tight.

"You too," I said to him. "Okay, cut."

"With what?" he asked me. "Did you bring anything?"

I hadn't and, it turned out, neither had Louie. We didn't have a knife between us. Eyes open again, we looked around the room for some sort of sharp implement to use but there was absolutely nothing.

"What'll we do?" I asked him, a tightness in my throat.

"I don't know. I don't know." He stopped to think. I heard his sharp intake of breath that always signified an idea. "Yes, I do. I do know something."

He grabbed my pants and yanked them down around my hips. This sharpness of this act also pulled down my shorts. Before I could say anything he did the same thing with his own pants and underwear.

"What are we doing?" I shouted at him.

"Blood and piss, my old man always says, is the same thing. So we can piss and touch peepees and it will be just like the blood, don't you see?"

Well that actually made sense to me, so I nodded and we each took a step closer and touched our peepees but neither one of us made water. We just stood there like that waiting. It felt silly. Then Louie got another bright idea.

"You hold mine and I'll hold yours. Then it will be like we are each other. See?"

I saw. So we did that and still nothing much happened. I say much. I'm wrong there.

That was the moment when the door opened and a woman walked in. I believe she screamed, then she shouted, then she groaned. We didn't know what to do, so we just stood there as we were, holding on tight to each other's infantile penises. We were looking at her, not sure what we should do, but in less than a moment we knew what had to be done.

She grabbed us both by our ears and began to pull us apart. I grabbed for my pants with my one free hand and Louie did the same thing. My mother's pad fell to the floor. More screams ensued. For some reason I never understood we were still holding on to each other's baby parts. The woman began shouting for help, calling out to whomever could hear her, for assistance. It didn't take a lot of shouting for a crowd to gather, each new person seemingly upset by what they saw, although a few of them seemed to be laughing more than they were doing anything else.

The woman, a Mrs. Lowry, found out our names and dragged us home to our parents. Louie's folks were very angry, more at me than at Louie it seemed. My mother was outwardly upset, but later on she laughed and laughed as she told the story to my father. He thought it was a pretty funny tale and so did Granny Elainie. I don't remember what Briana thought or if she even knew about it. Aunt Gussie was disgusted and called me some sort of name, but I forgot about that pretty quickly because my mother loved the story so much.

Louie and his family moved a week later to some other neighborhood and I never saw him again, but I always think of him as my best friend, my blood brother, and the only person I really want to come hold my peepee for me. Ever.

CHAPTER THREE

From the Reader's Digest, April, 1946:

> "Earl of Devon's Epitaph:
> What we gave, we have;
> What we spent, we had;
> What we left, we lost."

Granny Elainie died when I was still young. I mean, really young. I was in the second grade. Eisenhower was President. It was 1953. She wasn't sick or even old, not really old, not like some people are old. Granny Elainie was the youngest of us in so many ways. She had spirit and energy. She had life licked. She couldn?t be phased. Not really; well, not often, really. And she didn?t die, or live, on being Granny Elainie. For most of the people who knew her she was just Elainie. Mr. Compton, though, held on to the version of her when she was Lainie.

Lainie Silver was her name when she knew Mr. Compton. She showed me pictures of when she was Lainie Silver. She was beautiful. She looked like Elizabeth Taylor looked in the year that Granny died. The 1953 Liz was the 1931 Lainie, a version of the Liz from "Ivanhoe,' from "A Place in the Sun," shining and pure and almost too beautiful to look directly at her.

I still have the photo of her in front of the billiard parlor where she hung out with her friend Tooie. They had grown up together and even though Tooie was a lesbian, Lainie hung out with her. Granny Elainie was a faithful friend to those she pledged to love and Tooie was one of the first. I was the last one and she was always faithful to me, too.

But Mr. Compton was a story and a half.

Mr. Compton was the man who ruined Lainie for other men. My grandmother's words there, not mine. When they met, she told me, the earth moved for her and that had never happened before. It's not like she was a virgin when they met, not like she hadn't been sleeping with men for money or even for love sometimes. Lainie Silver was a career girl whose career started at the top and stayed there for a long, long time. She was a dominant lover, she told me - saying it was the best position. I didn't get it then. I do now, of course. But Mr. Compton changed her mind, turned her around, flipped her over, let her feel her power ebb as he made her happier than she felt she had any right to feel. She fell in love with Mr. Compton and he loved her just as much as she loved him. Of course, there were things he didn't know about her at that time and when he found out what she was, who she was, it hurt him and that hurt them.

Granny Elainie told me the story of his becoming aware. It went like this:

"We were in bed together, Maxie. We'd been in bed together for, I don't know, four hours or five maybe and I was thirsty, so I asked him for a drink. When he got up to fetch me water from the sink across the room, he tripped on my handbag. He fell hard on the floor, hitting his head on the Morris Chair in the corner where they kept it in this hotel room. But he laughed. He wasn't hurt, you see, and he laughed. But when he tried to stand back up, he fell again because his foot was caught in the strap on the handbag. That's what did it, Maxie. That's when the contents spilled out and he saw the photograph."

'What photograph?' I asked her each time she got to this point in the story. She liked to be prompted. She didn't need it, but she liked it.

"It was a picture of your mommy and me. You know the picture," and she'd turn to the photo album in her lap and open it automatically to the page where that very picture resided, tucked into its four black paper corners that held it fast to the black paper page. She'd point to the picture, then thump it with her fingernail. I always liked it when she did that. I liked the sound her fingernail made against the glossy paper. "This picture. The picture I love the best of your mommy and me."

It was a photograph taken when my mother was about ten years old. She was a true miniature of Granny Elainie. The two of them, so blonde, so perky, their faces in identical smiles with their high cheek bones shoved into blushes by the fun they seem to be having. When I asked Granny

Elainie who took the picture she just shrugged. "Not someone you'd like to know," was all she said.

"But you look so happy, you both look so happy," I'd exclaim.

"It's a look, Maxie. It's a look that suited us, that's all."

"But I want to know who...?"

"So, Mr. Compton saw the picture and he knew right away that the woman was me and he could see, from how much alike we were, that we were related and he could also see that I was a lot older than the little girl, so he knew right away that this wasn't my little sister, but my daughter, so he wasn't too happy about that."

When she would finish this speech about Mr. Compton's distress she would sometimes start to cry a little, but she could pull back from that quickly and she would and she'd go on with the story without needing a prompt.

"He never got me the water, Maxie. Instead he came back to the bed and he sat down and he held my hand in silence for a long time and then he looked up at me and there were tears in his eyes. That's when he asked me the hard question, that is it was hard for him to ask and not for me to answer. 'Lainie, tell me,' he said looking me straight in the face, 'this little girl...she's your daughter, so you weren't a virgin with me?' Well, Maxie, I wanted to laugh but he was so sincere and looking me in the face when he said it, so I told him 'no, I'm not a virgin, not now, not when we met, not for years already.'"

"Did that make him mad?" I asked her.

"Mad? Mr. Compton? No, he was never mad. He was never mean, not like some could be mean. He wasn't even so upset, really. He was just disappointed in me."

"What happened then?" I was back to prompting her, even though I knew what came next.

"So he got up from the bed and came around to stand in front of me. He was naked, you know. I sat up in the bed and looked at him, he was a magnificent specimen, and he was getting aroused a little bit. I let my breasts show on top of the sheet I was holding close to me and he said, 'Lainie, would you kiss it?' And I said, 'Mr. Compton, what do you think of me? I'm no whore.' And he cried and he knelt by the bed and he hugged me and he kissed my breasts and he swore he would always love me, always be true to me in his heart. It was so beautiful, but I knew what it meant. It meant the ecstasy that was Mr. Compton was over for me."

"Why was mommy a secret, Granny Elainie?"

17

"I wasn't such a youngster anymore, Maxie. For a man like Mr. Compton who wanted a virgin, a young and unspoiled woman, a mother wasn't in the cards."

"But he loved you, right?"

"He loved me, yes. But he loved the woman who was Lainie Silver, and not the mother who was Elainie Silverman."

"But you were both of them!" I always shouted at that point throwing my little arms in the air. Granny Elainie loved it when I did that. She would grab me high across the chest and hug me and my little arms would fall on her shoulders and I'd laugh because she was tickling me.

"And he was always true to you? Always faithful?"

"He never really married. All his life he was never truly married."

"And you were right not to kiss his peepee," I said, "because you weren't a whore."

"That's right. I wasn't a whore. I was a prostitute, but never with Mr. Compton. It's very possible, Maxie, that I loved Mr. Compton for more reasons than how he made me feel when he was on top. I think I loved him for his gentle ways and his polite manners. The first time we were in bed together and he made love to me he cried because he believed he had taken my youth from me. That last time, with the photograph," and here she would tap the picture once again, "I think he cried because he knew it must be the final time."

"But why? If he loved you, why?"

"He was a little bit disgraced, Maxie. He was ashamed he hadn't had the sense to know a woman from a girl. He was upset because now he understood that I knew he had been the virgin when we met. He was disgraced with himself."

"Did you ever see him again, Granny Elainie?"

"Did I ever see him again? Naturally. He married my girlfriend, Tooie, the lesbian. That way he could stay close to me and stay faithful to me as well because it's a well known fact that lesbians don't do sex with men. That's how he showed me how faithful he could be to me. But he ruined me for other men, Maxie. I could never love again either, so if it wasn't for money it wasn't happening."

Granny Elainie told me this story about twenty-five times in the years before she died. Each time the story was exactly the same as it had been the time before and the time before that time. She never varied in it. But it wasn't until she died that I ever met Mr. Compton or even saw him.

He came to the funeral. My mother pointed him out to me, because she knew that Granny Elainie had told me this particular story. He was across the room and when he saw us he nodded solemnly. My mother nodded back to him and beckoned him over. He put his hat on a chair and then walked over to where we were standing.

"You look a little like her," he said, but I wasn't sure if he meant my mother or me when he said it.

"Mr. Compton, this is my son, Maxwell, Elainie's grandchild."

I held out my hand, very manly, and he took it and gave it a perfect single shake.

"I'll miss your grandmother very much," he said. "Very much."

"She said you were always faithful," I told him.

"So she mentioned me?" He nodded a few times. "I'm very pleased to hear it."

"She loved you too," I whispered to him. He nodded again and then he put his hand over his eyes, his head still nodding slightly. When he stopped nodding and he removed his hand I could see the remains of his tears in the palm of his hand, but his face was dry. He looked up at my mother and he spoke.

"I made a mistake with Lainie. I should have asked her to marry me right then, right there."

"She wasn't the marrying kind," my mother said gently.

"So true," he said. Then he stood up very straight and looked at me again. "You remind me of her, Maxwell. You have her eyes." I blushed. "And you have her coloring, too," he said.

"They were very close," my mother added.

"It's a pleasure to finally meet you both," he said and he was turning away, about to return to his hat.

"How's Tooie?" I asked suddenly in a voice a bit too loud perhaps. He stopped and turned back to me and looked very hard at me. Then he smiled and I could see right away why Granny Elainie had loved him.

"That's a sweet question to ask. Would you care to meet her?"

"Is she here?" I asked him, a bit too eagerly.

"Here? No. She couldn't come here. But someday I could take you to her if you don't mind the trip. She would love to see you."

"Could I, Mommy?" I asked. My mother closed her eyes and bit her lower lip before answering. "We'll see, darling," was all she said to me.

Mr. Compton nodded again and went back to his seat being held by his hat. And then we buried Granny Elainie and what we left, we lost.

CHAPTER FOUR

FromThe Reader's Digest, April, 1946:

> From Collected Letters of John Q. Public: "A North
> Dakota radio station received a letter from a Minnesota
> listener which said: 'I know that you will be interested
> to know that after listening to your program for over
> a year I now have a baby.'"
>
> Editor & Publisher

My mother became well-acquainted with John Q. Public. Her mother,
Granny Elainie, introduced them around 1935, eleven years before I
was born. It was that night of sexual initiation that helped move the
family profession forward into a new generation and Granny Elainie was
determined to be the one who decided the when, where, how and who of
this first step into the big time for her daughter. Not that she was totally
inexperienced by then. She was nineteen, after all, and she'd been out with
boys, even with older men, by then, and she had learned a thing or two
about keeping her pride and her passions in reasonable balance. Quite a few
of her swains had made their moves and been politely rebuffed, although
one or two of them had made it to what was already quaintly being referred
to as 'second base.' Or at least that's what she told me one drunken night
in a rental apartment in Far Rockaway, New York where we spent the
summer I was eight years old.

So, at nineteen, Granny Elainie introduced her daughter to the delights of doing it "right" and "not for all night," as she liked to say. She also taught her child-turned-woman about doing it for cash.

"If you have to do it at all," she said to her daughter, Lana, "then make it worthwhile. Let me tell you how its done," and she proceeded to do exactly that. She explained everything from coitus to cunnilingus and all the various techniques a provocative woman could use with a man. She went into lengthy detailed descriptions of various hygiene practices and she was very deliberate in explaining about the money. "What they get to do depends on what they pay, and pay up front," she said. "You, the woman, are always in control. Never the man. You take the cash, count it, stash it safely and then, and only then, do you do anything."

My mother listened carefully to every word of the lecture on business, principals and habits. She was a good student, I guess, because she became very popular right away, at least according to her and to Granny Elainie. She had a career upswing at twenty-one when she met a man named Byron. Byron was wealthy, handsome and a confirmed bachelor. He was in the business of importing European antiques and he was in need of a classy looking woman to escort him to upper class affairs where he could do business. Lana, he decided, could be that one.

It was an odd move in her career. She basically had to give up all of the other men who came to see her, took her places and did her. It worked out, though, because Byron paid her very well for her time and she wasn't always having to wash places that were being used by clients. Instead she could dress well, go to parties, go to the theater and the opera and be admired by lots of people, women and men, who had no idea who she was or what she did for a living. Byron made up the difference in her life and for a while she even played with the concept of marrying him. But that wasn't in the cards.

First of all, he wasn't going to marry her or anyone. Secondly, sex with him only happened once in a while and she wasn't enjoying that part very much; he wasn't a good lover. Thirdly, she met my father.

They met at one of those parties Byron took her to as his lady-beard. It was held in a suite at the Excelsior Grande Hotel on West 38th Street, the hotel my father managed. When Byron and Lana arrived for the party, he had a small suitcase filled with beautiful platinum boxes from some estate in Austria. He had just acquired them and he had a client who was probably going to like them very much. They weighed a lot, so he had asked for someone to carry the suitcase for him and my father, as the manager, took that responsibility on himself. He knew that whatever Byron was selling was valuable, so he wouldn't trust this job to a bellhop. He and Lana met in the elevator going up to the nineteenth floor.

In those days the elevators were manually run by men in uniforms who opened and closed the grillwork inner doors. These men were trained to not see who was with whom and what was going on behind them. They were committed to their work and to the privacy of the people who came to their hotels. So, in this case, Lana and my father were standing in the rear of the car and Byron was in front of them, next to the elevator operator. My father barked out the floor number and the operator slid the gate closed, paused a second, then threw the throttle bar to the right and the elevator began its long, slow ascent.

"No stops for this car," my father said sternly. The operator nodded once without turning around. "That's fine, Barry," my dad added.

Byron never turned around to check on his suitcase or his girl. My father never looked at her either and, according to my mother, she kept her eyes trained front as well, her eyes on the back of Byron's head. But her hand slipped across the rear wall of the machined-room and over my father's hand, the one holding the handle of the suitcase. They stood there like that for fifteen floors, her hand over his, caressing the skin on the back of his fingers. He said it was the happiest vertical trip of his life because she was so beautiful that he had not been able to look at her for long in the lobby because Byron intimidated him. But for that trip he was in heaven.

After escorting them to the party, my father went back to his office and tried to work, but he found it difficult. His mind wasn't on papers, or bank accounts, or unpaid bills. He could only think about her. He was doubly surprised when, just about one hour later, the knock on his door revealed, when answered, the beautiful Lana and not his personal assistant.

"Come in, please," he said trying to contain his excitement. "Is there something wrong? Something you need?"

"No. Yes." Her answers were short and specific.

"Tell me," he said.

"I'm not supposed to tell you about myself," she said, "as my mother wouldn't approve of it."

"All right," he said, totally confused.

"But I haven't been able to think about anything but you since I came into the lobby and you came to greet us."

"I..." he hesitated. "I felt the same way."

"I work for a living," she said. "I'm a working girl."

"I didn't know that," he said not completely sure of what she was telling him.

"I come from a family of working girls," she said. "We're taught what to do and we do it."

A picture was emerging in his mind and although he was certain he was catching up with her tale, he wasn't the slightest bit offended by what he was hearing. That confused him. He had always considered himself a very moral man and if she was telling him what he assumed she was saying than he should have been deeply concerned.

"He's a client," she said. "But he's the best kind of client. I wanted you to know that. I only go places with him and look nice and intelligent. I help him impress his own customers and I don't do anything."

"All right, then," my father said.

"I like you, though," she continued. "There's something different about you, sort of like the boys I knew in high school. I can see the lust in your eyes, but I know you wouldn't try anything. You saw me with someone else and you respected that. I just wanted you to know I appreciated it."

"That's nice. Thanks."

"I'd like to get to know you though," she told him. "I really think I like you."

"It's awkward, isn't it, saying those things? I'm blushing from it, Miss."

"My name is Lana Silverman. My phone number is Trafalgar 9-401. I will be there all day tomorrow. I hope I haven't bothered you in vain."

She picked up his business card from the silver tray on his desk, turned around and headed out of his office. The story she told me is that he called her the next day and they met and then they met again a few times and he got to third base right away and then home run came just a few days before they married and my sister Briana was born almost immediately. With that short scenario, Lana Silverman went out of the family business. It was the shortest career anyone had enjoyed in the history of our clan.

Eleven years later I was born. In between I don't know much about, but certainly something had to have happened. My father changed jobs; my sister opted to take up the family business; my Granny Elainie died and she and my mother revealed a lot of secrets to me that they had never told anyone else. Those long nights with the two of them, together or on their own, were fascinating for me, enthralling even. What I learned from them, I'm willing to share, but there's a fee, of course. That much I've learned well. Ever thing comes for a price, and you get it up front.

CHAPTER FIVE

From Brewer's The Dictionary of Phrase and Fable:

"Frederick of Wales had a dog given to him by Alexander Pope, and on the collar were these words:

'I am his highness' dog at Kew;

Pray tell me, Sir, who's dog are you?'"

Freddy Wales sits silently in the classroom waiting for the constant hum of non-essential chatter to diminish. No one talks with her, but still the conversations abound and if she wants to she could inject herself into any of three confabulations surrounding her desk. She chooses to abstain. That is what marks the twelve year old as different, her reluctance, or rather her insistent removal. She will not be drawn into the all-important nonsense around her. Freddy is one of those students who actually studies, knows the answers to the questions that her teachers inevitably ask. "Who was the Duke of Aberdeen in 1720s?

Anyone?" Freddy's hand is already up but the teacher won't call on her yet. It's clear she always knows the right answer and a wrong answer is required: *What is the square root of 174? Quickly now?*" And again Freddy *would have the answer but is only called on as a last resort.* She has reached the stage of 'quiet resentment' and is not far away from the one called 'displaced anger.' She wants to answer the question, needs to be the one to say the right words at the appropriate moment. She is always the final alternative. Always and constantly.

"Remarks, students," Miss Wilson calls out to the room, "remarks on the verse we just read. Stuart Bilson. Remarks please."

Bilson pulls himself up from his desk and a hand on his shirt tugs him back down toward his seat. He jerks forward, trying to extricate himself from the large right hand of Charlie Towers, seated behind him. At just the right moment, Towers lets go and Bilson falls awkwardly over his desk. This gets the expected laugh.

"Bilson, the verse," Miss Wilson snaps at him. "Now, please."

"Yes, Ma'am," he stammers. "The poem is called Ellighee..."

"Elegy, soft g, please," Miss Wilson corrects him.

"...yes, Ma'am, Elegy, and its about somebody dead." He stops dead. "Is that all?"

"Yes, Ma'am." He stares down at his desktop. Freddy's hand is up, but Miss Wilson ignores her.

"Tell me, more, Stuart."

"Yes, Ma'am. It was written by Ed. Na. Street. Vincent Mullet and he says..."

"She says," Miss Wilson hastens to correct him, "and her name is Edna. Saint. Vincent. Millay. Say it that way, Bilson." He does and she compliments him. "Now, go on." Again Freddy's hand is up and again she is ignored.

"I don't know what you want me to say, Miss Wilson."

"I want to know how the verse made you feel. Or what it made you think. Anything at all."

"Oh," he says and he stands there making an 'Im thinking' face. Freddy's hand is up again. In exasperation Miss Wilson calls out her name. She stand s and begins immediately to analyze the poem.

"This is a protest poem about death and all that it means to us, the ones who are left behind to mourn."

"Yes. Very good."

"And it also paints a picture of hope when she says, quote, your young flesh that sat so neatly on your little bones will sweetly blossom in the air, unquote."

"What does that say to you, Frederica?" Freddy hates to be called by her whole name, but will accept it if she can answer a question.

"It tells me that the loved one who died will be pushing up the daisies, and the roses, and the peonies," Freddy responded. "The dead beloved is fertilizer for all that is beautiful and cherished." She paused. "Like Jean Harlow."

The class laughs instantly, and as a group. Red in the face, flushed with embarrassment Freddy sits down again.

"All right. Well done. Stuart Bilson, would you please thank Frederica for assisting you in the answer."

The boy sticks his tongue out at Freddy, put his thumbs in his ears and waggles his fingers as violently as he can manage. Another laugh and a sudden outbreak of chatter once again.

Class is over in another hour and Freddy, books nestled awkwardly in her cradled arms, walks down the hallway where three boys are waiting, obviously, for her. She slows her pace and begins to glance around the space, hoping for a friend, an ally. Seeing one, she digs her heels in and keeps walking their way.

"Teacher's Pet," one of the boys calls out to her.

"I'm not," she shouts back. "She hates me and you and everyone knows it."

"Cry baby!" A second voice responds. "Little baby boo-hoo!"

She sticks her own tongue out at this infant villain. She would call him a name but she knows better. This is not the time to start a fight. There are too many obstacles in her path.

She pushes past them and the third boy shoves her, his open hand colliding with her shoulder. She isn't toppled but her schoolbooks hit the floor in an instant creating an obstacle to anyone else trying to hurry past. She squats down in the midst of them and starts to gather them all back, rather like a Maine fisherman, she imagines, works to haul in his net of lobsters.

Freddy is always imagining such things. She has an imagination. That is why, she believes, she has no friends. People don't talk to her. No one invites her into their circle. Her circle is a dot and she the only mark within it.

After rounding the corner Freddy is in the homestretch back to her locker. She feels safe in this corridor of the school; everyone in this end of the school is a girl and she feels safer around her own kind. At the locker three down the line from hers is Linda Palozzi. Linda is two years older than Freddy, which is not surprising, for Freddy was an honors student, skipped ahead one grade. At twelve she should be in the sixth grade, finishing grammar school, but she is here in the junior high school as a seventh grader. She is proud of this accomplishment, but also intimidated by it. It is the reason, she is sure, that Miss Wilson won't call on her very often. That goes for all of her other teachers as well. But all she has to do, she keeps telling herself, is get through seventh and when she is in eighth, next term, it won't matter anymore. No one will care about her age, or notice it. She'll just be an A+ student and that will be enough of an identifier for her.

"Hi, Linda," she says, smiling for the first time all day.

"That's Miss Palozzi, squirt," comes the marginally hostile response.

"Sorry," Freddy says.

"It's okay." She speaks softly. "Just remember in public to call me by my grown-up name. When we're alone, you can call me Linda. I don't mind."

"Okay. Thanks."

"Don't mention it!" With a twirl and a turn, Linda Palozzi is off and on her way, her skirt flipping naturally as she bustles down the empty passageway toward her bus. Freddy wonders if her skirt ever flips and slaps that way, but she knows it doesn't. It can't. She doesn't know how to walk like that. She admires Linda Palozzi a lot. She wants to be like Linda Palozzi, be pretty and popular and not too smart and have people watch her walk away, her skirt flipping and flapping that way, her hair doing the same, but always the opposite way: right when the skirt going left and vice versa. Freddy knows she has a lot to learn and she want to learn it all fast before it's too late and not one boy will ask her to the seventh grade dance which comes up in three weeks.

Freddy has a lot to learn. Like who she is, what she's called, what she wants and what's important.

"Who are you, anyway?" she asks herself out loud.

"Whose dog are you?" says a voice from behind her. Freddy doesn't want to turn around and see this boy's face. She absolutely doesn't.

Very quietly, almost without sound, she says, "I'm no one's dog." The voice asks the question a second time. She stands very still and doesn't respond, pretends there is no voice, no person behind her. As though she was back in her class, only the teacher this time, she ignores this other person with all her might.

"I'm Mikhael Staffiev," the voice from behind her says. "I'm everyone's dog."

Freddy starts to slowly turn his way, but something holds her back. It's the question, the answer, the voice itself. She sees his shoes, a strange design of three colors of leather. His pants are cuffed and creased perfectly. It all seems so ... foreign.

CHAPTER SIX

From Brewer's The Dictionary of Phrase and Fable

> "Heir-Presumptive. One who will be heir if no one is born having a prior claim. Thus the Princess Royal was heir-presumptive till the Prince of Wales was born; and if the Prince of Wales had been king before any family had been born to him, then...his brother would have been heir-presumptive."

She sees Mikhail, finally, when the bell sounds. As she looks up at him, he is turning away from her, toward the classroom. She reaches out in his direction, but he is moving suddenly, lurching forward and away again.

"What did you say your name was?" she asks him, loudly enough for two other girls to turn in her direction but apparently not loud enough for him to hear and respond to her. "What's your name?" she shouts.

"Mikhael," he shouts back. "Don't shout at me." And he is gone. Freddy picks up her books and hurries off to her own class, hoping she'll find him there, but a quick scan of the room shows her that he is definitely not in the same class. "I'll find him later," she thinks, but she knows as surely as she knows her own lack of significance in the world that she won't find him later. Not soon, at any rate. After all, she's never even seen him before today and the term is more than half behind her.

The balance of her day goes as days usually went: nothing interesting happens and she only learns what she thought she had already known on any and every subject. At three o'clock, with no after-school activities scheduled, she boards her bus for the trip home. Once again she checks the conveyance, as she had all of her classes, in case Mikhael might be on her bus, but she is disappointed to discover that he isn't. Most likely he has headed in a different direction yet again.

As the schoolbus pulls away from the curb she spots someone she thinks might be Mikhael. The boy's hair is what she thinks she remembers and the shirt and jacket as well. The boy is entering a limousine and after the way he had described himself, as everyone's dog, she knows she is wrong about the boy she is watching.

There is no way this could be Mikhael. Only rich boys rode in cars that were chauffered. Only rich boys. Not people who talked to her.

Fridays are good for Freddy. On Fridays she understands that pressures are abating and her need to be special changes to a need to simply be. That includes the need to be with boys, her special need to be with one boy who likes her in a different way. So, without the need to excel at everything, Freddy often takes a more relaxed tone on a Friday. She actually flirts with the boys she liked and she always hopes that her flirting will bring about a movie date, or an invitation to a school dance or a party. What never occurrs to her is that her behavior switch is too late, comes too late in the week to impress a boy that she is date material. Instead they all just think she is tired from too much showing off her brains without letting those brains consider her body. And at least one group of boys really know it.

"Freddy has no breasts," Ian Carter says on this particular Friday to the other three boys who are close to him at the time. "I could see across the inside of that shirt she was wearing and she doesn't have any."

"That's 'cause she isn't a real girl," Jeremy Finn responds.

"Course she is," saya Barry Hedge. "My sister takes gym class with her and she told me Freddy has too got breasts and their pretty ones, too."

"What does your old sister know about breasts?" Ian says with a haughty tone in his voice.

"My sister has great boobs," Barry adds. "She knows what's what when it comes to them things."

"Aw, you've got better breasts than Freddy does, Barry," Ian spits back at him. "You got real girly breasts."

Barry, who is overweight and sensitive about it, rears back, swinging his arm above his head, his hand clenching hard into a fist. He is about to lay one on Ian, when Harry Barnett grabs his arm in mid-swing and whips him around to face the other way.

"Hey, what are you doing?" Barry snarls at him.

"Leave it alone, Barry, leave it alone, hear?" Harry says to him. "Ian's just being stupid, that's all."

"You just like Freddy too much, Harry," Jeremy says.

"I don't." Barry is almost stammering now.

"Yeah, you do," Ian agrees.

"You do," says Harry. "And it shows."

"She's a wise-ass," Barry says defensively.

"But you like that in your women," Ian adds. "You like 'em dominant."

"I don't even know what that means," Barry protests.

"You probably will one day," Harry says.

"Yeeeeeeaaaah!" Barry mutters, taking a step back away from the others. He pauses physically and vocally. "You all think you're so smart." He turns on his heels and ran off down the hallway.

"Think he's going to check out Freddy?" Ian asks the other two.

"Like a library book?" Jeremy asks.

"Like Marilyn Monroe, stupid," Barry told him. "He's going to look down Freddy's shirt and see for himself what she's got there."

"We should watch him do it, right?" Ian suggests in a question.

"Yeah," the other two chorus and the three of them move off down the hallway to see if they can catch up to Barry in his quest for cup-size truths.

Freddy, of course, is completely unaware of any of this. She is sitting, as she often does, on a Friday, on the third step of the rear staircase, the one furthest away from the cafeteria or the gym. It is usually a quiet spot in the late afternoon. The classrooms on the second and third floor on this side of the building were reserved for chemistry labs and industrial vocational classes. Most of those ended right after lunch and so there were fewer students or teachers using this particular stairwell. She finds it a perfect place to sit and read for eight minutes or just to think about things. On this Friday she is reading.

She doesn't look up when she hears the footsteps behind her. "Whoever it is," she thinks, "will go right by me." She pays so little attention to the slight clatter of feet that she doesn't notice the sudden lack of footfalls. What does finally attract her attention is the sound of breathing. It is coming from above her. With a sudden tug of apprehension she slowly glances up and sees the face of Barry Hedge staring, upside down, at her on the step below him.

"What are you doing?" she yells at him.

"Don't get angry," Barry says quickly, a fearful grab in his throat.

"What were you doing, Barry? Tell me."

"I was just... looking."

"Looking at what?"

"Your..."

"Oh."

They both remain silent for a while.

"Do you want to ask me out?" Freddy says, finally breaking the lull.

"Me? No. Why?"

"Nothing."

"Would you go out with me?"

She looks at him and thinks about the question. Then she replies. "You're not my type, Barry," she says, but she is secretly glad that he has asked her. It makes this Friday a perfect day. She instantly returns to her book and ignores him, hoping he'll go away.

She hears feet moving, but she isn't sure of their direction. When Barry doesn't appear in front of her, she assumes he'd gone back the way he came. But she is surprised and alarmed when another male voice speaks to her from below.

"I like your spirit," says the voice and she knows at once it is Mikhael. That touch of the foreign "something" in the air tells her it must be him.

"Who the hell are you?" Barry shouts from above her somewhere, close but not as close as he'd been.

"Don't answer him," Feddy says.

"Hey!" comes a shout from far above her. Ian has been unable to contain himself with the newcomer in the picture. "Hey, you! Dog boy! Get down and lick my boots!" This brings derisive laughter from the other boys with him. Barry is heading up in their direction now and Freddy is on her feet.

"Ian Carter, you wash your mouth out with soap!" She calls up to him. She follows this with a loud, long Bronx Cheer. "Don't let them talk to you like that," she says in Mikhael's direction.

"I don't care, really," he says quietly.

"Well, I do. I hate the way they talk down to me."

"Well, perhaps I can offer some solace," the boy says to her. "May I offer you a ride home at the end of the day?"

"A ride home, how?" But she remembers the sight of the boy she thought was him entering the limousine and she knows what he meant.

"I have a car that brings me here and takes me away," he says. "I would put it at your disposal."

A door slams above them and Freddy understands that to mean that Barry and the other boys are gone.

"Thanks. I'd love a ride."

"And you're not afraid to enter a strange person's car? Hasn't your mother cautioned you about doing such things?"

"My mother knows I have sound judgment," she says.

"And you will let me take you home?"

"I will."

He comes around the corner of the stairwell and stands looking up at her.

"If you have any questions, please feel free to ask them. I am here to answer all."

"You talk funny," she says. "Are you from a foreign country?"

"My family is, yes. I am born en route."

"And you have money, I guess, if you have a car and driver. Your family must be important folks."

"My father is heir-presumptive to an important position in the old world. Here he merely works in a bank."

"What does..." she is going to ask him to define the concept of heir-presumptive, but chooses instead to ask another question. "What does it feel like to be special?"

"I told you that already. I am everyone's dog. Here there is no respect for what is special in a person. That is something you should already know, Fredericka."

"I like the way you said my name just then," she tells him, "with that extra ick sound. You made it soft and ladylike."

"It is how we would say it in my father's land."

"Well, I like it."

This day, and for most of it and not just this one moment, Freddy cherishes being Frederica. Suddenly Friday has taken on the polish she had always imagined she could.

CHAPTER SEVEN

From Brewer's The Dictionary of Phrase and Fable:

> Strasbourg Goose. A goose fattened, crammed and
> confined in order to enlarge its liver. Metaphorically,
> one crammed with instruction and kept from healthy
> exercise in order to pass examinations.

Sitting in a chair that seems to be larger even than her bed at home, Freddy
Wales feels remarkably, no, stupendously, at home. She stretches out her
arms to reach the outside edges of the chair's arms. She is sitting upright
and all the way back against the high, tufted firmly stretched lavender
fabric that covers the chair. Her feet dangle over the edge of the seat
cushion, but don't dangle far as the seat is too deep to allow her to lean
back, sit upright and still bend her knees at the front end of the seat.

"This has to be the largest chair in the world," she says to Mikhael.
"It just has to be."

"You know it isn't so," the boy replies to her. "There are many much
bigger. Even in Washington the city there is an enormous chair in which
your former president Lincoln sits."

"But that's not a comfortable chair," she says quickly. "That's carved
from marble." She lets her fingers arch and grip then loose, arch and grip
again. "This is a very comfortable chair."

"For you, perhaps," Mikhael says. "But for me, and for my father too,
it is a chair that contains us and brings no joy at all."

"What do you mean, it contains you?"

"It is a seat of long tradition and it should not be here."

"What does that mean?"

"My father has taken it from his country without the permission of the state."

"Was it his chair?" she asks him.

"It was!" He says it proudly.

"Then what's the problem? He has a right to sit in his own chair." When Mikhael doesn't answer her, she goes on a bit.

"Well, doesn't he have that right?"

"No. That is our trouble."

"Well, I don't understand this at all. Mikhael you never tell me much. We've been friends now for a month and you never tell me anything."

"I tell you my secrets," he says sharply.

"Oh, yes, sure. But what secrets are they? 'Nobody likes me.' Well nobody likes me much either. 'I'm everyone's dog,' well that's no secret. You let them take advantage of you all the time. So what?"

"It is hurtful, Fredericka."

" 'It is hurtful'...well, duh! Of course it is. If you let it be. You have to be more like me and just ignore the stupid ones."

"That is why I like you. Well, it's one reason."

"And do you know why I like you?"

"Because I bring you home in a limousine. I know."

"No. Don't be an ass. I like you because you're smart, like me. I like you because you aren't surrounded by shallow ones, just like me."

"It's true."

"And I like you because you like me. That's the most important reason."

Mikhael comes over to where she is sitting in the grand seat and seats himself down on the small upholstered foot rest at the base of the chair. He reaches up and touches her foot which she jerks away from his hand.

"Why did you do that?" she demands.

"I just touched your foot."

"I know what you did. Why did you do it?"

"It seemed right, just then."

"Well, don't do it again, hear?" She waggles a forefinger in his direction.

"Yes, your highness," he says, acknowledging her command. He bows his head for a moment, then jerks it back upright to look at her. She is smiling, but trying not to and her smile becomes a smirk.

"You have the bearing of a queen," he says softly.

"I do not."

"You must not always be so adamant, or I will have to call you Queen Fredericka."

She is running her right hand forward and back along the swank arm of the big chair. Without taking her eyes off his she asks him, "Is that what this is, then? Is it a throne?"

His eyes stay on hers, locked on hers really, as he slowly bobs his head up and down a few times.

"So, does that mean your father is a king, then?" Mikhael doesn't reply.

"Is your dad a king, Mikhael? Is that what you tried to tell me?"

"No. I never tried to tell you that."

Freddy leans forward, cinching her waist as she bends close to his face.

"You always choose your words so carefully, my friend."

"And you always assume you have the correct answer at the ready, Freddy," he replies. She laughs at the unintentional rhyme, but then catches herself mid-chuckle when she realizes that he has indeed chosen his words with care, for he has deflected her question with humor.

"You're a clever boy."

"You're a clever girl."

"We should be friends, right?"

"Correct."

She pushes herself forward until her legs are really dangling down, in front of the plush, pillowed armchair. She reaches over and touches his hair gently, finger-combing it out of his eyes and back over his ear.

"You don't want me to say anything to anyone, do you, about this chair, about your father?"

"No, please."

She smiles at him, but not a sly smile or a mean smile. This is real friendship and a soft smile is called for here. "All right. Secret's safe."

Mikhael stands up and takes her hands and helps her off the throne.

"In this country, anyway, a throne has a different meaning, you know."

Mikhael stares at her, not catching her drift.

"Here when you say you were on the throne, it means the crapper." She laughs and in an instant he is laughing also.

"My father would like that word," he says. "He always seeks new words to describe his situation. This would suit his mood, I know."

"Can I meet him some time?" Freddy asks her friend.

"Perhaps. Some time. This is not the good time, though. For now he is not available to be met by strangers."

"I'm not a stranger. I'm your best friend." She grins. "Hell, I'm your only friend."

He shakes his head for a moment, his smile reverting to a frown. "No. There is another friend."

"Another...? Who?"

"Someone you have not met. My mentor."

"Your what?"

"My teacher and my guide. My Mentor. In the evening when I am alone here he comes and for many hours will talk with me and lecture to me and give me guidance as to my lessons, and as to my role."

"What's your role? What does that mean?"

"I am trained to succeed my father as heir-presumptive to... to what he would inherit if that was ever to be possible."

"So you study to be important? Mikhael, you're important just being you."

"I must be made ready if things ever change in our favor, Freddy."

"What are you king of? I want to know."

"I am not a king. I am not a prince. I am Mikhael Staffiev of 154th Street." His tone is one of recitation, a childlike recitation that gives too much information and says too little to satisfy Freddy. She holds him by his shoulders and gently shakes him twice. "Why did you do that?"

"You were gone, Mikhael. You were totally gone from here just then. It was like your voice was coming out of the chair and not you."

"I was here, Fredericka. I am always here," and as he says it he touches the chair itself.

She moves away from him, over to a couch that faces a fireplace at the other side of the room. He watches her as she saunters through the space, around the furniture and he watches her as she turns to look at him from this discreet distance she has now placed between them.

"I want to know," she says.

"What do you need to know?" he asks her.

"I want...."

He stops her before she can continue. "What do you need to know?" he repeats, emphasizing the word "need.

She catches the tone and amends her question.

"I guess I need to know who you are, really."

"And I have told you. You know my name and my age and where I live and where I go to school. Those things define who I am, really."

"Then, I guess," she says, pausing to find the way to put this correctly, "I need to know who you would be if things were different for you."

He smiles at her, takes two steps in her direction and stops before responding. "If things were different for me, Freddy, I would be Cary Grant." He claps his hands together twice, giggles and twirls in a circle, coming to a calm, complete stop facing her again.

Freddy laughs, then points at him. "You almost could be Cary Grant, you know. You have that cleft in your chin, just like his."

He pokes himself in the chin. "I know. It is strange for no one else in my family has such a cleft."

"And he came from somewhere foreign too," Freddy adds.

"And he was a stilt-walker, did you know that?" Mikhael asks. "I can do that. I can walk on stilts. Shall I show you?"

The boy's eagerness to show off exposed a whole new side of him to Freddy. He isn't being careful suddenly of everything he says and does. There is a sudden spontaneity about him that she is enjoying very much.

"Show me? That's not good enough. Can you teach me?"

"I can and I will do it." He races out of the room and she follows him. Wherever those stilts are, perhaps there will be another piece of the puzzle that was Mikhael Staffiev. That is something she can't afford to miss.

CHAPTER EIGHT

From Brewer's The Dictionary of Phrase and Fable:

> "Right Foot Foremost: In Rome a boy was stationed at the door of a mansion to caution visitors not to cross the threshold with their left foot, which would have been an ill omen."

For almost three weeks Mikhael Staffiev has coached Freddy Wales on stilt-walking. In that short time, with only an hour a day to practice she has gotten to be very good at it. She had been sure that should could master the art, even though her earliest attempts had proven to be awkward and dangerous. After her fifth fall, a topple that took her over a small embankment in the park near Mikhael's apartment, he has taken her off the long stilts, which kept her two feet above the ground and put her on the lower ones which only allow her to rise twelve inches. She does much better on those, but after a few days she is dying to try the higher ones again.

"I'm ready for them now," she tells Mikhael who agrees with her. Her balance has improved quickly on the lower pair and her confidence level has risen with her success. He switches her back to the two-foot high foot rests and watches her wend her way around the park on them. He definitely feels the pride that any parent or teacher experiences with the success of an effort by a youngster.

"You have mastered the art," he says to her midway through the third week.

"Thanks. It's not so hard." She smiles at him and from the way she smiles he knows there is a question coming and he already knows what it is. Before she can continue he answers her unspoken query.

"Yes, Freddy, I have higher ones. And yes, Freddy, you can try them tomorrow." She hugs him hard and is laughing with anticipation when she finally lets him go.

"You're wonderful," she says as she steps back a step. "Wonderful. A wonderful friend!"

"And you too are wonderful, Fredericka," he responds. "You are more wonderful because you have done so much so quickly."

"But it's easy," she laughs.

"Is it?" He looks just a tiny bit crestfallen. "I took much longer to master this art."

"You're a boy," she says, "and boys always take longer. Girls are quick studies and are naturally graceful. Boys are awkward."

"I am not awkward," he says trying to contain his annoyance at her pronouncement.

"No, not especially, awkward," she admits.

"Then why did you say that?"

"I don't know, Mikhael." She pauses. "It's what girls say, I guess."

"Well boys say things too."

"Don't I know it? They say a lot of them about me, I guess."

"You still worry about 'them'? You are being foolish. You don't need 'them.' You are better than them."

"Oh, Mikhael, you sometimes say the nicest things."

"You're welcome, Freddy."

"I didn't say thank you."

"You did, though," he tells her. "In your way, you did."

He takes the stilts from her and before she can say anything more, he is off, on his way home, the stilts balanced on his shoulder.

The next afternoon he meets her with two pairs of stilts, their foot rests set considerably higher than any Freddy has managed thus far. They kiss once briefly as he greets her before leading her by the hand to a nearby park bench. He climbs onto the seat, pulling her up alongside him. They face the upright crossbeams of the bench's back. Mikhael hands her a pair of stilts, keeping one for himself. These he plants on the ground behind the bench. Freddy follows his lead.

Mikhael climbs up on the back of the park bench, his arms held high on the upright beams of his stilts. He has chosen a position that will give him extra support, his feet flanking the two side of the cement that formed the brace arch for both seat and back support.

"Come on, do the same," he says to Freddy who is trying to pull herself up to his position. She is having a harder time than she has previously had when following his lead.

"I can't get my balance," she says.

"Here, watch me," he says clambering down to the seat again. "Do what I am doing. You hold both of the stilts in your right hand and to the right of the upright, see?"

She nods and follows suit.

"Then you place your left foot at the top of the seatback, like this." He does it and she does also. "Then you use your weight to balance as you pull yourself up there. Come on, do it. See, see how your right foot comes up to meet its mate?"

She does, actually, and she tells him so.

"Now you put down your right and you are home free."

Freddy does as she is told and finds it works.

"Now what?" she asks, but she already knows what comes next.

"Now separate the stilts and put one on each side of your feet, on the outside, Freddy. OK. Move one foot to the foot rest. Good. Now the other. You have it. Come. Let's walk together."

Awkwardly they move away from the park bench, Freddy a bit unsteady standing on the small wooden beams which are an extrusion from the stilts themselves. Mikhael moves naturally, but Freddy, at this new height, seems to be unsure of herself. The boy keeps reassuring her about her skills, her abilities, telling her how well she is doing, but he has no way to help her in case of emergency. This has worried him but he is sure she can manage the taller stilts and still manage to add the purchase of an ice cream cone if they are lucky enough to find a vendor.

They walk on their three-footers for almost a half mile, their steps lengthy, giving them the opportunity to cover four times as much ground in the same time. As they walk Freddy shouts questions at him, but he can easily let them pass if he wants too because he can feign an interest in his, or her, difficulties in passage. She only makes two attempts to ask him about his father this time before dropping the topic for the day. It no longer matters as much to her as it had a few weeks earlier. Now her thoughts are devoted to Mikhael and the stilts. She loves the stilts.

Unable to locate an ice cream vendor, Mikhael turns his steps in the direction of the Central Park Zoo; Freddy follows him instantly, thrilled at her sudden sharp turn not bringing her down to the ground.

"I'm much steadier today," she shouts after his retreating back.

"I know." His call comes from very far away, it seems. "Come on, catch up."

"I will, too," she calls back to him. She increases her pace, lifting her legs as best she can while holding on to her stilts at the top. She sees him veer off to the left and she decides to do the same thing, only sooner, to possibly head him off by so-doing. Using her hands to steer herself she moves to the left, lifting her left stilt and turning her leg in that same direction, pulling her right foot and stilt after her. It is a long, hard pull, much moreso than she had considered while making this drastic turn. Her miscalculation has obvious results: she trips herself forward, losing her balance and falling in the direction of the large granite stones that pile up the hillside on this side of the park. They loom up quickly, heading right for her face. She swivels her hips, hoping to break her fall and possibly even avoid the slabs of stone altogether. Instead she lands on her side, her hip protected from the natural obstruction by her stilt, but without anything to cushion her arm. She knows, before she even hears the sound, that she is about to break her bones. She is right.

The pain is intense. It is all she can do to not scream and carry on. She isn't going to be the prim and proper "girl" in this situation. She is going to tough it out like a boy, like a prince of a boy would. Several people, witnessing her fall and probably even hearing her body connect with the rocks, rushes to her side to offer what help they can. Mikhael is nowhere in sight, certainly not there among them.

"My stilts," she mutters. "Did I break my stilts?"

"No, not really," someone says, someone young she thought from the sound of his voice. "Are you an acrobat?"

"No." She grunts out her response to the question.

"Ok. Sorry," comes the voice in reply.

"What did you mean, not really?" she asks, gasping for air, still not screaming her pain.

"One of them looks chipped, is all," says the boy, she knows now it is a boy.

"Help me, please, someone," she says and she begins to cry. Her pain is suddenly overwhelming now that her lungs are providing her with the proper amount of air. "I'm hurt, I think."

"Can I help you stand?" the boy asks.

"Leave her alone, boy," says an older a person, a woman Freddy thinks. "You never move an accident victim."

"Here's a cop," someone else shouts. "Hey, officer, over here. This little acrobat girl has hurt herself."

Freddy hears, rather than sees, the crowd parting a bit to let the policeman through. She sees the brim of his hat, then his face, then his jacket with its dark uniform-blue hues. He holds out his hands and gently touches her arm and she shouts out words she hadn't known she remembered, none of them what people associated with young girls. A few of the by-standers stand back a bit. Not the boy, however.

"We need an ambulance, I think. Can someone go and call an ambulance?"

"Yeah, I will," says a man somewhere in the crowd.

"No need," the cop calls after him. "I'm radioing now." He holds up his walkie-talkie. "It's a done deal. Folks, please step back a bit. Give the kid a chance to breathe."

Officer Cathcart, his name on a steel pin over his jacket-pocket, asks her a few questions, her name, her age, her phone number so they could call her mother. She responds to everything as she normally would but with each question, or rather each answer, she is more and more in pain. When he is done, she asks about Mikhael, about her friend.

No one remembers seeing him. No one knows where he might be. She calls out his name, but there is no response.

"I'll be your friend for now," the boy says, the one who talked to her already, the one who had called in the police.

"I don't need another friend," Freddy says.

"I think you do," the boy replies. "I think you must because your other friend seems to have disappeared somewhere."

The logic of his reasoning makes sense, but Freddy isn't eager to accept it or to accept him. She calls out to Mikhael again and again gets no answer.

"He doesn't seem to be anywhere," the boy says.

"He must be close by. I was following him when I fell."

"He's gone now," someone else tells her.

"What does he look like?" a woman asks.

"He looks like... well, he's on stilts like mine," she says suddenly unsure how to describe Mikhael. She could see his face and even his clothing, but she can't quite describe them out loud.

Two people remove themselves from the rocks where Freddy lay in pain. They are back quickly to report on their findings. "No one on stilts out there," they both say, almost simultaneously.

"He must be," Freddy insists, but she knows they are right. She knows that Mikhael has gone on without her for some reason.

"I'm here," the boy says. "Let me help, please."

She thinks about this for minute, a long, long actual minute, before she speaks.

"Okay. My name is ...."

"Yes, I heard you tell the cop," he says. "My name is Maxwell Draper."

CHAPTER NINE

from The International Thesaurus of Quotations:

> "The most I ever did for you was to outlive you/
> But that is too much."
> Edna St. Vincent Millay, untitled,
> Make Bright the Arrows (1940)

"When I lost you for good and all, when I lost you I lost my heart." That's how I hear myself in the quiet of night sometimes. My own voice comes to me in the darkness, out loud, but not too loud for I don't want to wake Tooie. She is in the next room, in her own room, her own bed, but the door between our cells stands open so we can hear one another if there is an emergency. Or simply a need for a hand to hold. That happens sometimes. It's the way for married people, old married couples who are affectionate and deeply involved but not necessarily sexually so. Tooie and I are very close. She is dear. She is as much as I have in this life of the woman I loved and should have married. I was an ass. A pompous and deliberate ass.

Lainie told me she loved me and I believed her for as long as I did because I wanted to believe her. She had come to me in my life as someone indescribable. It was a miracle that she came to me at all. I should never have left her the way that I did, but I did what I had to do then because I didn't know what else to do. Oh, yes, I knew I could go the other way, but my two selves were at war, battle-fatigued by the fence that had been installed by my own hand.

I wanted to know more than just the betrayal. I wanted to know the beauty. I wanted to experience everything that was positive and nothing that was even the least bit disturbing. Tooie tells me that I am the world's last innocent, a soul without blemish, but that's not true. I was never an innocent, a blemish-free soul. I was a man who couldn't bear the thought of the thing that was perfect housing a shadowed flaw.

Lainie was flawed and I should have known it. I should have known it before my heart and my love were so much at stake. But I was an ass, as I said. I never asked and she never told. Accidents will happen and when our did, it was more than I could bear and I was a fool. I acted badly and I betrayed what was best in both of us. I have never forgiven myself.

Myself. What is that? Who is that? I don't even know any longer. Vincent Compton. Who is that? What is that? I don't know any more. I don't know.

✱

Vincent Compton got out of the automobile and reached for the newspaper the man at the stand was holding out for him. The nickel he handed the vendor was new and shiny and it sparkled in the bright sunlight. He returned to the driver's seat and slapped the periodical down on the seat next to him. It flopped open and its headline was too revealing, too important to ignore:

SACCO/VANZETTI DEAD.
DEMONSTRATORS ENRAGED

It was August 24, 1927. Two men, accused, tried and convicted of murder, but condemned for their radical politics, had inspired the creative minds of the nation and abroad to campaign for justice. Six years of hearings had taken their toll on many, including George Bernard Shaw, Einstein, H.G. Wells and the poet Edna St. Vincent Millay who had gone to jail for her vocal protestations of their innocence. Vincent Compton had not taken part in any protests or even attended a single seminar on the case. He was a closet Socialist himself and for his family's sake he had kept his profile low in these dangerous days.

Besides, it was the 1920s. Life was lived in the fast lane if you could pull over into it. Compton had tried to make that move but each time he started in that direction something pulled him back, called him up short. The vo-do-dee-do life was an elusive one even though he could see it, hear it, even taste it all around him. He loved the new jazz music. He liked to dance and could fox-trot and charleston as well as anyone.

Women's clothes, short, flimsy, decorated with beads and fringe attracted him, especially when there were long legs and bare arms attached to those dresses. He had natural appetites and he wanted to indulge them, but there was still an old moral sensibility that held him at bay. He hated it.

But this day, this particular day, with Sacco and Vanzetti gone, there was a new and terrible tremor in the city. It was unavoidable. It was like the new subway system that rocked and shook and made the subterranean walls shiver. Here it existed above ground, in every building, in every street. He parked the car, tossed the still unread newspaper into a trash can and walked down the street to the nearest speakeasy, determined to have a drink, to forget his inability to communicate his needs.

When he entered the Sparta Sportsman's Club on West 55th Street he thought, at first, that it was empty. There wasn't another soul at the bar, so he took a stool in the center of the row of nine and waited for the barman to take his order.

"A beer, I think," he said. The barman looked him over carefully, then spoke.

"I'm afraid you have to be a member here, Sir. Are you a member?"

"I'm not," Compton admitted. "I didn't know..."

"Give him a beer, Teddy," a woman said from somewhere in the gloom behind him. Compton turned and squinted in the dimness of the large room. He saw a slight flash of light from a corner, perhaps in a booth, he wasn't sure yet; his eyes had not adjusted to the change of light from the bright outdoors to this place with its few candles. "It's early. He needs a beer."

"Sure. Why not? And if we're busted, I'm calling you out on this, Lainie."

"Thanks...whoever you are," Compton said, adding quickly, "whereever you are."

"Think nothin'. You looked like you needed one."

"I don't need...well, I guess I could use...that is..."

"It's okay, kid. Just relax and enjoy it."

"Where are you?" Compton asked. "I can't see you."

"Your beer, sir," said the barman behind him. Compton turned to look at him, this man he could see. "Twenty cents, please."

"It's on me, Teddy. No charge."

"Okay, sister." The barman moved away and into his own dim corner at the end of the mahogany bar. Compton felt someone at his elbow and when he turned the woman who had bought him a beer was standing there, so close, so near to him. Her being there was a surprise, so sudden, so unannounced, and he took a moment to blink a few times, not sure whether she was actually near him or not.

"Enjoy your beer, Mister..."

"Compton," he said. "Vincent, please."

"Mr. Compton, then." Her voice was like a honey-coated purr. He found himself looking into her eyes and seeing himself reflected in them, two Comptons, both with that sad expression that came over his face when he felt uncertain of his next move, his motivations.

"Hello," he said. "And thanks."

"It's okay. I got the change."

"What do I call you?" he asked.

"Lainie. It's a simple name. Say it a few times. It'll be yours."

"Lainie," he said, and then he repeated it a few time, saying it differently each time.

"That was good," she told him. "You sounded sincere once or twice in there."

"Oh, I was. I am."

"Nice to know," she said. "Very nice to know you."

"Very nice to know you too, Lainie."

"Oh, Mr. Compton, you used my name in a complete sentence." Her cooing tone made him wonder about her own degree of sincerity, but it also made him smile so he decided not to think too much about her sincerity.

"It's a nice name. I'd like to use it often," he said in perhaps the most romantically motivated statement he'd ever made. "You're like a dozen red, red tea-roses, don't you know. I'll have to say your name a lot."

"We'll have to arrange that somehow."

She put her hands on top of his, tapping it a few times with her fingers. The sensation that produced in him was one he found verbally indescribable: soft and gooey with a hardening of arteries in parts of his body that didn't naturally harden. He had no male friends to talk with about the way Lainie made him feel at that moment, and he certainly couldn't describe it to his mother. He decided to leave it to memory alone and not try to talk about it.

✻

That memory of our meeting was with me when I stood in the funeral parlor so many years later looking at her daughter Lana and her grandson,

Maxwell. Between them, mother and son, daughter and grandson, I could see the Lainie I first knew on that strange summer afternoon in 1927. I had outlived this woman I should have loved better than I had. I had given that to both of us. I could fulfill the promise I made to her one night, long after we had parted, after I had married her best friend, Tooie the Lesbian. I could be the man I promised her I would be.

I just had to figure out how to do that. I have my limitations.

CHAPTER TEN

from The International Thesaurus of Quotations:

"A Man's womenfolk, whatever their outward show of
respect for his merit and authority, always regard him
secretly as an ass, and with something akin to pity."

H.L. Mencken, "The Feminine Mind"
In Defense of Women (1922)

Tooie, the Lesbian married me for reasons of her own. I married her
because she said yes. Well, that's not fair, is it? She wouldn't have said "yes"
if I hadn't said "marry me." Why did I say it, ask it, suggest it? Well, I'll tell
you. She was Lainie's best friend and I couldn't marry Lainie, so I thought
if I married Tooie I'd stay close to Lainie, still have her near me when I
needed her there. I couldn't have been more wrong. That's the problem,
the central problem, when a man marries: he thinks he knows the women
close to him, but he really doesn't. Not at all.

Lainie was a lot like my mother in some ways. She could look you
straight in the eye and make you believe in her. All the while, meanwhile,
behind your back she was thinking some things that had nothing to do
with what she said to you. My mother never told me the truth about
anything, but I didn't know that then. I didn't know that, actually, until
she was dying and then she told me lots of things. For example, she told
me my father was a man I never met. My real father was someone she had
known for a short time, a boarder in her brother's house where she worked.
"He was a traveling man," she told me, "which would account for your love
of faraway places." "The trouble with that theory," I told her back, "is that

I don't have a love for faraway places, Momma." "Sure you do," she said, "just like him." "Momma, the only faraway place I love is Montauk Point." "There you are," she said closing her eyes, "just like your papa."

What she didn't tell me was his name. She never said why she'd loved him or why he'd left her. She never told me anything except this curious legacy of bloodlust for faraway places. The truth is that right after that conversation I suddenly developed a yen for travel, longed to see Sugarloaf Mountain down in Rio, ached to touch the pyramids in ancient Egypt and wanted to board a ship in the harbor, any ship going anywhere. I told Tooie and she told me to calm down and grab a beer. Then she went out and found a lady who'd sleep with both of us and my father's yen for distant locations left me forever.

That was one way Tooie kept me sane. She could always find some woman, some nice woman usually, who'd accommodate us both. I don't know where she found them; I never asked her. I merely accepted the inevitable and got my kicks and went to sleep.

Like my mother Lainie told me the truth when she wanted to, when it was convenient for her. She could make me believe a lie if she wanted to do that. She could twist me around her little finger, to coin a cliche. What she couldn't do, like my mother could do, was make me forgive the lie. My mother was my blood; Lainie was my loins. Blood calls to blood no matter what, but loins are loins and they drift. If Lainie had been my mother, I would have forgiven the lies and laid them to rest, but then she wouldn't have been my love, only my mother, so the outcome would have been much the same anyway.

One thing, though. Like my mother for my father I never stopped loving Lainie. That's the truth.

But Tooie, that's the topic. Tooie the Lesbian whom I married to remain close to Lainie the Liar whom I left but wanted to keep close. I drift, I always drift, when I talk about Tooie and Lainie. How did we meet? Who was she to me that I would ask her, that's the topic. I'd been seeing Lainie for a while and we'd been sleeping together and I'd been helping her out with some cash now and then because she needed the money. She liked to dress up nice for me, and she didn't have a job, so I'd give her money when I saw her and the next time we'd be together she'd have something new to wear and to dazzle me with. I liked that. It made us both feel good, I mean really good. So maybe the fourth or fifth time I saw her, she introduced me to Tooie.

We were in a speakeasy up in Harlem to hear a singer Lainie was fond of whose name I've forgotten over time. She was a light-skinned negress with a beautiful voice and a beautiful body. Her hair was died red and against her mulatto-cream skin made quite an impression. I remember she was singing a torchy ballad called "Just Like a Butterfly That's Caught in the Rain," when Lainie waved to someone across the room. I don't know how she could make that someone out in the dark of the room, but she did, and the next thing this woman was joining us at our table and that was Tooie.

"Tooie, this is Mr. Compton," she said. "My friend, Tooie, Mr. Compton."

"You the guy been buying Lainie pretty things?" she asked me.

"I guess I am," I said.

"You got swell taste, Mr. Compton," Tooie said.

"Well, thanks, but I don't really buy the things, Lainie does. I just let her have some money to use."

They exchanged glances, but I didn't see anything in that.

"I meant your taste in Lainie, Mr. Compton, forgive me if I'm not clear."

"Isn't she something," Lainie added, "saying sweet things like that?"

I bought her a drink and she said a few more nice things about me. Then she was gone again.

"Nice friend you've got there, Lainie," I told her.

"She's been my pal for ever so long."

"How'd you meet her?"

"We were school chums. She was in my class and I was way out of hers." Lainie giggled as she said it.

"What does that mean?"

"Well, you see, Mr. Compton, it's like this. It was the sixth grade at school and she was in the next row over, one desk behind, so she was in my class. But I was a real girl and she was just a lezzy. So she wasn't anywhere near me, I was way out of her class, if you get me."

"I guess I do," I said, and the singer finished singing. There was thunderous applause and I leaned in close to Lainie. "So she and you are close?"

"Get that idea right out of your head, Mister," she snapped at me. "Tooie is a friend, that's all. Nothing funny goes on with me with her like me with you."

"Okey-dokey," I said, pulling back, sitting up straight.

"You wouldn't want me like that, would you?" she asked me.

"No. I like you like you are. I like you as my girl."

"You don't like the idea of sharing me around, do you, Mr. Compton?"

I know now that I should have asked Lainie, right then, to make an honest man of me and marry me, but I let it go by. I didn't take the plunge as it were, to coin another cliche. Instead, I asked her a different question.

"So you and Tooie are close friends and share your secrets, I guess, so what did you tell her about me?"

"I told her you were real sweet, and real kind."

"Is that all?"

"No." She gave me that coy smile I loved and still love to this day.

"What else then?"

"I told her that if I wasn't to marry you sometime, then she should and get herself some sweet and kind respectability."

"Marry your friend the Lez? Why would I do that?"

" 'Cause you're the nicest guy I know, is why."

"I don't get it," I said to her "Why would you want me to marry someone else?"

"I don't know if I can marry anybody," Lainie said. "I really don't know. It's a big thing, you know. It's not like having a kid, it's a real commitment. It's like giving up the life and making a new one with one other person only. That's a hard job if you ask me."

"You don't know what you're talking about," I told her. "My mother married my dad and they made a go of it and they had me and they had my brother and they had a life. Not so difficult, see?"

She gave me a soulful look, sad and deep and very intellectual. She took a deep breath and picked up the pearls I'd bought her myself and stuck them in her mouth and ran them back and forth across her lower teeth. Then she dropped them onto her bosom.

"Mr. Compton it isn't always like that," she said. "And don't you believe it for a second."

"You sound bitter," I said.

"Do I? Do I, really?"

Just then the red-headed singer started another song I loved and I got a little lost in the lyrics. It was the Gershwin hit, 'S Wonderful, a song that really hit home just then. I sang along with it, hoping Lainie would get the idea from the song, if not from me:

" '*S wonderful, 'S marvelous, you should care for me.*"

"Oh, Mr. Compton," she said, "you know I care for you."

" '*S awful nice, 'S paradise, 'S what I long to see.*"

"Mr. Compton, you can see it whenever you want to see it."

"*You've made my life so glamorous....*"

"That should be my line, Mr. Compton."

"*You can't blame me for feeling amorous...*"

"Like I feel for you."

I took her hand in mine and stroked it with my fingers while I held it fast. I was in love, I guess, and I really felt it just then. I don't know if it was the music or the booze or the lights, but I really felt it.

"You don't sound bitter now," I said to her.

"I'm not bitter," she replied, "just angry. It's the life, I guess. Sometimes it gets to me."

"Your life is okay with me," I said and I know now that was my undoing, because I had no idea what I was saying or what she was saying. I thought I was proposing to her and she thought I was agreeing with her about her choices. That was the mistake we both made. The big one.

Later, in her room, when I saw the photo of her and the little girl I knew I had been a fool and that I couldn't have the purest princess in the world for my own. She was someone else's already, had been someone else's and could never really be mine.

Her words came back to me about her friend, Tooie the Lesbian, and it occurred to me that someone like her could be true to one man, because she didn't even want one man. And knowing her I could be close to my Lainie and never lose sight of her. I just knew that I couldn't be close to her like I wanted to be, so second best would be the best choice for me.

That was before I knew that women can take you for a ride, before my mother told me about my father. That was before I knew who I really was, down deep. So much before.

CHAPTER ELEVEN

From The International Thesaurus of Quotations:

Credulity: People everywhere enjoy believing things that they know are not true. It spares them the ordeal of thinking for themselves and taking responsibility for what they know.

Brooks Atkinson, "February 2", Once Around the Sun (1951)

So, once I told myself that it was all over with Lainie I was free to move on to sweeter sea water. Something fresh and new was what was needed. I was determined to find a woman who had no past, no secrets and no shames. I knew it was possible to find such women. You just had to locate the convent, find the gate and hold out for the virgins.

That's a joke. I don't think, and I didn't think at the time, that this particular alternative was available, not in New York City and not in 1927. Remember, I told you, it was the jazz age. Everybody danced to some tune or other; everyone imbibed something potentially illegal: Gin, Wine, Reefer, Something. I don't think there were virgins any more, not over the age of twelve at any rate. I wasn't one, not even in my heart any longer. Lainie had taken that one piece of purity away from me. That was how I saw it just then. I thought she had robbed me of an innocence I probably never possessed.

I don't know for sure how long after that I bumped into Tooie, saw her face and remembered her name, and thought about marriage to her. Let me tell you some more about her, see if I can remember the details right.

She was about thirteen inches shorter than me. I'm 5-11. She was pert.

So were her breasts. I remember them all right. "No man's land," we used to call them for fun. She had a cupid's bow mouth, for real, not just with the lipstick outlining them that way. Her eyes were green and her hear was a pale red, almost blonde, but still with a definite fire-glow hue. She had flat shoulders and those dancing dresses in the 1920s looked great on her. Her arms were little bit long and her hands were too, with long tapering fingers and long tapering nails at the ends of them.

She liked the color maroon, that dark, brown-hued red, sort of a plum color but with too much brown. It was a color I'd never liked before I saw her wear it. She also liked jet beads sewn on to everything. I think she was the original "Image of the grave" girl. Her makeup was very, very white except for the kohl that lined her eyelids and the maroon lipstick on her pouty , bee-stung lips. Overall, the picture was a pretty one, if a bit on the bizarre side. I liked it. It was different. It was pure Tooie.

So, I was at this party and there she was. I didn't recognize her at first. I'd only seen her that one time and that night had faded into a singular, through the spy-glass sort of view. That way I didn't have to worry too much about what I thought about it. I just thought it was a night I didn't want to think about and that was just fine. But the party was one I had gone to on a dare. A guy at work told me about it, invited me and then dared me to show up. I always take a dare, so I showed up.

I hadn't been there ten minutes when she put in an appearance.

"So, Mr. Compton, long time...." said this short white, maroon woman.

"Yes, sure, right," I think I said. (Tooie always corrects me here and says I replied something else, like "Excuse me?" with attitude, but I don't think so.) I was trying to place her, but the lights and the costume and the situation were so different that it didn't really come to me.

"Tooie O'Brien," she said holding out her hand in my direction, palm up. I wasn't sure what to do, because the name O'Brien fooled me I guess, so I bent down and kissed the palm of her hand. "Oooooh, Mr. Compton, my friend was right, you are a gentleman." That's when it hit me. Tooie!, Lainie's friend Tooie, the Lesbian! I laughed, and she misunderstood the laughter.

"Oh, I see. Anything but," she said, withdrawing her hand.

"No, please, excuse me (that was where I said it and without attitude I want to assure you) but I just didn't recognize you Miss Tooie."

"I see."

"It's true. Believe me. I didn't expect to see anyone I knew and certainly not you."

"And why would that be?"

"I ... don't know." And I really didn't know why.

"Well, are you engaged for this next dance?" she asked me.

"I'm free, actually."

"Goody." She took my hand and led me to dance floor and we waltzed, and that was a surprise because the band had been blaring out the Charleston just a moment before.

There is something surprising about the waltz. It insists that someone take command and that someone, I suppose, is usually the man. The man leads in the waltz. So that's what I did. Tooie, for all her curvaceousness in this era of the sleek, slender line, was a wonderful dancer. She turned, she reversed, she kept up with me step after step, turn after turn. When I doubled the tempo of the graceful three-quarter time turns she followed along without anything more than a smile as comment on my daring. I don't know for sure how long we held the position, kept up the terpsichorical movements, but it seemed to be unending. When finally the music reached its emotional crescendo and brought us up tight and short, I know I was completely out of breath and Tooie seemed to be also.

"That was wonderful," I said to her.

"I was about to say that," she added.

I don't know what possessed me, but I leaned way down and kissed Tooie, the Lesbian. And I don't know what possessed her either, but she kissed me back

I was about to stand back up when she turned my head with her hands so that she could whisper into my ear and what she whispered entranced me: "I'm a virgin," her voice rustled in my ear. Then she let me go.

I took her to the kitchen for a beer and we talked and I took her home and she invited me up to her room and there she undressed for me and let me examine her so that I could see that she hadn't lied. And I proposed to her. Right there and then, I asked her to marry me. It hadn't been more than a few weeks since I parted company with Lainie and suddenly that fantasy, that unreal fantasy of marrying her best and closest friend and staying close to her but at a distance, was possible. I waited for her answer but it didn't come. Finally, after she had dressed herself again, she responded to my question.

"Mr. Compton, I'm flattered," she said, "but you have to know me before you ask me such a question."

"I know you," I told her. "I knew you when we danced."

"The waltz is a deceptive dance," Tooie said. "It is filled with all the romantic possibilities as you turn and swivel and swirl. The man's arm is the only support the woman has and she is totally dependent upon him for everything. He is the super man and she the compliant babe. I, Mr. Compton, am not the compliant babe, not for any man in this world."

"You mean because you're a lesbian?"

"I do mean that, yes, but I mean just a bit more, Mr. Compton. Do you know why I undressed for you like I did?"

I shook my head, for really I didn't. She knew that I was aware of her sexual preference, so there was nothing to achieve by undressing to seduce me. It hadn't been that.

"When I told you I was a virgin, I meant with a man." I nodded. "When I undressed to prove that to you it was because you had that look that men sometimes get that says, *'you'll be a virgin no longer, my sweet,'* which is silly because I could scratch out your eyes before you could find your penis. Do you understand that?" I did and I told her so. "When I undressed for you it was to show you no man's land, my breasts and my pudenda. I am not ashamed of it. It is perfect just the way it is and it will stay that way for as long as I care to keep it. Do you understand?"

"Tooie, I admire your frankness," I said. "I know what you mean and what you intend for your life, but I really like you and I think we could be happy together, even without the sex."

"You're naive, Mr. Compton."

"I'm not so naive as you think, Tooie. I've learned a lot these past few weeks."

"And Lainie?"

"We are done."

"And you would marry me?"

"I would."

"It would mean giving her up for me. If you could do that, I would help you with your life."

"How do you mean that?"

"I mean that I will provide you with the sex you need and you will provide me with the protection that I need from an unpleasant world."

"You'd give up women for me? I don't understand."

"No. Don't think that for a minute, Mr. Compton...."

"You should call me Vincent," I said. "I think we're beyond Mr. Compton now."

"Vincent, then, listen to me. I will bring you the women you need. I will provide for you with meals, and housekeeping, and cleaning your shirts and undies, and you will be proud to have me at your side when you need me there. Proud. I won't be shunted to the background. You'll have to be proud of me and make me proud to be seen with you. That's what I want."

"I would, of course. But I don't understand all this."

"You don't have to now. But if you seriously want to marry me that's the promise I need from you. Pride in me."

"I can do that. Easily. I will."

Without another word, she kissed me hard on the mouth. We were married two weeks later. And I never saw Lainie again after that wedding supper. Never. Not until I saw her in her coffin.

And Tooie was as good as her word. She brought me the women I needed and she dressed well and spoke well and read and listened to good music and I was proud, no, I am proud of her, always and forever. Proud. I know what's true about us and not everyone we know needs to know more than what I choose to show them about us. They can believe what they want but Tooie the Lesbian and Vincent the Ass are a couple for eternity and Proud to be so.

But, of course, during a long marriage that isn't the whole story. How could it be?

CHAPTER TWELVE

From The International Thesaurus of Quotations:
"Every path has its puddle." English Proverb

There was a time, when was it exactly - I want to be accurate - I can't remember, but I will, when Tooie and I almost called it quits. We were man and wife at that point for ten or twelve years. It was an even number of years, I know that, because I remember saying to her "why do odd things happen in even years?" If it was twelve years, and I believe now that it was, than it was 1939 and that must be right because it was the year that Gone With the Wind and The Wizard of Oz were playing and I know that the year of great movies was the year of our difficulty.

Tooie had taken a job working for Sachs Fifth Avenue as a gift-wrapper. She had a gift for it, and she had devised and designed a whole array of gift-wrap bows that no one else could create. She had gotten rather famous for it, and I was proud of her. People would come to Sachs for their present, just so Tooie could put the finishing touch on the package they took off to some loved one, or would-be loved one. Her hand-tied bow was the final grace said over their offerings. Sachs was grateful, they were no fools over there, and they rewarded her with bonuses and in-house endowments of all kinds.

All of that would have been just fine if it hadn't been for Hattie Marshall. When Tooie took the job, Hattie Marshall was her boss, the supervisor from Hell. Sachs had a standard gift-wrap, a standard ribbon and bow. She wouldn't put up with Tooie making any changes to the way things had always been done, but when Tooie began slipping in one or two of her own designs, and Hattie caught her at it, all Hell did indeed break loose.

Tooie was reprimanded a dozen times, her pay was docked and she was threatened with loss of her job if she didn't stop making things look different. But in New York, and this may not surprise anyone, word spread pretty quickly that a girl named Tooie could make your package something really special and she became the department store speakeasy, so to speak. You had to pretty much "knock three times and whisper low" before having your package done by anyone in the department. If you were in the know you waited for the lady with funny name badge that said "Tooie" before you left your gift to be assembled.

There were five women in the department and Hattie Marshall supervised them all. She was the big Number One. Even though she wasn't always there, she seemed to have spies among the other four and not even days off prevented Hattie Marshall from catching Tooie breaking the rules.

That's the thing about Tooie: she breaks rules. It doesn't matter if they're personal or professional, she breaks them. Look at us. Look at our marriage. Not exactly traditional, right? So, anyway, Hattie Marshall.

It finally got to the point where Tooie was getting really frustrated by Hattie's attitude and at her constant berating of her. She knew she was worth something more than just a modest clerk's salary. She had heard the sales girls on the floor talking about patron's questions before they bought a watch, or perfume, or something even more personal like a nightie. "Is Tooie working today?" patrons would ask and the sales girls would call the department to see if she was in or not. Sometimes the customers would hand back the item and say they'd come back another time. That's what moved this whole fracas to another level.

So, in May of 1939, Tooie got summoned to the personnel department and told she was fired. That didn't go down very well with Tooie.

"What's that about?" she demanded to know from Mr. Jimmy Nolan, a manager in a baggy, striped, out-of-style suit.

"Mrs. Compton, there are too many complaints from your supervisor. You don't do your work."

"I do my work. I do my work better than anyone else and I do more of it."

"Customers are leaving the store empty-handed because of you, Mrs. Compton."

"The Hell they are!" Tooie apparently slammed her fist down on his desk and upset the picture of his wife and two dogs at home.

"Watch yourself, Mrs. Compton, or I'll dock your final check."

"You wouldn't dare, Mr. Nolan. You wouldn't damn dare."

"Wouldn't I?" A smirk crossed his face. "And watch your language, young lady."

"Don't be calling me a Lady!" She hit the desk again. She could tell she had frightened him and she always liked to do that with men who tried to push her around.

"Must I call security?"

"No. You don't have to worry about being hurt by me. Not you, Mr. Nolan."

"Are you making a threat against Miss Marshall?"

"Her? I wouldn't sit on her face and fart. No. The only threat is to the future of Sachs. You're throwing me out and I'm a customer draw. Where I go, they will follow, Mr. Nolan. You tell me they walk out without buying anything because I'm not here to wrap for them? Well, that tells me a lot. I'll get another job where they like what I do and I'll take out ads in the New York Times, the Herald-Tribune and the Daily News. I'll tell the world where I am, I'll tie it in a ribbon with a pretty unusual bow, and I'll send it home to the millions. How do you like them apples?"

"You wouldn't do that," he shouted at her. Calmer, he said it again, "you really wouldn't do that."

"Watch me."

She stood up and turned to leave his office, but he dashed up from behind and then around his desk, planting himself in front of her.

"Mrs. Compton, please wait here a moment, will you?" He was cooing at her and being very nice, suddenly. "I'll be back, right back, in a moment, okay?" He urged her back to her chair and Tooie, being Tooie, stood her ground, holding onto the chair's high back.

"I'll wait, but I won't sit. Not yet."

Nodding, nodding, nodding, Nolan backed out of his office. When the door had closed tightly after him, Tooie took a deep breath and let out a typically Tooie-like chuckle. She turned away and picked up the photo she had knocked over of Nolan, his wife and the two dogs.

"Fag," she said. "No kids and a trophy wife."

He wasn't long away and she was still holding his family photo when he came back into the room. He was accompanied by another man, a bigger, darker, older man in a baggier, stripier, older suit.

"Mrs. Compton, this is Mr. Arnold. He's the manager of this department. I told him about your plight and about our difficulty with Miss Marshall."

"Our difficulty?" Tooie was grinning as she said it. "That old sow needs replacing, that's the difficulty."

"Yes. And Mr. Nolan here thinks you're the woman to do it," Arnold said quickly. Too quickly for Tooie.

"What's the offer, Mr. Arnold? This guy here just gave me my walking papers."

"That's in the past, of course. An oversight. A mis-step in the world of judgement."

"I am sorry about that," Nolan added. "But all I had was the bare facts."

"All you had, buster, was the bare fears," Tooie said. "You heard that woman's insecurities is what you heard."

"Yes, I suppose so."

"What we're proposing at this juncture, Tooie...I may call you Tooie, mayn't I?" Arnold asked her. She nodded. "What we're proposing at this juncture, then, Tooie, is that you take over the department as supervisor, that you create your wonderful bows and ribbons and wraps and that you teach your craft to the five women working under you."

"Say, if I'm the supervisor then there are only four women under me."

"No, no. We'd keep Miss Marshall on in the capacity of ribbon clerk, your old job."

"I can't do that to her," Tooie said. "I can replace her but I can't boss her. I tell you it wouldn't be right, 'cause I couldn't be fair to her or about her."

"What are you saying," Arnold asked.

"You'll have to fire her, I guess. If you want me, you'll have to get rid of her and quick." She took a breath. "I've already got a few other offers here on Fifth Avenue."

Arnold leaped into the breach. "It's as good as done." He held out his right hand to shake hers, but Tooie wasn't done yet.

"Nothin's as good as done and it's got to be today. And I've got to have a raise, a good one. I'm not just a supervisor, I'm a designer. People are gonna see my stuff and know it's a Sachs original. That's gotta be worth something."

"Yes, of course," Arnold agreed glaring at Nolan over Tooie's head. "We'll get that all worked out to your satisfaction, I'm sure."

"Okey dokey, then. It's a deal."

So, Tooie got the big job and Hattie Marshall was out. You wonder how this affected us, Tooie and Me. That's the really interesting part.

She came home from work and told me the story about her promotion but she left out one major section of the story which I learned a few weeks later. When I did I really hit the ceiling and Tooie and I had one of the few major rows in our relationship, one that brought us to the brink of disaster. And it was all on account of her treatment of Hattie Marshall, a woman I never even met, or saw, but only heard about, mostly in relation to this story I just told you.

Oh, Tooie had mentioned her a few times before this firing and hiring incident. She would come home pissed at the way she'd been treated by Hattie Marshall. She'd rail and cry and carry on, but I always took it to be a work-related thing and not something personal. That's where I was wrong. So very wrong it hurts me to admit even now, so much later, so far away from it all.

It seems that Tooie and Hattie had a thing. Usually when Tooie found a new friend to play with, she'd tell me about it, let me know. But with Hattie it was something secret and to me that meant it meant something that could threaten our happiness together. That's not a good thing. Our marriage was based on an openness that was special. It included the threesomes, of course, but each of us was free to find a person, now and then, to be with. The agreement between us was no secrets, though. We told each other about it right away.

She heard about my fling with Virginia Woods. She heard about my little romance with the woman down the hall from us which lasted a few weeks. She told me about her own little affairs with women named Judy, Ramona and Sallie (Sallie turned out to be a guy, but that's another story). But with Hattie Marshall she kept mum.

How I found out about it was this. Maybe three weeks after she got the new job at Sachs, the really good one replacing Hattie Marshall, I was on the subway going to my office just off Wall Street, when this woman came up to me and poked me in the arm. I usually ignore such things on public conveyances, but this time she was persistent and I realized she wasn't just poking, she was saying my name.

"I got to talk to you Mr. Compton," she was saying.

"Say, do I know you?"

"No, you don't. But your wife does."

"Well, what goes on between my wife and her lady friends is no concern of mine," I said, not meaning it, but making it sound like I did.

"You're gonna wanna know about this," she said. Her voice was like acid on glass, you could hear the hissing sound it made, smell the smoke, too.

"Well, what is this about?" I said in frustration, almost in anger.

"She cost me my job, that bitch did, and all because I threw her over."

"What are you talking about?" We were off the train now, on the platform on a bench. In true New York fashion people were hurrying by us, paying no attention and I appreciated that.

"My name is Hattie Marshall. Does that mean anything to you?"

"I know the name. I've heard it mentioned."

"Well, your wife, Mr. Compton, your wife came on to me hard. She got me alone and she stuck her tongue in my mouth and she touched me where no one should and she got me going."

"Yeah, she's good at that. What of it?"

"She and me went together for a while. It was good. But then I got over her, I guess and I left her."

"Better for her. You weren't exactly nice to her in a business sense."

"You don't know, do you?" she said. "You bought into the story."

"What do you mean?"

"She was going to leave you for me," Hattie Marshall said. "She told me she would leave you and live with me. We were going to revolutionize the place at Sachs. We were going to be partners in the designs. But she scared me, and there was someone else."

"What are you talking about?"

"Sure I was hard on her, after that. I was hard because I knew I was betrayed by her."

"You're nuts," I said. "Tooie's not like that."

"You don't know her," she said to me. "You don't know the kind of woman she really is."

With that she got up off the bench and ran down to the other end of the platform where the other exit is. I sat there a moment thinking about what she said, and then I went up the stairs, crossed over to the uptown platform and went to see Tooie.

When I told her about the confrontation she didn't laugh like I wanted her to. She sat still and silent and looked at me, no tears in her eyes, no remorse in her face, nothing at all to tell me that she was sorry, or that the story was a fake.

"I should have told you Vinnie," she said quietly. "I should have been honest with someone, especially with you."

"It's true, then?"

"Yeah. Sort of. Mostly."

"What am I supposed to know that I don't, Tooie?"

"There's no one else. I promise you that."

"So she was wrong about that?"

"She was wrong. Period."

"I don't know. I think... I don't know."

I left her at Sachs and I went to the movies. That's how I remember it was 1939, twelve years into the marriage. I went to see "Gone with the Wind." I hadn't read the book, so it was a new story to me and it was four hours long and when it was over I remembered to call my office and tell them I wouldn't be in. They already guessed that, I think.

It was Scarlett O'Hara that changed me a bit. Something about the way she lied to everyone, especially to the men in her life about the men in her life. There was something about that woman that made me realize that Tooie had simply made a mistake, well two mistakes, getting involved with Hattie Marshall and then not telling me about it. I thought I'd better go see her again and tell her that I'd been thinking, had an epiphany.

She saw me coming up to the counter with a package in my hand. I put it on the counter. She stood there looking at me.

"It's a special present for someone I care about," I said. "Can you do something really special with it, please."

Tooie nodded at me. This time I saw a tear in her eye, but she held it firm, wouldn't let it drop off her cheek.

"I was gonna leave you," I said. "I don't stand for lies. Remember Lainie?"

She nodded, but kept her eyes on the package she was wrapping for me.

"But I went to the movies instead of the apartment. I packed in a lot of technicolor drama instead of a suitcase or two."

She didn't respond to me yet. She kept on with the ribbons now, multi-colored ones, all wrapped together into a tight rope ribbon.

"Scarlett O'Hara is a bitch, Tooie. You're just a fool. There's a difference I figured out about three hours into it."

She was working on the bow. It was building up in layers, four of them all looped in different directions. It was like a big zinnia. Beautiful.

"What you've got is ambition, Tooie, ambition and talent. You just took the wrong road to success. I can handle that if you promise me you won't lie about things, not to me."

She handed me the finished package. It was sensational, beautiful, erotic even, and I was so proud of her work, so proud of her.

"In my way, I love you, Tooie."

I handed her back the package.

"Don't you like the way it looks?" she asked me.

"I love it, but it's not mine." She looked up at me. "It's yours."

That's what saved our marriage in that perilous time of the lie. She did it all, just like she always did for me. No straight, dry paths for us. But we jumped the puddle.

CHAPTER THIRTEEN

From The International Thesaurus of Quotations:

"Reputation: When we are dead we are praised by those who survive us, though we frequently have no other merit than that of being no longer alive."

LaBruyere, Characters (1688)

I came home from Elainie's funeral, Lainie's funeral, and found Tooie sitting alone in a dark room in our apartment. I wanted to ask her what was wrong, but I didn't need to ask the question because I already knew the answer. I stood there for a moment, watching her in the dark, light from the street playing delicately across her pudgy features, and thought about our years together, our losses and our gains. I wasn't in a mood for balance sheets just then. I couldn't handle numbers or statistics or even theories. My mind was on the woman in the box, my eyes on the woman in the dark and my heart tugged and strained by the boy, in the grips of the woman, with Lainie's looks. That boy. I had never seen a boy with such sadness in his face. And I had seen lots of sad, little boys.

Half of my working life I had commuted to Wall Street, to the brokerage firm that employed me, where I'd spend the day with numbers and with telephones and log books. I worked without contact with people directly. I watched trends and I counted dollars rather than relationships. There were no friends, companions or cohorts with whom I could convene after work. I had clients, but they were voices whose personalities were contained in signed checks. I did this through half of my married years and

Tooie, who was the center of my life, was the only source I had for contacts with living people. Everyone else was a compound fraction, a percentage point and a dollared return on an investment.

It was July 12, the day I passed the orphanage, just off of Great Jones Street in Greenwich Village, that changed all of this for me. I had taken to walking up town after work, just to avoid the crush of angered humanity that plunged into the confines of the sewer-like subway. It was a pleasant way to end a day. From 8 in the morning until 4:30 in the afternoon my world consisted of the phone, the notebooks, a small window that looked out on other small windows, and, of course, a personal collection of finely sharpened pencils. So, walking up the broad highway of Broadway to West Broadway gave me a chance to breathe real air, clear my head of the dust of numbers and see faces. There weren't many faces that inspired me to chat with any of them. Once or twice I thought about it, but I am not gregarious. I don't make first moves easily. And, anyway, Tooie was already supplying me with strangers for my physical communications.

Imagine my surprise, then, when the two boys grabbed me by the ankles and tussled me to the ground. I hadn't even noticed them; children had never made much of an impression on me. They ran out of a building, just ahead of me, and as I passed they lunged, tackled me with one on each leg and knocked me over. I fell over the one to my left and felt the one to my right reach up for my coat, stick his hand inside, brushing it along my chest and extending into my breast pocket where he came into contact with my wallet. I tried to snatch it back from him but I was so off-balance, and the other one had such a grip on my arm now, that I couldn't make the move quickly or definitely enough. I rolled, they ran and I was instantly up on my feet.

I could see them ahead of me on the crowded pavement and I took off after them like a shot. I am long-legged and a good runner - winner of several high school trophies actually - so I was soon up alongside them.

"Stop where you are, boys," I shouted, "or you will regret your actions."

"Keep off it, long and lanky," one of them screamed in my direction. "Pervert! Help! Pervert!"

The other one took up the cry and though they continued running, and calling me names, recreating me as a public nuisance for the gathering public, I kept up with them. "No, you don't," I thought to myself and I added a cry of my own to their loud, soprano voices.

"Stop thieves," I cried. "Help me, someone, catch them. Thieves."

The joint vociferations of "thief" and "pervert" attracted quite a crowd. Within seconds there was a circle around us and the boys had nowhere to run, nowhere to hide.

"Hit him, somebody," one of the boys shouted with pain in his voice. "He'll hurt me."

"Just give me back my pocketbook," I said loudly enough for everyone in the crowd to hear. "They shanghaied me and stole my wallet!" I added so my listeners would understand the situation. "Knocked me right over and snatched and ran." One sympathetic woman patted me on the arm. The man who stood closest to the boy who had stolen my wallet reached out instantly and grasped the youngster by his shoulder. The other boy, seeing his friend nabbed tried to push through the crowd, but New Yorkers know how to stand fast and hold a position and they didn't let him through.

"Which one, Mister?" someone shouted. "Which one done it?"

"This one robbed me," I said indicating the boy on my right, "but they both had a hand in

it. This one knocked me down."

"I never..." the youngster started to say, his defense not possible as the crowd shouted mean things in his direction.

"You did, though," I reminded him. There were cries of "show us the wallet," and "give us your proof" from different ends of the gathering. The first boy just laughed at the catcalls and his laughter seemed to say, "I don't have it. Prove your case, Mister," as it flashed in my direction.

"Here it is, Mister," a policeman spoke out from the far reaches of the throng. He pushed his way through and came abreast of me. "Your name, please."

"Vincent Compton." He opened the wallet that I knew was mine and looked into it, searching for an identification card. He found one quickly.

"That's the name, all right, sir. You're lucky. Spotted it about half a block back."

"He must have tossed it when I gave chase, then," I said.

"He's a liar. I never did. He's just after me, that's all. Pervert."

"Officer, don't listen to this. They knocked me over, tackled me, and stole that wallet from my coat pocket."

"Thank you, sir. I'll take it from here. We know young Cassius here. Know him well, don't we Cass?"

"How do, Officer Murphy?"

"I'll 'how do' you, Cassius. That I will, and your little accomplice too."

Just then a woman pushed through from the far side of the crowd. She was pretty, about 25 years old with pale orange hair and a freckled complexion, grey eyes and soft red lips. She was wearing a plain brown dress with pockets.

"Officer Murphy, please don't," she said in a sweet, pleading voice.

"Miss Levy, you know I have to write this up. You know it."

"For the sake of the orphanage, I beg you not to. I'm sure this nice man won't press charges now that he has his wallet back." She flashed a smile at me. "You will be kind to the children, won't you?"

I didn't mean to answer her, but I found myself nodding, making a visual promise that my lips couldn't speak.

"Thank you, sir. The children at St. Jason's thank you also."

"I'm not sure...."

"And on their patron saint's feast day, too. Thank you so much." She had both boys by the hands now. "St. Jason's is not a wealthy place and a fine would break us right now, so I thank you much.

I was compelled by this creature. She was so straightforward and so easy with me and with the police officer. "St. Jason's?" I said. "I'm not aware of it Miss...?"

"Arlene Levy," she said. "I'd shake your hand but I dare not let go of either boy just yet."

"Yes, of course, I understand....?"

"I'm headmistress this week," she said. "That is until the new head is picked and I go back to cleaning and cooking and such."

"But you're so good with them. You should always be surrounded by children."

"Now, don't get me started on that subject," she said. She nearly swung her small charges around as she turned away from me and headed for home. I wanted to stop her going, talk to her a while, but I found myself both tongue-tied and unable to think of anything to say. I followed them down the block and waited while they mounted the steps of a large, double-width brownstone, an old building on an older street, just off the Bowery. It was imposing and grand, once a fine home I could see, and still decent, at least in its facade. Once she had made it up the nine high stone steps to the large, glass double doors she turned to look at me on the sidewalk.

"You might as well come in, Mr. Compton," she said. "You look almost as lost as the rest of the children inside." I followed her in. Nothing was ever the same for me after that. There were the children and Arlene Levy and still there was Tooie at home. And I finally had a calling, a life-work, something to inspire and tire me. Surrounded by children, boys, I have spent the rest of my time in life raising money to keep St. Jason's Home alive. To finally put my best tools to work for something less than selfish was what I needed. It was what I found.

Max had reminded me of Lainie even more than his mother did when I saw her. Max, with Lainie's eyes and mouth, Lainie's way of moving her head to one side when she spoke or when she was seriously watching me. Max reminded of John Jack, and Louis and Robert John, Robert Joseph and Robert Paul. He put me in mind of so many of the boys at St. Jason's. Jason, the Saint, aided his cousin Paul and was himself the Bishop of Tarsus. We aid the boys at the home established in his name and I wanted nothing more than to come to the aid of this boy, Max, grandson of Lainie, St. Lainie, my Lainie.

CHAPTER FOURTEEN

From The Readers Digest, April, 1946"

> From Uniques: "A Vancouver woman told police that
> in 18 years of marriage she never had got along with
> her husband, that he had promised her a divorce but
> never got around to giving it to her. 'So please,' She
> asked, 'can I sue him for breach of promise?'" – UP

It was fifteen weeks after my Granny Elainie's funeral that Mr. Compton
kept his promise and came to see us. He brought along Tooie, the famous
Tooie. They were sitting in the foyer of our apartment building when
I came in from school. At first I didn't know who they were and I was
walking by them when the man on the bench called out my name.

"Max," he called. "Max, over here."

I turned to see who it was and recognized him at once. He rose and
held out his hand, ready to shake mine, I guess, but I walked right by him
to the woman sitting quite still on the upholstered leather bench against
the wall. I picked her hand up off her lap and held on to it, tight, and said,
"you must be Tooie." After a second or two she nodded but didn't speak.

"I'm glad to to meet you," I said. "I'm Max, Elainie's grandson."

She nodded again, but still said nothing.

"Cat got your tongue?" I asked her. She laughed, shook her head then
nodded.

"I can talk," she said. "Don't worry about that, kiddo."

She sounded so much like my Granny that I instantly burst into
tears on hearing her. She reached around and pulled me to her and held
me while I sobbed. I liked the very familiar scent of her. Here, too, she

reminded me of my loss. I cried there in the strong circle of her embrace, then pulled myself together and stood back up, alone and unsupported.

"Let me see you, kid," Tooie said. "let me see how you look."

I took a big step backward and stood up straight and tall, my shoulders thrown back and my chest out. I heard her laugh. It was a warm, enthralling sort of laughter and it made me smile just to hear it.

"You're a cute kid," she said, that laughter ringing through the words. "A darn cute kid. You're right Vin," she said, "he does look like Lainie."

"Everybody says I do," I told her.

"Everybody's right, then," she answered.

"My sister Brianna doesn't look like her at all."

"Is that so? Well, we'll have to see about that."

"It's so, Tooie," Mr. Compton told her.

"I can fix that," Tooie said. "I can fix that right up."

"No, don't," I said. "That look is mine."

"She won't then, Max," Mr. Compton said to me.

"Yeah, okay," Tooie said grudgingly.

I heard the elevator door opening, and I took Tooie's hand and pulled her up off the bench and over toward the elevator. Mr. Compton followed us and in silence we rode up to my floor. There was something so very right about their being here with me and I couldn't explain that rationally to myself, but it felt right. I hoped my mother would feel the same when we got to the apartment.

I didn't have to worry. She was gracious and welcoming. She was wearing a peach colored slip and high heels when we came in. I called out to her, to warn her that I had company with me. Sometimes when I came home she would only be wearing a girdle and a bra, no panties or anything else. But today she had on the slip and she looked almost fashionably dressed.

She came around the corner from the living room and I could feel the rush of fresh air she brought with her which meant that she had been sitting by the open terrace door. Before I could say anything more, Mr. Compton said hello and introduced his wife.

"Lana, this is Tooie. You've heard about Tooie, I'm sure."

"Of course I have, from my mother." Tooie was holding out her hand, but Lana reached out and hugged her, kissing her lightly on the cheek.

"Ooh, pert breasts," Tooie said, "hard nipples."

"Oh, forgive me, not being dressed, but it's so hot today," Lana said quickly. "Excuse me for just a minute while I throw something on."

"Don't do it for me," Tooie called out after her but Lana was out of the room already.

"Behave youself, now," Mr. Compton said to her, a bit harsh but not too harsh.

"Oh, all right. I was just kidding around anyway. I mean, that's Lainie's daughter, for God's sake."

"I know who she is, Tooie, and I'm glad to hear you do too."

"All right, already."

Mother was back in a flash, dressed and wearing her pearl earrings that had been her mother's favorites. Tooie recognized them immediately.

"I gave those to Elainie," she said.

"They are so beautiful," Mother said.

"They were a gift from me, a loan of a gift, actually."

Mother instinctively put one hand up to touch an earring. Instantly embarrassed by the gesture she moved her hand away and into the air near her head.

"Such a beautiful day, too," she said as she moved her hand and her arm around. "Can I get you anything, a drink perhaps?"

"Sure," Tooie replied. "A martini, please? Gin, not Vodka, and with olives and up," she added shaking her hand to indicate a tall glass.

"Like Mama's then," Mother said. She made the drink and there was a long, uncomfortable silence while she did it. I thought Mr. Compton would say something but he didn't, at least not until Mother was finished making Tooie's martini.

"You don't have to entertain us, Lana," he said. "We just came so Tooie could meet you both. I promised I'd do that, so I have."

"Why did you wait so long?" I asked him.

"Excuse me?"

"Why did you wait so long to come?" I repeated my question.

"I didn't want to intrude on your...sorrow," he said.

"You didn't think then," I told him. "Sorrow gets help from friends."

"You're a wise child," Tooie added.

"He is," Mother said, hugging me. "Both my children have brains."

"Brianna has brains?" I asked. Mother swatted me with the back of her hand across my shoulder. "Sorry."

"Brianna is my daughter," Mother explained. "She's gone into the family business."

Tooie and Mr. Compton gave each other a sidelong glance, then they both smiled and turned back to us.

"I'm sure Lainie would be proud," Tooie said sweetly, her smile plastered across her face.

"Oh, she was, she was," Mother told her. "She just wanted Brianna to be certain that she understood what she was getting into. My mother would never have guessed about Brianna's instant success and her meteoric climb up the ladder of prostitution."

"I didn't know there was a ladder," Mr. Compton said.

"Oh, my, yes. I made it half way up before I met my husband and got out of the business to raise a family."

"What's the halfway point, darling?" Tooie asked her.

"Well, the call girl slash escort is about half way. That's where I was working when we met. It's fairly clean because half the time there's no sex but you can get paid big bucks anyway."

"That must have been nice for you," Tooie said, smiling, "to get paid for only half the work."

"It was."

"Lainie was never a paid escort," Mr. Compton added.

"No, not Mama. She was pretty single-minded about what she would do for dough."

"We loved her, you know. Vinnie hoped to keep in touch with her through me, but after we wed that just wasn't possible."

"I know."

"It's sad, really. He always loved her best, but he couldn't stand the deception."

"I know. She told me. I was sorry that I was the cause of your splitting."

"Thank you, Lana. It wasn't you, exactly. It was the knowledge of you. I was the weak one, the one who couldn't handle it. Lainie was almost blameless when you get right down to it."

At that moment, when Mr. Compton said those words, I knew that I could like him very much. He was being nice, and being honest too, about a situation that he just couldn't handle when he was younger.

"You really loved her," I said to him.

"I did, Max, I did."

"And I loved her too, don't forget. She was my best friend. She was the first person I ever told about myself and she was there for me. She wouldn't just let me go with anyone, it had to be someone nice enough for me."

"Tooie's made a name for herself, you know, in the retail business."

"So you sell at a markup now?" Mother asked her.

"No! It's not that sort of thing at all." Tooie proceeded to tell us about her work at Sachs and her gift wrapping inventions. While she was talking about it, she opened her bag and took out some beautiful dark red ribbon, the color of blood, and began to fold and twist the ribbon into a sensational form that resembled a bird on a nest. I was really impressed that she could just do that, right there in the apartment, without even watching her fingers. I knew I loved her right then and there. I just knew it.

Mother was impressed also. I could see that in her face and in her body as she leaned forward to look at the finished art work. She picked it up carefully, keeping what she assumed to be delicate and easily destroyed cupped in her long fingers and her deep palm.

"Oh, honey, you can just toss that birdie around," Tooie told her. "You can't hurt it."

Mother grinned, an expression I had rarely seen on her face, and tossed the whole thing up into the air. She caught it coming down with both hands and clasped it tightly for a moment, then released it. The form of the bird in the nest immediately reappeared from the jumble of ribbons I was looking at. That was thrilling. I jumped up from my chair and hugged Tooie around the neck. "I knew I was going to like you. I knew it."

"Now you be careful young one," she said. "I'm liable to fall for you."

"Hey, hey there," Mr. Compton added.

"May we come again?" Tooie asked Mother as she stood up. Mother nodded and they hugged one another. Mr. Compton shook Mother's hand and then he shook mine as well.

"I'm sorry we have to go, but we were unexpected and we promised one another that we wouldn't stay and be a burden," he said.

"Oh, you're not," Mother said hastily. "And of course we'll see you again, soon."

"As for you youngster," he began, but Tooie corrected him "Kiddo, Vin, not youngster." He nodded to her and continued: "As for you, we'll be seeing a lot of you, I hope." I said something like "definitely!" with emphasis and we all began to walk to the door.

"You've got to promise me one thing, though," Mr. Compton said, and I agreed without knowing what he might ask. "If I don't come back sometime, you won't sue me for breach of promise." Then he laughed.

If I had only known what he meant by that, I wouldn't have laughed along with him. But that little secret would take years to discover.

CHAPTER FIFTEEN

From The Reader's Digest, April, 1946:

> From Cartoon Quips: "Boss replying to employee
> asking for a raise: 'Of course you're worth more than
> you're getting, Morton. Why don't you let up a bit?"
>
> B. Tobey in The Saturday Evening Post

How old was I when the work came up? I think I was already in my teens,
fifteen or almost sixteen. So much had changed for me after Granny
Elainie died and Mr. Compton and Tooie came along. For boys it's not
the same as with the girls. Girls have a natural tendency toward the work,
at least the girls in my family, my mother and my sister Brianna at least,
had a natural bent in that direction. Mother had given it all up when she
married father and got pregnant. I know she sometimes regretted that, but
she had been a good mother and she loved both of us so it wasn't exactly
the hardship it might have been for her. And she had father and he had
given up the straight and narrow for "the life." And we were all happy and
healthy and living well.

Mother was the first one to wonder about me. On my thirteenth
birthday she sat me down alone in the living room and talked to me about
the family business. We talked a long time and she told me many things.
Now, some of it I knew from my talks with Granny Elainie but some of
it was new and different... very different. Mother told me about boys and
what they sometimes did and I have to say it was a pretty horrible thing
to hear about from your mother.

"I don't need to know much more do I?" I asked her when she took a breath after discussing oral sex.

"Oh, yes, Maxie," she said, "there's so much more."

"I don't want to know about it."

"Well, all right, not today, then."

"Not ever," I said adamantly. "I don't want to know anything else."

"You're young. You'll get curious."

"Why? Why would I get curious?"

"You're a boy," she said. "Boys want to know things."

"Not me," I assured her. "I already know more than I want to know."

I was embarrassed because the talk about erections and things had given me one and I didn't like that sensation. It had happened to me several times that summer at the beach and, wearing a tight, stretchy bathing suit instead of the old-fashioned loose boxer short types I had been feeling terribly humiliated. I didn't know what was going on or why. I only knew it made me feel ashamed of myself, made me want to hide. I used a beach towel to cover my loins until the painful swelling went down.

Somehow I knew that I hadn't been bitten by a sandcrab or a mosquito, that this was the first flush of sexuality. That only increased my fears that someone would notice, might point or giggle or even laugh at me. I was insecure enough without people laughing at me. Later visits to the beach I always wore a big, long shirt that covered me to the knees, just in case it happened again and it always, invariably did. I felt better knowing I could hide beneath my Hawaiian tunic and not be revealed as the pervert I felt I was becoming.

Now, just a few weeks later, Mother was talking to me about sex and business. This wasn't what I wanted to talk about. I wanted to talk about cars and about school and about my new friend Freddy, a girl I had met in Central Park who had fallen off stilts. Freddy was the first girl I had met who didn't behave badly with me. She was accepting and nice and didn't challenge me too much and didn't seem to want to always grab me and kiss me. I wanted to tell Mother about her, but Mother never seemed to be interested in my friends. Except for Tooie and Mr. Compton, of course. She always wanted to know about them.

I had been seeing them from time to time and, just recently, just after my fifteenth birthday, they had taken me out to dinner at the Hotel Carlisle and we had gone, afterward, to a nightclub and heard Mel Tormé sing. That had been very special for me. I had seen him in the movies and on the Ed Sullivan Show on Sunday nights, but I had never seen him up close before.

I was surprised to learn that he wasn't much taller than me. I had suffered a growth spurt at twelve and again at fourteen and shot up five inches in each year. My clothes, naturally, didn't fit me too well and I looked a bit like an out-of-towner, some hick from the sticks who had come to New York to become something better without an inkling of how to go about it. But Mel was about my height and his clothes were perfect, a tuxedo with a frilly shirtfront and a thin black bow-tie. His blonde hair had a kind of flip in the front that gave him a jaunty, angular look that seemed to pull his mouth into a sly smile. He sang songs I loved, songs my Granny Elainie knew. I mentioned that to Tooie and to Mr. Compton and they just nodded.

"We knew he'd sing some of the old standards, Max," Tooie said. "We hoped that would be okay with you."

They knew it would be because they knew my taste was like my dead grandmother's taste. They both knew where my best education had come from when I was a kid.

"I love it," I said. "This is a great gift. Thanks."

Tormé had just broken into Judy Garland's big hit 'Over the Rainbow' and he shot a glance in our direction. I smiled at him and he smiled back on the words in the verse about someday wishing on a star and I knew, right then, what they really meant. I knew about longing for a different life, a different place but right then and there I was content to be where I was and who I was, knowing that the yearning could, and probably would, return for something else.

"Want a real drink?" Mr. Compton asked me. I smiled and was about to say that I had already had one, when Tooie slapped him on the wrist.

"Don't corrupt the boy, Vin," she said.

"Corrupt? I just thought he'd like a fruit drink like a Screwdriver."

"You're bad, you are."

"Tooie, it won't hurt him."

"I think it's a bad idea."

I shushed them. Tormé was singing beautifully and I didn't want to have to cup my hands over my ears just to hear him. It seemed like he was singing just for me and I was really getting into it. Besides, I thought quickly so I could get it over with, I didn't want a 'real' drink. I was fine with my Shirley Temple.

When the song ended and we were applauding I turned to Mr.

Compton and explained that I didn't want a drink, but he had already ordered me one, so I just took it, thanked him and took a sip before setting it down on the table. I liked the taste of it and in a few seconds I felt a kind of buzz in my gullet and then in my head that I couldn't explain, so I assumed it was the liquor in the mixture. I looked at Mr. Compton and he grinned at me, so I grinned back at him. I was having a smiley night.

When the set was over and the jazz singer had retired from the stage, we got into a conversation. Tooie was a big fan and Mr. Compton was too, so the three of us could compare our notes and feel confident that the discussion was worthwhile. While we talked I finished the drink.

It was getting late and I had school the next day, so Tooie suggested they take me home. Mr. Compton thought it a good idea, so he called for the check, but Tooie slapped him again and said she'd take care of it. I got up to go to the men's room and left them squabbling over the bill. I hadn't been in the toilet long when the door opened and Mr. Compton came in. He took up a position in the next stall and without a word we did our business. I felt odd standing next to him. I knew he was always comparing me to Granny Elainie, seeing in my face something of hers. While I liked that, it also made me uncomfortable and I felt his eyes on me there and then. Without speaking we both finished up, washed our hands and left the men's room.

"Where's Tooie?" I asked him. I had looked for her in the vestibule of the club but didn't see her.

"She's gone home, Max. I'll take you back to the apartment."

"You don't have to, Mr. Compton," I said. "I can get home."

"Nonsense," he replied. "I just gave you an alcoholic drink and you're just a kid. I'll take you home and no back-talk."

There seemed to be no other option so I nodded and we left the building. Cabs were lined up waiting for club patrons to emerge, so we had no wait. I got in and Mr. Compton followed quickly. He gave the cabbie my address and we sat back against the green leather seat. He put his arm around my shoulders and pulled me in close to him.

"How did you enjoy your birthday, Max?"

"It was great. Thanks so much."

"We wanted to be with you, Tooie and me both."

"Well, thank you for that. I love both of you."

"You're very sweet, young man."

"Okay, but I'm not really," I said. "I can be pretty bad at times."

"Oh? How bad is pretty bad?"

"Pretty bad."

"Do you know how much you remind me of your grandmother?" he asked me.

"I think I do, yes."

"No, I don't think so. I don't think you do."

He put his free hand under my chin and tipped my head backward a bit so that I was staring up at him.

"Close your eyes, Max. Please. I want to give you something."

"What?"

"Something of your Grandmother's. Something that belongs to Lainie."

"Oh." I was surprised and little nervous when he said that, but I did what he asked. For a second or two nothing happened, but then I felt his breath on my face, then his lips touching mine and then his tongue tickling my closed mouth. A rush of emotions engulfed me. My head felt feverish and my feet and hands were like ice. Then he was sitting up again and it was over. But I had an erection and I was embarrassed and I didn't know what to say.

"That was for her, Max, not for you," he said quietly. "I miss her so much."

"I miss her too, Mr. Compton," I said very quietly, so quietly I wasn't sure he heard me.

"I won't do that again, Max. I assure you. But I had to this time, okay?"

I nodded and shortly after that the cab pulled up to my building and I moved quickly to the door and opened it outward.

"Thank you for tonight, Mr. Compton. Please thank Tooie for me, too, please."

The cab pulled away and he was gone. I was feeling better, standing up in the cool night air. I went up to the apartment and by the time I got there I was fine.

It was sometime after that when my mother decided to talk to me about the work. I was either near sixteen, or just sixteen, but it was a time when birthdays no longer held any magic for me. She had talked about sex between consenting adult men and that had surprised me when I was thirteen. Now, as she brought it up again, I remembered the kiss in the cab and knew that was sort of where she was heading with her chat, but I didn't want her to know about Mr. Compton and his looks and his

89

touches and his kiss. I had never told anyone about it and I wasn't going to do that now.

She had told me about her life and about my sister's success. She had talked about a few other people we knew and about my Dad and his work at the hotel. She was discussing the practical aspects of prostitution and the care, cleanliness and attitude toward the work that had distinguished her family from the ordinary whores on the corners or the call girls. We were a family with a family business and we were different from the others.

I had moved away from her after we stopped talking and just outside the living room I had a thought, so I went back in. She was where I had left her, but she wasn't looking in my direction. Instead she was gazing at nothing, her eyes trained on the pull at the bottom of the braided cord on the window shade. I watched for a while, hoping she would break her concentration and notice me again, but she didn't.

"Momma," I said and she turned slowly to look at me, "why did you talk to me about sex and men when I was still a kid? And why are we talking about it again now?"

"You're a young man," she said. "You need to know about your nature and where it might take you."

"My nature?"

"I'm your mother, Maxie, and I know you better than you know yourself."

"What does that mean?"

"You're a pretty boy, Max. Pretty boys attract older men."

"I don't."

"You do." She said it so simply I had to believe it. "I watch when we're out and I see the effect you have on them."

"I didn't know...."

"I know that. You're an innocent, maybe the last one in the world, Maxie. I don't want you to be unprepared for things."

"I'm not such an innocent."

I had a secret and I wanted to share it with her but I hadn't because there were other people involved.

"What do you mean?" she asked. "What secrets are you hiding from me?"

"There's..." I couldn't go on.

"Max. Tell me, please."

"Not now, not today," I said and I ran from the room. My mother had seen my secret before I knew it myself. She had glimpsed the truths

I couldn't acknowledge because I had no words for them at the time. My mother was my confessor because she knew what I would say if I could say it.

And, at just about sixteen, I had a secret that was even more important than my little kiss in the cab with Mr. Compton. I just wasn't ready to share it with anyone. Not even with my mother.

CHAPTER SIXTEEN

From Brewer's The Dictionary of Phrase and Fable:

Lidskialfa [the terror of nations]. The throne of Alfader, whence he can view the whole universe.

(Scandinavian mythology)

She isn't laid up very long. The wounds had not been as severe as she first thought them. Once the doctors had looked her over, bound up the minor break in her leg and handed over the morphine to her mother, to be used only when the pain was too great to allow her some sleep, she could relax a little, think about Mikhael and about Max, too. Freddy had always been a healer, a quick one. The cut on her upper lip when the carving knife had slipped on an onion skin and flipped backward onto her face had healed in only two weeks. It left a tiny scar, a pencil-thin mark from the top of her lip to the side of her nose, but with a touch of powder it disappears almost completely now. The break in her bone was minor, the sort of scattering that heals most easily. Luckily, they told her, she is young and with the young the time it takes is minimal. She is up and about in just over a week.

During that time in bed, alone most of the time, she thinks a great deal about Mikhael and his father and the chair. He has never answered her about the chair. Instead he has distracted her with other things, with the stilts, with games. Now, with so much time on her hands, instead of on her feet, that chair and its secrets occupy her mind. What has he told her? What does she remember about it? What are the words?

"It is a chair that contains us and brings no joy at all." Those had been his words. "It is a seat of long tradition and my father has taken it from his country without the permission of the state."

She remembers their conversation vividly. She remembers how she had asked him about his father's rights and Mikhael's darkened expression when he tells her "That is our trouble." He has never explained this to her, but he has called her a Queen, called her Queen Fredericka and she recalls liking her name for the first time in her life. She misses that feeling of sudden and inexplicable pride in her name. It had been too new, too short-lived. She misses Mikhael and she wonders why he had disappeared in the park that day, left her alone to suffer in pain. She wants to hate him, but she likes him too much to do that, ever.

When her mother tells her that Mikhael Staffiev is at the door to see her, and starts to ask Freddy if she wants to see him, Freddy nearly leaps out of the chaise that holds her. It is almost as though her thoughts of him had somehow summoned him.

"Bring him in," she shouts. "I want to see him now."

She is so demonstrative that her mother backs out of the doorway and a moment later reopens the door to admit Mikhael. He comes in quickly, nodding to Mrs. Wales as he passes her. Freddy's mother closes the door, but leaves it unlatched...just as a precaution. Then, discreetly, she goes into the kitchen and shuts that door tight.

Mikhael throws himself down onto the carpet and bows his head low in front the reclining Freddy.

"You must forgive this boy," he says, almost too quietly to be heard, but Freddy hears him.

"I should be very mad at you," she says.

"I was the coward," he responds, looking up at her. "You fell and I did not know it instantly, but as I turned to look at you and found you not there, I wondered what I had done. Then I heard the crowd gather on the other side of the hill, heard the man who yelled that a girl was hurt, and I was frightened. I leaped from my stilts and dragged them with me as I ran from the park."

"That was wrong of you," Freddy says. "You should have come back for me."

"I could not. The chair."

"Oh, damn the chair. I hate that chair."

"But my father...."

"Who is your father," she cries, "that his chair means more to you than your only friend when she's hurt?"

"He is my father. Surely you understand what that means."

"I don't." Freddy doesn't want to sound the way she knew she sounded, but she couldn't help it, can't stop her voice from whining. "You have to help me, Mikhael. You have to tell me things and make me understand you."

"You know I must keep the secrets of my father."

"I know." She is calmer suddenly. Familiarity with this situation kicks in and she hears her voice grow softer.

"I would tell you much if the time was better." He is smiling up at her from his position on the floor. He reaches up and takes her hand. "I would tell you everything, Fredericka, if it was possible."

"Yes, I know you would."

"I love you, my sister."

For some reason this simple statement makes her blush, gives her chills and sends a shiver down her spine. The doorbell rings and she hears her mother move from the kitchen table, shoving back her chair and then hears her footsteps. Mikhael sits silent and Freddy holds her breath. Visitors are rare at their apartment. This is strange.

A moment later her mother opens the door to her room and looks in, reacting oddly to the sight of Mikhael on the floor, then smiles, then speaks.

"You have another one, another boy."

"Who?"

"Max? I think he said Max."

"Can he come in, too, please?" Her mother withdraws, then reopens the door one more time and lets Max enter her room. He also reacts sharply to the sight of Mikhael on the floor.

"I've never seen so many boys in your room, before," Mrs. Wales mutters.

"We'll be fine. Just close the door, please." Her mother does as she is asked and Freddy introduces the two boys.

"You're the kid on stilts, then?" Max asks.

"He was," Freddy tells him.

"You're a bigger kid than I supposed," Max continues. "I thought bigger kids were more responsible."

"I am responsible when it is convenient," Mikhael answers, "and in this instance it was not so. Too many people converged on our Fredericka too quickly."

"That's nuts," Max responds.

"My hero! My champion!"

"To whom do you refer with these accolades, Fredericka?"

"To Max, of course. Not to you, Mikhael."

"And Max, you would wish some sort of hero's wreath, I suppose? To be crowned with the laurels?"

"Not me, bub," Max said, as manly a man as he can muster under these odd circumstances.

Freddy giggles. She likes the differences between the boys almost more than the boys themselves.

"He talks funny. Really foreign," Max says to Freddy.

"I am from another world," Mikhael tells him.

"Yeah, like Jupiter or Saturn."

"Or Uranus," Freddy says and the words make her laugh, a laughter echoed by Max and finally, realizing the silliness of it, by Mikhael himself.

"Where are you from?"

"I've been trying to get him to tell me for weeks, Max."

"Are you ashamed of your place?"

"I am not. I may not speak of it easily, however."

"He has a chair his father stole from there, wherever there is."

"Freddy! You must not speak of the chair."

"It's a throne, Max. A real throne."

"I never heard of a throne being stolen," Max says.

"It is not stolen, it is appropriated by its rightful occupant."

"Occupant? Does your father sit in it all the time?" There is no reply.

"I've sat in it, Max, and not on his father's lap, either. His father wasn't there."

"You are irreverent, Fredericka," Mikhael says, standing up finally and brushing off his pants with his open hands.

"Mikhael, I am happy you came to see me but I'm still mad at you for leaving me like that."

"Yeah, why would you do that to her?"

"My reasons are based on sound judgement."

"I still want to know why," Freddy demands. "I know you have lots of secrets, but I want to know."

"Not in front of him," Mikhael says.

"So you will tell me, if Max goes away?"

"I will. I promise."

"But Max won't go away. I want him to stay."

"These are secrets!"

"Max, will you promise, will you swear, to keep whatever you hear in this room to yourself, always and forever?"

"Yeah, I will!"

"Does that satisfy you, Mikhael?" He crosses his arms over his chest and pouts. He is tapping his right foot in a strong and steady rhythm. Freddy watches him in silence and Max does likewise. "Does it?" She finally says.

"I accept this pledge."

"Good! Now, give!"

The three of them, seated, move close together and Mikhael proceeds to confess his secret, things he has told no one else ever since arriving in America. When he is done, he admits to them both, he feels better, freer than he has felt in a long time.

"The chair is the Lidskialfa, the throne of Alfader. This is the ancestral throne of our people. My country no longer is there, Freddy, a tiny place between Lapland and Poland with Russia just behind it. Alfader, the ruler of my place, is the ancestral name for what you would call the King. In that world he is not just a ruler, but the father of his people, the all-seeing father, the God or demi-God. My father was the last of these men, the last in our country which has disappeared, perhaps for always now. When this European war which devastated the world ended, the Russians claimed our land for their own and my family fled to Denmark, then to Holland, then France and then to America. In my lifetime I have dwelt in five countries. My father has dwelt in six. My mother in nine and my sister in ten of them. I am the guardian of the Lidskialfa, the only one who knows its importance. One day, when my country is ours again, we will return the chair to the room where the Alfader sits and watches over the entire universe that is his legacy. I will be the Alfader."

"Golly," says Max, "can I see this likkykalpher some time?"

"Lidskialfa. And one day, perhaps."

"I've sat in it, Max."

"And do you mean to tell us that you live alone?" Max asks. "You're just a kid."

"No. I have two servants who look after my needs."

"But no father at home? No mother or sister?"

"No."

"Max has a sister, too, an older sister."

"Mine is also older, but she may not inherit. She is a girl."

"My sister, Brianna, already owns the world," Max says, but when pressed for more information by Freddy, he won't say another word about her.

"When can I see this chair?" Max asks.

"There is no good time."

"You could take him home with you, Mikhael. You could show it to him now."

"I think it is not a good time, Fredericka."

"I have to take some medicine and that always makes me sleepy. You should both go and Mikhael, you should show Max the Lids...ski...al...fa. Is that it?"

"That is it."

"I'll come back soon," Max says. "I'll go and leave you two alone."

"No! You'll go home with the demi-God boy and see the chair. I don't want you to think we've been kidding you."

"Some other time."

"No. For Fredericka's sake, I will take you there now."

That settled among them, the two boys embrace Freddy and depart for Mikhael's 154th Street apartment. She watches them go, sees Mikhael slip an arm around Max's waist as though to escort him swiftly from the room. She hears them say goodbye to her mother and she hears the door close behind them. Somehow, she knows, that arm will remain around that waist for a longer time than necessary. Something about the way Mikhael had called her his sister.

"I need the morphine, now," she calls to her mother. "I need it bad."

CHAPTER SEVENTEEN

From The Reader's Digest, April, 1946

from Talkfest II - Unconventionally Speaking:

Henry Morton Robison, roving editor of the Reader?s Digest: "Gypsy, shall we assume that everyone knows what Unconventionality means—'and take off at once'?"

Gypsy Rose Lee, première stripteuse of burlesque and author of The G-String Murders: "Let's not be in such a hurry to take off anything. With all the amateurs at it, how do you expect a girl like me to make a living?"

We stood in the room with the chair, the Lidskialfa, just Mikhael and me, for a long time. It had a light shining down on it and the gold that was on it, at first, made it hard to see the fine carving and the details. I wanted to go right up to it and touch it, just to see what I couldn't see at a distance, but when I took that first step up to it, Mikhael put his hand on my shoulder and stopped me.

"We go no closer," he said in a soft voice.

I nodded, but then I shook my head.

"Freddy said she sat in it. What's that about?"

"For Fredericka it was different. She is already a queen in my heart."

"I see," I said. "She's a queen and I'm just a ... what? A vassal?"

"No, of course not."

"Then what? What am I?"

"You are a New York boy whom I know through odd circumstances. That is all you are to me."

"Mikhael, you are not a nice person at all. You're a snob."

"I am. I admit it."

I heard him laugh, or at least chuckle twice, right after he said that and although he was telling me I was right, it made me blush. I think it must have been the attitude in his voice. I think it had to be the terrible way it made me feel suddenly to be right in judging someone when I had no right to judge anyone.

"I'm sorry," I whispered.

"I accept this apology in the spirit in which it is given."

"What's that supposed to mean?"

"You apologize and I accept. That's all."

"No, it's not all. I can hear in your voice that it's not all."

"Can you?" He gave me a strange sort of look as though he could read something in my face that I didn't know was written there. "You can, I see it. You have a mind, Max. I was not aware of that."

"Of course I have a mind."

"I don't mean a brain, Max. Everyone has a brain. You have a mind. That is not the same thing at all. It means that you can reason and feel things at the same time and make a deliberate and honest decision on the two things at once. You may have the same double senses as King Solomon."

"You're putting me on," I said, almost embarrassed at saying it.

"No. I mean this completely. You may have the finest mind in my experience."

He put his hand on my shoulder again, only this time it was to lead me closer to the throne. I moved hesitantly in the direction in which he guided me and when we reached the edge of the platform on which the Lidskialfa sat we stopped. He put his other hand on the arm of the chair and gently guided me up the step to the seat.

"Sit there," he said. "Try the Lidskialfa and tell me what you see from there."

"I don't know what you mean," I replied. "What would I see? What could I see? We're in a room and I'll see the room and I'll see you."

"But how you will see me and how you will see the room. That is what interests me, Max."

"I don't know what..." But he was turning me around, moving me backward into the plush seat of the ancient chair. I placed my hands on the carved wooden arm rests and slowly descended into the large, ornate seat. When my butt touched the plush, he moved his hands to my waist and gently shoved me backward until my back had reached the upright of the chair's back. I blinked a few times. There were tears in my eyes for some reason. My hands hald the end carvings of the chair's arms tight and when my vision cleared a bit from the lachrymal secretions I did see things differently. I couldn't understand it, but I did.

"What do you see now, Max?" Mikhael's disembodied voice inquired of me.

"I see a man and a woman and a boy and a girl," I said. "I see a room all red and covered in gold flocked wallpaper. I see sorrow and I see pain."

I couldn't believe what I was saying out loud to him.

"I see loss and I see gain as well. The man holds the boy close to him and the woman does the same with the girl. The girl is very frightened and the boy is also scared but he is braver. He stands erect and tall. The man is the least comfortable. He is weeping and ashamed of it. He is holding tightly the shoulders of the boy and the woman. He is afraid for them more than for himself."

"Yes, it was so," Mikhael said from some distance.

"I see a room like this filled with other people who hold guns in their hands. I cannot see their faces clearly but they are not smiling, I know that much."

"They did not smile that day."

"I see the room again, see it empty of people, completely empty. I see the room more red and gold than it was before and the gold is not steady but moving and the red is not red but drying to a purple and brown. What do I see, Mikhael? What is it?"

"You see a room where people have died, Max. You see a room where blood has been violently shed on the gold-flocked walls of red. You see the flames of willful destruction and madness, Max. You see it all, just as I see it, just as I have seen it every night of my life."

"I need to leave this room, Mikhael. I need to."

"No," he said abruptly. "I will come to you in the Lidskialfa."

He leapt up onto the chair and sat there with me, his body pressed hard against mine. We were together, trapped between the hard, carved arms of the large chair. His arm was around my shoulder and his other hand was on my chest, over my heart. I could feel him breathing, he was so close, as close as anyone had ever been to me up until that moment. His breathing was hard and empty, no healthy oxygen in it in either direction. I wanted to give him good air, but I had no idea what that meant, what I could do to achieve that.

"Mikhael," I whispered, "was that you? That little boy I saw...was that you?"

"Hush," he whispered back at me. "You may not know more."

I turned to look at him. Sitting there together I realized that he was about two inches taller than me. His eyes were a cold and burning green color and his sandy hair fell over his brow as he looked down at me. I stared up into them, wondering how we would ever get out of this chair, out of this uncomfortable position we shared when I felt his hand leave my heart.

"You are excited too, Max," he whispered. "I could feel it in your heart."

"I don't know what's happening yet," I said.

"I do," he responded and he leaned down those two inches, his eyes never leaving mine, and he kissed me.

What I felt then, when his lips and mine met, was something I had never felt before. No kiss of any kind from anyone had ever lit me up within before. It was as though I had caught the flame of the room I had seen in the vision given me by the Lidskialfa. I burned hot and then cold and then hot again. His hand touched my cheek and my chin as we kissed and the flames leaped downward through my loins and into my legs. We parted, but his face stayed very close to mine.

"This is the gift of the Lidskiala," he said softly. "It is not the memory it shared with you, but the memory it makes for you."

"This is crazy," I said.

"This, Max, is love." And he kissed me again.

We talked in his room for hours. Much of that first flush of passion had past and we were ourselves again. We agreed that for the present, at least, no one should know about what had happened between us. He was wise enough to realize that this sort of thing would not be acceptable in his school or in mine. Even Freddy was not to be told. Mikhael feared that she would be upset and never see him, or either of us really, ever again. We never spoke about the future, though. What had happened, it seemed, was already behind us. He never suggested that anything more would occur of a similar nature.

He used that phrase, "a similar nature," and I knew what he meant.

What he didn't know, though, was my family history and the open acceptance of the worst of what we did. I made the promise he secured, however, and would not speak about what had happened, even to my mother, for a long time. He had created the secret that I kept. He had brought me to a place of privacy that my own family had never even suggested could exist.

It was a place that never felt as comfortable as it might have if my life had been different. It was not the sort of place our family could acknowledge. I knew what my father would say, what Granny Elainie would say, if they knew about this new friendship with Mikhael. I would be a bargaining chip for improvements of all sorts. I would be the pawn in a chess game where the outcome was the betterment of our situation. I knew that and I kept the secret for that reason alone.

My life would have been a happier one if I could have told someone about my feelings, but not even Mikhael would tolerate hearing about them. I had been revealed to myself, once and for all, not as a gigolo or a pimp, but as a man who craved other men, who responded to other men. I was an amateur in these ranks, but one who could, with my family history, become the best in this business. That was totally different from anything I had ever seen before in myself. I could be a King among my peers and a queen among kings.

It was my awakening.

CHAPTER EIGHTEEN

From Brewer's The Dictionary of Phrase and Fable:

> "Sin-eaters: Persons hired at funerals in ancient times,
> to take upon themselves the sins of the deceased, that
> the soul might be delivered from purgatory."

Mikhael sits by one window in the apartment, gazing out at the growing gray winter sky. At the other window sits Max staring at the same thing in his own slightly wicked way. As she watches them both from her perch across the room Freddy can only marvel at how different the two boys are, how differently they watch the same sky. Freddy notices such things and she catalogues them for future use, if any there could be, of these peculiarities.

To her, it seems, Mikhael is actually studying the sky, absorbing every aspect of its color and the speed of clouds and the refraction of light through the thickening wind. If she concentrates hard she can practically enter his mind and hear his inner monologue which, she is sure, goes something like:

"Less blue now, more gray, more gray even, and grayer still. The wind at twenty knots bends branches which reach furtively for a passing cloud. The sun breaks into three colors at this juncture, including a persimmon color foreign to any sky." That is how she hears him in her mind. There is a stilted, foreign romanticism to his thoughts about the weather.

Max, on the other hand, is handling it all with a more practical attitude. Freddy, again, moves to read that mind and hear those words:

"Wow, the way the gray eats up the blue. And that breeze that works its charms on the sticks and leaves of the ash tree, so powerful it hugs you. I like the way the sun keeps trying to change it all into colors, like reddish-orange-clay or mustard-yellow-blue." Max is the more practical mind, Freddy thinks. She can understand his reactions to things much more easily than she can Mikhael, but she still feels closer to the foreign boy than to the native. She isn't sure just why.

"Can we do something, please," she almost whines at the two of them. "I'm bored."

"Fredericka, how is it you can be bored when nature is putting on this show for us, for only us three, I think."

"Yeah, Freddy, come on. Come watch with us. It's great stuff."

"I don't want to watch the sky turn gray. That's not fun."

"You've been cooped up here too long," Max says. "You need a break from all this getting well."

"I do."

"We must take you out then, to some place extraordinary and unusual, I think."

"And just what would that be, Mikhael?"

"I shall think on it and tell you when we're almost there, Fredericka."

"Hey, no fair. Just because you have money for surprises doesn't mean you get Freddy all to yourself."

"Maximiliano, whatever I decide, you shall be a partner with us, a full and complete partner, naturally."

"Isn't he swell, Max?"

"Swell." And Max thinks about their last afternoon alone together and how the word swell was immediately appropriate. His face changed and Freddy noticed it right away.

"What are you thinking?" she asks Max.

"Oh! Nothing. Nothing, really." Mikhael breaks into a smile and Freddy is aware of it. She gives him an odd look.

"And what are you suddenly thinking about?" she demands of him.

"I cannot be addressed in this tone of voice, Fredericka."

"You can and you will. What was that grin on your face about?"

"I was...shall I really say it, Max?" Max waves his open palm at Mikhael who either misunderstands the gesture or chooses to ignore it. Freddy isn't sure which it is.

"Something's going on between you two. What is it?" She sees Max blush and Mikhael smile again at Max's embarrassment. "Are you two planning some sort of surprise for me?"

"Yes, of course we are," Mikhael says quickly. "You cannot ask us what it is, because then the surprise would be diminished."

"What's the surprise, Max?"

"Well, you heard Mikhael. My lips are sealed."

Mikhael laughs out loud, a bursting of sound and air, nothing subtle. Freddy and Max both turn to look at him. His hands are clasped across his mouth and nose but his eyes, very visible in his otherwise concealed face, are still dancing with merriment and mirth.

"Come on, guys, this isn't fair."

"You'll have to wait, Freddy"

"But I don't want to. I've been cooped up here for weeks. I'm bored. I want my surprise now."

Mikhael lets go of his face and holds out both hands to Freddy.

"Come to the window, Fredericka. See the show that nature puts on just for us."

With pain in her eyes and her shoulders she pulls herself up from the easy chair and makes her way over to the window seat where Mikhael is perched. The closer she comes to the window the easier it is for her see the vast expanse of weather-related show the boys have been watching so closely. The sky is only showing distant, tiny patches of blue. All the rest is a multitude of gray shades, an almost infinite number of them from near jet black to distinctly pure white. The rising and falling of the wind moves the clouds through this half-tone world at variable speeds and with varying positions in the sky, sometimes rising upward, sometimes sinking close to the ground or at least to the trees and the building roofs.

"It is sort of pretty, isn't it?" she says reluctantly.

"Yeah," Max replies from his own seat.

"Come over here, Max," Freddy says to him. "There's plenty of room for three on this seat."

"I'm okay."

"Come. On."

They repeat this exchange a few more times and finally Max pulls himself up onto his knees and edges his way backward until his feet hit the floor. He walks a bit stiff-legged over to the other window where Freddy had joined Mikhael. Slowly he sits down on the far edge.

"You're too far away, Max," Freddy says to him. "Move over here, closer."

"Why? I'm okay here."

"We should all see the same thing, the exact same thing," Freddy continues. "Come and sit really close. We'll put our heads together and see exactly the same things."

"I'm really just fine."

"Max! I'm the invalid and this is what I want from you. Now, please."

He thinks for a moment, then speaks again. "Won't I be too heavy for you? Freddy, you'll be pressed between Mikhael and me and that will put a lot of weight on your body."

"I won't mind. If it hurts I'll tell you. Okay?"

"I guess." He moves over and slowly leans in against Freddy who is already being supported by Mikhael's body, his outstretched left arm cradling her shoulders. "Is this all right? I'm not too heavy, right?"

"No. You're fine." The three of them press their heads together and, as close as their six eyes could possibly be, they stare out at the impending storm. Freddy notices that Mikhael's hand is no longer holding firmly the muscles in her shoulder. She can still feel the weight of his arm across her shoulder blades, but his hand has moved elsewhere. She tries to stare out of the side of her eyes, to see if she can find his hand, but the Olympian task of moving her eyes that far to the left is painful and she lets it go. Instead she closes her eyes and tries to imagine his hand and where it could be.

What she sees, or at any rate imagined she could see, was Mikhael's hand on the back of Max's neck. It is obvious, she feels, when she thinks about it. It is about as far as any arm could reach and it made Max more a part of their triad. Held close in this way, Freddy can imagine their relationship to the property itself, how their bodies relate to the building and its own position on the street. Her mind goes directly to these things and not to anything more personal.

"Are you okay, Max?" she asks.

"Yeah, fine."

"Mikhael? You?"

"This is good with me."

"Okay then." She is aware of Mikhael's hand moving against Max's neck now. The tendons and the muscles in his arm move rhythmically against her upper back and she knows without knowing how she knew it, that the end result of all that rhythmic pulsation means his fingers are moving into a clench and relax, clench and relax, massaging of Max's body. She feels a rush of jealousy which she submerges with a gulping of air.

"I know the surprise," she thinks to herself. "I know the surprise."

As the sky fills in its blue bits with gray, as the wind tosses the clouds about with its merciless gusts, Freddy chokes back a sob and a sigh. She crouches there, sandwiched in by her two best friends who, she now knows, have something between them that doesn't involve her. She has no idea what took place between the boys that she couldn't share, she only knows it is there and it is true.

"Do you see the way the clouds move against one another, Fredericka? Max?"

They both nod and the gesture nods Mikhael's head as well.

"That is us, my friends," he continues. "That is us."

"I sure hope so," Max says earnestly.

"Now and always," Freddy adds, and the three heads continue to bob in accord. "And I'll always be here, in the middle, taking both of your sins onto myself. That's what a best friend does," she adds.

The grey sky nods with them. Nature agreeing with natures, secrets held tight in the grip of trade-winds, is all there is now and it is everything.

CHAPTER NINETEEN

From The Reader's Digest, April, 1946

> "What humbugs we are, who pretend to live for Beauty, and never see the Dawn!"
>
> Logan Pearsall Smith, All Trivia (Harcourt, Brace)

How old was I? How old? How very old, indeed: seventeen, a high-school graduate and pretty. My mother told me I was pretty and she told me I was smart. Our talks about sex and men and other things had continued on an irregular basis but they always ended with the thought of my being a pretty boy, one who could succeed in the family business on my looks alone. Of course, she would always say, I had more than just my looks. I had the music I had listened to all my life, the books I had absorbed in spongelike fashion, the inherent good taste in clothing, jewelry, art, all of which I had inherited from Granny Elainie. I was very special. I should use my talents well. Those were the thoughts drummed into my head between the ages of thirteen and seventeen.

As I stood on the platform at my high school graduation, wearing a snappy yellow cap and gown, holding my diploma in my left hand and shaking hands with the dean of boys, the principal and the guest presenter for the day with my right hand, nothing could have been clearer to me: I was pretty. I came with additional advantages, but I was pretty. That was that.

My graduation was special because Mr. Compton and Tooie were there and Freddy came as well. Mikhael declined the invitation, but he presented me with a special, private one of his own, for later in the evening. I had, of course, accepted his gracious gesture and said I would be there when I could. My family were doing a dinner in a restaurant and those were always special affairs. Even Brianna, my sister, was going to be there.

I hadn't seen Brianna for three months. She had gone to Europe with the man she was "devoted" to at that time. It was difficult to arrange, but she had flown home to New York to be with me, with the family, on this occasion and I was supposed to be grateful to her. For some reason I wasn't.

It was 1963 and the whole social structure around us had changed. The first disco in the United States, Whiskey-a-Go-Go, had just opened, Charles DeGaulle had vetoed England out of the European Economic Committee, and the "Jesus cloud" had appeared in Arizona. The Beatles were the biggest thing in music and Tab, the first diet soda, had just appeared on the soft drink market. Nuclear proliferation protesters marched on London, "Dr. No," with the hunky James Bond of Sean Connery was playing in theaters and, on the day of my graduation, Pope Paul VI succeeded Pope John XXIII as the 262nd Pope.

Freddy was all agog over the Pope thing. I don't know why it meant so much to her, but she called me on the phone to talk about it in the early morning.

"Do you think it will change things for Mikhael and his father?" she asked me.

"No. Why would it?" I asked.

"Well, they come from a Catholic country, Max. Maybe this new Pope will get in there and intercede for them to return."

"Bring back the throne, you mean, and face the consequences."

"Not just the throne, but them."

"You put too much credence in Mikhael's story," I said to her.

"You don't think he's the heir to the throne?" she asked.

"Well, I think one day he'll get the chair," I said, and I laughed heartily at that, but Freddy didn't.

"You're being mean-spirited, Max."

I didn't think I was, but I agreed with her, humbly, just to keep the conversation moving. Freddy could be so adamant about things when they related to Mikhael and she still had no idea about our romantic arrangement. It had been more than two years and she still hadn't caught on to us. It always struck me as funny. She was about three years older than me, but it had never hindered our friendship, but they were both older, further along in most things, and they should have been more adult than me, but I always felt like their elder when we were together.

"Have you seen him lately?" I asked her.

"No. He's always so busy. I wish I knew with what."

"I see him now and then," I said selfishly, almost with a meanness that was new for me.

"I know you do. You mention it a lot."

"Sorry. I don't want to rub it in."

"It's just a phase," she said and that took me aback.

"What do you mean?" I mumbled.

"Well, you know, there's a time when boys need the companionship of other boys. That's where he's at right now."

I was stumbling into dangerous territory here. I was going to have to be very careful how I spoke and how I sounded.

"All boys need time alone, without women around," I said.

"Oh, I know," she said. "My mother warned me that boys...men...boys could be difficult and secretive and such."

"Yeah, well, we're still searching for, you know, identity."

"I know, but he's 21. How much searching is there anyhow? Girls don't have to do that."

"Girls are lucky."

"Yeah, right, lucky."

That had taken place that morning. By afternoon, when she turned up and sat with my parents, she was different, more truculent.

"I thought Mikhael would be here," she said abruptly.

"He couldn't come."

"Well, why not? What's more important than this today? Not that stupid Pope thing!"

"He just couldn't come. He had other plans."

"I'll kick his royal butt," she said. "Friends don't just blow off friends for a Pope newsbite. I'll have to tell him a thing or two."

"Whoa, Freddy, slow down." I was about to make a mistake like none I had ever made before. "What's with you? Are you angry at him for not coming to my graduation or angry with him for not being here with you?"

"You little snob," she shouted at me. "Why would you think I was making myself more important than you?"

"Freddy, hold on!"

"I don't care what you think about me, but I'm not selfish. I'm not the

113

one in yellow here. I'm in a sedate dark blue. I don't have to be the center of anyone's attention."

"Hey, we had choices and I liked this color."

"Well, you look like a pea-hen, Max. It's ridiculous."

"Freddy, that's...."

"I don't care how it sounds. You should have been more of a boy."

"More of a boy?"

"Yellow is not a boy's color."

I gasped as she shouted that out at me in front of my family and my schoolmates.

"You're supposed to be my friend, Freddy, not my critic!"

"It's no wonder Mikhael stayed away today. He would have been gagging at the sight of you in that gown."

"Mikhael loves me in yellow," I shouted back at her not hearing my own words and how they sounded. "He says it's a color that complements my complexion. I wore this for him and he didn't even bother to show up!"

There was a silence that followed that statement that someone really could have cut with a trowel. I don't remember ever hearing so little sound before or since.

"What are you telling me?" she said quietly after the long silence threatened to become pre-civil war in its intensity.

"Nothing," I said hastily.

"Max," my mother chimed in, "what is all this?"

"Nothing!" I repeated emphatically.

"Maxie, we need to talk," my dad said.

"I don't need to talk about anything," I declared. "I'm going to change my clothes now and we'll just go out to dinner like we planned."

"Maxie, don't walk away like that. You insult your mother."

"I don't... and I don't care either."

I stormed off toward the changing room, unaware that Brianna was right behind me.

"Hey," she said touching me on the shoulder, "don't just storm off like that. Not from them, and not from me. I came a long way to be with you today and if you're about to say what I think you're about to say, I want to be close by and the first to shake your horny little hand."

"I don't know what you're talking about," I said to my sister.

She shoved me down onto a long bench in the boy's locker room and straddled it, looking straight at me.

"You know, kid, it took me a long time to get where I am. And here you are, at seventeen, still a kid, and you've got a prince on a string."

"I don't know what you're saying."

"You've got a god-damned prince dangling."

"I don't...."

"Come off it, it's as plain as plain can be." She laughed. She threw back her head, the way she used to when we were both still kids living at home, and she laughed a deep, dark, Colleen Dewhurst sort of laugh. It was sexy and it was dirty and it was infectious. I found myself laughing too.

"Come on, tell me everything. Brianna wants to know."

Her hands were on my shoulders and her eyes were staring directly into mine and, for the first time since Mikhael and I had shared that first kiss, I confessed it all to someone. Every detail of our affair came out, everything about my experience in the chair, the Lidskialfa. By the time we finished talking she knew more about my affair with Mikhael than I thought I knew.

"It can't go on, you know," she said, "you're not in his league."

"I know."

"We've got to talk to Daddy about this. He needs to know what levels of love you've attained. He's got to do something for you."

"No," I told her. "I'm going to college. I'm not going into the business."

"The hell you're not. You're a natural. You're Granny Elainie all over again."

"No."

"Oh, yeah. If I could take you to Europe with me you'd be set up in a day. A day, Maxie. You're a looker and you're smart and, except for this yellow thing, you've got good taste. One day. I promise you. You'll never have to worry again about your future. One day in my hands with my connections...."

"NO!"

"Keep your voice down," she said calmly, almost serenely. "Get dressed and let's go out to dinner like we all planned."

I waited ten minutes, my sulk hard to endure. Then I did as she instructed me and joined the party.

It was fun. I can say that about the dinner party. Freddy had calmed down again and no one spoke about Mikhael or Freddy's outburst or anything having to do with my verbal indiscretion. The party was focused on my graduation and its celebration.

115

Tooie had wrapped a gift for me and it was so beautiful I was reluctant to open it, but she showed me how to preserve the bow by removing the lid of the box on one side only and so I did it and found, inside, a beautiful suit of shantung silk.

"Wear it well, kiddo," Mr. Compton said. "Success in how we dress is true success."

"Crap," said his wife, Tooie the lesbian. "Success, kiddo, is measured in who we dress with."

"That's weird," Freddy whispered to me.

"Yeah, but it's okay," I reassured her.

My parents gifts would come later, privately at home, but Freddy had brought something to give me and she handed it to me after giving me a sweet kiss.

"I hope you understand it," she said, and she blushed. My mother applauded her quietly and Tooie leaned over the table to kiss Freddy, but Mr. Compton pulled her gently back into her seat. In the box was a small statue of three monkeys. One had its arms wrapped around its mouth, one around its eyes and one around its head, covering its ears. I looked at it for a moment, not quite realizing what she was saying in her present. I didn't have to wonder for long.

"Remember the day, when I was still recovering?"she asked. "Remember how we all sat there together, with our heads together and our hearts together too?"

"Sure I do."

"That's us." She smiled the sweetest little smile imaginable.

"That's the hear no evil, see no evil, speak no evil chimps," my father said.

"It's more than that," Freddy said. "It's Max, Mikhael and me."

"How do you see that?" Brianna asked her.

"Well, Max never says an evil word, I see nothing bad in anyone and Mikhael won't hear about anything that isn't pleasant."

"That's so clever," my mother said to her. "How did you ever think that up?"

"I just notice how we are," she replied.

"Well, it's a lovely present for Max, dear."

"I love it," I said to her. "I'll always love it."

"It's a thing of beauty," Tooie added.

"You're my best friend, Freddy. We'll always be that. We'll always be best friends." I hugged her and what she whispered in my ear as we hugged sent a chill down my spine.

"We'll always be best friends, Max, we will, even after Mikhael and me are married. With all this excitement about you, you didn't even notice my engagement ring."

Came the dawn.

END OF PART ONE

PART TWO

CHAPTER TWENTY

From Theatre Language: A Dictionary by Walter Parker Bowman & Robert Hamilton Ball:

"Play of situation: A play in which events rather than character or atmosphere dominate."

I look at him there, sitting on the settee, leaning to the left, his feet tucked up under his long, lean legs, his right arm resting on a cushion, his left crooked on the small couch's arm, his fingers caressing his chin. He stares down at the book his right hand holds before him, tilted backward slightly, catching the light from the floor lamp behind him. It shines on his hair as well as on the printed page, his hair which shines with brilliantine, combed to perfection. He wears a shirt open to the third button revealing his neck and his clavicle, the tiny Adam's apple which surprisingly hasn't made his voice tinny or high-pitched, the space between his pectorals. The shirt hangs limp there moving with his even breathing. I want to ask him what he reads, but I don't. I don't really care to know, I just want him to speak to me.

I don't know what I'd do without him here. Max. How long has it been? How long have I known him? When did I even know that I knew him? Does it really matter now? He's here. He helps me with things. That's all that matters.

He is my valet. He helps me dress, cares for my costumes, cleans and restocks my stage makeup, powders and finger-waves my wigs for me. He keeps track of my rehearsals, my appointments, my performances and my aprés-performance needs. He even does the dirty for me, when I need that little act performed before I sing. He is my perfect friend, my little helpmate. He is Max.

Of course I knew his parents. Of course I did. Years back, in New York, at the Metropolitan and at the hotel, his father was the one, the Max of his own day. He made certain that I always had the room I liked, the sheets I liked, and the champagne I preferred. He would usher Helga into my room and we were free to love, to make love, to work at love at any rate, for as long as we wished. Helga Meerstadt. Where is she today, I wonder? What could have happened to that grand bosom, those amazing hips and those thighs, those eternal thighs that held me in their grip? Helga. So long ago now. Twenty years ago.

Our affair lasted for eleven years. Some would say that this is a sign that we shared a true affection for one another, perhaps loved one another. Some would say. I say only that we shared one another unstintingly. We gave to one another the physical attention that no one else would provide us, in spite of our stature in those days: Helga the leading soprano in the key Wagner roles and I, the perfect basso, the ideal Don Giovanni, the consummate Boris Godunov, the flawless Sarastro.

We were an ideal match in voice, temperament and sensual pleasure. We were both married in those days, Meerstadt to an analyst, a pscho-analyst, and I to a woman who designed all-white furniture for all-white rooms with all-white carpeting and all-white lights. I am a basso, filled with light, color and patches of darkness in my spirit. I suffocate in all-white spaces. The day I left Miranda at the house in Rancho Mirage, told her we were through, I thought Helga might do the same with Meerstadt, her Georg. It was a day of major losses for me, as it turned out. Helga turned her back on me, called me every vile name under the Deutsche sun, refused to speak to me ever again and Miranda added a great deal of color to the rooms we had once inhabited by slitting her wrists and proving that red was her other color. Before she expired she added orange, blue and gold to the decor by immolating herself in the room she had drawn with such pale attitudes.

I think I would have died, more of embarrassment than anything at that time, if it hadn't been for Max's parents. They opened the doors wide to their lives and took me in. The opera company cancelled my contracts. The Hurok office, that fat old Sol with his Russian accent and his cigars, cancelled my concert tours. RCA Victor put my new records on a back shelf, to wait out the scandals they said, and within a week I had totally disappeared professionally. I went from being the highest paid, most avidly sought-after male American singer since Lawrence Tibbett to being just another out-of-work, unemployable, unsaleable drug-store basso. Paul Donner no longer existed. I was only "poor old Paul Donner" from that point on.

Max, I recall was kind to me. Nothing he knew about me could have altered his childish generosity and that meant something to me. At the time I had no idea where that gratitude would lead me. That would only reveal itself in time. But just then, in 1956, when he was ten and I was forty-three, his sweetness made me reconsider my present and my future.

I stayed with them for about a month, and then, with a firmer grip on the ways of my world, I left them. I wouldn't see them again, any of them for many years. I went back to California and made my third and final film, my best role in the cinema actually and one which helped to cleanse the image that my wife's odd suicide had created for me.

The role was El Perpetua, the man who cannot die. Not a vampire film, not a horror film of any kind, but movie about a man who has made himself immortal through his tonsilaria. El, as the character was always called, was a singer, a great man in Vienna. As with my own career this El had created many of the great opera roles and even though he was aging he had maintained the voice. This was where the acting, my greatest talent actually, came into play. I was forty-four now and the man I played was supposed to be over one hundred years old. He looked great for that age, especially as played by me, and his sang with the gusto and interpretive genius of a man of, well, forty-four. In love with a woman much younger than himself he had to pretend to be someone else, someone new and young and vital, in order to win her hand. When she discovered, on her wedding night, that she had married El Perpetua, she wants to kill herself, but his sweet serenade, his song of love and devotion, halts her in her pathway to damnation and she promises to love and honor him for himself alone and not for who he has been for a century.

I loved that part. I sang five arias and a new song written just for me by Harry Warren and Sammy Fain, called "I Can Live It Again." It hit the charts within a week of the single coming out, one for the first classical singers to make an EP recording, a 45rpm for those who don't understand the technical language. In two weeks it was number three on the pop charts, right behind a Bobby Darrin song and one by a group called Mudlarks. Suddenly I was back on top and even though the film wasn't a hit, the song was and I was again.

Three years later I was on the concert circuit and opera companies were requesting me and by 1961 I was back. I hadn't visited New York since 1956 and my quick trip there was hampered only by the knowledge that a new opera house was in the planning stages. I so wanted to open it. I visited the top agencies hoping for some interest in the restart of my stage career, but no one took th e bait. Even with my records selling well and my excellent notices for the concerts and recitals, the opera world had closed its doors.

That was when Helga came back to me. Meerstadt had died and she was alone. I thought she returned to me for the sex, but all she wanted was the voice. She wanted to pair with me for recitals. She wanted to blend our musical elements, but not our physical ones, and I turned her down. I didn't want a washed up Wagnerian rising again on my musical coat-tails. I turned her down flat.

But in 1967, on a Carnegie Hall date in New York, I met Max. I met the boy who was almost a man, just twenty-one to my fifty-four. He was looking for work and, he said, not interested in his family's *"business,"* and I needed an assistant and I offered him the work. He took it. He took to it. And he took to me. He didn't mind my special requests now and then. He had no objections to my odd quirks and my unusual needs. I could use his talents for my own pleasure and my own purposes and so, without meaning to, he stepped into that family profession in his own peculiar way.

Now, on May 27, 1973, there he sits, reading, thinking, but not cogitating on the exigencies, the pressing needs, the urgent requirements of an aging basso profundo, the man who pays the bills. Max has his own world now. His place in the world, one not given or taken, but one earned and held. I would like to think that he thinks of me, of thanking me, but he doesn't. This is not the boy, any longer, this is the man. My man Max. Max.

CHAPTER TWENTY-ONE

From Theater Language: A Dictionary by Walter Parker Bowman & Robert Hamilton Ball

> "in order of appearance: Said of actors, in listing their names on a program: In the order of their entrance or in the order in which they speak onstage, rather than in the order of their importance in the cast."

"Max, I need you," I call out to him in the next room.

"What is it, Paul?" he answers me. I can tell he hasn't moved an inch from whereever he is next door.

"I don't want to shout out everything. Come in here, please."

"What is it?" He is standing in the doorway looking at me sitting there at my dressing table staring into my mirror. I know that from the closeness, the proximity of his voice and by the slight creaking of the door hinge just above the level of his hand, obviously leaned against it.

"Why do you always do that? Why make me call for you twice?"

"I'm sorry, Paul. I was studying."

"Studying?" I do look up at him when I say that.

"Yes. You know I have my exams coming up in a fortnight." No one else I know would ever use the word fortnight.

"Of course you do."

"So, what is it? I'm here. How can I be of help?"

"Would you just take a look, please, Max, at my makeup box and see if there's a number three pencil there. I don't dare leave this eyelid without applying that line I like that takes off ten years. I'm afraid if I let go, I'll never get the angle right again."

"A number three? Let me look." I hear him rummage in the top section of the kit, and I know it has to be there. There had always been a number three, slightly gray, almost white when applied delicately.

"No, Paul, I don't see it."

"It must be there, Max. Look again."

"It's not there, I tell you."

"Well, look in the lower section. Maybe you threw it in instead of placing it where it ought to be." I can hear him moving the compartmented upper piece out of the kit and then I hear him moving things about in the deeper pocket of the box. His fingers halt. Then start up again, moving things carefully to search for the pencil that I had already removed from the kit and placed carefully under the makeup towel on the table.

"I still don't see one, Paul. You must have lost it."

"It's not my job to lose these things, Max. That would seem to be your bailiwick these days."

"Nonsense, Paul."

"Nonsense! Indeed. Anyone would think you were accusing me, now, of something."

"Well, they are your things. I only help with them. They're your responsibility."

"I took you on to take care of such matter, Max. Remember that."

"Yes, Paul. Yes, Paul. I will remember, and be grateful, Paul." The tone of his voice is insolent and resentful, but the words are nice to hear. I admonish him anyway.

"Watch that tone, please. Remember how that alters my performance." I drop the eyelid and turn to look up at the boy, the young man, Max. He stares for a moment into my eyes and then he smiles. I can't help myself. I return the gesture.

"I'm sorry, Paul. I'll find you another one somewhere. Give me a minute, please."

He is heading for the door when I decide to make things right between us again. I reach under the towel and pull out the pencil. I drop it quickly onto the floor at my feet and move it slightly out of sight. Then I turn and call out to him before he can leave the dressing room.

"Max, wait," I say with a certain tone of urgency. "Let me...what's this?" I move my foot and give a little kick. Then I lean forward to see the pencil that I know would be there. "Why, Max, you must have knocked it to the floor when you were ransacking the kit. Naughty, Max."

"I'm sorry, Paul. I'm..."

"It's all right now, Max. I have the damn thing and I'll make my youthful line and all will be right with the world again."

"Can I go back to studying, Paul, or do you need me for any more little chores?"

"Of course you can study. Of course. I'll be just fine. Thank you, Max."

I watch him go back into the other room and hear the slight skriech of the divan's springs as he sat and stretched out his long, slender legs. I reassert myself with the eyelid, hold it fast and make the mark that takes away the tired look of aging eyes. Now, even in the front row, I would appear younger, stronger, more virile, more well-suited to my voice. I would fool some of the people for some of the time and a few for a little while longer during the performance. I would fool no one all of the time, not even myself. That was my future and I knew it. Still it is good to be singing again, live and in person, and it is a help to have Max with me.

He is studying for his exams, earning at last his diploma from the school he has dragged himself to, day after day for six of the seven years he has been with me. I never understood what it is he wants to achieve. A diploma, of course, but for what purpose? He works for me, lives with me, has a life than many men would envy. This new knowledge he pursues isn't going to make a shard of difference in the way of the world, not of his world certainly. He is destined for the performance venues as an able and effective assistant to the star. That is what he does so well. Why would this knowledge of European history he craves ever be useful to him in the life we forge together, or even in the life he has put behind him to be with me? I don't understand.

"Max?"

"What now, Paul?"

"Max, I need you a moment. Just a moment, please."

"Don't beg, Paul," he says, coming into my inner sanctum. I stand up.

"How do I look?"

"Lovely."

"How old do I look?"

"Thirty-five and not a day older." I can hear the gentle exasperation in his voice but I go on with our ritual.

"Who is the handsomest man in the world?"

"Phineas."

"Phineas?"

"...as played by you, Paul."

"And who's the hero the women adore?"

"That's Phineas, too, Paul."

"And who gets to sing the loveliest song in all creation?"

"It's you."

"Thank you, Max."

Phineas was the role in the new operetta I starred in. The producers had offered it to me in the fall of the previous season, but it wasn't right for me then. Max read it and made two suggestions which I passed along to the authors and, as in days of old, they made the changes to suit the artist. Now the role is me and I am the role. What was done for me was simply this: Phineas had youthened from a man of 45 to a youth of 38 and secondly Phineas had the two songs that closed the two acts. No longer did a younger man sing the plaintive ballads about love lost and love never recovered, but Phineas, the man of strength and character could reveal his deepest emotions through those gems of song. Max had known where they belonged and to whom and he had set things aright.

"Do you ever miss her, Paul?"

"Who? Helga?"

"Yes, of course, who else?"

"No one, naturally. Helga. Miss her. Those two concepts no longer fit together."

"Why? You loved her once. I remember that."

"Like a baby craves mother?s milk after being weaned from the teat I craved Helga Meerstadt in her day. She was mine for a time, but never mine in reality."

"You're such a phony." That comment brings me up short. I lose my sense of person.

"What the hell do you mean by that?"

"Listen to yourself, sometime, Paul. You can't say anything honest in an honest way. It always has to be "special" for you."

"Max, you're getting out of hand."

"A bit. Yes."

"What is it, baby?" I ask him.

"I don't know."

"Well, Papa Paul has an appointment in five minutes with 1,836 people who came and paid to hear him sing and watch him act, so" – and my voice goes deeper here, into my singing range, "stay put and wait for me. We'll fix you up later."

As if on cue the knock on my door alerts me to the fact that I have said the right thing at the right time. I am needed on stage.

A good performance is always a joy in which to be holding center stage and this night is a very good performance. Everyone is into it. There isn't one slaggard. Light cues are perfect and the audience gets into the emotional swings and we are on fire. It happens now and then, just that way. The stars are aligned or something, I don't really understand it, but electricity strikes through the empty space between stage and audience and illuminates the heart and soul of every participant on either side of the orchestra pit. At the end of Act One I come back to the dressing room drenched with sweat and needing my Max.

"Max, I need you, now boy." I drop onto the chaise and kick off my shoes. "Max, now please!"

There is a knock on the door and before I can shout "no visitors" the door opens and she is there. Suddenly I knew what has been bothering my baby boy earlier. SHE is there.

"Helga," I say softly.

"Paul, before you must say something, try to listen, yes."

"Helga, this is not the time. I have to rest and prepare for the second act."

"Paul, I am coming to tell you of the mistakes of the past."

"But this is not the time." I take a deep breath and let it all out in one syllable.

"MAX!"

"He is not available. I am on an errands sending him."

"How dare you! Helga, leave my dressing room."

"And who, if not Helga, will help you prepare. She knows your ways."

I am about to protest but she has dropped to her knees before me and places her mouth where it hadn't been in far too many years. As she closes her lips tight, I lean my head back against the pillow and settle in for what I know will make me even more brilliant between 9:55 and 10:48 this evening.

When she has completed her task and I am wiping myself dry again she sits down on the chair at my table. She is smiling the smile I recall from all of those trysts that had been arranged so well for us in the old days at the Metropolitan. I am smiling mine as well. I know that from the itch that always attended the broad, Helga-smile providing deep dimples in both my cheeks.

"Have you missed me, Paul?" she asks in perfect English.

"Of course, I have," I tell her.

"I was, of course, wrong to betray our love, Liebling," she says. "You put aside your California girl and I could not desert the man who was husband. I was unfair to the pride of our affection."

"You had scruples, Helga."

"I had baby in the oven," she says.

"His?" I ask.

"What do you think?" she replies.

"Mine, then?"

"My son must carry the legal name of his legal father," she replies.

"So, his?"

"You can ask this?"

"Then, mine."

"I am a moral wife, even if I am an immoral mistress."

"Helga, I'm confused. I have a performance. I must think of my Phineas."

"As I think of mine."

"Your what?"

"Phineas."

"Thank you." I move to kiss her, but she takes a step back from me.

"Phineas." She says it again.

"You must call me Paul. I only play Phineas."

"It is his name."

"Yes, the character I play."

"No. Baby Phineas."

"There is no baby Phineas, Helga. In the play I am unmarried, but sympathetic in spite of that."

"The baby Phineas."

"You said that. It makes no sense."

"Her baby, Phineas, Paul," says a voice from behind me. Max's voice.

"Her..? Who? Helga," I say, turning back in her direction, "is there a baby named Phineas?"

"Mein Gott," says the Meerstadt. "Mein Lieber Gott!"

"Her baby is named Phineas. She sees this as a psychic connection,

Paul. She thinks the baby must be yours, calling out to you. That's what she told me."

"Max, it's ridiculous."

"Why, Paul? You were lovers once."

"Max, you know my tastes. Do you think that's only with you? I may not know much about science, but I know this much...no intercourse in the whim-wham and no baby."

"So you never....?"

"Max. I repeat. You know my tastes."

There is a knock on my door and the stage manager calls five minutes.

"Helga, out, I must change. Max, my costume. Helga, later, please. Goodbye."

Max escorts her gently to the door and moves her through it. I hear it close again.

"Max, you do believe me, don't you?"

"Paul," he says sweetly, kissing me on the forehead, "how could I ever have doubted you?"

All is well. Order of appearance in perfect alignment. Costume in place. Music to sing. An evening in perfect harmony with itself.

CHAPTER TWENTY-TWO

From The Reader's Digest, April, 1946:

> From Cartoon Quips: "One glamour girl to another:
> 'We're practically engaged. He's just waiting for his
> fiancée to return the ring.'"

When I saw Paul Donner backstage and introduced myself to him I wasn't really expecting much, I promise you that. He was just an old acquaintance, a friend of the family. I was just the kid who used to sit and listen in rapturous silence while he sang or spoke to us. There were no expectations on my part. I just wanted to say hello. Still, his reaction to me, standing there looking innocent, was one of utter and complete lust. I don't remember anything like it ever.

Not that I was bothered by that. I'd been through a few things already that certainly mirrored this new experience, but the intensity of this one was different. So when I told him I was single and looking for work and that my parents were still in the game, so to speak, he parried that minor thrust with an offer to be his assistant, his valet and driver. Naturally I accepted the offer.

I knew, I suppose, that those three-pronged duties would expand quickly to include a fourth, the one I'd been avoiding since my teens, the one my mother liked to talk to me about. No "family business" interest for me, I promised myself. I was going to go to school, get a degree in something useful and marry Freddy, even if she was older than me. Maybe I'd keep seeing Mikhael, but that would be the extent of my outside sex life. I was aiming for a normal-as-American-Apple-Pie life. But Paul was clearly over the top about me and he made an awfully nice offer and Brianna said I'd be hanged by my cohonies if I didn't take the position, so to speak, so I agreed. And oddly enough, it worked out and I wasn't too personally offended by it. Accidental decisions create our fate, I guess, and my fate was certainly to be the object of my family's history no matter how hard I tried to change all that.

I did have real responsibilities beside the blow jobs and such. I did have his back on appointments and I pressed his suits and his ties, kept his household running and I did drive him to the concert halls, theaters and opera houses. When he had students, and there were always three students, I kept them in line, kept them waiting, kept them paying their bills on time. Now and then I'd cook something too. I wasn't too bad. Mikhael had shown me a few tricks in the kitchen when we were still friendly. He had some weird Scandinavian recipes that were actually pretty tasty if you made them just so.

So Paul was happy he had hired me and I was pleased about making the connection after so many years. My mother was pleased with my professional "progress" and my dad was delighted to reunite with an old friend, which was totally weird since I expected him to reject this "old guy-young guy" thing, especially with an old friend like Paul Donner. It was strange watching them together, like two old bowling buddies, except that one was screwing the other one's son. Strange, indeed. I guess we never really know our parents in spite of ourselves.

It wasn't until Helga Meerstadt appeared at the dressing room door that there was even a slight shadow in this sunlit path. She cast a huge, dark spot over the easy happiness I was having, but that wasn't something I was willing to show to anyone, least of all Paul. I had learned early that giving him an advantage over me was not a good thing. This is what had happened.

I'd been working for him, sharing a life with him actually, for about three months when I got a call from my mother. Freddy, who had pretty much disappeared from my life for a while, had called looking for me. My mother, being a good and protective soul, had taken down her information and passed it along to me, rather than passing Freddy through the gauntlet and giving her any information about my life, my whereabouts, anything except that I was well. I held on to the contact numbers for a while, and then, when I was ready to face her, I phoned.

Just hearing her voice gave me chills. Old times, good ones, rushed backward at me, stunning me. It was as though I was fifteen again and not in my mid-twenties.

"It's so good to hear your voice, Max," she cooed at me through the receiver.

"Yeah, it's nice to hear yours, too, Freddy," I responded, a bit cooler than she.

"I've wanted to call you for so long."

"Well, what took you so long, then?"

"Well, you know how we got the last time...? I wasn't sure..."

"Hey, I never hold a grudge, Freddy. I really don't."

"I know. You'd said that. But you know how I am, right?"

"Sure."

"Can we get together? Coffee, maybe? Or a drink somewhere?"

"Still taking the initiative, I note."

"Max, come on. It's not a date, just meet."

"Where?" I said. "When?" She gave me a few possibilities but they were awkward ones for me, either a class or an appointment for Paul. I suggested an alternative when my schedule looked pretty clear and she took it as a date without even batting an eyelash. I know I'd have heard her if she had batted one.

"I can't wait, Max."

"Me, too," I said.

And so we met. The place: Bloomingdale's on Lexington Avenue, the restaurant. The time: a Monday afternoon at three. The weather: gloomy and unpredictable. I wore a grey suit, striped shirt, no tie, moccasins. She wore a grey suit - wouldn't you know - striped blouse and a flowered tie, asters on a black background, which she kept knotted but not secured to the collar, and three inch heels. We looked like a committee meeting of some sort, sitting at the small steel and enamel table sipping tea and eating tiny cakes. You had to love it, or at least see it to believe it.

We beat around the bush for a few minutes, shared a reminiscence or two, laughed uncomfortably, and then got down to brass tacks.

"How long has it really been?" she asked me.

"How long has what really been? Be specific, okay?"

"Since we last sat and talked? Was it your party? Your graduation party?"

"No. We talked again after that."

"I don't remember, Max. I only remember how angry you were with me that time."

"Well, it was my party, after all, until you made it about you. You did shock me with your good news, Freddy."

"I should have known, but I was naive, I guess."

"Yes. Naive. A good word for it."

"Be good, Max. I'm trying to be nice here."

"You have to be nice, Freddy. This whole thing is your idea, this get-together."

"I know. I'll be nice."

We sipped our tea again.

"You're looking very handsome, Max, very mature, too."

"I'm not a little kid anymore. Neither are you, by the way."

"What? A little kid or handsome? Or mature for that matter?"

"A kid, of course. You're very handsome, Freddy. And frankly, you haven't matured much, at least not physically. I guess marriage hasn't brought you the breasts you always wanted."

"Oh," she said too quietly. "I'm not married, Max."

"You're... what happened? I thought..."

"Yes, so did I."

"I'm sorry."

"I'm not."

We sat in silence and sipped again.

"What does one say in these situations?" I asked, not expecting an answer.

"Depends on who you are." She giggled, but there was no humor in it. "We were almost married. That's something."

"I guess."

"It wasn't anyone's fault, Max. We were just two kids and we thought it could work. It couldn't."

"Was it his... you know... his tendencies?"

"No." Again quiet, and again quick. "That would have been okay with me. As long as it wasn't you."

"Then what, Sweetie?" I hadn't called her that, ever, in my life but it just came out of me.

"That damned chair."

"The liddy-skiffy thing, or whatever."

"Yes, that one, the Lidskialfa. I'll never forget how to say it, believe me."

"What happened?"

"I see you don't read the big news magazines, Max. It made them all."

"I do, but I don't read the right parts, it seems."

"Well, this was a scandal. Just the way Mikhael always said it might be."

"You mean someone got wind of the chair and the theft and all that?"

"Uh huh." She blushed and I knew that somehow she was connected to the bad news about the bad news. "My mother wanted a photo of me in the chair, just for herself, she said. So I convinced Mikhael to take one. It was an okay photo. I looked all right and the chair was pretty big so it photographed well. Too well."

"Don't tell me.."

"Yep. She sent it to the Times with a wedding announcement and they printed it without knowing anything about the chair, but the international sections of Newsweek, and a bunch of other tomes picked it up and made a scandalous report about some American girl who had possession of this missing European heirloom. You'd have thought it was a Nazi treasure trove the way they descended on us."

"It was almost the same thing, Freddy."

"It was worse. It seems that Mikhael's father was not the heir presumptive. He was only an 'assumptive,' a usurper wanted by Interpol. That's partially why we never saw the man. He was truly on the lam."

"That must have been so hard for Mikhael," I said without thinking.

"Of course it was. And it was hard for me because of the wrath I suffered from Mikhael. I had never heard so much abusive language in my life, not even in high school. It devastated me."

"That's awful."

"It got worse, Max. The FBI got into it. They seized the damn chair, arrested Mikhael and detained me as a material witness.

"Really!"

"I was in a holding cell for five days while they continually isolated me and questioned me, and grilled me and questioned me. I didn't know if I was coming or going some of the time."

"Why you? You were only the fiancée."

"That was why. They assumed I knew something. How stupid was I? they asked me. How stupid were they? I wondered. If I had known what was going on why would I allow myself to be photographed like that. That's what I told them."

"And...?"

"And finally they believed me, bought my story and let me go."

"Mikhael?"

"I have no idea. He just disappeared into the system somewhere. I've never heard from him, or about him, again."

"That's ridiculous!" I shouted, then turned my volume down. "They can't just detain someone like that. He was a kid when they got here. He had a family that slowly disappeared and he was alone. What was he supposed to do?"

There was a short breath of deep silence between us after my outburst.

"So you do still care about Mikhael, Max." It was a statement of absolute fact and not a question this time.

"I don't...really."

"You do. I can hear it. I can see it in your eyes."

"I don't. Not anymore. Not after...this."

"Well, we're not engaged any longer, Max. I sold the ring, took the dough and went to Atlantic City for a long weekend."

"Oh. How was that, then?"

"You won't believe this, Max, but it was cathartic. I met Mikhael's father there."

"The heir assumptive."

"The very one. He looked me up at my hotel, bought me a drink and told me, in no uncertain terms, what he would like to do to me. I threw my drink in his face and headed for the bus station and came home. It was definitely the final straw."

"So, you're free and you came to find me."

"Not exactly. I waited a while. A long while actually. I was too ashamed, I think of the way I treated you all those years ago."

"Yeah, well," and I took a breath before I said this next, "that's water under the bridge, I guess."

"That was gracious of you, Max."

I couldn't think of anything to say to that, so I sat there and I looked at Freddy and I reached across the table and took her hand and held it firmly within mine. She smiled at me and I smiled at her and I knew we probably wouldn't have many more of these dates.

"I'm free and on the loose," she sang to me, a quote from some musical show I didn't know.

I gave her a thin-lipped smile and nodded, then I turned it into a negative and slowly shook my head.

"But I'm not," I said, and I let her hand slip out of mine.

"What do you mean?" She gave me a skewed smile and her eyes seemed to soften and, at the same time, to diminish in both size and color.

"I'm not exactly free. I have...professional...commitments." I touched her hand and she pulled it away instantly. "Let me explain." And I did.

CHAPTER TWENTY-THREE

From the Reader's Digest, April, 1946:

> From: Life in These United States: "My wife, whose feminine logic always baffles me, returned from a shopping trip lyrical in her description of a 'dream dress' she had seen in a shop window. After a week of badgering I gave in as usual, and she went gaily off to buy her heart's desire. But to my amazement she returned empty-handed. 'It was still in the window,' she explained. 'So I decided that if no one else wanted it neither did I.'"
>
> Donald L. Whitaker (Omaha, Neb.)

Not too long after my "date" with Freddy I heard from our mutual friend, Mikhael. While I had often thought fondly about her, his place in my memory had grown consistently grim. Gone were the happy times when we were still kids. Those moments remained in my memory but they took on a darker aspect, an abuser and abused personality. I could look back on those times only as the exploitation of the relentlessly foolish. With my family and that personal education I got I should have known better, been smarter about what was real and what was merely stupid in my actions. To hear from Freddy's lips the story of her ill treatment by him and then by his father really did the trick. I had no use for these people and they could certainly have no use for me.

Besides, my life with Paul Donner was just perfect. I had clothes, food, a place to be in the evening when school was done. I had the music I loved and fine apartments as homes in New York and London and superb hotels suites when we traveled. I wasn't ever treated like a servant, but always as a cared for best friend. There was nothing I was seeking, nothing I was missing. It was the perfect situation for me.

Things were just fine. That's the truth of it. I had no need for Mikhael.

Mikhael, though, had need of me. Uprooted and alone, ignored by his father who apparently believed that Mikhael had betrayed him, the only man I had ever cared about was in need of a friend, of me. When he phoned me, and how he got the number I never discovered, and I heard his voice through the receiver I thought I would die.

"Max, don't hang up on me too," was how he started the conversation.

"Too?" was all I said. I never acknowledged I knew him, knew his name, said his name. I just repeated the word he had said.

"They all do it, now," he said. "Everyone. Freddy. My father. Even the strangers I speak to at banks."

"Banks?" I asked him.

"I must have some money, soon. I have nothing left to me. All was taken away. My father has closed the apartment and fled from me."

"Fled?" Boy, was I being difficult with him.

"To Canada, I think. To safety."

I said nothing. There was nothing I could say.

"Max, see me please. See me today. I need to hold you and have your arms enfold me once more."

"No," I said. "I'm too busy."

"You are too busy for an old sweetheart such as me?"

"Yes. Too busy."

"But I have nothing, Maxie, and you have everything. Spare an old flame a minute."

I held my breath, knowing I should just hang up the phone, but I didn't. Instead I listened in as much silence as I could muster.

"Max!" He was in a commanding mood suddenly. "You will let me come up to see you, yes." It was a statement and not a question.

"If you find me here, so be it," I said as placidly as I could. In truth my heart was racing a mile a minute.

"I will come to you, then," Mikhael said ending the conversation. I put the receiver back in its cradle and stood there looking at it for a long time.

Then I went to my room to shower, shave and change. I knew instantly that I had made too many poor choices in the past few moments, but I did what I set out to do and when I was done I decided to make a run for it. I would get out of the apartment and not be here when Mikhael showed up. That was the best decision I ever made. Sadly I made it too late.

He was standing outside the door as I opened it. He looked at me, his dark eyes burning into mine. I tried to blink, but couldn't. My focus was caught in his stare and my eyes were no longer mine to command.

"Hello, Max," he said simply. I nodded at him and after the briefest interlude I took a step backward and gestured to him to enter. He did so. "This is a fine place you inhabit. Very grand befitting your station."

"What does that mean, exactly?"

"Nothing at all, Max. Don't be offended."

"Offended?" I was doing it again.

"I mean no harm, Max. I just wanted to see you after so long."

"You broke your engagement, and a long one at that, to Freddy," I said.

"You have seen her then?" he asked a little too eagerly.

"I did." I paused. "Yes."

"She is well?"

"She's fine." I decided not to go into details with him.

"And you will be seeing her again, I trust?"

"I don't know. I don't think so."

"You are the unforgiving man, Max." He laughed a little bit.

"Not so," I said.

"So we both have a chance with you then," Mikhael said grinning from ear to ear.

"No," I said instantly. "No chance. Not a chance in Hell."

"Max, so demonstrative!"

"What do you want, Mikhael? I have a life. I'm busy."

"I want the hug you promised me, Max."

That's presumptive of you, Mikhael. I never mentioned a hug. I think that was your idea."

"Who cares. Between us a hug is insignificant. Come and embrace me, Maxie."

"I don't want to. Thank you."

"But I want you to. This much I require of you and not more."

"You mean *'not the whole enchilada.'* "

"Yes, of course I mean the enchilada. Whatever that may be."

141

He laughed and I found myself joining in. I didn't want to but I couldn't stop it.

"Come in. Have a seat. Can I get you anything?"

"Just my little hug of welcome, Max."

I didn't want to. I new where it would lead. I hugged him anyway and an hour later, one enchilada later, we were talking, finally.

"That was nice, Max. Better than old times."

"That is one thing we won't talk about," I said abruptly.

"You withhold from me. I understand."

"I'm not compensation for your losses, Mikhael. I'm not and I won't be."

"You think that was pity sex?"

"I don't know what it was. But it's behind us."

"You act as though you did not want to see me."

"I don't. You haven't been a part of my life for years, Mikhael. I wrote you off as a bad check that wouldn't bounce twice."

"So much in the business world, Max."

"I'm sorry. But I'm not here to be played with again."

"You have aged."

"I'm older, wiser and self-protective, yes."

"But not me, Max. I am the same."

"You're not. The old Mikhael, the former one, would never have treated Freddy the way you did."

"Always it was Freddy between us, Max."

"No. She was the glue that kept us together."

"It was not your affection for me that did that?"

"No."

"You say I have misjudged Fredericka and have misunderstood you. This is a claim I cannot communicate with, Max."

"It's the truth."

"Your truth only." He sounded angry and vicious when he said this.

"You can't make me believe otherwise, Mikhael."

"You have no idea what she has done to my life, then. The betrayal of my family secret has completely overwhelmed me. It has taken away my purpose in life and had robbed me of my father's affection."

"When did he ever express any? When did you ever see him?"

"You think you know my life so well? Why? Because we spent some time together? You were never a big part of my life. Neither one of you played a role in the fullness of my life."

"So then you can take the rest of your life away with you, Mikhael. I don't need to be a part of it and neither does Freddy."

"What do you think I am, Max? What do you think I can be alone with nothing and with no one?"

"I don't care to think about it. I don't care at all!" I was shouting now and trying not to. Paul was due home any minute and I wanted to remain calm but that was almost impossible.

"Little Max, so big and tall and so very small and insignificant in reality."

"Just get out of here, Mikhael. I don't want you here."

"You were delighted to have me here, Max. Don't for an instant think otherwise."

"Still the bossy bastard," I snarled at him.

"I could always get what I want from you, Max. Always. Always."

Each time he said the word my anger increased. Finally I shoved him hard, in the direction of the apartment's door. With each shove he took a large, awkward step backwards. He never said anything to me except that word, over and over, "always, always, always." Finally we reached the door and I reached for him, turned him away from me and shoved him hard, one more time against the closed door.

"Get out, Mikhael. Just get out and stay out."

"You think its that easy to not want me? You will learn."

"I know who I am and what I want," I said. I reached around him and grabbed the doorknob, pulling it towards us, The pressure of the opening door shoved him hard against me and my free arm went around his waist to support him and keep us both from falling down.

Paul stood in the doorway, his key in his hand. Mikhael looked at him watching us in that awkward embrace. He gave his harshest snicker, then laughed and pulled himself free from my arms.

"Goodbye, then, boy from prostitutes. I have no further need of you."

He pushed past Paul and went out into the hallway. Paul stood there watching him retreat toward the stairwell. Then he turned to look at me. I didn?t want to see his face just then. I didn't want to read in it what must be in his mind.

"Good afternoon, Max," he said finally. "Is supper ready?"

CHAPTER TWENTY-FOUR

From Brewer's Dictionary of Phrase and Fable:

"Sugar and Honey: Rhyming slang for 'money.'"

She remembers everything. Every word he ever spoke to her, every response she ever made. Mostly she remembers the good things because the bad ones are just too bad to be remembered, but some of those she would never be able to shake.

"Sugar and Honey," he used to call out to her when he came in from wherever he'd been all day. It had seemed to her that he couldn't make up his mind about a nickname for her so he called her both. It had charmed her. Once she asked him about it and he had merely smiled at her, kissed her lightly on the cheek and went about doing whatever it was he had to do. She never knew what drew him from her so often. Once Freddy had actually asked him that question.

"What is it you do, Mikhael? I don't understand what it is you do."

"Sugar and Honey, leave it alone," was how he'd reply to her question.

It would take her years to discover the secret behind the words. Once she knew it, she knew she couldn't live with it. Some secrets are not to be borne lightly. So once again she had confronted the man she loved, had pledged to marry one day, with the question of his occupation.

"Mikhael, you know what I do. You know how I earn a living. It's only fair that you share with me as much as I share with you."

"Don't be foolish, Fredericka. Leave this alone."

"But why won't you discuss this? What can possibly be so terrible that I can't be a part of it?"

"If I told you, I would have to kill you," he said, and he laughed instantly after saying it as though it was a joke, a mighty joke. But Freddy knew it wasn't a joke. She knew from deep experience now that this was not a joke at all.

"You've pulled that one time too many, Mikhael."

"Have I now, Fredericka? That is a sad statement."

"You have no idea how sad it is," she said.

"Why do you say things such as that which appear to be threats?"

"There's no threat, Mikhael. There is only honesty."

"Honesty can be threatening to someone in my position."

"Then tell me about your position, Mikhael, and remove the threat by doing so."

"Fredericka, you have been reading too much fiction."

He sounded so superior when he said that, so overwhelmingly haughty and Freddy couldn't bear it another moment longer. She reached into her handbag and drew out the small, folded piece of light blue stationery she'd been carrying for days.

"Here," she said. "Open it, read it."

He took it from her and slowly, very slowly, his eyes never leaving her eyes, unfolded it. He laid it on the table and smoothed it out with the lowest, outside edge of his left hand, his thumb pointed up at his own face as did it. When it was flat and squared, he lowered his eyes to look at it. She watched him, watching his face for a change, a sense of recognition. There was nothing. He looked at the paper, and not at her, long enough to read what it contained, then he slowly raised his eyes again to look at her.

"You believe this to be true?" he asked her.

"I do."

"Then you cannot love me any longer, Fredericka."

"I love you, Mikhael. I love you, but I don't trust you. I can't."

"And you truly believe all this?"

She nodded.

"And what would you have me do, now, Fredericka?"

"Give it up," she said quickly. "Just turn your back on it and give it up."

"My life has been about protecting what is, and what shall be, mine. I cannot simply 'give it up' as you would have me do."

"Mikhael, your father destroyed his family and his world for a chair.

You don't have to do that, too. I'm your family now and I urge you to give back what was taken illegally. Save yourself."

"I cannot do this thing you ask of me. I will not."

"Mikhael, you're a fool. You really are."

"I am what I was made to be. I cannot be something other than that."

"You can. We all can. Max has made himself other than what he was brought up to be."

"Max!" He looked angry when he said his former friend's name. "You compare me to Max?"

"Max is a better man than you will ever be, I'm afraid."

"You have slept with Max?" Mikhael asked her. "You, also?"

"No, I never...what do you mean me also?"

"I mean...it is his world to sleep with many."

"No you don't, didn't, don't. You meant something else, didn't you?"

"I meant only what I said."

"I knew it." She gasped for a breath, "I always knew it."

She rushed from the room with his call of "Sugar and Honey" sounding somewhere behind her. She tore her clothing off her body and stepped into the bathroom naked and burning. She turned on the shower and stepped into it not knowing if the water would be cool, hot or tepid. It was hot. Steam rose from around her feet and suffused the curtained porcelain chamber in which she stood. Water spilled over her breasts and her abdomen, entered her and left the way it came.

In her mind's eye she could see the two of them, Mikhael whom she loved and Max whom she adored, together, naked, legs intertwined, sexually interlaced. She closed her eyes and opened them and she felt betrayed by the visions she summoned and couldn't send away again. She was crying, she realized, a soundless, noiseless sort of crying with tears and no sobs. There was regret and anger but no passion in her pain. The hot water, the steam and the thrust of it, was slowly cleansing the memory of moments she had never witnessed but could now see as clearly as if she had. She remembered that awful party at Max's graduation and the anger she had witnessed at Mikhael's reluctance to come to celebrate with them. She recalled the day in her mother's apartment when she had watched the two of them at the window. She understood, finally, the pain she felt kneeling there between them. Suddenly it all made sense.

Then she heard him behind her, standing in the doorway watching her.

"Go away, you horrible pretender," she shouted at Mikhael, never turning around to look at him.

"I will do so when it is appropriate to do so," he responded. "At this time I want to talk to you."

"I don't want to talk to you."

"You think you know something, Fredericka, that you never knew before."

"I know what I know."

"And you know what? That once a little boy fell in love with another boy? That is nothing. That is what boys do."

"Not the boys I used to know."

"Nonsense. We were the boys you used to know."

"I knew boys before you, Mikhael," she said turning to face him.

"But you never knew boys like me before you knew me."

"No."

"You can be very silly, Fredericka, when you say things like you are saying today."

"Can I?" She turned off the tap, leaving only a trickle of water from the shower head nozzle dripping on her shoulder. "Hand me a towel, please."

He did and she took it to dry her hair. She was standing naked before him, facing him full on. He had seen her like this many times before and so it meant nothing to him. She was unembarrassed, as always with him.

"And I already know what you do, Mikhael."

"How would you know this?"

"I am not as stupid as you think. I watch and I learn."

"Fredericka, I have never conceived that you are stupid, or foolish."

"Good, then we understand one another."

"And you will still marry me, Fredericka, when the time comes."

"I suppose I will. If you'll have me."

"And when that time comes, I will no longer be in this business you know about."

"No. You will have moved up from pretender to king and I guess you won't need to be selling drugs any longer."

"I will not."

"And that's that, I guess."

She moved into the bedroom again, a trail of watery pockmarks appearing on the carpet in the room. She opened her closet and took out a dress, one that he had purchased for her. She turned to show it to him.

"You like me in this dress?"

"I do."

"I'll wear it, then, for the photograph."

"Ah, yes, the photograph for your mother, of course. That is today."

"Yes."

"And this picture will be for her alone, as you promised."

"Yes."

"Then, my darling Fredericka, enjoy the time with your mother."

He bowed to her, then kissed her lightly on the mouth. His tongue darted in between her lips and she licked the tip of it with her own tongue. Then he moved away.

"You shouldn't have lied to me all this time, Mikhael, about what you do and who you are. It would have been so much better just to tell me the truth."

He turned in the doorway to look at her. "As you always tell the truth?" he asked.

"Yes. As I always have."

"And always will, my darling Sugar and Honey?"

"I always have," she said. She smiled at him. "I always have."

It was a scene she would try never to relive, she promised herself, and if she did replay it in her mind she would always see it exactly as it happened.

She was ready, dressed and made up, when her mother arrived ten minutes later to take her picture with Mikhael's father's chair. She was prepared to answer her mother's question about sending the photo to the papers, too. She was ready to take on the world, if she had to, just to put an end to all these memories she could only imagine, not real, yet too real to be forgotten.

She sees this movie in her mind. She watches it every few nights as she lies alone in her bed that once was shared with Mikhael. She ponders her future without him. She wonders about Max. She cannot discover a tomorrow any longer, she can only relive this past. She remembers what she she remembers, most of it good. Some of it is only money.

CHAPTER TWENTY-FIVE

From The International Book of Quotations:

"Mothers: 'Every beatle is a gazelle in the eyes of its mother.'"   Moorish Proverb

When Tooie became more involved with herself and her own interests than she was with me, I knew it was time to consider the direction my life was taking. This was after Max moved on to his own life, you see. I had my work with the boys and Tooie had hers at the store. We were both busy, all the time. I'd make appointments with her for meals and sometimes she wouldn't show up for them. That made no sense to me. I mean dinner is dinner. What woman doesn't want to join her husband for dinner, especially when he's buying and she's not slaving over a hot stove after a long day at work.

I suspected she had another girl-friend, of course. So I asked her, point blank, about it. She denied it and I had to believe her. That's what a good man does. He believes his wife when she says she has no lovers, but is just working far too hard. I learned later that what she wasn't saying was just as important, and just as big a part of the truth, as what she was saying. She was working too hard. That was true. She was putting in extra hours. She was designing a whole new gift wrap item, one that was going to revolutionize that whole entire industry, not that it was an industry, but it was a business. Tooie was inventing the stick-on, pre-made bow.

But that wasn't the whole story. No. She had a secret again and this time it was one I really couldn't guess. Tooie, it seemed, had developed a mother fixation.

Here's what I learned. And how I discovered it.

We were in bed one Sunday morning, just snuggling like we liked to do. I had made us coffee and we each had a mug of it. I was balancing mine on my knees which I'd pulled up close to my chest. It sat there, rocking just a little bit as I tried not to move. I could smell the brew, dark and strong, made from fresh-ground beans that I mixed from three different kinds of coffee: mocha-java, Vienna Roast Columbian and Jamaican Blue Mountain. Tooie was holding hers in both her hands, her palms pressed hard against the mug. She'd been having trouble with one of her hands. It stiffened up on her and it hurt.

"You doing okay?" I asked her, sweetly.

"I'm aces," she said.

"You don't look it," I told her. "Your lips may say 'okay' but there's 'ouch-ouch' in your eyes."

"Don't get so cute," she snarled at me.

"What's going on, Tooie, my love?"

"Mr. C,. there's a saying that goes like this," she replied, 'Man comes and tills the field and lies beneath//And after many a summer dies the swan.'" She paused and looked at me. "What the hell does that mean?"

"Why does it bother you?"

"Because it's a stupid quote, that's why."

"Stupid? How?"

"The first part I get. Man works the land, then gets buried beneath it, right?" I nodded. "But what's that second part got to do with anything? It takes a number of summers, Mr. Compton, to live your life and then you die! Bingo! So this swan dies eventually, what does that have to do with anything?"

"It's a reflection, my dear Tooie, on relationships. You're missing the point."

"Enlighten me, already."

"Man represents a man, do you understand that?"

"Sure."

"And man, this particular man, works hard and when he dies they lay him down where he worked."

"I knew that. I told you that." She snarled at me. "But what's this swan thing?"

"Well, you won't like this very much, Tooie."

"I can take it. Dish it out."

"The swan is a reference to his mate, lovely, useless, decorative. She lives on after him, but without him to serve and delight she ultimately goes the same way."

"You mean she dies."

"That's what the poem says."

"You mean she has no life after he's gone, and she finally gives in and gives up?"

"Uh huh."

"Is that what you think will happen with us?"

"Tooie, I doubt it very much. You're an independent soul, always was and always will be I guess. You'll go on a long time after I've given up the ghost."

"You bet I will!"

I took my coffee mug off my knees and leaned over to give her a little kiss on the cheek. She smiled, but she still gave me a tap on the chin to show she didn't really want me kissing her like that.

"I only want you to know I care about you, Tooie. Nothing more or less."

She looked at me a while, sipping her coffee as she did it. I could feel a blush rising from the middle of my chest up my neck, heading for my face. But before I could completely embarrass myself with it, Tooie spoke again.

"I know you been wondering about me," she said.

"What do you mean?"

"You know very well, Mister, what I mean. You been wondering what's up with me, who the woman is in my life. Hell, you even asked me once."

"You have been distant lately," I said to her.

"Yeah, well, I have my reasons."

"More than one reason?"

"Yeah, yeah, more than one."

"Can you talk about it, Tooie? Can you give me a hint, at least?"

"I miss the kid."

"We never had a kid." I wasn't thinking, I suppose, when I said that.

"Sure we had a kid, Lainie's grand-kid. Whatever happened to that kid?"

I had never told her about the kiss in the cab or about my very unnatural feelings for Max. I had told her that Max was growing up and didn't seem to have the same interest in us any longer. That was true, of course. Max was no longer a teenager, no longer a child. He was a young man starting a life away from the life he'd known. He was living with an opera singer and working as his valet. It wasn't my choice of a career for him, but he was going to school, his mother told me, and she wasn't too unhappy about the situation.

"You know he has his own life, now, Tooie,"

"I want to see him, Mr. C." She sounded petulant, like a child of four or five. "Vinnie, go get him for me. Please."

"I don't think he'd come around if I asked him," I said, regretting it instantly.

"Why? What did you do, Mr. Compton? What did you say to him?"

"Nothing. Really, nothing."

"You can't lie to me and get away with it, you know," she snapped at me.

"Tooie, please, there's nothing, really nothing. A kiss, a harmless kiss."

"You did what to that boy?"

"Nothing. I swear it."

"Don't you come swearing your swears at me. If you harmed that child, I will have to deal with you."

"Tooie, it was a little kiss. I was... drunk and he looked so very much like Lainie. I kissed him. There was never anything else again. Truth!"

"Well, you go get him and bring him here to me. I need to see him."

She was shouting at me and jumping up and down in a seated position, spilling the coffee all over the bedspread and behaving like an infant. I'd never seen her like that before, so I promised her I'd fetch Max and bring him back home with me for her to talk to if she'd only stop making such a fuss. It calmed her down right away. I left the room to fetch my clothes and when I was dressed I took that long delayed walk over to where Max worked, to see if I could persuade him to accompany me home. It didn't seem too likely. Except for a polite word at his high school graduation he had never spoken to me again after the cab ride home on his birthday.

To my surprise Max answered the door when I identified myself. He opened it wide and gestured me inside. I took the step and entered a world like none I'd ever seen outside of a Jeanette MacDonald movie. The reception room was grand and decorated in all white. The floor was white marble and the walls were white flocked paper. There were white velvet drapes and three chairs upholstered in the same white fabric. A small white carpet served as the central point for them, creating a pure white conversation area. A white Chippendale table rested delicately on the white carpet. The lamps and shades were white and a curved white staircase dominated, or would have if it had been any color other than white, the far wall as it reached up past the white bordered, pale, pale blue ceiling to the next level up. That blue, so pale it was almost white, gave them room a grounding it would have never had without that touch of blue.

"Quite a room," I said. Max said nothing. "Thanks for seeing me, Max."

"It's been a quite while," he said.

"It has. I wasn't sure you'd want to let me in."

"Why wouldn't I? You didn't do anything wrong. It was a moment, Mr. Compton. Just a moment."

"That's very generous of you, Maxie."

"It's nothing. How've you been? How's Tooie, the Lesbian?"

"That's the thing, Maxie," I said, coming right to the point. "She's pining for you. I don't know what's up with her. She made me come here to fetch you home for her."

Well, he stood there and he smiled, just broke into a grin and let it grow into a smile.

"That's so sweet," he said. Then he laughed. "I'm sorry, Mr. Compton. I didn't mean to laugh like that."

"It's okay with me."

"You just don't know how funny this is for me. Just this week two people I'd lost track of showed up here and tried to change my life for me, and now you with your strange request for your wife. There must be something in the stars, I guess. It's like everyone I used to know is coming out of the woodwork. Must be a full moon or something."

"I don't get you," I said.

"It's not important."

"Still, Maxie, they say things come in threes. Like this."

"They do say that, don't they?" he asked and then he laughed again.

"You wait a minute. I think I will take the plunge this time," he said and he disappeared into a room that seemed to have green, brown and blue colors in it from where I stood. I was going to follow him, even though he'd said to wait, but then he came back into the room clutching a hat and coat. "Let's go," he said, and he bustled me right out the door into the hallway.

Tooie was still in bed when I got back to the apartment with Max. She didn't look too good. Something had gone wrong while I was out doing her errand.

"You feeling okay?" I asked her quietly.

"Nah, it's nothing. Just that swan kicking up in me, I guess."

"Swan? What swan, Tooie?"

"You got the memory of a dead elephant, Mr. C.?" she asked.

"My memory is fine."

"No shit!" she said. She was looking over my shoulder and she spotted Maxie. "Max! Honey. Come over here. Let me see you, let me feel your arm and your warmth."

Max came over and sat down next to her, right there on the bed. He leaned in and kissed her gently on the mouth and she giggled like a child might.

"You look terrific, Tooie," he said and I knew it was a lie, but I watched her believe it.

"So do you, kiddo," she said. "God your grandma would be proud of you."

"You think so?"

"Do I? I just said so, didn't I?"

"You did. You surely did." Max laughed that really engaging laugh of his again and I laughed along with him.

"Mr. C, we got some coffee for this young man? Go see, and fetch me some fresh, too, please."

"You sure, Tooie? That last cup I gave you got you kind of hot and bothered."

"I can handle it. I can take it." She gave me a little nod and I went to do what she asked me to do. Like always.

I was out of the room for maybe ten minutes and I could hear the sound of their voices talking, laughing, carrying on. After a while they got quieter and when I came back with the coffee what I saw sent chills right through me and weakened my spine and my legs right down to the knees. Max was still sitting there, where I'd left him, but Tooie wasn't leaning against the pillows any more. Max was holding her, her head on his shoulder, her arms kind of limp, one at her side and one around his back. They weren't talking. They weren't moving. They were just sitting there like that.

I made noise in my throat, so I wouldn't frighten them or upset them. Max turned to look at me, but Tooie never budged. Max gave me a look, moved his eyes up to heaven and then back to Tooie. He didn't say a word, didn't have to, because I knew exactly what he was telling me. I knew that there'd be no more coffee drunk in that room that day. I knew that Tooie wasn't interested in coffee. Tooie wasn't interested in much of anything anymore.

You want to cry when you lose the person you spent your life with. You want to, but sometimes you just can't do it. That was who I was right then. I wanted to say something, sob something, but nothing would come. I just stayed there looking at her and Max and wanted to say or do or need or feel something special, but all I could do was stand there and look at them.

It was as though they had robbed me of an important possession, a moment in time that meant more than jewels or rewards or anything like that. I wanted back what was mine, but I didn't know what it was I wanted. It's a terrible feeling not to know what you want when all you feel is the need of something lost.

Finally, Max spoke up.

"It was how she wanted to go, Vin," he said.

"She wanted?"

"She didn't want you to be hurt. She told me she was holding on for you, but you couldn't be holding on to her or you might go first."

"How could she...? That's a terrible...."

"Vin, she really loved you, I think."

"I loved her, Max." There. I'd said it out loud. I'd finally had the chance to declare something I'd known for years and almost never said aloud. "She was the best thing to ever come my way."

"Her mother died, did you know that, Vin? Had she told you that?"

"Her mother died years ago."

"No. Her mother died two weeks ago, she told me."

"Her mother died before she married me."

I was trying to look at Max, and not at Tooie, but my eyes couldn't refrain from a glance in her direction right then. Revelation does that to you. It makes you turn in the direction from which it is coming, to look at the source of new truths. Max was still talking.

"Nope. Two weeks ago. That's what took the heart out of her, Vin. She kept her in a home all these years and when she died, she just lost more of herself than she ever imagined."

"You're telling me she never told me the truth about her mother?"

"I'm sorry Vin, but that's what she told me just before she...before she let go."

"She never told me." I was feeling like my chest had been crushed in. I couldn't get my breath. Max was laying her back down on the bed, now.

He was letting loose his tender hold on the woman I loved. I was alone with a corpse of someone who had hidden big, very big, secrets from me for years and a man who was once a boy I almost ruined myself over.

What I did then, was what I had wanted to do before. I cried. But I didn't know what I was crying over just then. I didn't know that until much later.

CHAPTER TWENTY-SIX

From The International Book of Quotations:

Profligacy: "Not joy but joylessness is the mother of debauchery."

Nietzche, Miscellaneous Maxims and Opinions (1879)

It isn't how long you wait for your life to improve that matters. It's what happens during the waiting time, the waking hours and the dream-filled ones as well. It's where the mind goes during that time. After Tooie's death I wasn't really sure where my life was any longer. Or what it was about. Or even why it was still a life. I only knew that my dreams were filled with her, with Lainie and Max, with the boys at the home and with a woman named Suzanne Aurelia Pitts.

Lainie, Tooie, Max, even the boys, were real. Suzanne Aurelia Pitts was a dream. I had invented her out of whole cloth, cut away the incidentals and left on the table the shape, the form, the concept of a woman who could be all of the people I loved, all rolled into one special person. I had dreamed her up one of those nights when I thought everything was going well for me. My work was satisfying,; I had stopped missing Lainie and Max was on his own and doing well; Tooie was inventing new bows and wraps and I couldn't have asked for more. But for some reason, I did. I wanted that perfect something, someone, in my life.

Suzanne Aurelia Pitts was the woman I created in my imagination and made into something wonderful, real and attainable. She was thirty-seven, a widow with money, had a great figure, dark blonde hair, not brassy or yellow, but dark, nearly brown but not ever brown really. She was my height, exactly, so in heels she was just a bit taller than me. She had long slender legs, almost a shade too thin, really, her only flaw. Her mouth was a natural red with an equally natural upturn into a subtle smile. Her eyes were green with flecks of brown and red in them. Her fingers were long and slender too, but they were perfect. Her breasts were cuppable in my hands and felt warm and solid and fleshy. Her hips were their match. So was her ass.

I loved Suzanne Aurelia Pitts. That was all there was to that. I loved her. I wanted her. She just wasn't real. So I dreamed of her all the time, awake or asleep. And after Tooie died, I cried for both of them, for the double loss I felt for the woman I'd lived with in reality and the woman I'd lived with in my imagination. They were both lost to me somehow.

Until I opened the book and found her. I'm speaking now of the telephone directory book. I opened it up and looked for her name and there she was. At least I thought there she was. S.A. Pitts was how the listing read. I knew that many women wouldn't put their first name in the phone book for fear of being discovered to be single women. They used initials only. There was no address given either, but just a telephone number. I closed the book.

I tried to forget that I'd found an S.A. Pitts in the local directory. I didn't want to think she might be real, that I might have met her once, not invented her, but just remembered her somehow. I needed to talk to someone about this, but there wasn't anyone I could call or meet and drink a cup of coffee with and chat about all this. I just didn't know anyone I could trust with this stuff. And then I thought about Max's father. If there was anyone who might be able to handle such stuff it could be him.

When I phoned him at home he sounded surprised. I suppose that was due to the fact that I had never called him before. Usually it was Lana I talked with. Not Jimmy.

"Jimmy, it's Vinnie Compton."

"Vinnie, yeah, how are you doing, man?"

"Thanks for asking. I'm going to be fine."

"That's great. I know how fond Lana is of you."

"Yeah, she's been a good friend to us."

"So, hold on, let me get her for you."

I had to speak quickly. "No, Jimmy, actually, I was calling you." There was a silence at the other end and I was sure I'd not spoken fast enough to catch him. Then I heard his voice again.

"Me? Really?"

"Yeah, yeah." I paused a second. "I need your help...your advice, I guess."

"My advice? Well, sure, okay. What do you need?"

"Jimmy, there's a...a woman..."

"Oh, I see. You need a room."

"No. Not that. I need to know... well, how to go about..." I just couldn't say it all at once. It felt so strange to be talking about Suzanne.

"Surely by now, Vinnie, you've had a woman."

"Oh, yeah, it's not that. I know how...I mean I know what to do."

"Okay." He sounded a trifle impatient suddenly, so I just blurted out the whole sordid tale about inventing this woman and finding her in the phone book. He laughed. I mean he laughed out loud and I blushed. Halfway across town I blushed.

"So what's your problem, Vinnie. Call her up and see if she is this Suzanne Aurelia Pitts or if the initials don't even come close. If they don't it's over. Simple."

"But what if they do, Jimmy?"

"Then, maybe, you didn't invent the woman. Maybe you met her somewhere once and remembered her and later on you thought you made her up."

"And then what?"

"Hell, I don't know. Ask her out?"

"What good would that do? I'm an old man and she's a beautiful young woman."

"Well, you don't know that for sure, do you? You haven't met the real one, at least not for a while."

"I don't know. Jimmy"

"Call her." He sounded so sure of himself. "Call her and ask if she's the woman you met...maybe even through Tooie."

"I don't know."

But he was right and I knew it. It was the only way to find out who she might be. I thanked him and he asked me to let him know if there was anything "practical" he could do to help me out. I promised to let him know.

I waited about a week before I tried the number. I was nervous as I dialed it. I had poured myself a pretty stiff drink and put it down on the telephone table in the front hallway. I seated myself and took a sip, then put it down, picked up the receiver and dialed her number. I waited, listening, as it rang. On the fifth ring I was about to hang up when I heard someone pick up the handset on the other end of the line.

"Hello?" said a female voice. It was sensual, quiet and almost whispered.

"Miss Pitts?" I said, asking the question that I knew would get an affirmative answer.

"Who is this, please?"

"Suzanne Pitts?" I asked without answering her question.

"Yes, who is this?"

"Well, I...,my name is Vincent Compton and I...."

"Really? Vinnie Compton?"

I took a deep breath. This was going much better than I'd imagined it could.

"Yes," I said, "Vinnie Compton."

"I can't believe you?re calling me," she said.

"This is Suzanne Aurelia Pitts, right?" I muttered.

"Vinnie, you know I hate that awful middle name."

My mind was raging over the blank pages of memory that had no real remembrance of this woman. Nothing was imprinted there.

"I didn't know that," I said blankly.

"Yes, you did. We talked about it."

"I don't remember that," I said.

"Shall I tell you all the details?" she asked me. I gulped and said yes. "We were in my father's car and you pushed and pushed and pushed me to tell you my middle name. You were guessing at it and coming up miles away from it, things like Alice and Annie and Arabella. When I wouldn't tell you, you started to tickle me and when I couldn't stand that any longer, I blurted it out. Boy, it took you by surprise. I practically had to deny it to get you to look at me again."

I didn't remember this at all.

"Oh sure," I said. "I remember it now." I didn't, as I said, but it was easier and more polite to just say I did.

"Good." I could hear her smiling through the wires. "So how are you?"

"My wife died recently. I'm okay, though."

"Your wife? Oh, God, I'm sorry. Poor Tooie."

"It's okay."

"Are you doing all right, Vinnie?"

"I'll be okay. I've been thinking about you, though."

"About me? Why?"

"I'm not really sure. I just was."

"How did you find me? It's been years, Vinnie."

"I...I looked you up in the phone book and there you were. Real."

"Well, of course I'm real."

"I just thought...I wondered if maybe I made you up in my head sometime."

"Well, it has been years since I saw you."

"Suzanne, it's been eons."

"Okay. Eons."

"And you're not...married?"

"Me? Vinnie, come on. Who'd marry me?"

That set me back. Maybe I'd remembered her name somehow but not who or what she was. Maybe she was ugly, or something worse.

"I'm sure you've had your chances, Suzanne."

"Well, I wouldn't say no one ever asked me, Vinnie."

That was good. That was better.

"So why didn't you?"

"Maybe I was waiting for the right guy. Some ticklish guy, maybe, to call me up and ask me."

"Okay."

"Was that a question, Vinnie?"

"No, no. A statement. Just a statement."

"So, tell me about you," she invited, so I told her about me and Tooie and about my work and about a lot of other things too. It ended with me inviting her for a cup of coffee the next morning and with her accepting. When we hung up I felt okay about it all, but worried. I didn't know what she looked like or what to expect. I didn't know how to handle a date. I called Jimmy back and told him how it all went.

"So, man, what can I do for you now?"

"Come with me," I said immediately.

"On your date? I don't think so."

"Please, please, come with me as a friend."

"She'll think you're into orgies or something."

"No, no. I'll say I just ran into you and while waiting we got to talking. That's all. She'll buy that, won't she?"

"I don't know. I don't think I would."

"Jimmy, please do this. I don't want to be alone with her."

"You're scared she won't be the girl of your dreams," he said.

"I'm scared, sure, but not of that exactly. I'm scared she will be the girl in my dreams. I'm not sure I could handle that."

I described the girl, Suzanne Aurelia Pitts, that I dreamt about. I had given him the details before, and now I repeated them all.

"She sounds like a dish."

"I know. That's what scares me. How am I supposed to handle all that?"

"Like in your dreams, Man."

"I don't think so."

"Look. Here's the deal, Vinnie. I'll come with you, have a cup and then leave. I'll leave no matter what she looks like. Unless you ask me for a place to go. Then I'll do what I do, okay? No charge for you."

"That's not going to happen, Jimmy. After this coffee I have to get to work."

"Yeah, that's what men always say before they book the room." He laughed again. Then he hung up. I was more confident, knowing that I wouldn't have to start out alone with this strange woman who had memories of me that I didn't share.

The next morning he met me near the Schraffts on Central Park South about nine in the morning. We went in, got a corner table and ordered some coffee. A few other folks drifted in and sat in pairs at tables or at the counter. Then, at 20 minutes after the hour, the door opened and a woman came in. I looked at her and I knew she was Suzanne Aurelia Pitts. She had to be.

She had dark blonde hair, not brassy or yellow, but dark, nearly brown but not ever brown really, just the way she did in my dreams. Her mouth was a natural red with an equally natural upturn into a subtle smile. Again it was the smile I knew so well. Her eyes were green with flecks of brown and red in them, but they had small, gray bags under them where the skin was too tender, too soft. She was sixty or so, not a young woman at all. I waved at her until she spotted me, than I put my hand down and watched her walk over to the table.

She had long slender legs, almost a shade too thin. Her skirt was short and the coat she wore missed hitting her hemline by about an inch. The colors weren't a good match. She sat down and looked at me.

"You got old, Vinnie," she said. "I never thought of you as old."

"You're not the same young girl you were, Suzanne," I said, knew it was not gallant, and hated myself for it. "This is my friend. Jimmy. I bumped into him outside and asked him to join me while I waited for you."

She gave him a smile and a nod, then turned back to me.

"Did you always look like that?" she said. "Weren't you much handsomer?"

"Probably. Death takes its toll."

"Yeah. It does."

"So you've lost someone too." I said simply.

"I've lost everyone. My husband divorced me and I went back to my old name, so I even lost the name I acquired. My son died young. My parents are gone. I'm alone, now."

"Wow." I bit my lip after saying that. I felt so stupid.

"Yeah, wow. I have no friends any more. My husband took the ones we had together and I'm not easy with people like I used to be with you."

I was wracking my brain trying to remember something about her other than how she looked. Nothing was there.

"So, how did you and Vinnie know each other?" Jimmy asked her, coming to my rescue. I breathed a sigh.

"He didn't tell you?" she asked Jimmy who shook his head, then punched me in the shoulder gently.

"He never says anything, this one. He's Mister Discretion, he is."

I smiled wanly and looked away from him.

"Okay," she said, "if he won't tell you I will."

"Nice," said Jimmy.

"You don't mind if I skip a few details, Vinnie, do you?"

I nodded, than shook my head, then nodded again.

"I'll call that a yes," she said. "It was in bed we met," she said next, like a lyric from a song in a Julius Monk revue I'd seen at the Upstairs at the Downstairs not long before this, maybe eight or nine years earlier.

"That's a funny thing," Jimmy said.

"Yeah, I guess it was. His wife, Tooie, did you ever know her?" I could hear Jimmy nodding. "Well, Tooie met me at a party and invited me over to her place for a party, so I went and Vinnie was there and we had a fun little time and then he took me home. It was a sweet gesture, I thought at the time. I mean it was an orgy and then he took me home. I was still living at home with my folks and I had my dad's car that night, so I didn't really need an escort, but he insisted. I figured he just wanted to get into my pants again, without Tooie watching, but no. He just wanted to be a gentleman and see me home."

I turned to look at her again. This time, the story on the table, she looked instantly familiar and I remembered her. Every word she said was absolutely true. I smiled again, but this time I felt warm when I smiled and not at all uncertain about things. She returned my smile.

"I should get going, I think," Jimmy said, and he stood up and held out his hand to her. "Nice to meet you, Suzanne." He bent over and kissed the back of her hand and then he turned to me, smiled, nodded and moved off. I was alone with the girl of my dreams.

"I've been dreaming about you," I said without meaning to say it.

"So, you looked me up?"

"Yeah. So you got married? You said yesterday, 'who'd marry me?' What did you mean by that?"

"I meant, now. I was married for a few years to a guy I never really got to know well. He ignored me most of the time and I ignored him."

"How could he possibly ignore a looker like you?" I asked her.

"Well, he wasn't much on looks and I'm not much of an intellect, I guess."

"I don't see that."

"And after the kid died, he had a bad attack of influenza when he was ten and they lost him in the hospital, Mike and me just drifted."

"Tooie and I never had kids."

"Yeah, well, I'm not surprised."

I wanted to be hurt by that, but I wasn't. She was just being honest and I knew it.

"So, what do you do now?" I asked her.

"I wait."

I took a breath. I shut my eyes. I saw the girl I remembered, I dreamt. I opened my eyes and looked at the real flesh and blood woman in front me.

"I know what you mean."

CHAPTER TWENTY-SEVEN

From Theater Language; A Dictionary of Terms in English of the Drama and Stage from Medieval to Modern Times by Walter Parker Bowman and Robert Hamilton Ball:

> "Asphaleia stage: A stage of iron, with metal cables
> and a hydraulic lifting system, used to render a theater
> fireproof."

There are cages in our lives. We build them ourselves, or others build them for us - it really doesn't matter, and we live within them for the protection of others and the containment of our feelings. We can pull the wires that attach them to the ceilings of our emotions, to the floors of our realities, and raise or lower ourselves in these confines to a point that is comfortable for us. We can do that. We are humans and we know how to do that. We know how. We learn the trick of manipulating our tiny worlds, our cages, in order to do this. Those of us who cannot adjust our places in the room that is our relationships sometimes crash to the floor and, as our world shatters into hard metal strips and shards, we hopefully pick our way out of the debris in which we find ourselves. Those of us who can do otherwise, do so. I am one of the latter. Usually.

When I was a boy I had a puppy who tore newspaper into strips. She would hold down the remnants of the day's news and with her teeth she would rip those lengthy strips of over-inked newsprint. That was her way of dealing with the loneliness she felt when she was being ignored by me. Max has his own methods and they are not very dissimilar from my puppy's.

He lowers his particular cage to a halfway spot in his underwhelming world and he rips my heart into long, empty strips. He does it slowly and methodically, like the puppy, and he does it without even knowing he's doing it.

I can handle the pain of being torn to shreds, but I cannot abide not knowing what is behind such an action. It is not my nature, my operatic nature, to just stand there and not reach for the high note, the low note, the middle register and the words that those notes amplify. I am forced, ultimately, to speak. That is the journey I take in my cage, my hydraulic stage of life.

"Are you going to explain this?" I asked him.

Max didn't answer me. He stood there, looking forlorn and not speaking a word.

"Max, you have to say something. Even if you don't explain what's been happening, you must say something."

"Hello, Paul."

"Well, that's something anyway," I said. "Now, would you mind saying something worthwhile."

"There's really nothing to say. He's an old friend."

"He didn't seem very friendly to me."

"He wasn't. He's had a bad week."

"A week? Really?" I wanted to laugh at that, but I couldn't. I'd been having a bad month and Max hadn't reacted this way.

"He's not like you, Paul."

"No one is, dear boy."

"No. No one is." Max came over to where I was standing and he placed his hands on my shoulders. "I've admired you my whole life, Paul."

"Oh, tush!" I pulled away from his grasp.

"It's true. In the darkest times I had your voice and your music to soothe me. You know that. I've told you that before."

"Yes," I said. Just that.

"And you've been great to let me live here and work for you and go to school."

"Every boy needs an education," I replied.

"It's not just that, Paul, you know it. You've let me into your life, your world. I'm very grateful for that."

"Then show your gratitude and talk to me. Tell me what's bothering you."

He shook his head, too slowly I thought, before speaking and then, after a tentative "I..." he stopped speaking and looked away.

"Who was that man?" I was whining, I could hear it, and I didn't care.

"An old friend."

"And?"

"And now he's not a friend. That's hard for me."

"Well, what is he now?"

"He's nothing. Not a friend. Not an enemy. Nothing. That's hard."

"I don't understand, Max."

"I don't know how to explain it. We were close friends. He was my first lover. Then he stopped being either and went away. Just like that. No reason. No explanation. I was very hurt by that. Then suddenly, there he was. And the man he was just wasn't the boy I knew."

"He'd moved on, Max. That's all."

"All?"

"It happens to everyone. We grow out of the people we knew."

"I don't like it, Paul. It means I'll likely grow out of you, too."

I took a deep breath and said what I had not wanted to say, ever. "You will."

"How will I know..."

"...when that happens, Max? You'll just know. Then you will do what you must."

I reached for his hands and held them in mine. I smiled my most radiant smile and pulled him toward me.

"I've never wanted to own a person, Max. It was never part my psychological make-up. However, if I did ever want to have someone made a permanent part of my life, I think it would be you."

He didn't respond to this. He stood there, held firmly by my hands, and he looked straight into my eyes, seeing behind them, I could sense, seeing into my brain, into my thought patterns, trying to read the heart in my head, seeking the deepest recesses of my brain to find the real meaning in my words. It hurt me to stand there like that. It pained me deeply. It made me wish that my particular cage had an electrical button I could push, perhaps with my nose considering that my hands were full, a button that would take me way high up, away from this confrontation that was making me so uncomfortable.

"It wouldn't be me, Paul," he said suddenly and I felt my cage begin to descend, rapidly, slightly out of control, rocking a bit from side to side.

The hand in my mind reached for the cable, grabbed it and lost its grip instantly as the burning flesh was stripped away by the metal cable rushing through it. I waited for the crash, that terrible, anticipated crash, but it never came. I just kept going down further and further, hotter and hotter, without pause.

"Paul, are you all right?" I heard Max say from somewhere far away.

"I'll be fine," I shouted.

"Paul! Don't go away from me."

There was something in the sincerity of that statement that enforced a natural braking system in my mind's cage. I slowed and stuttered and the sense of descending ended abruptly. I was on solid flooring again. There was no movement in my world. It was growing cooler again.

"I want to tell you about Mikhael," Max said from somewhere above me. "Let's sit down, and let me tell you everything I can remember."

I nodded and was suddenly standing there next to him again. We were the same two people we'd been before, close, companionable. I sat down on the sofa and Max sat down next to me. He was still holding onto my hands. I looked at him, nodded and he told me the story, from the beginning, about himself and Mikhael and a girl named Freddy. I heard the words, but I wasn't truly listening, for all I cared about was that he had opened his cage door, left it and entered mine.

The hydraulic motor that moved me up and down took over and we started on a very slow ascent and the world was shining again. Max was confiding in me. Finally.

CHAPTER TWENTY-EIGHT

From The Reader's Digest, April, 1946:

> From Hollywood Round-up: "Jack Philbin, an admirer of Edmond Lowe, had never met Lowe but kept staring at him in a restaurant until Lowe nodded and said, 'Hello.'
>
> 'What do you think of that?' asked Philbin. 'I've gone to so many of his movies, he thinks he knows me!'"

We were sailing on the Cunard Line ship, QE-2. It was still new, bright, shiny, smelling of wax and polish. Our suite was the second largest one possible to book with two bedrooms, a sitting room with a grand piano, two terraces - one forward and one on the starboard side, a dining room, two bathrooms and a powder room. We had our own, well-stocked bar as well. Meals were available to us night and day, prepared and served by our own steward. Our suite could accommodate thirty-five people for a party, we had discovered earlier that afternoon, as old friends and my family swarmed in and out wishing a bon voyage, a swell trip, all of that stuff. It was great fun until someone burst into song. Naturally she sang 'Bye, Bye, Baby' from "Gentlemen Prefer Blondes,' now the inevitable ineffable sailing-off-on-a-ship song. The woman's voice was almost on pitch and I knew how that would irritate Paul. If there's one thing about him that never fails him it's that sense of pitch.

I looked around to see who had started this foolishness and discovered, to my shame, that it was my mother. I hurried over to her, just as she reached the penultimate line: ""Although I know that you care..." I grabbed her on cue and gave her big kiss on the mouth, the only way to halt her in those odd vocal moments of hers. She looked startled, as though she hadn't recognized the man in whose arms she found herself. When I pulled back and looked into her eyes, she giggled, then broke in hearty laughter. That was better than her singing.

"Oh, baby, I'm going to miss you," she said to me.

"I know. I'll miss you too." I didn't plan to miss her, but it was a nice thing to say.

"Happy Birthday, honey!" She kissed me this time.

"Thanks, Mom."

"All ashore that's going ashore!" came the British-accented cry from the companionway.

"That's you dear," I said to my mother.

"Must I?" I nodded assent. "Must I really?"

"Yes," I said.

"But I don't take up much room. You could keep me in the closet."

We both giggled at that and I had to slap my own hand across my own mouth to contain it. When I was sober again, a moment later, I put my arm around her and turned her around in the direction of the cabin's door.

"Now scoot, Lana. I'll write to you. I promise."

"And bring home a nice present or two, too," she said looking over her shoulder at me.

"I will. I promise."

"Something silky," she added. "Or sparkly. I don't care which."

"Okay. I'll find something appropriate."

"No! Nothing appropriate." She was clearly drunk on champagne. "Something special!"

"Okay. I've got it." I gently nudged her forward. She took the hint and grabbed for my father who was leaning against the wall.

"Help me home, Jimmy," she said to him.

"Help you? I can barely stand up on this bucket. I think I'm seasick."

"Seasick?" I said breezily. "We've been tied up at the Cunard pier all afternoon, Dad."

"I know, and I'm sick of it," he said, slapping his hand against his hip. He leaned over in my direction and gave me a short busky kiss on the lips. "You have a good time son. Remember that. This trip isn't just for work, Max. Have fun."

"I will. I will."

They were heading out the door, the last of our departure party guests to leave. I turned back to look at Paul lingering near the piano.

"Do you want to be up on deck for our departure?" I called out to him.

"You go on, dear boy. I'll join you in a few."

He was nodding to me, encouraging me to leave the stateroom. I wasn't sure I should, but as this was my first time on a liner I thought it only right to see and experience everything. I nodded in return, turned away and shut the cabin door behind me.

I could still see my parents backs ahead of me in the corridor. I rushed to catch up to them and just as they found the stairwell to take them back to the gangway, I stopped them.

"I'm going up to the Promenade deck, my dears," I said to them. "You find a place on the dock to watch and I'll find you and wave."

"And don't forget those yellow and pink streamers I brought you," Lana said.

"No, I won't. They're in my pocket. When the whistle blows the third time and we're free, I'll unleash them. You'll see them, all at once, and know where I am if you haven't already spotted me."

"We'll find you," she said. Then she said it again. I hugged them and headed up the stairs to my right as they joined the throngs heading down two decks to the visitor's gangway. As I turned on the landing and headed up the next flight of steps I saw my mother's hat disappearing below me. I didn't know how poignant a moment that could be until that very moment. Suddenly I was very much alone in a strange place, an alien atmosphere and I wasn't prepared for it. I felt tears welling up in my eyes and, inadvertently, I missed the next step and staggered, catching myself at the handrail.

Another hand grabbed me from behind and helped to steady me.

"Are you all right?" asked an unfamiliar voice.

"Oh. Yes. Thanks. I just missed the step," I said.

"And we're not even shoving off yet." His voice was charming and slightly accented. I turned to see who this man might be and was confronted by a face like none other I'd seen in my life.

His face was wider than it was long, very pale and smattered with freckles. His eyes were hazel, almost amber actually, and they were quite far apart, highlighted by long blond lashes and arched brows that seemed almost unreal. He had a very straight, very long nose, more than an inch and a half at the tip from his face itself. His nostrils flared up and the mouth below that nose was wide, thin-lipped and seemingly perpetually dour, its corners turned downward. His chin disappeared into his neck and his neck was long, slender and revealed an enormous adam's-apple. His hair was a sandy blonde color, very straight and cut badly, the tresses falling haphazardly over one another and over his high brow. I realized that I was staring at this face when the mouth's corners turned up to smile, revealing beautiful teeth, but even in a smile his mouth retained that odd, downward-turned aspect...a grimace, really

I turned away, not wanting him to think I was staring.

"My name is Drew Hatton," he said.

"Hello, I'm Max," I answered him.

"Just Max?"

"Well, no," I blushed, "the Incomparable Max, actually."

I turned away and continued up the stairs, knowing he was directly behind me.

When I reached the Promenade Deck I moved out onto the long stretch of newly waxed wooden flooring and looked in both directions for a place at the railing that wasn't already crowded with other folks. There was only one spot and it was all the way aft. I hurried to it, not knowing if Drew Hatton would follow me, or if he was meeting his own friends, family or companion. As I squeezed into the railing's tiny open space, between a man who might have been a New Jersey butcher and an elderly woman who was clearly a British Dame of some sort, I heard Drew's voice again.

"Ah, churl," he said, "took all and left not a drop for me." When I turned to look at him he had the potty face again.

"Juliet, isn't it?" I asked him.

"No, Drew."

"The line, fool," I said, knowing I was now in flirtation mode.

"Ah, yes, the Shakespeare. Rather like Juliet, I imagine."

"I would move over and offer you half of what I have here," I said, "but I'm rather hemmed in, as you can see."

"No matter," he replied. "I'm taller than you and can see quite well if I squeeze up against you, like this..." and he moved in very close indeed, "Then if I put my arm about your shoulder, like so, and lean across your other shoulder, just so, I am almost where you are and still have a perfect view."

"Yes, you do," I said.

"Oh. Am I being too forward on such short acquaintance?"

"Well, this is a bit intimate and awkward," I said.

"How true. How delightful."

"I beg your pardon?"

"Delightful of you, that is, to be so frank about this awkward situation."

"Why delightful?" I was curious now.

"Well, some other person might see this as an advantage, but you obviously don't. That's refreshing."

"Advantage? How?"

"Oh, so you don't actually know who I am, then." He sounded a bit disappointed.

"No."

"Well, I shan't tell you. I mean why spoil such a perfect moment."

"Okay." I turned away to look at the dock and see where we might be en route to departure. Two of the three heavy ropes were gone and the gangway was being pulled away from the ship. I turned back to Drew.

"We're almost off," I said barely able to contain my excitement.

"You sound thrilled," he said. "Don't tell me this is the first time for you."

"It is, though."

"My God, a virgin."

I was about to dispute that, but let it rest.

"Well, we need champagne, Max. It's imperative, you know. A Cunard tradition." He shouted for a waiter and one appeared instantly. He ordered two champagne cocktails and turned back to lean on me again and to peer over my shoulder.

The third rope was being wound up on the lower dock area and the ship gave the first big blast of its horn. It was deafening. I put my hands up to my ears, to block the sound of it, but Drew gently put his hands around my wrists and lowered my arms.

"You mustn't," he said. "It's bad luck."

"Really?"

"It is. The ship will give three blasts and on this final one the tugs will begin to move us out into the river. The tradition is that the first blast notifies the Gods above that we're praying for good weather and an easy voyage. No one can shut that prayer out."

"What's the second one signify?"

"That is to remind those on shore that we are not merely leaving their sight, but we are asking them to pray for safe harbor and safe return."

"Nice. And the third one?"

"Well, the third one, Max, that's the most important call of all...." Our champagne arrived and he took both glasses, handing me one and keeping the other. "It means champagne! What should we toast to? A happy voyage?"

"Sure," I said.

"And how about to you, Max?"

"Me? No, I don't think so."

"But it's your first trip. It must be to you."

"Well, it's also my birthday, so okay, why not?"

"So that would make this your 'maidenhead' voyage."

He raised his glass and started to say something, but the second blast of the ship's horn drowned him out.

"What's the third horn for?" I asked ignoring the missed toast.

"Well, Max, that's the most important one, as I said. It reminds us that lifeboat drill is only twenty minutes on."

"Lifeboat drill?" I asked him. He filled me on the procedure, the need to return to the cabin, read our instructions, find the life-jackets, put them on and reconvene on deck under our assigned lifeboats. "Sounds silly," I said.

"It's not. It's imperative. And if you miss it, and they do take attendance, then you pay the penalty."

"What's the penalty."

"The brig, my dear. The brig." There was a silence and then he burst into laughter. A moment later I heard, from below us, the clang of the heavy metal gangway door being shut into place. I could feel the ship floating free now and I wanted to see if I could find my parents on the upper deck of the pier.

"Excuse me, Drew, but I have to look for someone." I turned back to look at the land we were about to leave. I reached into my jacket pocket for the streamers my mother had given me. I held them, now, in readiness for the right moment, the third blast of the horn. The tugs were in place and starting to guide us into the channel. I couldn't see my father anywhere but I thought I recognized Lana's hat again. I raised my hand to wave goodbye and then the final blast from the ship's horn occurred.

It was long and loud and didn't disturb me a bit this time. I had become accustomed to its tone and volume. I tossed my hand forward and then jerked it back suddenly, allowing the streamers to unleash and float on the light breeze. Their combined pink and yellow colors seemed quite distinct to me as I watched others down the line doing the same thing.

The woman in the hat was waving her hand and I felt certain it must be Lana. I waved hard and the streamers danced on the light wind. Then I let go of them and watched them float slowly backward and downward until I couldn't find them any longer.

The ship was turning now in the channel and starting to move down river. I realized I was now staring at New Jersey and I turned back to face Drew. But he was gone. I was alone.

I suddenly thought about Paul, alone in the suite. I wondered if I should head back there and check on him. I finished my champagne cocktail and was heading down the outside staircase to the deck below when the announcement about the lifeboat drill began to come over the loudspeaker system. Drew had been correct. I moved on to find Paul and find my life jacket.

I entered the suite through the salon door, one of three to the suite, expecting to find him there, on the sofa or out on the terrace watching the processing shoreline. He wasn't in either location, so I went to his bedroom door and knocked gently. There was no response.

I had noticed, during the bon voyage party, that he had remained a bit aloof and distant from the crowd of friends, relatives and well-wishers. I had thought it odd. It wasn't his style to avoid the middle of a room, to limit the attention paid to him. I had spoken to him about it, briefly, while a friend of his, Mitzi Kronos - born Martha Maloney - was singing a medley of hits from her Broadway years but he had dismissed my concern with a simple gesture. Even Jimmy, my Dad, had noticed his peculiar behavior and commented on it to me. Now there was this new wrinkle. No sign of the man in our rooms.

I went to the closet in the front hall and opened it, hoping to find only one life jacket there, indicating that he had taken his and gone above to our assigned boat station, but there were two life jackets in the cupboard. That concept wouldn't hold water. I began to worry.

I went back to his bedroom door and knocked louder, calling out his name, hoping to hear his voice. There was no response. I was going to try again, but instead I just gripped the doorknob and gave it a turn. The door opened easily and I stepped inside Paul's room. His trunks stood open, but unpacked on one side of his bed. A closet door was open and there were a few things there, mostly the coat he had worn to board the ship and three hats, his suit jacket and his shoes, the ones he'd been wearing at the party. I knew these oxfords well, having helped him off with them many times. Now I was really starting to worry.

I checked his bathroom, but it was empty. The bed, still perfectly made up was not where Paul was to be found. His room, in fact, was devoid of its occupant.

I exited and crossed the salon to my stateroom hoping that he had gone there and was lying on my bed asleep. That would have been wonderful, but it turned out to not be the case either. My room was just as empty as his had been. I decided that he must have come up onto the Promenade deck during our shoving off to find me and might still be up there looking for me. That was the simplest explanation. He was on deck. When he didn't find me and realized that lifeboat drill was on, he would return to the cabin for his jacket and I'd be waiting.

I waited for ten minutes and he never came. Two more messages were broadcast over the loudspeakers about the drill and then, after a lull, there sirens commenced, summoning people to places. I hesitated. I didn't know what to do. Finally, as the final call was given, I dragged myself into the modified Mae West vest and hurried back out and up to my place. Perhaps he would be there, I thought. I'd see him there in line, sans vest, but there.

The deck was crowded and I pushed past several groups of people to get to my assigned place on deck. Once there, in my proper group, I searched the three-deep cluster of people for Paul. I couldn't see him.

A junior officer of some sort began to call the roll, by cabin number. When he got to ours I answered to my name, but Paul made no reply. They called his name four times and I finally spoke up.

"He seems to be missing," I said. "I tried to find him in our suite, and I waited for him, but he never showed up."

"Where is he, then?" the officer asked. I shrugged and looked as uninformed as I could. I'm sure it wasn't a stretch. I really had no idea.

"Please wait here when we're done," the officer said.

Fifteen minutes later the hordes were officially dismissed. People filed past me, looking sympathetic or annoyed, depending on whether they were female or male. Finally the officer approached me.

"I've radioed the Purser and the Captain. They would like to see you."

"Me? What have I done?"

"We don't know, of course. That's why they want to see you."

I shrugged, asked where, was told where to go, and I went there.

Neither the Captain nor the Purser had any knowledge about Paul Donner's whereabouts. I was instructed to contact both of them as soon as he showed his face. I promised to do that and returned to the suite.

There was no sign of Paul. A thought hit me, and I telephoned the purser's office and asked for the man. In an instant he was on the line

"By any chance is there a Helga Meerstadt on board?" I asked him.

"Why?"

"Well, she and Mr. Donner are great friends and former lovers. If he found her on board he might be with her. That would explain a lot," I said.

"Give me a moment." I listened to the awkward silence as he thumbed through his registers. Then he was back on the line. "No, I'm sorry. She is not with us on this trip."

"Well, then, I'm stumped," I said.

"Please keep us informed, Sir, of any changes."

"I will," I said. I hung up the phone and sat down on the sofa. I was at a total loss about Paul and what had happened to him. I decided to wait for him, right there. I wouldn't change or dine or anything until I knew where he was, what had happened to him. I waited a long while.

In fact, I waited until midnight without any word of him. I fell asleep on the couch on my first night on a ship, still dressed in the clothing I'd worn all day. When I woke it was dawn, we were at sea and I was losing hope, all hope, of finding my lost friend.

Paul Donner was missing.

The phone rang. I grabbed it, hoping for good news.

"Good morning," said a familiar voice.

"Hello," I replied, a bit diffident I realized, but I was exhausted.

"Care for a spot of breakfast?"

"Look, Drew, this isn't the best time...."

"It's the only time for breakfast, dear," he said.

"Well, not today, thank you." I knew I sounded curt and dismissive, but I couldn't help it. He noted the tone and changed his into something softer, sweeter, more solicitous.

"Can I help you with something, dear? You sound so defeated."

I explained about Paul and his current status of "missing." Drew was sweetly conciliatory. He offered to do some searching for me in the public rooms, the bars, the tiny secret spaces where people went to play games, or cards, or simply be alone. Grateful for his help, I thanked him and hung up the phone.

He called back a half hour later to say that he had found sign of Paul, but by that time it didn't matter. I knew the answer already.

Paul Donner was dead.

CHAPTER TWENTY-NINE

From the Reader's Digest, April, 1946:

> From Picturesque Speech and Patter: "Join the Navy
> and See What's Left of the World" (A. Cramer)

When you're a day out to sea there's very little that anyone can do to help you if you've a man overboard. Actually there's very little to be done for either of you. The instant I was sure that Paul Donner was not on the ship I went to the purser and he called the captain and together they assured me of the above. They certainly couldn't turn the boat around and slow down to a walk just to search through the open waters that surrounded our long-lost wake. They contacted the coast guard and gave them our position and our relative position and our approximate path through the calm seas.

"You're lucky," someone said to me, "that we've had calm seas so far. Otherwise a search wouldn't even be practical let alone possible."

"Lucky," I thought. "How lucky can I get?"

"If he's alive," Captain von Milzner told me, "they'll find him and get him back to safe harbor in New York."

"If he is alive, he's got to be on this ship," I said. "He's got contracts in Europe and London."

"Contracts?"

"Yes. He's Paul Donner. The Opera star?"

"So, you're saying he's someone important, then?"

"He's very important," I informed this Norwegian lout who, it turned out, wasn't the captain, but only a staff captain - a very different position on board a liner. The real captain was upstairs somewhere in his cabin keeping us on course and on time. Clearly that was more important to him than finding the passenger he'd lost on his first night out of port.

"We'll inform you when there's news," said the staff captain.

"Instantly!" I shouted at him. "Do you understand that command? Instantly!"

I hadn't meant it to sound so huffy and imperious, but the demanding goddess in me, that little piece of me that comes from Granny Elainie, comes out in times of deep stress.

"In the meantime, sir," the Norwegian said to me, "would you mind very much if we continue with the work that will both protect our other passengers and impress you with our care for your person."

"Just find him," I said, adding a "please" at the end. He actually gave me an encouraging nod and extended his right arm to give my left shoulder a double pat.

What I really wanted and needed was for someone to find Paul, find him well and unharmed. That was all I wanted. It didn't seem a daunting task, not to me. It seemed very doable, very achievable a goal. By mid-day, however, after a second life-boat drill during which they hoped to discover, what..? that someone else was missing too? It seemed like a solution. It felt possible that Paul had met someone else and spent the night and day away.

With the sounding of the alarm came that inevitable combination of shock and anger as people shuffled to their assigned places a second time in two days. You could see that there was an excitement level at work here. It made sense to believe that there was a danger at hand. The seas were calm, the sky was clear, the ship wasn't rocking, but there was that odd touch of autumn in the air, a chill that couldn't be defined. When the captain finally called the all-clear and people were shuffling along the decks to their stairwells, that sense of 'strange' had clearly altered into something harsh and hostile.

I was taken to the purser's office and told to wait there. Apparently there was news. I waited. I waited a while, almost a half hour, before I got antsy. I picked up the telephone on the purser's desk and jiggled the button until the operator responded.

"What exchange?" she said.

"Just get the captain," I responded.

"Aye, aye," came her response.

I waited a moment, then there was a clicking sound in the ear-piece, then a whistle, then some more clicking. Then a voice came on.

"This is the Bridge."

"I want to speak to the captain," I said.

"Captain's on his way below," said the man.

"To where?"

"Purser's office," came the reply.

"Thanks!" I quickly hung up the phone and waited again. It wasn't even a minute before the purser and the captain arrived. At a gesture from the captain, I sat down again.

"There is no good news, I'm afraid," said the man in charge.

"What does that mean?"

"It means, sir, that we have not found a trace of your companion aboard this ship. He was the only person not at his station during the drill."

"I see."

"Are you certain, sir, that he was aboard at the time we weighed anchor?"

"Of course he was! We had a bon voyage party, said goodbye to the guests and then I went up onto the Promenade deck for our departure. He was here."

"He was with you at that time, for departure?"

"Well, no. He was in the cabin, I think."

"But you're not certain." I shook my head. I really wasn't sure at all about what he had done, or where he might have gone after I left him there.

"Can anyone attest to the facts of your whereabouts, sir?" That startled me.

"Well, I...yes, I think so. I fell coming up to the Promenade deck and another passenger helped me up and stayed with me on deck." I gave them Drew's name and his cabin number. They thanked me and told me I could return to my own cabin, if I liked. I got up, a bit numb, wondering if I was suddenly a suspect in something. That was how it felt. I was at the door when the captain's voice, asking one more question, stopped me.

"One last thing, sir. When did you know your friend was missing? And how?"

"I explained about the ship turning and Drew's advice about lifeboat drill and my returning to the cabin in time to hear the announcement. I told him about checking for Paul, waiting for Paul, not waiting for Paul and not finding Paul. I gave every detail I could remember. He nodded as I spoke, than he thanked me again when I'd finished. I exited the room feeling hot flashes and perspiring. I was a suspect, I knew. I was the object of observation and witness endorsement. They thought I had done something to Paul. It was ridiculous, but that was the operating theory.

I wondered if I should try to contact Drew and warn him about this, but I instantly knew that if I did that I would be even more a suspect. I decided to go to one of the many bars on the ship and order a drink. My nerves were truly jangled by now and I needed something to steady them.

I went aft to a nice cocktail bar with a piano and a dark corner or two. I ordered a scotch and soda, took a seat and watched the ship's wake in the distance. One or two other people were seated in the room and there was a hush in the place which, along with the scotch, soothed my spirits. I started to regain my composure. I was mellowing out when a steward approached my table and, without a word, placed a folded note on the table before me.

"What's this?" I asked.

"From Mr. Donner, sir," the steward said. I must have jumped a foot in the air without trying.

"What? What does that mean?"

"Mr. Donner, sir. He left this note for you yesterday. He said when you came in I was to give it to you."

"When did you see him? Jeffers?" I could see his name on the metal bar over the pocket of his pristine white jacket.

"He came in just before we left the dock, sir. I was the only one in here at that time, and he handed me the note, pointed you out to me, there at the railing with the other gentleman, and told me to give you this note when you came in, and not a moment before."

"He..." I wanted to read the note. I gave him a nod, but he stood where he was. I reached into my pocket and took out a dollar and handed it to him. He gave me a smile and backed up a step. "Wait. Please call the purser's office and tell him I'm here and want to see him."

"Certainly, sir." And he was gone.

I opened the note that Paul Donner had left for me. I read it, couldn't quite believe what it said, closed it, reopened it as though I hadn't seen it before and read it again.

"I believed you, Max," it began, "when you said that your chum, Mikhael, meant nothing to you. I believed you. I did so because I wanted to believe you. This voyage was to cement our relationship, to restore the faith I had in you when I brought you into this world of mine. But we haven't even left port and you are in another man's arms. That is more than I can bear. I'm leaving the ship. You will pack my things and have them placed in Cunard's care when the ship arrives in England. I will have them picked up. I don't want you to contact me. I don't want you to come back to me. I finally know you for the man you are, and probably were trained to be. I have never felt so betrayed before, Max. Never felt so insulted. Enjoy your stay in Europe. You know the itinerary. It is all paid for. I won't stop you from enjoying it. I just don't want to see you again. Ever. You are on your own now. I am dead to you. Paul"

When the Purser arrived I handed him the note without a word. I motioned to the steward to join us and he did. He told his story about Paul writing and handing him the note. The purser asked to keep it for a while, to show the captain. I nodded and the two of them went away again, leaving me alone to wonder how stupid the world around could possibly be, how stupid, jealous and odd. I was wronged, not trusted by the one person in whom I had confided and trusted. Everything I had built was demolished. There was nothing left for me.

"There you are. I've been wondering," came the words in the voice of the man whose accidental encounter with me had triggered this life-altering change. "Are you all right? Is there anything, anything at all, I can do?"

I didn't want to say yes, but I knew now that I must say yes. My fate was indeed what my mother had foreseen so many years earlier. I was in need, for real. Here was my route, laid out before me. Here was my answer. I hated myself for a moment, then I smiled nicely at Drew and moved over on the banquette, making room for a new protector.

CHAPTER THIRTY

From the Reader's Digest, April, 1946:

From "What's your Eye-Q?" condensed from The American Magazine by Joseph Samachson, Ph.D.:

> "One quarter of your bodily energy is used in seeing. True, according to Dr. Charles Sheard, of the Mayo Clinic. Which explains why the condition of your eyes can affect your general health."

The morning I arrived in London I telephoned New York, hoping to catch Paul Donner at the apartment. There was no answer. I tried him two more times over the next five hours, always with the same results and then I remembered that he was due in London for a singing engagement so he was probably on his way or already here. I had followed his directions and disembarked his luggage and hadn't waited to see who was retrieving it. For all I knew it might have been Paul himself. He might have flown over a day or two after leaving the ship. He might be on another ocean liner arriving a day later than ours. I had no way of knowing for sure.

I called down to the desk to ask if Mr. Donner had reserved another room or suite, other than the one I was now in, the one I had reserved for us in his name more than two weeks earlier. The desk clerk was pleasant, in that way the Brits have, but he couldn't tell me if Mr. Donner had reserved another suite for himself. Or wouldn't, I thought. It seemed quite likely that he had. This was where he always stayed when he sang in London. There was no logical way in which he would have altered those plans.

I took up a position in the lobby the next morning, hoping to catch a glimpse of Paul coming out of one of the seven elevators that dumped their passengers into the wide lobby. I waited from eight o'clock until well after eleven but there was no sign of him. I walked up to the front desk and asked for note paper and when I had it wrote Paul a note. I placed it in an envelope and handed it to the desk clerk.

"For Mr. Donner," I said. Then I gave him a pleasant nod and turned to walk away and out of the building. The voice of the clerk stopped me in my tracks.

"Do you want this sent directly up to your room?" he asked me.

"No. To Mr. Donner's other room, please." I was sure that would do the trick.

"Mr. Donner only has the one suite reserved, sir, the one you're in."

"Are you sure?" I asked returning to the desk.

"Yes, sir, absolutely."

"I see. Thank you." I took back the note, shoved it into my jacket pocket and headed out to the street. Cunard's offices were only a step or two down the Strand, so I went there next. The young woman behind the counter was all business.

"Yes, sir, Mr. Donner's trunks were picked up instantly and taken to his hotel," she said.

"Wonderful," I replied. "Thank you all very much." I took a breath. "I should just check to see that they all arrived in perfect condition. Which hotel where they taken to?" I asked.

"I'm terribly sorry, sir, but I am not at liberty to disclose their destination."

"I'm Mr. Donner's assistant," I told her and I gave her my name. "It's my job to keep track of these things."

"It is my understanding, sir," and she picked up an official piece of Cunard stationery to hold on to as she said this, "that Mr. Donner has asked that no one be told his whereabouts in London. He has particularly named you in this note."

"That's impossible!"

"I'm so sorry sir, but that is what it says here."

"I want to see your supervisor, instantly," I said, sounding as much like Paul as I possibly could under the circumstances.

"Of course, sir. Please have a seat." She picked up her desk telephone and punched in three numbers. After a moment, still smiling at me, she said into the receiver, "Yes, Mr. Orton please to the front desk. Thank you."

She nodded to me and gestured to the three leather chairs at the other end of the room. I dutifully went, sat, and waited. The wait was a short one. Mr. Orton was a stout, short man with a Hitler moustache and a snatch of red hair at the back of an otherwise bald head.

"How may I be of service?" he asked. I told him what I wanted and he slowly shook his head, side to side, while strumming his chin with his splayed fingers. "I'm sorry, of course, but the privacy (and he said 'priv' with a short 'i') of our guests is a matter of great propriety to us. I cannot possibly reveal his placement in London. Not to anyone."

"You people have been of absolutely no help, whatsoever."

"I'm sorry sir. I really am."

I got up to go. I had no desire to shake this man's hand or to thank him for anything including his insufferable, intolerable attitude. He had brought me nothing of value.

"One thing, before you go," he said.

"Yes? What is it?"

"Your return ticket with us in three weeks, sir. Mr. Donner has canceled your ticket, received a refund for it actually. We'll have to ask you for the documentation at your earliest convenience."

"My ticket? How am I supposed to return to the States without my ticket?"

"I'm sorry, sir I have no idea. Perhaps you could purchase a less expensive, lower class ticket for yourself."

"With what?" I stopped myself from saying too much more. My financial status here was not something I wanted to disclose in a public place. At least my hotel room was paid for and assured, I thought. At least that.

I walked back to the hotel. I was weak, now. Hurt and weakened by all that had happened to me at Paul Donner's hand. None of this was fair. I had done nothing to hurt him. I had tried to keep myself aloof from Drew at departure, but an accident had changed all that and changed everything else. I was sure that none of what happened at departure would have mattered if it hadn't been for that awful scene in the apartment with Mikhael. It was Mikhael who had destroyed everything for me. How typical, I thought, of Mikhael to come between two people who actually care for one another. He had managed it with Freddy and me and now with Paul and me. There was no one else, I thought. That's what I thought.

At the hotel I checked in with the desk to see if there were any calls waiting for me. No calls, no messages, no callers either. I went back up to the room, tired and hungry for the long day had brought me little rest and no food. I was wondering how to remedy all that when the phone suddenly jangled, its sharp, harsh belltones rattling my brain for an instant.

"Hello?" I said. "I mean, are you there?" I added, trying to sound British. I had remembered that phrase from a Kay Kendall movie.

"Hullo, Max?" came a now familiar voice. "It's Drew. Drew Hatton. Is this a bad time?"

"No. No, Drew, not at all. This is a perfect time, actually."

"Oh, super. I've waited all day to chat with you and I thought you might be free for a spot of tea."

"Tea....tea sounds sort of ... insipid, actually," I said, dragging out the syllables since I didn't know as yet what I might be ready to do.

"Still no luck then, locating the man?"

"No. None."

"So sorry to hear that. Let me pick you up in half an hour then."

"You always seem to be picking me up, Drew."

"Now, come on, dear boy. I've already told you my intentions are honorable."

"Yes, but you don't expect me to believe that, do you?"

"And why not? I am older than you and wiser than you, too."

"Doesn't mean you're not the same sort of lecher everyone else is."

"Why 'everyone else' Max? What's that for?"

"Well, everyone today seems to be hitting on me, on the straight, at the bird. I'm like the center of some large, general target practice. That's what I think."

"Poor little Max. Attracting the fish like a worm on a hook, are you? Sad."

"Look, it's not like that. I'm not enticing today. I'm ugly as sin."

"Well, I think you need someone to take you out for a meal, out for a drink or out to a show. Something should be changing your mind."

"A show?" I said, suddenly remembering the one thing I'd forgotten. "Sounds great."

"Excellent! Where shall I take you, then?"

"Wigmore Hall," I said, naming the concert hall where Paul was scheduled to give a recital in just two days.

"Wiggy Hall? Done," he said. "What's on tonight?"

"Oh, I don't care, but we should get going now, don't you think?"

"Absolutely. I'll pick you up in ten minutes. That's room....?" I told him the number. "Excellent. So get your war paint on, Max."

"Never wear the stuff, Drew. Never needed to."

"Well, dear heart, we don't stay young and flawless forever, now do we?"

"Don't be bitchy." He was gone. I freshened up, changed my shirt and tie and was just tucking in when the buzzer at the door sounded.

We cabbed it over to Wigmore Hall. It was still only early afternoon and when we walked into the lobby the first thing I saw was the three-sheet poster for Paul's concert just two days later. Drew saw it also.

"Oh, I see," he said, "still yearning for your Camelot?"

"You do spend a lot of time in America, Drew," I said. "To hear about our Broadway musicals..."

"Musical," he said thinking hard about what he was saying. "Oh, you mean that Richard Burton thing with the Andrews girl. No, dear boy, I was referring to the place where our King Arthur and his wife Guinevere lived."

"Yes, I know, Drew. It's all in the show.'

"All? I seriously doubt it. Put it all in and there'd be no room for the songs."

I started to hum "If Ever I Would Leave You," and he nodded as though he knew exactly what it was and what it meant. I stepped up to the box office window and inquired about tickets for Paul's recital. There was very little from which to choose, so I opted for two seats in the rear of the gallery. "At least," I thought, "he'll never see me up there."

Drew wanted to pay for them, but I wouldn't accept his generosity. There was nothing else to buy at Wigmore Hall, so we left and re-entered the cab which Drew had held for us.

"Where to?" he asked me.

"I don't know. This is your town, so you choose."

"It's not my town, Max. New York is my home now."

"Yes, so you said, but you're from here so this is always going to be your town."

He nodded sweetly, suggesting a fish restaurant where the Dover Sole was superb and the place was awash with 'common clay' so I wouldn't feel out of place. We went and gorged ourselves on fish and potatoes with parsley and frozen peas. It was a tiny restaurant off a tiny alley just off a large square in the West End. I almost knew where I was, but not really. London at dusk is a place that's too easy to get lost in, even when you know where you're going. But here, at Mazzeo's the food was really good and I was having a good time in spite of myself.

Drew had ordered wine and we drank freely with our dinners. At the end, I reached for my wallet to pay for the food, but Drew put his hand over mine and squeezed tight.

"Don't think of it, dear boy. They know me here and they won't take your money when you're dining with me."

"Why is that?"

"I'm a regular, you see. I have a house account."

"Well, let me relieve you of the burden of payment, Drew."

"No, Max. It can't be done."

"I don't know what you think you're buying here....."

I didn't get any further with that statement, for Drew stood up suddenly and walked away. I turned around and watched him depart the room, sure I'd really done it this time with my pig-headed, New York attitude. I threw down a five-pound note as a tip, and grabbed my coat off the chair as I rushed out after him.

The tiny vestibule which only held three people without crushing the walls was empty and I opened the door, sure I'd find him outside waiting for me. The street was crowded but there was no sign of Drew. I knew he couldn't have gotten far and the taxi wasn't waiting for us this time. I was starting down the alley when I heard my name being called from above. I stopped dead in my tracks and looked around, finally spotting Drew in a third floor window.

"What are you doing up there?" I shouted.

"Up here is where I live when I'm in London," he replied.

"Above the restaurant?" I asked loudly.

"Absolutely."

"That's incredible!"

"Why? London is filled with such places."

"I'm sorry, Drew, about what I said in there. Terribly sorry."

"Oh. Think nothing of it. I've forgotten it already."

"Thanks. Well.... I guess I should get back to my hotel."

"No, no. It's early. Come up for a drink"

"Now?" He nodded. "How?"

"Just come back in and walk up the two flights. It's easy. See you."

He pulled back into the room and shut the window quickly. I did as I was told.

The staircase was narrow and tipped in a hundred different directions, each tread moving my body a different way. It was almost as though the staircase had been created by Charles Dickens, or by Lewis Carroll for his Alice books. At the first landing there was a short corridor in each direction, each one clearly connecting with a second hallway that went off to the rear of the building. There were also a lot of doors. I made the tight turn to the next staircase and repeated my experience of the first one all over again.

At the second landing there were only three doors in a short hall. I wasn't sure which one would lead me in the right direction, so I just stood and waited for a minute, convinced that Drew would ultimately open one of the three. I was right. He did. It was the one on the left. It opened into a sumptuous apartment that seemed to go on for a long way. The room I stood in was filled with antiques, and photographs and paintings and lamps and small divans and overstuffed chairs. The windows were framed with ornate ruby and gold drapes and hangings. The doorway into the long hallway was shrouded in a similar drape. The carpets were lush and oriental and overlapped one another covering the entirety of the wood floor.

"I'll take that coat, Max," he said doing it.

"Thanks." He could see I was studying his room.

"You like?"

"It's fabulous, Drew. Utterly fabulous."

"Fabulous enough to make you forget your troubles for a few minutes, do you think? I can pour you a drink while you look around."

"Thanks, but I don't need one. Just climbing those stairs of yours has gotten me drunk."

"Yes," he chortled, "they're known to do that."

He was pouring a drink for me anyway. I could hear the liquid as my eyes, now hurting me from the quick attempt I was making to absorb it all, blinked over and over. He handed me the glass. I took a quick look, and saw it was wine again, the same wine we'd had below with our fish.

"I thought it best not to mix and match, Max."

"Yes. Thanks for that."

He clinked his glass to mine and said something in French and drank his glass dry. I sipped mine. My headache was increasing from the profusion of colors, fabrics, lights in the room.

"It's a bit much to take, Drew, all this stuff in one small space."

"It's me, Max. Very much me."

"Yes, I'm sure it is."

"Sweet or rude, Max? Which was that?"

"Oh, sweet, definitely sweet."

"Good. I prefer sweet."

I had moved into the center of this room and found a chair. I sat down, still holding my glass, but the chair's plush interior gave way and sank me down close to the floor, with my knees pointing upward in front of me. I nearly dropped my wine, but Drew was right there and he took it from my slipping grip.

"I should have warned you about that Morris chair," he said. "It's so old. Hardly gives any lap at all."

"None, I would say," I said. "Why do you keep it then?"

"Sentimentality, Max. Mere sentiment."

I wanted to say something nice to him. I was having difficulty with that though.

"Thanks for today, Drew. I really appreciate your time and attention."

"Easy commodities for me. Max, I have a lot of time on my hands while I'm here. My mother is in hospital and visiting hours are limited, so I have both days and nights free. I place them at your disposal."

"I didn't know you had a mother," I said, regretting it instantly. "I mean a mother in the hospital. What's wrong with her?"

"Actually," he said and he smiled wanly, "she's dying, Max. She's very old and very tired and she's dying. She doesn't want visitors, just me for an hour each day, and she doesn't want to live."

"At least she wants you every day," I said.

"Yes, the torture of it gives her some enjoyment, I think."

"Torture?"

"Yes, she gets in her one hour harangue about my life, my lifestyle, my lifelessness. She loves to pull out her stiletto and stick it in between my third and fourth ribs. It gives her hope, I think."

"My God, hope of what?"

"Hope of some reaction, I suppose. I think she'd like it if her nastiness got to me in a way that would make me violent enough to smother the last breath of life out of her."

"That's horrible."

"If I could shorten her final hours, Max, I would do it. I would. She's a horrid person. She's never been kind to me. I'm all she has, though, and so it's my duty to remain silent and let her have her say. After all, when she's gone, I inherit it all, so how can I be anything other than the son she abuses."

"Why is she like that? Was she always so?"

"Ever since my father died, yes."

"It's hard for me to understand, Drew. I come from a very different sort of family."

"Do you? Yes, I suppose you must."

"How ill is your mother? How close to the end of all this is she?"

"We don't know. It could go on for a year, I imagine. She seems hearty and strong to me, at least for the hour I'm allowed to suffer for her."

"Is there anything I can do? Any way I can help?"

"Well, I hesitate to ask, you know how I am Max. You have quite captured my heart and my attention, ever since our departure from New York and you've put up with so much yourself. I wouldn't want to complicate things for you, but if you'd care to step down the hall, disrobe and wait for me, that would be comfort to me."

"I see."

"Would you, Max? Just this once?"

"Well, you know Paul thinks that we..."

"Yes, but we didn't. Not for six days at romantic sea."

"Exactly. And I'll hear him on Thursday night."

"And you want to return to him pure."

"Well, pure isn't exactly the description I'd use, Drew."

"I'm tired of this game, Max. You know what I'd like. You're entirely free to go or stay. I'd like you to stay, just this once. Please. If Thursday goes well for you, I shall step back and never trouble you again, but if it doesn't go well, and if this little experience piques your interest at all, at least there'd be a place for you to return to, a place where the two of us could equally solace one another for the troubles in our lives."

"That's quite a speech, Drew."

"Wasn't it, though." He grinned, I suppose. That odd mouth of his altered, anyway.

I sipped my wine and he watched me drink as he gauged my decision through my actions. I kicked off one shoe and stood up to kick off the other one. I had little left to lose, so why not lose it here, I thought.

"That's my Maxie," he said softly.

I walked softly past him, through the heavily curtained door and down the dimly lit corridor into the next phase of my odd life. My eyes hurt and my body felt just a tad weak which I thought was odd so soon after a hearty meal. For an instant I flashed on the face of my sister, Brianna, and wondered if she had ever done anything quite like this in her career.

CHAPTER THIRTY-ONE

From Brewer's The Dictionary of Phrase and Fable:

"Prudent Tree: Pliny calls the mulberry the most prudent of all trees because it waits until winter is well over before it puts forth its leaves."

Leaving is never easy, she tells herself over and over, but proving that leaving is never easy is even harder. She has decided now that her long love affair with Mikhael has ended that she should leave New York and start again somewhere else. It is a clear and straightforward decision, an inevitable conclusion to a sordid liaison. His abuse of her after the newspaper debacle, his revilement of her after their twin visits to Max have been the axe-drops through her heart and her brain. It is obvious to her, and to Mikhael as well, that they couldn't go on together any longer. What is difficult is the leaving and the leave-taking.

It should have been a no-brainer, actually. Mikhael had disappeared from their apartment almost immediately. He had walked out, taking little or nothing - she isn't sure - and she had been alone to do whatever she chose to do with her life. Freddy's only problem is in the choices.

She could leave him and their life together and move back in with her mother. That is one idea

She could strike out on her own, find a place to live and a new life to go with it. That is an alternate.

She could leave New York and find an entirely new existence elsewhere, perhaps in Europe or Canada or California. She somehow can't imagine such an idea bearing fruit.

She could find Max, marry him and set up a new defense system against all she had known in the past. That one seems impossible, not to say silly.

With no clear vision of her own future she hesitates. She stays on in the apartment, goes to her office every day, comes back home every night worried that Mikhael would have returned and been waiting for her, seeking some sort of revenge. Each morning she wakes with dread of the day ahead and each night, on entering her apartment, her heart leaps into her throat as she snaps on lights and quickly searches cabinets, closets and rooms for any sign of Mikhael. Every morning dawns bright and clear, however, and every night provides no evidence of his handiwork.

The lack of anything dire works in the favor of no decision making. Freddy can kick off her shoes, make herself a drink and relax for one more night. A fifth alternative presents itself in the course of all this fear and uncertainty: she could wait until spring to make a change and leave when the leaving was easy.

"When the leaving is easy," she would sing to herself to a Gershwin tune from Porgy and Bess, and the spring thaw extended itself, in her mind, from spring to summertime. "Summertime, when the leaving is easy," goes her positive refrain. Her life continues as though nothing has happened and only the sudden pangs of fear, the anxiety connected with Mikhael, keep her vividly alive

Hardest of all to deal with is the idea that she is alone. She has never been alone before. The lack of a body to lean against, an arm to touch and a mind to reason with over the smallest concepts is hard for Freddy. She and her mother had been such constant contenders. Her double friendship with Max and Mikhael had always given her great joy as one or the other was always at hand. Finally the years of living with Mikhael had given her daily contact with a man who challenged her and brought out her best and worst qualities in equal measure. But "alone" is so different. The challenges are smaller, less interesting. There is no "other" wall, no opposite, no negative to her positive. There is only her own voice, her own thoughts. She is not accustomed to such privacy and she doesn't think she likes it very much.

When a man at her office asks her out for dinner she accepts instantly even though she doesn't like the man at all. It would be someone to talk with, to argue with perhaps. That is what she misses, not Mikhael and certainly not Max or Momma. It is that wrestling arena of the minds that has evaded her for weeks that she missed.

He takes her to a nice restaurant on the West Side, a Greek cantina with excellent food and imported wines. She meets him there, rather than just going there together after work. She wants time to transition from one concept - work, to another - play. She needs to make the leap over the stream of everyday life. When she gets to the address he has given her, he is waiting for her on the sidewalk outside the place.

"Good," he says, "you found it with no trouble."

"I know New York. You tell me a street number and I can usually find it, Bert."

"Ah, Freddy, you're a peach!"

Bert Grogan is a simple man with simple, ordinary tastes. Born and raised in Passaic, New Jersey, he still lives across the Hudson, though now he is dwelling in the town of Elizabeth. Divorced, with no kids, he is similarly alone. He lives in a one-bedroom apartment with a view of another one-bedroom apartment in the next building. It is decorated in IKEA's best and barely resembles a person's home - it is much more a showroom for the import chain store. Bert has assembled most of the pieces himself from the kit versions he invariably purchased. His clothing came from New Jersey shops that advertised their wares, and low prices, on television. His education came from the schools that profited from grants from the sales of furniture and clothing that those stores made to people just like him.

"Can we sit down, Bert? My feet are killing me." Freddy doesn't like standing on sidewalks in front of restaurants. It is something she has never done.

"Hey, sure, why not?" He takes her arm and escorts her up the nine steps to the doorway of the fine eating establishment. A man greets them just inside and seems to know Bert, or so it seems to Freddy.

"Table for two tonight?" the man says to Bert who nods. "You come with me, this way, please. Walk this way." He moves off, his hips swaying like Marilyn Monroe's hips in a 1920's fringed dress.

Freddy wants to make the usual joke over this, but restrains herself. The man leads them to a table at the rear of the room, a corner table with two chairs placed so that their occupants could easily watch the rest of the small dining room if they so wished. Freddy thinks she might have to do that, just to keep awake on this date.

As they sit down, the man, whose name she could now see is Stavros from the pin on his shirt, handed them over-sized menus, nods and moves away, snapping his fingers as he does so. She watches those Monroe hips for a moment, then picks up her menu.

"What's good?" she asks Bert.

"Oh, everything is good here. It's just like being on a Greek island, in fact."

"You've been to the Greek Islands, then?" she asks him.

"Me? No. Never."

"Then how would you know this is so similar?"

"Oh, you can tell, Freddy. Just look around. The checked tablecloths, the pictures on the walls and the smells?"

She is left without a reply that isn't smart-alecky and she is reluctant to pull one of those out of her hat at this early stage of the date. She thinks she at least deserves a dinner before letting out the insults and slams. She studies her menu instead, deciding on a few things she recognizes and nothing very dangerous. Stavros returns with water and bread and a bottle of ouzo, out of which he pours two small glasses of the potent liquid.

"For you, to toast," he says as he places them in front of her and Bert.

She looks up at him with a quizzical expression, but he pays no attention to her. He is watching her companion instead. Bert picks up his small glass and gestures to her to do the same. He clears his throat and speaks:

"To Greece, and her children," Bert says boldly, "and to the woman at the table, a Goddess in green and a darn good sport." He knocks back his Ouzo, taking it all in one quick slurp. Freddy follows suit, without a word, and finds herself choking on the potent alcohol. She coughs once, then once again after a moment. Stavros pats her on the back for a moment, then reaches for the two empty glasses and turns on his heels and moves off.

"Are you okay, Freddy?" Bert asks her.

"I'll be fine," she chokes out in a hoarse whisper. "I'm just not used to that stuff."

"Ouzo. Yes. It can take its toll."

"You seemed to take it in stride."

"I eat here a lot."

"Okay." She jams her finger up against the closed menu. "So, what's good here?"

"Avgelomono is good," he says. "Spanakopita I like and the stuffed grape leaves and the Pastitsio too." He smiles at her. They were the very items she had already chosen. Now she feels odd ordering them, as though she is doing it all at his suggestion. She knows that is stupid of her, that she should just order what she had planned on having no matter what. She is finding this dating thing hard to pull off.

They both order the identical menu and he makes the comment that they might just as well have gone back to her place, or his, and cooked a meal. Then he laughs and Freddy does also. They eat in relative silence, occasionally exchanging an office story or an observation about something in the restaurant that catches at least one pair of their eyes.

When dinner is over and they have solved their argument over the check by splitting it down the middle, they stand once again on the pavement below. Freddy extends her hand to her co-worker.

"Bert, thanks, but I'm not a great date. I guess I'm just not ready yet."

"Same here, Freddy," he echoes her. "Not great. Not ready."

"But thanks for asking me anyway," she finishes.

"Thanks for coming."

"It's an awfully good restaurant, you were right."

"Well, thanks for that, too."

"I'll see you tomorrow," she says, moving off a step to avoid the inevitable attempt at a good-bye kiss.

"It's a date!" he says moving a step in the opposite direction. She gives him a quick smile and a little wave and turns to move off toward the nearby corner at Eighth Avenue. She doesn't turn to see if he is following her or going off toward Ninth Avenue instead. She just keeps walking.

"Nope, not ready, not yet," she mutters to herself. "I'll just have to adjust to this solitary thing." Two men, one of them Hispanic, turn to look at her as she passes them, muttering her minor incantation. She realizes she is attracting attention and she closes her mouth and increases her pace a bit.

She decides, long before she arrives back at her apartment, that she should reexamine her options and find another way. Even if it isn't until summer that she takes a decisive step.

CHAPTER THIRTY-TWO

From Theater Language; A Dictionary of Terms in English of the Drama and Stage from Medieval to Modern Times by Walter Parker Bowman and Robert Hamilton Ball:

Scène à faire: A French expression used in English for an obligatory scene. Usually italicized.

I knew, of course, that he would come. He had to be there, had to see me once more, talk to me if I would permit it. He had no choice in this matter. I had left him none. The life he knew and would attempt to continue to know was the life I had brought him into as my aide. He loved it all, much more than he had ever said, but still I knew what was real. I knew that Max enjoyed the company of great, and even near-great, artists and that was the world in which I lived and worked. So dumping him on the ship, allowing him to live on his own for a week and telling him in a letter that we were done, all of that was for the desired effect. He would have to come and see me.

I know I sound manipulative. In truth, I am. I simply cannot be plainer that that on this subject. Max thought he knew me but in reality he only knew a part of me, a third of me perhaps, but surely not me in my entirety. No one knew all that made up the soul of Paul Donner.

So I wasn't surprised when the stage door man brought back the slip of paper with Max's name written on it. I looked at it for a moment while the man watched me, waiting for an answer of some sort. I milked the moment for all it was worth, staring at the name on the paper. Then I very deliberately crumpled the paper up and tossed it over my shoulder into some sort of oblivion somewhere in the dressing room, somewhere the woman would find it when she cleaned this room up, readying it for another artist to temporarily occupy.

"You don't want to see 'em?" came the Cockney question from the mouth of the man.

"No," I said. "I'll see him. Give me five minutes, then send him up." I gave the man a smile but he scowled back at me. "Please," I amended my statement. He broke into a broad grin, showing one broken tooth and one capped in gold. He nodded twice at me and backed out of my dressing room door, closing it firmly but silently as he did so. "I'll definitely see him," I muttered to myself. "Oh, yes."

I spent the intervening minutes combing my hair, daubing my forehead with cologne and generally making myself irresistible. I was ready for him when he knocked on the door. I was good and ready, rehearsed and prepared and ready to work the lad over until the apology I'd get would come from the depths of the heart, not merely from the formulations of the mind.

He knocked.

I didn't respond.

He knocked a second time and without waiting for my call, he opened the door and came in. That, I will confess, took me by surprise. Even if it shouldn't have, it did.

"Well. Max," I said. He stood in the doorway without saying a word. He was looking at me, waiting for me to make a first move, but I could find no reason to be the first one to weaken here. I was the victim, after all, the victim of a distinct form of betrayal, after all.

"You looked good out there, Paul," he said. "You sounded good too."

"A compliment," I said.

"Well, yes. You sang beautifully and you looked wonderful. I thought you needed to hear that." He was good at this," I thought to myself, "so good."

My heart was leaping around in my chest. I could feel it dancing a gavotte or some such movement. It wasn't directly responsible for, or responding to, Max's words. They had been hard enough to pick up and write, eventually, pausing for a moment or two at the last movement. That has been my specialty for years, but I was wrong - there was no doubt about t.

"Well, I have no doubt you have similar engagements elsewhere, Maxie," I said to him. He blanched, then recovered and was about to say something when I intervened once again with a new thought.

"If you don't, dear boy, I can recommend a few of the needier artists currently in London. Surely you will find someone among them who cares, or who desperately needs to play the show to its concluding measures."

"That's cruel, Paul," Max said to me in return. "I knew you could be hard, but I never imagined such cruelty coming from you."

"You don't know what human cruelty is, Max. You've never had to live within its borders."

"And you have, I suppose?"

"Max, you think you know me. What you know, dear boy, is a fraction of my life, a mere fraction, perhaps two tenths, perhaps less."

"I think I'd surprise you, now."

"Do you?"

"I do."

"Come here, Max. Sit down while I work on this face again," I said. I was only forestalling the inevitable and I knew it.

When he was seated and less intense I spoke to him again.

"Will you please tell me what you want, Max. You know I consider *us* to be at an end."

"I don't Paul." He smiled and I could feel that smile with the back of my neck as I watched it emerge in my dressing table mirror. "We're both here, Paul, and we're both helpless in this situation."

"Oh, you think so, Max. Well, let me tell you something you should have known from the beginning of our relationship....."

"There's that stupid word," he shouted. "Why does everyone use that word when it means so very little. I meet you, we shake hands and smile, we part. That is now, now has become, a relationship. It's crap, Paul. We had a whole lot more than just that."

"Max, if you insist on glamorizing our situation with imagery you had better do a good job of it."

"Oh, please, Paul. Pay attention, please. I want to talk about where we are and where we're going."

"All right, Max. Where are we? Where are we going?" I smiled at him as I turned to look at him again. "Be precise, now."

And he proceeded to tell me his concept of our arrangement. I listened to all of the sordid details and the more humane ones as well. I paid close attention to every word of this scene, so obviously rehearsed by Max before he arrived. He told me everything except the two most important facts and I wasn't ready to ask him to go over those points. He never mentioned love in our equation and he never included sex either. Please note: I consider them very different things. I never confuse the two.

By the time our talk concluded Max had brought me to confess that I wanted him on the next three legs of my tour in Britain and on the Continent. I had seven concerts and a dozen or so radio appearances scheduled and I did need him to do the dirty jobs that were just beneath the level at which an artist would be comfortable operating. Max would join me in a week in Glasgow for a recital and we would move on together from there going to Manchester, Liverpool, Brussels, Paris, Lyon, Zurich, Venice, Lake Como, Stuttgart, Berlin, Copenhagen and finally Warsaw. As he programmed the schedule in his head I was already preparing to desert him in Poland, to leave him there among the hateful crew who never forgave anyone for the holocaust, but blamed it on the Jews, the Austrians, the Bavarians and the American blacks who came there at the end of the war. Yes, I thought, leaving Max stranded in Warsaw was revenge enough for his desertion of me on the ship for that man.

There was a moment in our conversation that made this plan seem all the more plausible and reasonable. He had apologized five or six times for what he insisted was only a misunderstanding. I had accepted his apologies but, at that point, made no concessions. That was when he brought up Drew, his new 'friend.'

"He has been kind to me Paul. I feel I must not just walk away from him. I have to do this right, Paul."

"And that is...?"

"I have to tell him about our conversation - oh, he knew I was coming here."

"He tried to dissuade you, no doubt."

"He did, but I persisted and finally he understood what I had to do."

"And you'll tell him it's all over."

"I'll tell him what's real. I think that's more reasonable."

"And what is real, Max"

"That I am going to be with you now. That we've talked and all is understood."

"I see."

"It's not enough for you, is it Paul?"

"No." I paused a moment, then laughed - oh, so sincerely. "It could never be quite enough, Max. You know how I am."

"Then what would you want?"

"Max, I would want you to stay where you are, right there and never to speak to or see, him again. That's what I would want."

"You'd want me to be to him what you were to me on the ship."

"Yes. Exactly."

"I'm not you, Paul. I can't do that."

"Then go to him and not to me."

"Paul, I'm trying to correct mistakes here. Yours as well as my own."

"So, you think I've been behaving improperly."

"Yes, I do."

"How sweet of you, boy."

"I think I'm being the mature adult, Paul, and you're the little spoiled brat in this. You're the one who acted badly without even hurling an accusation at me."

"Hurling an accusation. What would that have brought? More lies? Most likely, I say."

"I can't do this, Paul," he said, standing up and moving away from me.

"Oh, sit down, Max. You wanted to talk all this out and that's what we're doing. You're having your way with me."

"I'm not."

"You are, but let's not press the point if it makes you so uncomfortable."

"Thank you."

"Welcome."

What followed was the calming, and the petting, and the pandering, and the lies and the quibbles, and, well, you know how these chats go, I'm sure. I agreed to this and that and he agreed to the other thing and when he left to return to this Drew it was with the understanding that he would end whatever was between them and come back to me and we would tour Europe together.

But I had my ace tucked up my sleeve. I'd leave him in Warsaw and that would, after all this time, actually be that. Having my cake and eating it too. There's a small irony in all that decision-making. A very small irony indeed. An obligatory scene between us had played out according the pattern normally pursued. But there was one little element that only I knew about.

Smiling, at my age, reverses the wrinkles and allows me to present a much more youthful portrait of myself to an adoring public. With Max on his way back to me I could face those lovely fans and dazzle them with my eternal youth.

CHAPTER THIRTY-THREE

From The Readers Digest, April, 1946:
From We Have Solved Our Housing Problem:

> "Some of our friends have told us we're crazy, and
> some that we're very brave. But we think we're just
> plain sensible. We have a place to live and are living
> well. And we're well paid besides.

> Frank, 26, a Yale graduate, came back from the Pacific
> with the rank of Lieutenant, senior grade. I'm a college
> graduate too, and an experienced secretary. We have
> hired out as household servants."

Margery Ellen Wolf, Minneapolis Sun-Journal

We were back together, it seemed, and that was all that mattered. We had
cleared up the misunderstanding, Paul and me, and now all I had to do
was clear up the other one with Drew. Of course, that would be easier. He
already knew my goal was to patch things up with Paul and move on. Also,
it was clear to me that moving on from Drew would be a no-brainer. We
had only spent the shortest time together and though I could see, already,
that he had a serious intent, I had been fairly clear about not returning
those feelings. I told Paul what I had to do, sort of, and left to do it.

I said "sort of" because I hadn't really told Paul everything.

"I stayed with a friend," I said to him. "I have to go collect my things."
He had known it was Drew. We had fought over it, but finally he had given

in, allowed me to end things cleanly with Drew, and not to leave this kind man in the way Paul had deserted me on the ship.

"I won't be long, Paul," I said. "It's a quick goodbye and I'll be back here."

"Of course, dear boy. You know where you'll find me."

"Thank you, Paul, for finally understanding."

"When one is as ol' .... when one is as experienced as I am," he said, "one can understand a great many things." He smiled at me with that warm smile he used when he was serious. "You go finish up with your 'friend' and I'll make a few calls to reconfirm arrangements. Don't be long, Max."

"I won't. I promise." I leaned up to kiss him on the cheek. I thought that was a nice, friendly gesture. Paul held me by the shoulders and changed the chaste buss into something more sensual, more erotic. When he pulled himself away from my lips I could still smell his stage makeup, could hardly breathe in, in fact, without smelling it.

"Don't be long," he repeated. I nodded as I backed out of his dressing room door. There had been something in the tone of his voice as he said those three words that made me tremble, just a bit. It was as though the request had been more of a warning than anything else, as though the phrase "or else" had been left off at the end of it.

Outside his dressing room I paused to lean against the wall and recompose myself. I took a few short breaths, my hand pressed to the side of my face. I was sweating. I was panting. My legs felt none too steady. When my breathing slowed to a more normal pattern, which happily didn't take long, I left the building and headed back to Leicester Square and Drew's flat.

"You're back," he said, and he smiled the broadest smile I'd ever seen.

"I'm not, actually," I said to Drew. "I only came for my things."

He was silent. He looked at me carefully, examining my eyes and my mouth and my neck for any signs of tension or indecision.

"I see," he said, "that things have gone well for you with your old friend."

The kindness in his statement was clear to me when he said "old friend" and never stressed the word "old" but did emphatically endorse the word "friend."

"He understands the mistakes that were made," I said.

"And he forgives you and he forgives himself."

"Well, yes, sort of."

"And now what happens, Maxie?"

"Now we go on as before."

"How very Noel Coward of you both."

"Yes, sure. Whatever." I wasn't really sure what that meant but it seemed like agreeing would be the easiest way to go.

"You've come for your things, the few things you've left here."

"I came to tell you that this was the course I've set for myself. Most of my stuff is still at the hotel, you know that."

"You didn't want to just abandon me then?"

"No, of course not." I reached out to touch him but he pulled back a few inches. "You've been kind to me Drew. And I know you're interested in me. I didn't want to just disappear on you, not the way Paul did on me."

"You're really very sweet, aren't you?" He sat down on the chintz divan near the window.

"No. I'm not. You really don't know much about me, Drew. You don't know about my family and our ways."

"Of course I do." He smiled at me again. "You don't think I take any young baggage into my life without knowing a bit of background, do you? When we first met on the ship and I found myself so attracted to you I set a few people moving around New York to make a few inquiries. I know something of your history."

"You do," I said, not a question, not a statement, just a few words to bring the conversation back into my ballpark.

"I know about your mother and your father and how they have lived. I know about your sister, too. In fact, I know your sister."

"You know..."

"Brianna, yes. She's been attached to a friend of mine for some time now."

"You never said anything."

"And I probably wouldn't have if this moment in our friendship hadn't happened, Max."

"What were you expecting from me, Drew?"

"Just what occurred."

"You mean...?"

"Precisely. I knew you would spend the night, do the tricks, satisfy the need."

"And then what, Drew? What did you think would happen next?"

He gave me a curious look, then patted the cushion of the divan where he had seated himself and indicated that I should sit down next to him. I hesitated, but then I went there and sat.

"I thought," he said quietly, "that you would ask me for money. I'm sorry, but I did. Knowing what I know I thought you would expect to be paid for services rendered."

"I have never..." I started to say, angry and hurt.

"I know," he said stopping my rant before it could begin. "I know you have never done that. But we had what most people would call 'circumstances' going here Maxie. We had the oddness of desperation - on both our parts. I thought you'd fall into family pattern, that's all. But you didn't. You were sweet. You were gentle. You were honest with me. You did what I wanted because you wanted to do it. I realized that soon enough."

"Well, thanks for that!"

"Maxie, don't be angry with me. I'm just a stupid, lonely man fixated on the son of prostitutes. How could I think anything other than I did?"

"I don't know, Drew, but at least I know that Paul has never thought of me the way you did."

As I said those words I remembered the final moments in his dressing room, when he had kissed me the way he had. It was the first time I had ever felt the way I did with him or anyone. Mikhael who had abused me in so many ways had never made me feel like a whore and Paul had done exactly that with his goodbye kiss, not an hour before. Now Drew was telling me that he had expected me to make him feel like a client, a "john" but I hadn't. He was telling me that I was better than he had thought me. I leaned back against the arm of the divan and my head leaned further back toward the open window. I sucked in the air of London, not fresh but at least not stale.

"I'm wrong," I said. "I'm so wrong."

"Max, what is it?" Drew's voice was deeply, honestly concerned.

"I'm like a five year old, suddenly. I trust the older folks because I should, because I've been taught that my elders know best."

"Max?"

"Drew, you knew about me and offered me your friendship, yes?"

"Yes."

"And Paul knew about me and offered me his."

"All right."

"But there's a difference, Drew. Until this moment I never saw it, but there's a difference."

"Explain, please."

"You used me because you thought you could, but when I didn't use you, you honestly thought we could be something to each other. Is that right?"

"Yes. You know that."

"Paul, who needs me desperately, only needs me while he needs me."

"I'm not following you here, Max."

"There's something wrong, Drew, something wrong with the way Paul needs me. There's a trick buried in it somewhere. He wants more from me, but he wants it...I don't know...now."

"What are you trying to say, dear heart?"

"Paul is through with me. Somehow I know that from his, well, his way with me when I left the theater."

"The concert hall, Max."

"Yes, whichever, it doesn't matter. He is used to me doing for him, picking up after him, packing him up, moving him, overseeing his things. He needs me to do that, and to make him feel young and handsome and virile. His calling card on stage is that eternal youth. He needs me for that."

"I'm sure you do your job, Max."

"It's more than a job, Drew. It's a vitality he draws from me, through my work, through the sex, through whatever else he can get from me."

"He sounds vaguely vampirish to me."

"That's exactly right, Drew. That's what he is - without the teeth and blood stuff, but it is like that somehow."

"How does one get mixed up with such a person?"

"He's an old family friend. I've known him since I was a kid."

"Max, what are you going to do now?"

"What do you mean?"

"Well, you cannot go back to him, obviously, not now, not knowing what you now know. And I doubt you'd want to stay with me, either. Not now, not knowing what you now know I know. What are going to do?"

"I don't know."

I sat there, leaning hard against the corner of the divan. Drew got up and went into the kitchen, coming back instantly with a glass and a bottle. He uncorked the wine and poured me a large tumbler of the deep, red liquid which I downed without a breath. He refilled the glass and handed it back to me.

"Better?" he asked.

"No, but it will be in a minute or two."

"I have a thought," he said. "May I suggest something?"

I nodded.

"I could call a friend of mine. Have him come over. Introduce you to him. See where that takes you."

"What? Be my pimp?" I jumped up from the couch, horrified at the concept.

"No, no. You misunderstand me, Max. The friend I refer to is your sister's ... man."

"Oh! You mean, bring Brianna into this mess."

"Only if Geoffrey thinks it wise. I'd want him to meet you first."

"You would do that?"

"Of course. You may not have gathered this, but I do like you. Sincerely."

"Well. Okay."

I knew at that moment that I would not return to Paul Donner's rooms, that I would not accompany him and lose myself in servitude to him. That phase of my life was truly over, really behind me. He had been good to me for as long as he believed that I had no interest in anyone else but him and myself. He had turned on me, would likely do it again when he could. I had sensed that somehow when I left him at Wigmore Hall, but hadn't understood it. Drew was a better person than either Paul or me, but there was still something hard for me to grasp in him. I didn't know where he stood, or where I stood for that matter, on the reality of my past and my family's past. But here he was calling in the troops, my sister's keeper. He was doing it openly, and without the slightest hesitation. He was a friend to me, a friend indeed.

"Can I stay here, in the meantime?" I asked him. "No strings attached?"

"No strings, no threads," he replied. "I've only the one bed, as you know, but I promise to be entirely chaste where you're concerned. You need have no fears on that score."

"Call Geoffrey, then," I said, "and thanks for that. You have no idea how much I appreciate it."

"We'll just see what transpires, shall we?" I nodded. "Max, you are welcome to stay here for as long as I can handle the burden of you being here. I want you to know that. I'll let you know when it's too much for me, if that time arrives. If nothing else, you'll be an unburdening place after my hours with Mum."

He went into the other room to place his call to Brianna's friend and, for the first time since I had left Paul's dressing room, I breathed normally and without any pain in my chest. Even my heart felt right again, no angst, or pain, or fear constricting it. I was without funds, without future, without much else but the unfettered friendship of Drew Hatton.

I didn't feel alone, and that was a miracle.

CHAPTER THIRTY-FOUR

From: The International Thesaurus of Quotations:

"In married life three is company and two is none."

Oscar Wilde, The Importance of Being Earnest (1895)

When you think about it, and I often do think about it, Susanne Aurelia Pitts should never have married me. Come on, admit it, I was too old for her. I was too old for anybody. Add to that the way we met, the way we found each other after Tooie had died and there was bound to be a disaster ahead for us. Still, she was so sweet and pretty, in her way, and I was so lonesome after my wife passed, and so much in need, and so much alone without Max to talk to, that marriage to someone must have been inevitable. And there was Susanne.

She's a very nice woman. That's the worst of it. Very nice women tend to "like" me and I am far too carnal a beast to like "like" when what I want is someone who's lust is just heating up. Susanne was carnal, but her appetite went to the mixed buffet and not just the meats. My appeal, for her, was solidly vested in the triple, not the double. She had come to me through Tooie and it was the two of us she had enjoyed so much, not me. Of course neither of us was willing to admit this for the first few months of our marriage.

Oh, she tried to be a single spouse. She cooked for me, cleaned for me, kept my clothing neat and tidy, kept the apartment the same. We'd go out to a movie or over to Roseland Ballroom for some dancing. She liked wine tastings and I went along with her trying to drink as much in case she needed a solid arm. I liked book signings and readings and she would accompany me, sit by me, hold my hand and try not to yawn. We were very capable, if not compatible, companions.

We'd been legally joined for about six months when she decided to have the "conversation" with me. It was her doing, not mine, her choice, not mine. When it was over, things were permanently different. Permanently.

"Vinnie, I'm not happy," she started, even before I could sit down with my glass of Scotch and cross my legs.

"What's wrong, sweetheart?" I asked her. I already had a theory, that's who I am, but I wasn't letting on.

"It's us," she said. "It's just us."

"Us?"

"Us, yes." She frowned and shook her finger at me. "We're nice people, but we're dull, just us. I don't know...but I think we're both in need of further stimulation."

"What does that mean, Susanne?"

"You know."

"I don't. If I did, I would say so."

"Well, when you and Tooie were married you had others to help you both with your sexual needs."

"That's correct." I was right, I knew, about my theory and here it was, coming at me like gangbusters.

"I need others, too," she added.

"I see."

"Don't you, Vinnie?"

"You're my dream girl," I said simply, "my dream wife. I'm perfectly happy with you alone."

There was a pause, a silence between us, or between her and me as there really was no "us" just then.

"That was sweet," she said.

"It's the truth, Susanne."

Another pause. I could almost watch her thinking, see her thoughts played out on her face.

"I think we should try," she said.

"Try to make this work, you mean?"

"Try it with others," she replied.

"What do you mean, exactly? What do you really want to do?" I was afraid she'd tell me that she wanted to take a lover. In fact, I was sure that was the way she wanted to go.

"I think a threesome now and then, Vin, would be stimulating."

My mind and my loins jumped back a decade. This had been Tooie's idea also. The difference was that she was a Lesbian and she and I only had sex together a dozen times or so in our marriage. All of the rest of the time it was with another woman. Somehow she could find satisfaction in my pleasure with a pretty girl. This time, however, things were slated to be different.

"What do you really want?" I asked her.

"I want you to make love to me, Vin, like always, but I want another man involved at the same time."

"I don't understand," I said.

"I want to watch," she said.

"You want to watch what?"

"I want to watch you and another man making love."

That was her declaration of independence, I thought. She would make me over into a homosexual man and then expect me to pleasure her in some way. I wasn't sure how, or if, this could work. I told her so.

"Well, it wouldn't be anything so radically new for you, Vin. You made love to Max, you told me."

"I kissed him once. He looked Lainie, his grandmother. I was drunk and got carried away. That's not being attracted to men."

"I don't know that I want you attracted to men, Vin, just screwing one now and then, for me, for my pleasure."

"Susanne, you are something else," I said, not knowing what else to say and not wanting to offend her or hurt her feelings.

"I'm your wife, Vinnie, and I want to go on being your wife, but sex with you is ... dull. I don't want dull."

"Dull?"

"Yes. Dull. Almost humiliating it's so dull."

"Susanne.... I ...." I was speechless.

"You try, dear, and you try and you try and you try. And all you try is my patience."

"What does that mean?" I could hear my voice rising - louder and higher.

"Can I speak frankly?"

I thought that was a bizarre question, with a "can" and not a "may," after such a conversation, and I told her so. She laughed, or rather giggled out loud, then coughed a few times to regain her composure.

"I haven't had an orgasm since we married," she said.

"Well, that's pretty direct," I remarked.

"It's the truth. I don't know what to do. I went to my doctor and he talked about auto-stimulation, but I don't know."

"So you want us to take a lover, then?"

"No. Not a lover. Pickups. One-night stands. And, not a lot, not often Vinnie, but now and then."

"Susanne, I don't know what to say to this. It's not the lifestyle I want."

"Well, we can try to behave, I guess," she said, "but I'm afraid I'll just get bored with you and bored with us and want to leave you."

"So, you're threatening to leave me."

"It's not a threat, Vinnie. How can you say that? It's just the natural progression of a dull marriage."

"You know," I said to her, "I never thought you were an ordinary girl, a person without colors. I always imagined you were special. You have been for me, Susanne. You really have satisfied that part of the dream for me. But now you bring me an idea that is so much the opposite of what I hoped for that I don't know how to handle it."

"I'm a little bit surprised myself," she said. "I thought with your wonderful history as Tooie's husband that this would seem natural, ideal almost."

"It doesn't."

"So what do we do now, then?"

"Sleep on it?" I suggested.

"Okay, but maybe in separate beds," she replied.

"Okay. For now."

"Okay."

I leaned over to kiss her, for I really do love her you know, and she leaned in for it. It was a sweet kiss, tasty and sweet, gentle and sweet. I licked her lips with my tongue and she smiled - I could feel that smile. When we parted I sat looking at her, into her beautiful, trusting eyes and I realized that she had taken a giant leap in our relationship, telling me how she felt and what she felt she needed. I also knew that I wasn't all that interested in doing what she was asking of me.

"I'll think about it," I said.

"Three's company," she said.

I nodded but added, "Apparently two isn't."

She shook her head. This was the shortest time I'd ever spent contemplating the changes in my life. Different faces, different times were playing out in my head like a melange of delicate fruits and nuts. There was Lainie, of course, and Tooie and Max and Lana and a hundred nameless faces and limbs, women who had spent a few furtive hours between Tooie and me. They all swam around now in my memory's lake of love-making. In all this time Max had been the only man I had ever kissed. It had been pleasant, refreshing and frightening. I wondered if I could attempt that again with another man, with a stranger.

"How would it work?" I asked my wife. And she proceeded to tell me. When she finished, I knew I would do it. After all, she was my wife and I loved her and her happiness was sacred to me. It's what husbands do, or should do: please their women.

But my life was permanently altered. Permanently. And every time I climbed into the threesome-bed, unlike the years with Tooie when I thought about Lainie during our intercourse, now I thought about Max. Permanently.

221

CHAPTER THIRTY-FIVE

From Brewer's The Dictionary of Phrase and Fable:

"Goody-Goody: Very religious or moral, but with no strength of mind or independence of spirit."

She has nothing to wake up for any longer. She finds herself without reason for another day, certainly none for another night. The reality of striking out for herself is that she is left alone with herself, Freddy discovers. This had not been the goal. She had wanted to make him hurt, grieve for her, and work himself back into her good graces. The idea was to make Mikhael mad enough to find himself rather than to just reflect the miserable man who was his father.

How, she wondered afterward, could she have so misjudged Mikhael? How could she not have seen, have known after so long a time, who the man she was to marry actually was in real life? That she had deluded herself, or been so completely confused by him, served to beat her down almost as much as her mother had been beaten down by her father. Freddy's father had been an abusive beast of a man, constantly berating his wife for even the smallest mishaps. He had brought this into his relationship with his child as well, constantly impugning her every desire. To have grown up with this, to have understood it as she had done throughout her life and to not have seen the pattern in the man she loved was all Freddy needed to acknowledge she feels wretched, stupid, ill-used.

She has no one to blame. She knows she is smart, had always been smart. At least where books were concerned she is smart. Her intelligence focused into studies and not into the human heart. Her mind controlled everything except her emotions and when they were in play, her mind clicked off to protect what it could control leaving her vulnerable and foolish.

Mikhael, who had fond names for her and sweet affection when it suited him, had often accused her of myopia where Max was concerned. What she hadn't realized, when she heard those words, was that the same visual enhancement applied to her view of Mikhael. She saw only what she wanted to see, heard and understood the little things, but never the bigger pictures. She had erred in judgement. She had misunderstood the world she built around her to protect her from the memory of a father whom she hated. And she had destroyed her special place through a small series of mistaken acts and reactions.

And now she has no reason to greet a day. She has no control over her future and she finds she couldn't care less. At least, she tells herself, she knows that this is a bad thing. Even so, it is the thing she has and she will do what she can, if she ever cares to do anything.

Abuse at the hands of Mikhael was bad enough, but to be denounced and refused by Max had hurt her more. If that proved anything it proved that after all she had endured she could still be stunned by change and surprised by the brutality of friendship. Both of those elements are present when she finally answers a phone call.

For weeks the phone had rung and her answering machine had dutifully told its bitter story: "You have reached the number you have called. Leave a message and it will be noted. Returned is another matter. Beep. Beep, you idiot. Beep." She had recorded it within minutes of returning home from her surprise visit to Max. The bitterness she hears in her own voice each time it plays out leaves her even colder than she had felt the day she laid it down. What changed in her, she wasn't sure, but when she hears the outgoing message playing on this particular day it feels awful, it pains her, and she cries a bit.

The incoming message was something else again.

"Freddy, it's Bradley Wilner at the agency. I know you've been a bit, well, 'under the weather' shall we say, but I have a prospect for you, and honey you're the only one I know who can reel this big *fish* in for us. Please, please, please pretty please, call me when you get this message. No more "Goody- Goody," dear. Life beckons, sweetie, and you have so much life to live."

"So much life to live," he said. She breathed a sigh as she replayed the

message and heard that tag line again. Bradley Wilner. Such a slime bag. She truly hated his guts. His theory of work was a simple one: you do everything you can to take everything someone else has away from them. Hard work wasn't enough for Wilner. For him there was the energy cone to deal with. Wilner's energy cone, his work theory, was simply this. You stuffed your energy into a small opening and let it play out in a wider and wider circle until it blared its way through the difficulties and the various walls that people lived behind. You were Joshua at the walls of Jericho and you made a sound that nothing could resist. The walls would crumble under the force of your voice uttering the agency notes. That was how Wilner worked and how he had trained Freddy. It was, she realized, the force that had blown apart her relationship with Mikhael. She had trusted it and misused it. She had abandoned good judgement for the big noise.

For whatever reason, and she couldn't quite come to grips with what that might be, Wilner's message doesn't sit like a chilled wine in a tankard. It bubbles and she wants to meet it for some reason.

"I'm getting better," she thinks. "I'm changing again, finally."

She gets up from her deep chair and goes into the kitchen to scrounge up something to eat. She is ravenous suddenly, hungry for substance of some sort. The refrigerator yields nothing consumable. It has been too long and there has been too little to begin with in there. It is the same story with the cabinets until she finds a Ramen cup, a soup with Japanese noodles. All it requires is boiling water.

She fills a small saucepan and turns on the gas. The pilot light takes the hint and flares the escaping fumes in the jet into a circle of blue flames. Freddy heats up the water and while it is slowly coming to a boil, she goes into the bathroom and throws cold water on her face, her hair, her arms. It feels good. It is refreshing. She pauses for a moment to ponder on how long it has been since she last engaged her body with the chill of cool, reviewing substances. It has been too long.

When she returns to the kitchen, her water is ready. She pours it into the plastic bowl containing the noodles and the herbs and spices. She watches it percolate in the dish, which she hurriedly recovers with its paper lid, then she lays a spoon on top of it to hold it in place while the hot water simultaneously boils and steams the contents of the soup mix. It will take three minutes, she knows, to finish. She thinks she should call Wilner back while waiting.

"Brad? It's Freddy. What's up?" she says the instant she hears his voice on the other end of the line.

"Freddy? Doll! You're still with the living."

"Yeah. Still among *them*, Brad." She over-emphasizes the 'them.'

"Listen, Babe, I want to talk to you, but this is not the best time, okay?"

"I don't care what else you're doing, Bradley. You asked for me and here I am. Now what's the game?"

"Oh, well, it's...hold on a second." She can hear his voice, but not his words for a short time. He has obviously put his hand over the mouthpiece making it impossible for her to listen in on his other conversation. Then he is back with her. "Freddy, you remember the fish people in London, don't you?"

"Sure."

She had spent almost a week with them about a year previous. Nice people but without much ambition. Good food but without a large marketplace. Interesting digs but not rentable to an international clientele. She said as much to Bradley Wilner.

"Well, that's changing, Doll. They came back to us a week ago with a proposition and you're the best man for the job."

"Am I?" she asks him rhetorically. "I brought them to you, remember?"

"Natch," Wilner replies. "So that's why I'm calling on you."

"What do you need?"

"I need you to be in London, pronto. I need you to scout the new location and make it happen. I need you to be on them every step of the way. I need you to clinch the deal and to make whatever happens a Wilner production deal."

"Oh, so, just the usual."

He laughs at that. It is an easy, almost dirty, laugh and it somehow strengthens her.

"I can do it, Bradley, but what do I get out of it?"

"Well, let's see....salary, benefits, travel expenses, a bonus for a job well done and the satisfaction of knowing that I cannot do this without you."

"It's not enough."

"Oh, Sweetie, please. Not enough? What else is there?"

"I want out."

"Out? Doll, I don't get it. What exactly does that mean?"

"It means out. I want out of New York. I want out of this roller coaster ride in the press. I want out of the reach of the government cretins who hound me now for more information than I was ever likely to have."

"Oh, out of that," he says. "Well, we can do that, I'm sure."

"No more goody goody."

"I'm not sure you ever were a goody-goody, Doll."

She takes a deep breath and lets it out slowly, exhaling directly into the phone without realizing it.

"Oooh, sexy, Sweetie," he says in a softer voice than she is used to hearing.

"Don't be gross, Bradley. I'm just breathing."

"Freddy, when you breathe, it's...well...never mind..."

"When do we go, then?"

"How soon can you be ready?"

"Give me a few days, say Friday or Saturday. Will that work?"

"I'll set it up."

They chat about the details for a few minutes and when they are done, Freddy hangs up the phone with a deliberate sense of finality and turns around, a full 360, and takes in every aspect of her apartment.

"I won't miss you," she says allowed to the walls, the furniture, the furnishings. "I won't miss you a bit."

CHAPTER THIRTY-SIX

From Brewer's The Dictionary of Phrase and Fable:

Kissing the Pope's Toe: "Matthew of Westminster says, it was customary to kiss the hand of his Holiness; but that a certain woman, in the eighth century, not only kissed the Pope's hand but "squeezed it." The Church magnate, seeing the danger to which he was exposed, cut off his hand, and was compelled in future to offer his foot, a custom which has continued to the present hour."

She sits alone in the large, outer office waiting for him to summon her inside the inner sanctum of business and marketing expertise. She has her portfolio on her lap, feels a great confidence in her readiness. She has prepared her paperwork carefully and she is ready. Her fingers drum, almost silently, on the grained leather of the case in which her work rests easily, sealed in plexi-pages or tucked neatly into the large pockets, available for closer scrutiny. She is ready.

She has been waiting almost an hour already and that fact is disturbing to her peace of mind. Her appointment had been for 1:30 and now, she notes as she checks her best wristwatch, the silver and platinum one with the thirty-eight diamonds that Mikhael had given to her, it is 2:27. The quiet, almost imperceptible tick of the ornamental watch grows ominously loud. Hastily she pulls down the sleeve of her blouse and the jacket over it, trying to smother that irritating sound. It is too loud, she says inside her head, and surely the receptionist can hear it now too. She puts her right hand over the sleeve, over the watch, and tries to contain the noise inside the palm of her hand. It doesn't work. In fact, it seems louder than ever.

Now her teeth are clicking in time to the watch's faithful timekeeping tick. "Tick. Click. Tick. Click." It is all she can hear now, all, that is, until the blood pumping into her brain begins to pump in a rhythmic counterpoint to the watch and to her teeth. She is sure she has reached the hour by now and she listens to the miniature symphony she is now making, all by herself: "Tick, pump, Click. Tick, pump, Click." It is too much to bear.

She stands up, ready to leave. It is clear now that he won't see her. He has kept her waiting for an hour. It is time to leave. She steps away from the chair she'd been sitting in for so long. A single step is all she'd need to free herself from this anxiety, this noise; she is sure of it. But a single step isn't enough after all. She takes another, and another, is three steps away from the chair. The blood pumping in her mind lessens in intensity. That is good. That is very good.

She turns to face another direction, a half-turn, not a full-turn. She is looking at the window that separates this room from the outer hallway She takes two steps in that direction and notices that her teeth are no longer clicking in response to the sound her timepiece makes. There is just the tick now, just the tick. She walks slowly toward the glass door, there in the center of the glass window. She is close to it, safely close to it when her watch ceases its tiresome, ceaseless ticking. She reaches for the knob in the glass door, a handle really, not a knob she notices. A brass handle with a crystal inset that helps to hide it from view. She touches it, holds it, moves it slowly, silently downward, releasing the barely visible latch set into the framework around the vast, wide window.

"He'll see you now, if you're ready," says the receptionist, her clipped British accent so foreign to her American ears. "He'll see you now."

"I don't think so," Freddy replies.

"Is there a problem? He's ready to meet with you."

Freddy turns to look at the other woman.

"I've been here for over an hour already," she says.

"Yes. He's ready for you now."

"I..." she stops without making a statement. She realizes she is still clutching the portfolio to herself and that her hand is now gripping the leather with a claw-like intensity. She relaxes her hand and with the other one takes the two plastic handles in a firm grasp and she lets the sample book drop to her side. She takes a large step forward, toward the receptionist's desk. "I'm ready," she says.

The receptionist stands up and moves to a large oak door in the wall behind her desk. Gesturing toward it, she says to Freddy, "this way, then, please."

Freddy nods once and moves quickly past the woman and into Marc Pope's office. He is behind his desk with his back to her, but the instant he hears the door moving on its hinges he swivels about, looks at her in the doorway and stands up.

"Hello there," Pope says with a grin growing on his face. "Come in, please, and find a seat."

"Where?" Freddy asks him. "Which one?"

"Doesn't matter. Wherever you choose to sit, I'll sit nearby." He smiles fully now revealing an excellent set of perfectly straight, well-matched teeth, so "un-English" she thinks to herself. Freddy nods at him, quickly surveys the room and chooses a green and gold Captain's chair with its back to the window, a view of Westminster Abbey no longer able to distract her. The light will be good for her and would be for her drawings, she thinks. Marc Pope draws up a similar chair directly next to her, but not between her and her light source. She notes that he has clearly made this choice and she admires him for it.

"Shall we have a look, now?" he asks her. She nods and unzips the portfolio, opening it across her lap. He reaches over and taking one of the handles with his fingers he slowly sweeps it across her lap and onto his. They are sharing the book now. His knee moves carefully in her direction, finally just barely touching hers.

Freddy sighs once, then looks away, taking in his desk and the window once again. She hears him turning a page and then another before she dares to look in his direction once more.

"I like this one very much," he says. Freddy looks at it, not recognizing it for an instant and then, suddenly, understanding what it was.

"Thank you," she says. "That was created for the new pillow campaign for the goose-down people."

"Yes, I can see that. It's very clear."

"Thank you again," she says. "Notice, if you haven't already, the way the two pillows rest on each other."

"Yes. Very sensual. Sexual even."

"Yes. It's meant to imply to even the most casual observer that the pillows are doing the work for the people whose heads will rest there."

"It's very nice work."

She nods at him and smiles. She doesn't want to keep saying "thank you" over and over and over like a parrot with only one carefully learned phrase.

She reaches across the portfolio and turns two more pages, smoothing them out as she lays them carefully on his side of the book. She reaches into the plexi-page and pulls out a large, folded piece of foolscap. She unfoldeds it three times, spreading it out across the entire folder, smoothing it once again.

"I've seen this," he says. "Oh, not this, of course, but the real thing, the double billboard on 45th Street. It's very impressive."

"You can see here what I was doing, what I was going for" Freddy begins and her explanation for her choices spill out of her in one, two, three and four syllable words. As she continues to speak she becomes more verbal and more intelligent. Within moments she is feeling like herself again and that feels good. She can tell that her confidence in her work and in herself is paying off. Marc Pope is smiling and nodding and patting the drawing in front of him. Freddy feels all right again. All those nervous energy sounds that had caused her grief are gone, contained in their various sources. She is selling herself and doing it well.

"Can I ask you a question?" Marc Pope says suddenly, clearly about to change the subject.

"Of course," Freddy replies, then regrets it. Usually when someone asks her that question they had something specific in mind and ordinarily that something was about Mikhael and the damn chair. She doesn't really think that Marc Pope is going to ask her those questions, but she knows it is possible.

"The chair..." he says, and she instantly puts up her hand to stop him from going any further.

"I don't talk about that," she says.

"Oh. No. You misunderstand me," he adds quickly. He is thumping the drawing on their twin laps. She turns to look and sees that he is gesturing at the small collection of furniture in her drawing. "This chair, this one here. It seems out of place with the other pieces."

She looks at the item he is pointing at. "Oh, that," she says. "Yes, it does throw the picture off kilter but that was the goal. Look at the piece again and tell me what draws your eye, Mr. Pope."

He turns to look at it. Instantly he says, "The two lamps and then the drapes."

"Exactly," she says exultantly. "That's the goal here. The chair, placed where it is, draws your focus to the floor lamp behind it. It's shade, matching the other one over here, draws your attention to it and then across the drawing and what lies between those lamps is the drape. You can't help but see them as your eyes pass over them to meet the other lampshade. The chair, so unattractive and placed as it is, takes your attention, but you forget it through the symmetry of the other two pieces and your eyes and mind are focused on the curtain. That's what we're selling here."

"It doesn't take that long to work, though," he says.

"No, of course not. It shouldn't. That's the goal."

"Very successful," he says.

"Thank you."

"I think I've seen enough. I definitely want you for this job."

Freddy is folding up the paper drawing and tucking it back into its plexi-page holder. She doesn't want to seem too eager, answer too quickly. But she wants the job desperately and she feels he knows that.

"I'd like to work for you," she says simply.

"Is that eagerness I hear?"

"No," and she laughs, "just agreement."

"It sounded like eagerness to me."

"You know, Mr. Pope, I waited an hour for this chance to show you my work. If that doesn't connote eagerness, I suppose, nothing would."

"That's right."

"So I'll have to admit I am eager to take on this job."

"It will mean a lot of traveling, you realize."

"I do."

"You won't be able to remain in New York for very long. I'll need you over here, in London."

"It would be nice to get away from there for a while."

"Yes, I suppose it would." He smiles at her again. "Especially after what you've been through these last few months."

"Oh. You do know about all that."

"Of course I do." His smile wanes a bit. "Your whole city must know."

"Yes, I suppose so."

He has returned now to his desk and she is sitting, still with her back to the sun, looking at him.

"How soon could you be ready to come back over here?"

"A week, I think. I'd have to spend some time with my mother, of course. This is going to be a shock to her, my leaving town, leaving the country actually."

"Take two weeks. We're not in a rush. We want this done right, Fredericka."

The sound of that name, so formal and unused by anyone other than Mikhael makes her shudder involuntarily. "Freddy, please. It's... easier for everyone."

"All right, Freddy."

"Two weeks? Are you sure, Mr. Pope?"

"It's fine. We have a bunch of arrangements to make. Your passport and visa, your accommodations, a staff to support your work." He pauses and she has the remarkable sensation that his smile is detaching itself from his face and moving toward her. He has turned his head slightly, moving his gaze from the full sunlight behind her to a point more closely aligned with her shoulder. "And please call me Marc from now on. We're colleagues."

He stands up and extends his right hand in her direction. She stand up instantly and holds out her own, dropping the portfolio to floor as she makes her unanticipated move.

"Oh, dear," is all she can say. She can't take a step toward Marc Pope with her papers now scattering around her, but she couldn't afford, she feels, to leave him awkwardly standing there waiting to shake her hand and seal the deal.

"Indeed," he responds, still smiling. "Well, one of us ought to do something about that."

"Yes, of course." She squats down and quickly pulls things back into her book. She reaches over the far edge, finding the zipper and, still squatting, she closes and seals in her work. As she rises to her feet, the portfolio clutched in her left hand, she sees that he is still waiting, still standing with his arm outstretched. She grabs his hand with her right hand and gives it a less than tentative, single. affirmative shake.

"Two weeks, Freddy. Then back here in London."

"London," she says, smiling back at him. "I'm looking forward to it."

END OF PART TWO

PART THREE

CHAPTER THIRTY-SEVEN

From The Reader's Digest, April, 1946: from Hollywood Round-Up:

"'Hollywood,' says comedian Phil Silvers, 'is the place where people spend more than they earn to please people they don't like.'"

I was sitting alone, sipping my tea, reading a magazine. I was on the terrace. It was August. A wood thrush was warbling somewhere nearby. The dogs were napping under the shade my table umbrella provided. The fountain splashed in its irregular pattern and I heard the sound of a auto engine somewhere nearby. It spluttered twice and then went quiet. Then I heard the footfalls and a change in the water splashes in the fountain and I knew she was here. I didn't turn around, or change my position or do anything else that might let her know I was interested. Until I spoke, of course.

"Hello, Freddy," I said quietly, still not looking at her. "Welcome to Farnham Hall."

"Happy birthday, Max," she said without moving any closer.

"It's not my birthday."

"I know."

"So you didn't mean it?"

"Well, you weren't too sincere over that 'welcome,' were you?"

"No," I said. "I suppose I wasn't."

I turned in my chair to look at her, the magazine dangling from my clenched fingers. She looked good. Still identifiably Freddy, she was dressed in a fashionable suit, with a hat on, a clutch bag and high-heeled shoes. Even so, the girl I had known and adored was still there under the brim, behind the silk scarf at her neck, above the three-inch stilettos.

"You look tall today," I said.

"Like a little girl on stilts?" she said sweetly. I blushed, remembering how we'd met, that day, so long ago, in Central Park.

"That's how I think of you all the time," I answered her.

"Well, please come and kiss me, then." She held out her arms. "I'm really still that girl, you know."

"It's hard to believe, but okay," I said, springing up, disturbing the dogs, dropping the magazine. I took the four steps needed to reach her, my own arms now ready and available and I took her into my embrace and she closed her circle of arms around me. It felt good to stand there with her, hugging her, being hugged. It had been too long without a touch of home, of my real life. I hadn't realized how much I'd missed it all.

I'd been in England for two years. I'd been living here at Farnham Hall in the Cotswolds for more than half that time. I had spoken to my parents, seen Brianna on occasion, but hadn't maintained any other contacts with my past in all that time. There had been no reason. None at all.

"Can I pour you some tea, Freddy'" I asked her, not wanting to dwell on my own life but rather hoping to get down to hers.

"Tea? On a hot day like this?"

"Hot tea is the best thing for you. Take my word."

"I'd really rather go straight to a martini if it's all right with you."

"Ah. Well, There I can't help you. The bar doesn't open for another half hour. Rules, you know."

"Not even for me?" She winked as she said it.

"Not even for the Queen," I said.

"Which queen?"

"Now, Freddy! Behave yourself." I was spluttering. "These ancient walls may well have ears."

"How old is this place, Max?"

"Built in 1574, inhabited by one family until the mid-1800s when

Drew's ancestor acquired it through some shady dealing in stocks, I think."

"Incredible." She smiled that lovely broad smile I'd always liked. "Growing up where we did, it always seemed like anything older than sixty years was ancient and should be replaced."

"It's true. Things are different here. Slower. Much, much slower."

"So, no drink?" I shook my head. "Well, then, tea it is."

I pulled out the other chair at the table, displacing Alexei, the borzoi. He lumbered off in the direction of the hedgerow and Freddy took his place. I picked up the teacup and saucer, the teapot with the other hand and brought them to shoulder height at precisely the same moment, curving one hand slightly to pour the still warm brown liquid into the cup. Freddy applauded.

"You do that perfectly, Max," she said, and I could hear the genuine delight in her voice.

"Thanks."

"You're like a Geisha," she added and I felt myself blush. "Oh, stop that. You know you are. You know what you do and who you are and. . .who you do."

"Freddy, stop it. Things are different here."

"You think I don't know that by now Max? I've been in England for nearly fifteen months. I know how different things are here."

"Has it been that long, really?"

"It has."

"You must be nearly done with the project."

"Nearly. yes."

"So, what happens next for you? Back to New York, the old life?"

"I... I don't know, Max. I haven't made any decisions yet. Marc wants me to stay on."

"Well, have you anything back there to go home to?"

She was quiet, holding her teacup, taking her time before answering me. I was looking straight at her and she was avoiding my eyes.

"If you mean Mikhael, no. That's done. You know that." I shushed her and she smiled, then went on. "I've never heard another word from him. And, before you ask, I don't miss him anymore. My mother's dead. So there's no real hold on me there either."

"What about your father?" We had never really talked about her dad, but the little I'd learned hadn't been very good.

"I wouldn't see him, Max. Not now."

237

"Too late for that? Or still too soon?"

"Both, I think. There's be no reason for a reconciliation and I'm not sure I could control my emotions if I was thrust into a room with him at this point. My best memories of him are still too painful."

"You know with my family it's so very different."

"You're the lucky one, Max. You have the perfect family."

"Oh, absolutely. Dad's a pimp, mom's a call girl, granny's a whore and my sister has been a kept woman since the age of sixteen. An Ideal Family by Oscar Wilde."

"You're funny, Max."

"Am I? Sometimes when I think about us all, I wonder how I've managed to have even a semblance of a sense of humor."

"Max, your family are kind, sensitive, gentle people who always think about other folks pleasure and needs. They're around when you need them and they don't criticize you harshly for your decisions."

"Freddy, you have no idea what you're talking about." I could hear the telephone in the drawing room ringing off the hook. I wondered if I should excuse myself, rush in and answer it when the ringing stopped. "My family willingly trained me for prostitution, encouraged my homosexual side, and literally sold me to Paul Donner when he took an interest in me. Drew's the only decision I ever made for myself and that was just one more step in the pattern established for me as a child."

"You underestimate yourself, Max. You always did"

I could see Hilary, the housekeeper advancing with the phone in her hand. I nodded to her and she moved closer quicker.

"It's Master Drew, sir, for you," she said, handing me the ornate, gilt-edged phone. I took it, nodded to her and turned to Freddy.

"Excuse me, please, for a moment." She smiled, waggled her fingers in my direction and turned away, the teacup in her hand. "Hello?"

"Not hello, dear. I've told you. 'Are you there?' is the proper greeting." It was Drew, all right.

"Yes, I know, but the reality is I already knew it was you because Hilary told me and I was sure you were there, because you called me."

"It's form, dear. Form."

"I'll try to remember. I promise. So, what's going on?"

"Is she there?" he whispered into my ear through the receiver.

"Yes," I whispered back. He guffawed, as I now knew to call the small spurt of laughter that often issued from his throat.

"You don't have to whisper," he said.

"Neither do you," I responded. "We're on the phone and you're in London."

"Oh, yes, quite right."

"Thanks. Now, what's up?"

"Well, Maxie, now that the flat's been redone and the restaurant is on better footing, I thought we should all celebrate."

"Okay." I smiled at Freddy who had turned her attention back in my direction, then I shrugged and made a little, odd face.

"Why don't you and that girl powder your pretty faces and come into town for dinner tonight. We'll inaugurate the new dining room, tickle the new ivories and tackle the new bed. What do you think?"

"Okay," I said again, still smiling at Freddy.

"Well, that's not the enthusiastic response I'd hoped for, dear, but it will do for the moment."

"Anything special you'd like?" I asked him.

"Yes, wear the new Malcolm McLaren thing. You and The Sex Pistols look good in his things. Yes, I definitely like you in that."

"All right. I'll order the car and we'll meet at 7:15."

"7:15, Max?"

"Sorry, quarter past."

"Better. Much better." He guffawed again. "Ta!" And he was off, the line was dead.

I smiled at Freddy. "Drew wants us for dinner at quarter past seven. At the building."

"Oh, dear. I was hoping not to have to go back there just yet."

"Well, the grand opening is, what, Sunday, so there's still three more days in which to stay away. You could consider this an aberration. Marc would want you to do this, you know."

She smiled at that, but didn't comment. "Do you want to go in, Max?"

"I was quite happy here with the dogs, actually. I hadn't planned on moving from this spot at all."

"It is beautiful. Bucolic, really."

"Yes, it is."

We sat in silence letting the country beauty wash over us, the lightly aromatic air waft through our heads. I leaned back in my chair and let my legs stretch forward as far as they could go. There was a yelp as my heel dug into the side of the Spaniel, Floria. She leapt to her feet and shook herself violently as I pulled back my legs and sat up. She was wagging her tail, but she was clearly annoyed with me for invading the solitude of her nap. Without any more noise or fuss she trotted away, toward the same hedgerow that Alexei had found as a refuge earlier.

"The dogs don't like me today, it seems," I said to Freddy. "I might as well go into town and see what Drew's been cooking up. And if I have to, you have to."

"All right, Massa Max." She stood up and came round the table to where I was standing. She put her arms around me and kissed me gently on the lips. "How long are we going on this way, Max?" she asked.

"Just as long as we must, dear," I said. "Just as long as we must."

It was silly, I thought, that we always played these little scenes out for the servants. We'd been at this for months and months and I was getting tired of the tiny deceptions. We played at being old friends, which we were. We played at casual interest which was just plain wrong. We feigned a sexual disinterest which hadn't been the case for five months already. We did it for "form" for what Drew considered the proper way of doing things. I was hating it more and more and I thought Freddy was also.

"I could support you, you know, " she said to me, loosening her hold on my neck.

"I can't do that."

"Of course you can. You always have."

"Not with you. Freddy, it wouldn't work with you."

"I am the older woman in this relationship."

"Three years. It's always only been three years."

"I'm a woman, Max. We age faster than you men. Your one year is my four years. I am significantly older. Twelve years older, silly."

"You're not. I won't have it that way."

"Well, you go put on your frock for the gentleman in town. We can talk about this later. Over a martini, for God's sake."

I laughed at her persistence in these things, gave her a quick, light kiss on the cheek and trotted up to the house. At the French doors I stopped and turned.

"Bring the phone in, won't you? Please?"

She nodded and waved.

"And you might just give Marc a call, let him know you're keeping the client happy."

I didn't wait for her answer. I went upstairs to make myself attractive.

CHAPTER THIRTY-EIGHT

From The Reader's Digest, April, 1946:

> From Vive la Diff'rence!: "From a harassed teacher comes this tale: Initiating my young pupils into the mysteries of the French language, I explained that 'Madame' was used in speaking of a married woman; 'Mademoiselle' an unmarried woman; and 'Monsieur' a gentleman. To see if the children understood I turned to a boy who seemed rather bored and asked: 'What is the difference between 'Madame' and 'Mademoiselle'?'
>
> 'Monsieur,' came his prompt reply."
>
> Samuel Pepys Teucer, in Hamilton, Bermuda, Royal Gazette

I didn't want to go to London just to be told we were turning back around to the country again. I thought we'd take in a show, go to a club, roam the streets into the light of dawn and end up back at the flat having sherry. That was what I anticipated, always, with Drew. That was what I wanted but Drew, I knew, had other plans: dinner, an interminable evening at the piano while he pretended, badly, to be Noel Coward and Ivor Novello combined, then what he considered a hot roll in the hay. I had reached the point where none of this was really appealing.

With Freddy along it seemed to be an even worse idea spending the evening this way. In the car I thought I'd chat about this with her. To my surprise, she wasn't the least disturbed by the prospect of a quiet, family evening, even with the sexual encounter afterward which would, naturally, exclude her.

"Don't be silly, boy," she said. She punched me in the thigh as she said it. "I know you want me and not Drew, but he is the work and he is the man. Do what you must."

"And you don't mind it?" I wasn't sure I could believe her words.

"No. I get it. I know what the deal is, Max."

"Well, I wish I did. This wasn't meant to be my life, you know. It was a single roll in the hay, to thank him for kindnesses and consideration after Paul...."

"Yes, I know. You've told me the whole story before."

"Look, Freddy, if I didn't think we were meant to be together - once all of this work is over - then I wouldn't be keeping up this front right now."

"Max, if its meant to be, it will be. If I've learned nothing else in my life, I've learned that much."

I looked carefully at her as she said this, and I watched her eyes, her nostrils and her chin for moments afterward. I was anticipating a tear, a flare, a shudder, but there was none of those things. She was steady and regular, nerves tight and pleasant at the same time. She seemed to be the person she said she was and the "lesson" she'd learned seemed to be at the core of her being.

"I envy you, then," I answered her. "I don't have such personal knowledge."

"But you do, Max. You've known it longer than I have, much longer in fact. I think I first learned all this from you."

"How do you figure that'"

She reminded me of a time I'd forgotten, a period in our early friendship when she and I had banded together to fight off Mikhael whose urges were getting the better of both of us. We had never explained our motives to one another, but we were very much in agreement about not wanting him to 'push us around.' That was our bond. He was abusing me sexually and abusing her intellectually. It was my senior year in high school and I was very vulnerable. Freddy was already a sophomore at Hunter College and Mikhael, who seemed to feel that education was not something that he would need to support himself in the future, was demanding far too much for us.

"Don't be a stupid ass, Max," he said to me as he pulled himself up off of me. "Just be my ass, and carry me where and when I want you."

"I'm not stupid, Mikhael," I said to him, letting my exasperation at this attitude show through my words. "And I won't be your jackass any longer."

"You will be mine for as long as I need you."

"I won't. I'm tired of this."

"And how do you intend to make this different, Max?" He had that smirk on his face that I always thought was so attractive, until now. "Just what do you intend to do about this?"

"I'm not coming back here," I said. We were, as usual, in his apartment. "And I'm telling Freddy everything."

"You won't do that." He sounded so calm, so in control, that it frightened me.

"Won't I?"

"No, Max. I shan't allow it."

"How do you intend to stop me, then?"

"Like this, naturally." He grabbed me suddenly and pulled me forcefully into an embrace and then he kissed me hard, his tongue grappling with my clenched lips. As he held me I felt myself slowly give up the struggle and in a minute or less we were back at the sexual acts that seemed to please him and to aggravate me.

When it was over, this reprise of our fun, he lay on his side, his hand tickling the seven or eight hairs on my chest. "Was that so difficult to understand, Max?"

"What do you mean?"

"You cannot say no to me. It is impossible for you."

"I will someday."

"Yes, on the day I marry Freddy, you will be free of me, at least as my playmate. But I will still find a place for you, if you want it."

"I won't be your servant. You're not my king, Mikhael."

"No, of course not. You are an American boy, free to choose. I am not free. I have no choice in these matters. I must do what the chair demands, what my father would have me do."

"You and that chair, that Skialatum or whatever it is...."

"Lidskialfa, Max."

"Whatever."

"And you won't say a word about our afternoons to Freddy."

I was frowning hard and it hurt my face. "I won't."

"What a good boy it is," he said.

Meanwhile Freddy was having her own hard time with him. No suggestion she made about things they might do together hit home with him. He was always calling the shots with her, just as he did with me. It made her mad and it was frustrating. She would want to see a show, and he would refuse to go to something "frivolous" with her. She might want to go dancing or to a party, but refused saying that being in her company was all he needed and she should feel the same way - of course she didn't know about me at that point, about me and Mikhael and our afternoons.

One day we had ice cream together at Schrafft's, as she was now reminding me, and Mikhael became the subject of our dialogue. I was shocked to hear about the way he treated her. To me he always spoke of her as his Queen and I thought that meant he adored her enough to do whatever would please her.

"Why does he call you his Queen, then?" I asked her.

"He means 'consort' I think," she said. "Just someone to stand on his right side, look nice and obey his every whim."

"Do you do that?" I asked, a bit shocked, thinking of my own relationship with him.

"No. Don't be stupid."

That, of course, hurt a lot coming as it did so soon after he had called me stupid. They seemed too much in league for that moment.

"What are you going to do, Freddy?"

"I'm going to start going out with other guys."

"Could you ever...?" I stopped, thinking what I was thinking about, being one of those others.

"Ever what?" she said, sounding almost too demanding as she said it.

"Oh, nothing." I took a deep, long sip of my soda, the ice cream clogging up the end of the straw.

"You're such a baby, sometimes," she said, smiling, "but I love you anyway. You give me something, you know."

"I give you something. What does that mean?"

"Max, you give me hope. And strength. I know you'd never be the dumb one in a friendship. You'd always stand up for yourself."

"I do that?"

"Yes, you do. And you always seem to know that if something is meant to be, it will be. I see that in you."

"Wow!"

I smiled as she told me the story from her point of view, reminding of that time from our childhood. I didn't tell her about the scene that preceded our ice cream date. I didn't think she needed to hear about that now.

We were approaching London and Drew was waiting to entertain us. We had to pass through one dark stretch of road and I knew the driver wouldn't be able to see us for a while. I was counting on those seconds with Freddy, in the dark, in the car, to let us hold each other, not as friends, but as lovers. When the time came, she moved gracefully into my arms and we kissed, not as we had earlier, but in deep, romantic earnest, the way I knew we should. As the lights of the city began to intrude on us we pulled apart again. She took a small compact out of her bag and looked at her reflection in its mirror, adjusting a curl, removing a small smudge from the corner of her mouth.

She snapped it shut and smiled at me. Then she put her hand over mine on the seat between us.

"We're going to be fine, Max. If I hadn't known you since childhood I might not think it, but I have and I do."

"I hope you're right," I said. I smiled, hoping the smile was sincere enough to get me by, but deep in my heart I was dreading this night, dreading its outcome, I suppose. More and more my time alone with Drew was changing me into someone I didn't know, didn't like and had to find excuses for in my relationships with Freddy, my parents and even Brianna. Frequently I found myself wondering if any of my decisions over the past two years had any honesty contained in them. I hoped I was being overly self-judgmental and that time would prove me too self-conscious. I hoped.

CHAPTER THIRTY-NINE

From The International Book of Quotations:

> "Moderation has been created a virtue to limit the ambition of great men, and to console undistinguished people for their want of fortune and their lack of merit."

La Rochefoucauld, Maxims (1665) tr, Kenneth Pratt

We worked at our love. We did it slowly, though, in stages. She'd find a man who was eager to have her and she'd bring him home, having alerted him to the fact that she was married and that her husband might be home. Most of the time, believing me to be too old to care, or to get involved, they'd follow her home, escort her home, ready to give her their seed as she seemingly wished. I'd be there, waiting, pajamaed and slippered, a drink in my hand, the "old gent" or "hale fellow, well met" in the picture. It never seemed to bother any of them, or perhaps just one, that the husband was there, didn't seem to care.

My wife would get cozy, change into something soft and seductive and easy to take off. The man would have a drink that I made for him. They would kiss and I would comment on how lovely a picture they made. I must say that it was humiliating but I did it for her because I loved her. It made me seem so ineffectual, so much a shadow on their wall.

At the point where they would begin to heat it up, Susanne would always ask me to light a few candles and I would do it. The room would take on a soft glow, a romantic look and she always thanked me, bringing me back into the picture as her pickup would be nuzzling her, biting her earlobe or lapping at her long neck. Somewhere in this process I would admire the picture, tell them how beautiful they looked together, all of this in the script that Susanne and I had concocted together. Unlike the threesomes of my past, with Tooie and other women, this had an air of artificiality about it that always stuck in my throat. There was less of love here than there was of utilitarianism.

When the man seemed securely seduced by the aspect of final pleasure with her, she would always suggest that I stop watching them, that I join them on the bed. This I always did. She would reach over to me, comment on my firmness, my hardness, my possibility. The man, suddenly aware of my presence would ask what I wanted. He always did. This never failed. I would shrug and say something like 'my bit of fun, too," and then the man would smirk and kiss Susanne again.

She would hold his face tight against hers and then, I'd slip out of my pajama bottoms and do the dirty, as it were. Slowly and carefully so as not to hurt, I would enter my wife's lover, just as he would enter her. The double sensation usually made the man jump and shudder and her reaction would be to hold hard against him. We would be three joined at the groin. Ultimately we three would make the music that is sexual and the final moments of rapture would be special.

I had to admit that each time it was over and Susanne and I were alone again, our own love-making took on a peculiar intensity and pleasure. It was nothing at all like the lackluster sex she had complained about. It was the youthful experience once more, the initial exploration of a new type of relationship that so inspires the young. It embarrassed me the most when it pleased me much.

Susanne was happy with me after these encounters and loving and sweet. She would extol the virtues of her handsome husband and for days, or even weeks, she would be pleasant about our private selves. But then the urge would come again, the need to have this triple exorcism of ghosts and demons, the demand of the loins for that new mixed grill of partners.

Had it been a year already, I wondered aloud one day. Had we been doing this thing that long already?

"You know it, Vin," she replied.

"And it's good for you?" I asked her.

"It's better than good, Vin, it's God for me."

"I'm getting a bit long in the tooth, Susanne. I don't know how much longer I can keep doing this."

"A bit longer, Vin, Please. I need it."

"I know."

"And it's not so bad for you, is it? It's only one man's ass now and then. It's not like you've been converted or anything."

"No, no. Nothing like that."

"Still, you do it so well, Vin. Like you were made for it."

"I'm not. It's not my favorite thing, you know."

"Do you still think about him when you do it?"

"Him? Max? Yes, I suppose I must."

"Suppose? You're not sure?"

"I never put his face on it, Susanne. I never do that. It's just that his name comes into my head occasionally."

"When? At ecstasy?"

She was always using words like that. "Yes, just then, at that moment."

"Then you're thinking about him, all right."

"Yes," I sighed. "I guess I am, after all."

Two nights later she decided it was time again. I kissed her for good luck and she went off to wherever she'd go to find these men and I showered and put on the pajamas, poured myself a drink and sat down to wait. I turned on the television and watched some mindless situation comedy that didn't make me laugh and then switched over to the eleven o'clock news. There was the usual trouble in middle east and the usual weather report and the usual sports scores to get through and then, there was an item that finally piqued my interest.

A face on the screen was largely familiar, a youngish man with a brutal look, but not a savage face, not the usual street crime face, but an aristocratic one instead. I wasn't sure at first and the news reader didn't give me much help. But by the time the story was done, I knew I'd been right. It was that old chum of Max's, that foreign boy, Mikhael.

The anchorman had called him Michael, or rather Miguel, as though he was Spanish instead of Scandinavian. In truth, his dark hair and eyebrows, his unshaven face with its scrabbly stubble, did make him look Hispanic, even when he and Max were still friends. He had been caught in some federal sting operation over drugs, it seemed, and that too gave him a more Hispanic, street-culture drug involvement than anything more appropriate to his background. I wasn't clear about the details, probably because his face and the name hadn't made sense to me and I'd ignored a few facts while trying to piece together the reality here.

I switched to another channel hoping to find out more details, but it was too late. The news was ending. I switched back to the first station, only to find that the late night talk show music was blaring away. I switched off the set and wondered what I should do, if there was someone I could call. It was 11:30 already and I knew it would be too late to start a phone trail for some news. I'd have to wait until the morning, hope that the daily papers had something about all this, or that a morning news recap would bring me the details I'd missed.

Of course, I thought about Max almost instantly. He was still in England somewhere with that man he'd met. His letter to me, almost a year old, had given me some details about his break up with Paul Donner and about this strange Mama's boy he had become attached to in Donner's absence. I still wasn't quite clear about all of that either. I took a sip of my drink and wondered if, perhaps, I was getting too old to keep up with the world around me. I was missing out on the details - everywhere. I didn't even bother to get the names of the men I was screwing for my wife's pleasure. I wasn't even doing that!

I heard the elevator door opening and heard Susanne's laughter in the hallway. I hurried back to my seat and switched the set back on so it wouldn't seem as though I'd ben waiting for them. When Susanne opened the door and led the man in I was back in the usual nonchalant pose, acting surprised and delighted at having her home and meeting her guest.

She and I went through the ordinary charade we played for the benefit of the "guest." He had given me an odd look when we were introduced, but that had been the only thing that separated him from the other men we'd been through in the past year. Separated him, I thought. Made him different. Perhaps they had all, really, given me that look or something like it. Perhaps I'd not been paying attention for a lot longer than I realized, was missing the details that should have stood out in my mind. I wasn't young. I could admit that to myself without much pain. I wasn't the eager lad who had fallen in love with an older woman, a prostitute, and never realized that I was with a professional. But even then, it was now certain, I hadn't been paying attention to the details, the clues. This wasn't something new, then, this missing a look, a tidbit of news. I had always been like this. It wasn't advanced age. It was simply me, who I was, how I was with others.

Thinking this, and much more to boot, I was physically playing the game that my wife and I had rehearsed and played out over and over again. We were in bed, now, all three of us and it was my moment, but just as I took my position and began my awkward thrust, the man, this latest 'trick' spoke to me. That hadn't happened before.

"You're Compton, aren't you?" said the man I was about to impale with my prick.

"I beg your pardon?" I said, swallowing the words even as I said them.

"You're Mr. Compton. I thought it was you."

"What's happening here?" Susanne asked from what sounded like a mile away.

My ears were ringing and the veins in my forehead were throbbing. This stranger knew my name. The man stretched out naked between my naked wife and the naked me knew my name.

"Who are you?" I demanded far too loudly.

"You know me," he said. "You know me."

"What is all this?" Susanne demanded. I could hear the frustration in her voice.

"I don't know him," I said.

"Yeah, you do. Sure you do." He was nodding and I was staring into his face trying to understand what was happening, who he was, how this had happened.

"Who are you?" I repeated.

He extricated himself from between Susanne and me and sat upright, his back against the wall, his knees pulled up under his chin. He stared at me, waiting for me to remember him, it seemed. Nothing came to me.

"Do you know him, Vin?" Susanne asked me. I shook my head slowly, but I wasn't sure now. I couldn't be sure. He had known me, certainly, but I couldn't name him or recall him at all.

"Who are you?" I asked a third time.

"I'm Cass. Remember? Cassius Finnerty, from St. Jason's School."

Of course I knew him. Of course I knew him. Of course I did.

"You stole my wallet," I said, choking out the words. "You knocked me down."

He laughed. "Yeah, I did. That was me."

"You changed my life," I said, a bit louder, stronger. "You called me a pervert!"

"Yeah. And it looks like I'm doing it again, Mr. Compton."

"Don't say that, don't use my name."

"It's just a name, Mr. Compton."

"Don't say it. Don't say my name."

I could feel an odd clutch in my chest. It was as though a long, hard metal rod had suddenly been inserted somewhere in my side and it was poking its way up into my lungs. I gagged, tried to breathe hard and, without another thought, I fell over onto my side, grabbed the bed sheets for support and fell to the floor.

I could hear my wife screaming and I thought I heard the man, Cass, Cassius, say something else, but his words were quiet, indistinct. I remembered very little else except that the candles in the room seemed to be going out, one after the other. One after the other.

Then it was dark and I wasn't hearing much of anything other than my own anguished deep breaths.

CHAPTER FORTY

From The Reader's Digest, April, 1946:

> from "What's Your Hurry" condensed from This Week Magazine by Constance J. Foster: "We are new farm owners, and at first we were inclined to apply all the high-pressure hurry of city living to our 60 acres. But Ben, our tenant farmer, took us down a peg. Asked if he had finished plowing the cornfield, he squinted at the setting sun and said serenely, "No, but the land'll be there tomorrow."

When a phone rings in the next room, and you're laughing hard at something that you, yourself, have just said, it's never a good sign. It's all right to laugh that way at something said by another person. That's fine. But to laugh so heartily, so without humility, is apparently not fine. When it's someone else's joke or bon mot and a phone rings, then its just a phone. However, to enjoy your own humorous jibe too much and have that damned phone go off is a comeuppance in progress.

I know this because it's happened that way twice recently. The first time hurt. I wasn't too surprised about it, but it hurt me nonetheless. Freddy had only been with us for a week at that time and she and I were busy reminiscing about something we'd done as kids, something that I'd long forgotten, but which came back to me, back to both of us really, through an odd set of circumstances.

Drew had ordered us dinner. He wanted us to meet, not knowing that we knew one another. She had come over to supervise the work on his building, to make over the restaurant and the suites above. Even that was a rare and peculiar story, her employers in New York had chosen her for this job and she had objected, left them, gone to another company and been sent over anyway to do the same work she had turned down the first time. She had no idea that being here, taking on this job, would throw us together once again. The nature of coincidence had intruded itself into her life and brought her into mine. When Drew told me about this woman who was doing such a good job for him he neglected to tell me her name.

"You've simply got to meet her, Max," he'd said, gushing outrageously. "She's like no one else. No one, darling."

"Do I have to?" I asked.

"She's a lonely young American, like you, so yes, you must. I'll arrange it."

And so he had. I came into London and we met over dinner. Imagine, if you can, the shockingly expressive face of odd, old Drew when, on introducing us, we fell into each other's arms and kissed. It was a priceless look on that odd, silly face of his.

"Well, my dears," he said, fanning himself with his flattened, open hand, "I never imagined that even two Americans could be so. . .so informal."

"Drew, this is. . ." I started to say, but Freddy put her hand over my mouth to stop me.

"Actually, we've met before," she said. I laughed at that.

"Well, I say," said Drew.

"We've met many, many times before," she said.

"Indeed?"

"Drew, we've known each other since childhood," I said quickly, hoping to stop that fertile mind of his in its tracks. I didn't need him imagining anything between us, not if we were to see each other again while she was working for him.

"Oh!" he said. "Oh, I see." He laughed a bit. "How extraordinary then. Such an odd thing to have happen."

"It is," I agreed.

"It is," she echoed.

We were having a nice evening until the phone-ringing incident. We had been sharing some old times with Drew, telling him about Central Park and about the times when she and I and Mikhael used to play tricks on other people, just because we could. We hadn't been too clear about Mikhael, about who he was or who he became to either of us. We talked about him as though he was just another friend.

I was telling this particular story about how we once stole a live chicken from the marketplace owner down the street from my parents' apartment and let it loose in the lobby of the ritzy hotel/residence where Mikhael lived and chuckling away mightily as I told it. Freddy kept slapping me on the shoulder, urging me on, keeping me at my silliest when that phone rang in the next room. I ignored it, of course. We were in the restaurant and the slabs of Dover Sole on our plates were growing cold as we chatted and the parsleyed potatoes were getting that oily look they can take on when their warmth dwindles. I was laughing so hard at my own story, I was losing my place in it, it getting as cold as the food in front of me.

Arlene, the waitress, came over to the table, a French telephone clutched in her right hand and the receiver held against her bosom. She glanced at Drew, then at me. I was chortling at something I'd just said when I realized that she was staring at me. Her look chilled me and stopped me mid-word.

"You're wanted, Sir," she said, and she held out the receiver in my direction.

"For me? But how...?"

"The house sent the call on." She attempted a grin, but only a grimace crossed her face. She was still holding both the phone and the receiver.

"Take it Max," Drew said. "It must be important."

"Yeah, sure," I said reaching out tentatively for the instrument.

"Max, I hope...." Freddy added, but she went no further.

I put the receiver to my ear and reached for the cradle which I took from Arlene's hand. I said "hello," and heard my father's voice on the other end of the line, mutter my name. There was something in the sound of that word, my name, in his voice, spoken that way, that told me instantly that there was very bad news on the way. I put down the telephone, not realizing that I'd put it on top of my cold dinner, right smack into the oily fish.

"Max," he said again. "I'm so sorry."

"What is it? Dad, what's going on?"

"Then you haven't heard?"

"No. I haven't heard anything bad. What's going on?"

"Max. Paul Donner is dead. He died last night, on stage, in Hamburg."

"What?" I know that I squeaked on the word. Freddy told me that later. "How?"

"I don't have all the details, Max. I thought you would have known about it, being there in Europe."

"I didn't see anything, Dad. I didn't know."

Freddy squeezed my arm sympathetically, although she hadn't heard the news and neither had Drew.

"I'm here with Freddy, Dad, remember Freddy?"

"Oh, sure. Of course I do."

"Hold on, Dad. Let me tell them what's..." I put the receiver against my own chest, the way Arlene had. I looked at Freddy and I could feel the tears welling up in my eyes. Her look of anxious curiosity was replaced by Drew's own peculiar expression as I turned to look at him. I told them the news, looking at Drew and not Freddy.

"Apparently he died on stage last night. I didn't even know he was still in Europe."

"Talk to your father, Max. Talk to him. We'll be here," Drew said with such a sweetness that I almost wept right then. I picked up the receiver again.

"What do you know?" I asked him.

"Well, all I've heard for sure, Max, is that he was singing an encore, so he'd finished his concert by then, and he had a heart attack or a seizure and he collapsed."

"My God," I said, my thoughts running curiously through photos, lists, memories of things lost. "What was he singing?"

"I don't know, Max. I don't know."

"What do you think I should do?"

"What can you do? You have no responsibility in this, Max."

"I should do something. I came to Europe with him. I was supposed to be there with him."

"No. He changed all that. He dropped you, Max. You have no more duties to perform for him."

"But I should, Dad. I should. That would only be right."

"Whatever you say, Max. But you have no honest part in this. It had nothing to do with you."

"I'll let you know what happens, Dad. I will."

There was a sob in my ear, a sob that shook me. I didn't quite grasp what was going on at that moment, but a second later I realized what I'd heard and why.

"Dad, I'm so sorry for you. I know how much you loved him, too."

"I miss him already, Max."

"I'm sure." They had been such close friends when I was still just a kid, and I'd forgotten that. I'd forgotten that he was telling me about a mutual friend's death, and not just about *my* friend's death. My own world crashed and at the same time exploded outward. I think I felt worse about my selfishness than I did about my loss. I hung up the phone and whispered hoarsely to Drew and Freddy that I had to leave.

Without another word, I got up and went outside and leaned against the old brick wall of the theatre building across the alleyway from our building and I cried. That was the first time a phone ringing in another room while I was laughing at my own story had such an impact. I should have remembered it when the second incident happened.

But for that moment, that first time, with Freddy suddenly back in my life, the coincidence had little resonance. Freddy was back in my life again and that was almost enough to keep me sane as I went about the business of extracting Paul Donner's body from the German authorities, having him prepared and boxed and shipped home for a funeral and burial. I had all the numbers in my head, and my notebooks, for friends and acquaintances. From London I arranged his funeral in New York. I arranged his burial in California and a memorial service in Chicago. I did it all with Freddy at my side, a faithful friend and assistant taking over the chores that were too painful, assisting in the ones that needed two heads or four hands. I don't know how I could have done more than I did, not without her help. It was the work of the living to honor the dead that brought us so much closer than we'd been in years. And I was so grateful to have her with me. All the old feelings re-emerged and I was falling in love with her all over again. This time, though, it seemed those feelings were mutual. Maybe that's why the oddness of the phone and my laughter never had the impact, never made the impression they should have. Love was stronger than death.

So the second time, so many months later, came as a real shock.

It was the three of us, again, Freddy, Drew and me. And it was cocktails this time, no fish on the table, when the second incident occurred. By this time Freddy and I were deep into our affair. Drew knew nothing about it. She had just told him about our argument at my high school graduation party and I was feeling particularly rotten about my brattiness and my lack of a sense of humor.

"I was only seventeen," I said, making the only excuse I could think of.

"And I was rotten to you," Freddy added, "and you were such a child that day."

"I was feeling old, though."

"In that yellow gown of yours?" And she laughed again at that outfit I'd chosen.

"I wish I had a photo of that," Drew said.

"No, you don't. You really don't, Drew. He looked ridiculous."

"I did not. I looked. . .I don't know. . .lovely."

That set Freddy into gales of laughter. I was feeling just a bit non-plussed at that, so I thought I'd tell a story of my own, one that turned the tables on my old friend this time.

I began regaling them with the stupid story of Freddy and her mother and the old chair that Mikhael's father had stolen from his country when I became aware of a cold, hard look on Freddy's face. I didn't let that stop me, though I did pause to take a long sip of the wine I'd been drinking.

"So she let her mother bring a photographer into the apartment and the two of them posed with the damn thing, like the Gish sisters or something. Picture it, Drew. Picture the two of them. One sits and one kneels. Then they reverse. Then they both get photographed kneeling and bowing. And the photographer is snapping away, happy as a clam, and these two women are just about getting into the silliest poses you can imagine." I was laughing so hard as I said this that I could barely get the words out. One image after another was flooding away as I told the story of how they forgot the agreement and let the man snap one too many awful picture. That was when the phone began to ring in the other room.

I didn't have more than a passing flicker of memory of the last time this had happened, a phone somewhere counterpointing my laughter at my own words. I kept on until I realized that the phone was being handed to me by a very sober-looking Drew. I stopped laughing, looked at him, but didn't reach for the phone.

"Take it, Max. It's for you."

"I don't want to," I said. "I don't want to."

"It's important." Drew was so sober suddenly, so quiet and firm. I took the phone from him and spoke quietly into it.

"Yes," I said, "this is Max."

"I'm so sorry to have to tell you this, this way," said the voice I didn't recognize. It spoke nonstop until it said these words. During that brief monologue I guess my face fell a mile and Drew came and sat close to me, his hand around my shoulder and Freddy knelt down on the floor in front of me and placed her arm around my waist. "There was nothing anyone could have done," the voice concluded. "They were sitting there, so close, and it happened so suddenly," the voice told me.

"It was quick, then?"

"It was. I was on the other side of the room, Max. I wasn't close. And even if I had been, there was no way I could have reached them in time."

"Tell me your name, again," I asked. This was near the end of our conversation and the details were only a part of the horror story she'd been relating to me.

"Susanne Compton. Vinnie's wife."

"Yes, Susanne. I remember now."

"Max, I'm so sorry."

"But you and Vin are all right?"

"Yes, we're fine, but your parents, Max. I don't know how you must feel."

"No. No. You couldn't."

"But it was quick, Max. It was so quick. There wasn't any pain. It was a tragic moment, but no pain."

"Thank you for telling me that," I said.

"And they were together. Think of that. No grief for either of them. That love lasted forever and ended together. That's like a miracle, Max."

"A miracle. Right." I wasn't taking it all in as yet. It wasn't making any sense.

"Is there anything I can do, Max? Until you come, that is?"

"No. Of course not. How could there be?" I asked her. "Like you said, there's no one to grieve."

"Oh, Max, I didn't mean..."

"No. I know. I know what you meant." I went silent as the enormity of this awful news finally hit me in that deep place where you go to protect yourself from tragedy. "I'll call you back. In the morning, Susanne. In the morning. Tell Vin I. . .in the morning." I hung up the phone.

Freddy was still sitting to my right, on the floor. Drew was still beside me on the divan. They had heard my side of the conversation and they knew the news was awful. Still, they didn't know the fullest measure of the horrors. So I told them. I was dispassionate and calm about it, holding in the worst of the nightmare I was suddenly inside of in spite of myself.

"My parents were killed in a freak accident last night. They were visiting friends, old friends, you remember Vinnie Compton, Freddy, don't you?" She nodded. "They were visiting him and his wife, I don't know her, at their apartment in Harlem and there was a parade or something outside on 125th Street and they were leaning out the window to see it better and the building was an old one and something I don't get happened and the brownstone work on the top of the building loosened or got pushed or something and it hit them, hit them both at the same time and it. . ."

I was getting emotional as I told it. I could hear the tears in my voice, hear the rising pitch in my words. "It was quick, she said. Very quick and they didn't suffer. They fell from the window, Freddy, fell six stories and hit the grillwork fence - do you remember it - with the sharp, pointy fleur-de-lis top. They hit it, they fell on it." I was crying fully, sobbing at the image that I couldn't pull from my mind.

"Max, what can I do?" Drew asked me, holding me close, protecting me with his arm.

"Nothing. Nothing." I choked back a sob. "I have to do it. I have to be the one."

"The one?" Freddy asked.

"I have to call Brianna," I said. "We have to go home."

"Oh, my God," Freddy muttered. "Brianna." She stood up. "Let me, Max. You don't have to do this."

"I do, Freddy. I'm the man, today. I have to do it."

And, somehow, I did.

CHAPTER FORTY-ONE

From The International Thesaurus of Quotations:

"Weep him dead and mourn as you may,
Me, I sing as I must:
Blessed be death, that cuts in marble
What would have sung to dust!"

Edna St. Vincent Millay, "Keen,"
The Harp Weaver and other Poems, (1923)

As he stood there in front of me, tall and firm and still younger than he had the right to be after so much, all I could think about was his grandmother. I know you think that was inevitable. I always said he reminded me of her so very much, but he was a child when I said that. A child. And now he was a man, and not a very young man after all. He was thirty. Or thirty-one. I wasn't sure which, but still and all, not young.

And speaking of "not young" there was no one at the funeral "not younger" than me. I was eighty-two. Max was thirty or so. His parents, laid together, side by side in their coffins, were in their sixties. I was the survivor, the one who lived, the one who had always lived, outlived lovers, loved-ones, the beloved of a lifetime.

Max was sitting between two women, his older sister Brianna who resembled her father now, much more than her mother or her mother, my best beloved lover. She looked like him, much more than Max did, more like Jimmy. He had been a good looking man, handsome and with strong, definitive features. Brianna looked a lot like him. Her chin was firm and had that same little uplift. Her eyes were wideset and surrounded her strong, virile nose. She made the look her own, made it pretty, but you could still definitely see her father in that nose, chin and eyes. She was being strong, too, the way he would have been. There were no tears in her eyes, but her arm was hard and rigid, her fingers clasped, hand to hand, around Max's arm. Somehow, from the looks, the very different looks, on their two faces, it appeared that she was supporting him, his emotions, his loss.

The woman on the other side of him was Freddy, naturally, that same old childhood girlfriend I remembered so well. She was clutching his other arm, but instead of giving him support she was stealing away whatever she could of his inner strength. I wanted to walk over and slap her, remove her hand from his arm and take her place. I wanted to help somehow. I mean, I already did feel guilty about their deaths. After all, it had happened at my apartment. They were dead on my watch. Lainie's girl, Lana, and her sweet husband, the man who helped me find Susanne, were dead and I had been watching them, saw it happen, failed to save them.

Really, there was nothing I could have done. Instantaneous stuff bears no interference from bystanders. That's what I was, again, a bystander. I was someone who let things happen around him, in front of him, and never interfered. A naturalist in the real sense of that word. What happened naturally happened. I was without power, without choice, without any reasonable options. I was powerless. As usual.

Susanne was sitting next to me, tugging my sleeve, urging me to sit also. I felt unable to sit at this funeral. I felt totally out of place here. Guilty. Guilty as not charged, your honor. Guilty.

I looked down at my wife and gave her an encouraging smile, then slowly removed her fingers from my wrist. I unpealed them, one by one. Then I let her hand loose and let it drop into her own lap. She turned away from me, just turned her head and let me stand there, isolated and alone. The funeral director was speaking now, saying innocuous things that meant very little. He had been speaking for a long time and when he finally stopped and nodded in Max's direction and then stepped down off the dais, I felt a sudden clutch at my throat and a rapid turn at my stomach. Max was going to speak.

He stood up and turned and kissed his sister. He had both of her hands in his own and he moved carefully, so as not to harm her in any way. He never turned his back on her, but moved step by step, backwards toward the podium. And then he was there. Suddenly there. He cleared his throat, smiled, frowned, started to tear up, I'm certain, but held himself together as a man would, then cleared his throat again.

"Thank you all for coming," he said. "My sister and I are very grateful that so many people who knew our parents thought enough of them to come out today. Brianna and I have been living in England and we just flew in this morning, on the red-eye flight, so we're not very prepared, not very sober or sane either, are we, honey? Well, we're pleased you're here. I wanted to talk about them, about Lana and about Jimmy, my parents. You may think you knew them, but you didn't. You couldn't. These were people no one knew very well, no matter how much or for how long you knew them. They were private people. They lived inside the walls of their apartment and they only really lived when they were alone together. Not with you. Not with Brianna and certainly not with me."

I almost cried when he said that. What he said about them, and us in relation to them, was how I'd felt when Lainie had died. Exactly how I'd felt. Exactly.

"I want to paint a picture for you, if I can and I can only try, of who they really were for each other. Lana had her career and she gave it up when she married him, actually when she met him, not when they married. He became the center of her world and what he wanted was what she gave him. It was sort of like centrifugal force in reverse, really. His spin in the world drew her in instead of throwing her outward. No matter how fast he spinned, she was always coming closer and closer to his heart. That was how their love for each other worked. He always attracted her closer to him and she danced only for him, spun in those ever tightening circles just for him. It was the sort of love affair that couldn't die, because the attraction was one of speed and direction and an unfailing intent to remain close."

'Oh, God, Lainie,' I thought. That had been her hold on me and I had somehow managed to plummet out of the orbit we had established. How different things might have been if I had just trusted her a bit more than I had. There would have been no Tooie, no Susanne, no corrupted morals, no boys. It would have been Lainie and Vin. Vin and Lainie. I would have been that moon drawn in by the force that was my earth.

"As for Jimmy, well, any of you who knew him knew that there was no one else for him but my mother. I don't think he ever looked at another woman seriously. Not professionally, not personally. He did what he needed to do to make a living and to support us all, but no other woman played a part in his life. Not ever."

Brianna stood up and walked slowly to the podium where Max was speaking. She looked strong, she looked fine. She moved to stand at his side and she put her arm around his waist. For a moment they looked like their parents, like Lana and Jimmy, except that Max looked like her and Brianna like him.

"My sister and I want you to remember them the way we do. We want you to remember Lana and Jimmy in the way they would want to be remembered. They were the folks next door. They were the family unit that never split, never cracked, never altered in any way. In the world of middle American values they were the parents from Hell."

"They were, indeed," Brianna said nodding her head gently.

"He was the college kid with the career and she was the happy homemaker, baking pies, washing dishes, wearing an apron," Max continued. "They took care of their offspring. . ."

"Us," Brianna said grinning.

". . .guiding us to our own careers, hoping that we'd follow in the family business, in their footsteps somehow. . ."

"Which we have," Brianna added.

". . .and making our marks in that special world of theirs."

"What we have done in our lives reflects well on theirs, I think," Brianna said. "As they would have no regrets about their decisions, we have none about ours. As they would cherish the good times, so do my brother and me. As they might greet the difficult times, we do likewise. We are their children. We are their legacy."

"We are their children," Max echoed her. "We are their legacy."

They kissed each other gently, delicately, the way devoted siblings would, and they went, hand-in-hand, back to their front row seats. I don't think there was a dry eye in the house. I was certainly weeping, crying those silent tears that come to the elderly when the present subsumes the past, making everything the same thing, making all the losses the same loss.

Susanne reached up for me again, took my hand and gently used my solid frame to bolster her more delicate one as she stood up and moved her body over to become as one with mine. Our fingers clenched tightly; our arms were linked by the peculiar fit that two arms leaning hard against one another can assume. Our shoulders touched and we walked forward, our inner legs together, our outer legs together. It was the march of time, the procession of death. We went up and peered at the coffins, their lids tightly sealed. I kissed the fingertips of my loose right hand and touched Jimmy's coffin, then repeated the gesture with Lana's. Susanne began to cry and I moved her quickly off in another direction. We walked out of the room without looking at Max and Brianna and that girl with them. We went into the reception area and I reached for a drink, handed it to Susanne and got another for myself.

People were coming out now from the parlor and there was a buzz around us. No one spoke to either of us, blaming us somehow for this accident that had robbed us all of dear friends, of family really. I was beginning to think that we had best move out, find our coats and leave this place when I felt a hand on my right shoulder. I turned to see who it was and saw that it was Freddy.

"Hello, Mr. Compton, I don't know if you remember me," she said, but my nodding stopped her quickly. She could see that I did. "And this is your wife?"

"Yes," I said and I introduced them.

"This must be so difficult for you," she said to us. "I cannot imagine what it would be like to witness such a tragedy."

"Horrible," Susanne said quietly. "Horrible," she repeated almost too loudly. I patted her on the shoulder and she moved in close to me again.

"How did you hear...?" I asked her.

"I was with Max, in London, when your call came."

"How lucky for him to have a friend nearby, then," I said.

"He was devastated, Mr. Compton. The man you see today isn't the man he was two days ago, believe me. I don't know how he had the strength to speak like that. I really don't."

"It was beautiful," Susanne said softly.

"It really was," I agreed.

"He asked me to come out and find you both. He'd like to talk with you, inside if you don't mind. He wants a private word, I think."

I froze instantly. I hadn't been alone, or even nearly alone with Max since he was a child. And today, for some reason today, he reminded me of Lainie even more than he had that other time.

"I don't think so. It's not appropriate..."

"Please, Mr. Compton. He asked especially."

"Must I, then?" She nodded firmly and I nodded in response. Susanne was standing even more rigid than before and as I moved a step forward the heaviness she assumed stopped me dead in my tracks. I turned to her, smiled and nodded and she smiled and nodded but she still didn't move. "Please. Susanne, please." Her shoulder softened at that and I could impel her forward. Slowly we made our way through the throng, following Freddy into the ceremonial room.

The lights had been dimmed and I was aware, instantly, that the coffins had been removed. Max and Brianna were still down front, in the same seats they had taken earlier. Freddy escorted us down the aisle toward them. I think she coughed once and Max immediately turned and saw us hesitantly approaching. He was up instantly, his arms outstretched to us. Before I knew it he was holding Susanne and me and he was crying and we were crying and my arm was around his back and Susanne's was also and our hands were grasped holding him close to us, to our bosoms as they say. We were three mad adults, wailing and embracing and it was bad and it was good and something was released that hadn't been let go of before.

I don't know, I really don't, how long we stood like that. But finally we were done with that stage of our reunion and we were letting each other go, loosening that hold, that age-old tie of emotions. I watched him drag the last tears from his eyes with his clenched fists, tossing them to one side, to the other side. He smiled at us, and his reddened cheeks and moist lips were somehow wrong, not the image, not the right look, but I understood them. I knew I looked the same and without glancing at my wife I knew she was a match for us.

"Vin, I wanted to say...." and he choked. I smiled. I patted him on the shoulder. "Vin, I wanted to say this to you when we were alone. I know how much you always cared about us, about my family. You were that special friend who knew us generations back and still know us. There's no one else who's been there like you have. I don't think I treated you so well when I was a kid. I didn't understand then what I do now about friends, about family. Vin, you were always family."

I broke down and sobbed, right there, in front of Susanne and in front of Max and his sister and a stranger, that girl. It didn't matter if I was being an idiot. I was one of the family. I was what I had wanted to be for fifty years and I was finally there. I didn't know how to deal with that.

"Will he be all right, Susanne?" I heard Max whisper to my wife.

"He'll be fine. He survived a heart attack. He'll handle this too."

Max put a hand on my shoulder and gripped me firmly. Though there was no pain, no distinct pressure, just a sense of connection in that grip, I tried to resist it, tried to pull away.

"We love you, Vin. Brianna and I, we love you."

"I..." There were no words. I couldn't say a thing. I turned away from him so he wouldn't see the hesitation in my face.

"Vinnie loves you like no one else, Maxie," Susanne said. I could hear her words and hear the sincerity in them. That frightened me, horrified me, really. "As long as I've known him he's always talked about you and about your grannie and his love for you both. If he'd had a kid, it would have been one like you, Maxie."

"Thanks, Susanne," he said. "That means a lot."

"We hope we'll see you sometime," Brianna said, a lot cooler than her brother, but she was always like that, even as a child.

"I hope so," my wife said. "Vin, we gotta go, we really do." I nodded, still not looking at Max and Brianna.

"Thanks," I said. "Thanks for being so nice." I took a step toward the door, but Max put both his hands on my shoulders and easily, for there was no resistance in me any longer, turned me around to face him. "From Lainie," he said, and then he leaned into me and kissed me hard on the mouth, embracing me with his soul, that spirit he shared with the only woman who totally captured my heart and soul. I stood there unable to participate in this loving exchange. I could only see him in my mind, the way he had looked in the back seat of the cab when he was a kid and I was a predator who didn't know he was one. When he removed his hands, then his lips and stepped back I was finally released, not just from this embrace, but from the fantasy that had haunted me for so very long.

I opened my eyes. I looked at Max. I saw the man he was and there was nothing of the boy about him, nothing of Lainie either. He was a handsome man who had given me the one thing I had never had: the marble kiss of death that separates us from those beloved few who are with the Eternal. I nodded to him. It was all I could do to express this new feeling. I smiled. I smiled without any control of the smile. It felt to me like it really did go ear to ear. I took Susanne's hand and nodded at Freddy, then at Brianna and finally at Max.

"Let's go home, Susanne," I said. "My family doesn't need me right now and I need to be with you."

She smiled at me and turned and smiled at them. We went home and for the first time, ever, we made love - just the two of us, alone - and it was enough for both of us.

CHAPTER FORTY-TWO

From Brewer's The Dictionary of Phrase and Fable:

> "Perfectionists: A society founded by Father Noyes in Oneida Creek. They take St. Paul for their law-giver, but read his epistles in a new light. They reject all law, saying the guidance of the Spirit is superior to all human codes. If they would know how to act in matters affecting others, they consult 'public opinion,' expressed by a committee; and the 'law of sympathy' so expressed is their law of action. In material prosperity this Society is unmatched by all the societies of North America."

She is watching him for signs of depression. He has been oddly silent, for Max, since the funeral and Freddy is concerned about him. Trying not to allow him to see her vexation, she forces laughter, makes cruder than usual remarks and then shuts herself up by slapping her face lightly with the back of her hand. Rather than serving as a distraction for Max, this merely makes him more aware of the difficulties he now faces. All of this, however, does bring about a desired result as he concentrates more on her odd behavior than on his own troubles.

Brianna has stayed with him at the apartment for a week, but then gone back to London to the man who supported her style of living. She had been more affectionate with her brother than she had ever allowed herself to be in the past and that had soothed him somewhat. Brianna had even been kind to Freddy who managed to turn up every morning at breakfast time and stayed at Max's side until he was in bed and asleep.

"Don't you have something to do?" Brianna asks her on the third morning.

"No," Freddy responds. She resents Brianna's question.

"Well, isn't there somewhere else you could do this? Some other sick friend, perhaps, or a member of your own family you could watch?"

"I'm here for Max," she said, not looking at his older sister.

"We're here for each other," she responds with a slightly edgy tone in her voice.

"Are you?" Freddy asks her. "Aren't you involved elsewhere? Don't you have a ...I was going to say home, but I hesitate. . .to go to?"

Brianna glowered at her. Freddy could feel the heat behind the eyes that stared daggers into her own.

"Where have you been all these years, Freddy? All the years when Max struggled alone with people who couldn't help him, or wouldn't help him? Where were you, his best friend?"

"Don't moralize with me, Brianna. Where were you?"

"I was doing what I was brought up to do, thank you. I was doing my part for this family of mine. My. . .family. . ." She breaks through the sob in her voice and turns her head away so that Freddy can't see her eyes redden as she squeezes back the tears that longed to fall. Freddy can feel them however and she moves to the older woman and puts her hand on Brianna's shoulder.

"You're allowed to cry, you know," she says softly. "You and Max both. You're allowed to cry."

Brianna swivels in her direction causing Freddy's hand to cross her chest as she stands facing Freddy now.

"Am I? Really?" She pauses and Freddy can't read in her face what might come next. "Let me tell you something about crying. It spoils the makeup. It spots the dress. It ages the skin. It wrinkles the corners of the eyes, nose and mouth. It tastes bad. It accomplishes nothing."

"It relieves the heart," Freddy says. "It opens the soul. It freshens the air. It creates a void that can be filled with love."

"I never thought of you as a sentimentalist," Brianna says having regained her composure completely.

"I'm not. I'm just a realist."

"A realist? Nonsense. I'm a realist."

"No. You're not. You're too pragmatic for that, Brianna. You alter your reality as needed. Right now you want to be alone with Max so that he sees you care about him and eventually will share with you whatever is realized from your parents' estates. That's how I see you in all this."

"You're a cynic, not a realist, then. You don't trust even the best instincts in people."

"I don't hear you denying the accusation, Brianna."

"No. You don't." She pauses, licks her lips to moisten them. "But why don't I make a few accusations instead? You think you can convert a homosexual, don't you? You think your womanly ways can turn my brother into a perfect lover for you. You're a fool."

"You don't know what you're talking about," Freddy spits at her.

"Don't I? You think I'm so self-involved that I haven't seen you when you're with him? Think what you like about me and what I do to survive, but I've seen my brother with both of his men and I've seen him with you. With Paul Donner he was the perfect helpmate. With Drew he was becoming the natural wild thing that he was bred to be. With you he's a docile performing seal. You each get what you want from him. He has the same genes my mother and grandmother had, the same genes that inform me and my lifestyle. He has our father's instincts for survival, too. Within him is the knowledge that nothing is secure unless you own it. He is malleable, Freddy. But his nature is what it is."

"That's all you know. Max is in love with me. He has been in love with me since we were children."

Brianna throws back her head and roars with laughter. It is so loud, so abrasive and strong, that Freddy instinctively takes a few steps backward away from her. There is something truly animal about that laughter.

"You want me out of his life, then." Brianna stops laughing and looks at her.

"No, Freddy, I want you out of the apartment for two daylight hours. I want him to myself. I know you think I'm a bitch, heartless, manipulative. I'm all that, sure, but with Max I'm only his sister. Try to believe that if you can. His sister. I love him with the only kind of love I understand and, yes, it is an animal instinct, a form of love that may not be available to you. You're an only child. You have no one of your own blood to care about. For me, it's this. I need to be here with him, just us, to pull us both through this."

"I don't want to leave him with you. I don't trust you. I don't trust that you won't do something to turn him against me."

"What if I give you something, then, Freddy. Something to bind the ties between us and guarantee that when I leave him Max will be returned to your ministrations."

"What could you give me?"

"I don't know." She smiles. "Name something."

"Your passport then. You can't leave this country without it. I'll hold it until I'm sure you haven't killed me in there."

"What a child." Brianna opens her purse and produces the government-issued booklet, holding it between her first and second fingers. "Here. Take it. And get out, please."

"I'll be back."

"In two hours. Two. Is that too much to ask?"

Freddy shakes her head, finds herself smiling a bit, then turns away to hide her self-righteousness. She picks up her coat and her handbag and leaves the apartment.

She wanders through Central Park in the late morning light watching joggers flash past and nannies with their carriages strolling the lanes and byways. The late spring air is bracing, a bit too chilly and yet invigorating and refreshing at the same time. She is trying not to think about Brianna and Max and the strange conversation that has brought her outside. She is trying, in fact, to enjoy the unusual freedom of just being in the park by herself.

She emerges from the clump of dense foliage overhead and realizes she is near the Sheep Meadow, a wide expanse of parkland in which concerts were held, and the Metropolitan Opera sang in summer. From its center, she knows, she could see all of the buildings that bordered the park on the east, south and west sides. It is a view she hasn't permitted herself since childhood but this is a day like no other, and she takes advantage of it. She hurries across the slightly muddy grass and when she thinks she has reached that fulcrum point she stops moving and stands as still as she can, her eyelids clenched and her hands in fists at the ends of her extended arms. She turns around three times, slowly in place and opens her eyes.

The city is swimming circles around her. Buildings are playing with one another as they seemingly butt up against others. The low-lying trees, their fresh green leaves still in bud in places, make a frame border for the city and the sky above it. She closes her eyes again, extends her arms and fists and repeats her twirl, but in the opposite direction. With her eyes closed she feels like a child again, not a woman at all, but the girl she had been when she first met Max, here in the park, when he came to her aid in the stilt-walking accident.

She is thinking about that when she feels the arms come around her, pulling her arms to their sides tightly, and the mouth meeting her own. She is trapped, caught in the grip of a madman who is about to rape her, here, in full daylight, in the middle of the largest open space in a city crowded with structures and people. Panic grips her and then, suddenly, it flees leaving her in full control of her senses. She knows this mouth.

Opening her eyes she finds herself staring into the open eyes of Mikhael. With strength she hadn't known existed, she wrenches herself free of his arms.

"What the hell do you think you're doing?" she screams at him.

"Kissing my wife," Mikhael says in his still slightly accented voice.

"I'm not your wife. I never was. I never will be."

"Aren't you even glad to see me again?"

"No."

"That's it, Fredericka? One word to say so much?"

"One word said it. NO."

"Why are you like this? You were my love."

"You betrayed me in every way, Mikhael. Every way possible."

"And you didn't betray me in the one way you could?"

"How do you know about that?"

"How do I know about the chair? Are you crazy, Fredericka?"

She realizes that she had blundered, has almost given away the secret of her new passion for Max. She pauses, takes a breath, licks her lips as she remembered Brianna doing.

"Sorry. You took me by surprise, that's all." Her voice is calm, steady, soft again.

"I have missed you."

"Where have you been? You disappeared like a magician's rabbit."

"I have been where I have been. Now I am here."

"So I take it that the authorities are no longer looking for you, Mikhael."

"Not any longer."

"And your country? Your father's people?"

"Gone. Poof."

"And you're back in New York. What are you doing here?"

"I am talking with you."

"Funny. What are you really doing here?"

"Business. Of a personal nature, Fredericka."

"What does that mean?"

"It means 'personal' and 'private' and not 'public.'"

"In other words, shut up and don't ask questions, Freddy."

"Precisely, my dear."

"How did you find me?"

"I didn't exactly. I was crossing the park, on my way to keep an appointment when I saw you doing funny turns. I remembered you here in the park, in this place and I wanted to see you."

"Well, if you have an appointment, you shouldn't dawdle."

"So cold, Fredericka. Is there no hint of the love any more?"

"None. Sorry."

"I wish I could say the same thing."

"Of course you can. You disappeared without a word and suddenly here you are. You never contacted me. Never. There's no love in you, Mikhael."

"What is in me, Fredericka, is something to discuss with you at another time."

He turns and moves away from her swiftly. She stands and watches him go, but she has questions, suddenly, that she wants answered.

"When will that be, Mikhael? When?"

"Another time," he shouts belligerently. She watches him walking away, one more time, from her, just as he had done on stilts so many years earlier. She watches him until he is out of view and then she kicks the dirt, dislodging grass and weeds as she did it. This is not turning out to be her favorite day.

CHAPTER FORTY-THREE

From Brewer's Dictionary of Phrase and Fable:

> "Gone to Jericho: No one knows where. The Manor of Blackmore, near Chelmsford, was called Jericho, and was one of the houses of pleasure of Henry VIII. When this lascivious prince had a mind to be lost in the embraces of his courtesans, the cant phrase among his courtiers was 'He is gone to Jericho.' Hence a place of concealment."

It is night when she returned to the apartment. She isn't exactly sure how long the darkness has overtaken the city, she only knows that the change was specific and that she has been gone for much more than the two hours Brianna had demanded. She rings the bell several times, finally with impatience and a long, hard thumb on the button, but no one comes to let her in. The hallway is oddly dark, she thinks, not bright as it had been when she left for her walk in the park. She looks furtively at the far end, hoping for an explanation and there it is, plain as the nose on her face. A large window, clearly facing west, graces the wall at the end of the corridor. It had been afternoon when she left so, naturally, there had been sunlight. That could account, she thinks, for this change in light, this change of mood.

She tries the bell again, then pounds on the door.

"Open up, someone. It's Freddy," she shouts, her mouth pressed up against the glass opening that allowed occupants to stare out into the hallway to check out visitors. She can hear sounds, she thinks, from inside the apartment, but still no one comes to let her in. "Max?" Nothing. No reaction. "Brianna? Please?" She waits, her ear pressed up against the metal door, but she cand hear nothing more from inside. "I must have been projecting sounds," she thinks. It is clear that they have gone out. Perhaps they had been hungry and gone to get some food, to a nearby restaurant. She thinks it odd they hadn't left her a note telling her where to meet them. Then she remembers how cold Brianna had been toward her. Perhaps no note makes sense. Still, she has Max's sister's passport and that should mean something to the woman. Why piss her off when she had the means of making Brianna's return to England impossible? That was Brianna, Freddy thinks. Impossible.

Unsure of how to proceed, Freddy decides to return to the lobby and check with the doorman, see if he has a message for her. She finds an elevator waiting for her, the one that had brought her up a few minutes earlier, and she punches the G-button and waits impatiently for the door to reopen and let her out. The doorman, the one who had simply bowed her in on her return, is still in the foyer. She approaches him, taps him on the shoulder and smiles as he turned to look at her.

"My friends seem to have gone out while I was away," Freddy says to him. "Did they leave any message for me, by any chance?"

"I'll check, Miss." She hands him her business card so he'll have her name in front of him while he checks. He is back quickly with a folded piece of paper in his hand. She takes it from him, gives him another smile, then turns away to read the note. It is from Max.

"You weren't back and we needed to eat, so we've gone around the corner to a little French Bistro called 'Croque Monsieur.' Come and meet us there. Max"

She thanks the doorman and sets out briskly but only gets a few feet before she turns around and approaches the building again.

"Excuse me, which way is the restaurant called Croque Monsieur?" she asks her new best friend at the door. He directs her and she sets off again.

It is, literally, around the corner and around the corner again. Like children, denied the opportunity to cross the street, she stays on the continuous sidewalk until she is there. It seems a gay place, people crowding the bar and filling the small tables inside and outside on the sidewalk. The lights are moderately low and there are candles everywhere. Music from a jukebox blares jazz. There seem to be bursts of laughter from all sides. She stands gazing in the window, trying to spot Max or his sister, but she can't see them. Finally, sure they must be in the rear of the place, she takes the two steps down and enters the bistro.

It is even more densely crowded than it had appeared to be from her place at the window. She edges her way through the crowded corridor between bar and tables keeping an eye out for the others. It takes her a few minutes to make her way to the rear of the restaurant, but there is no sign of either Max or Brianna, not at the bar, nor at a table or in a booth. A waitress comes briskly out of the kitchen, nearly colliding with Freddy where she stands.

"Ooops, sorry, Ma'amselle."

"Oh, not a problem." The waitress is already moving away from her. "Wait a minute, Miss. Miss."

The waitress stops and turns to look at her. "I'm looking for two friends who said they'd be here, but I don't see them. Do you have another room, a dining room?"

"Nah, this is it, Ma'amselle."

"Why do you keep calling me that?"

"We're a French joint."

"And there's no where else here they might be seated?"

"Nah. Like I told you, this is it." She turns away again and continues her trek to the table she is serving. Freddy stands where she is, unsure of her next course of action. Then she follows in the waitress' wake and heads past her for the door.

Outside, she checks the occupants of the street-side tables just to be sure she hadn't missed something. Max is definitely not there. Not knowing what else to do, Freddy heads back to the apartment building.

She has just reached the awning that stretches from the curb to the doorway when she hears her name being called. She stops and looks around, not seeing anyone she knows, when she hears her name again.

"Where are you?" she shouts.

"Down here, silly," she hears Max say. This time she lets her eyes drift lower, to the cars parked along the avenue. There, in a faded gray Chevy, sit Max and Brianna. "Get in," Max says. "We're going for a drive."

"I don't think so, Max. I'm tired. I just came from that French place and you weren't there."

"It was too crowded. We couldn't talk."

"Well, I'm really tired, Max. I. . ." she hesitates. She wants to tell him about Mikhael, but she doesn't want to talk about this in front of Max's sister.

"Get in," Brianna growls from the driver's seat. It is too much an order to be ignored and Freddy immediately opens the back door and drops down onto the seat. She pulls the door hard after her, slamming it. "Good. Now we can get out of here."

Brianna starts the car and deftly pulled it away from the curb and into the dynamic traffic on the avenue. They are headed north and Freddy could see that Max's sister drove like a race car driver, huddled over the wheel, both hands clenching the steering wheel, eyes glued to the road for any opportunity to speed forward, to advance to the next rung in the race for prominence.

"Where are we going?" Freddy asked.

"Somewhere not crowded," Max says. "We're starving. You must be also."

"I'm. . .all right. A bit squeamish, actually."

"You? I don't believe it."

"Something happened, Max."

"What? What happened? Where? When?"

"My brother the reporter, always asking too many pointed questions," Brianna ventures.

"I'll tell you later. When we're alone."

"Oh, don't mind me, children. You can talk."

"I don't like your tone, Brianna," Freddy says, instantly regretting it.

"With luck, my dear, it's the last night I'll be spending here with the two of you, so don't mind me. I'm just the chauffeur."

Max, his body turned in the front seat to look at Freddy, winks. The gesture pulls the corners of his mouth up into that sweet smile she so enjoys. She waves him back toward her and sits way back in her seat. Max turns to look at Brianna, and he cocks his head in Freddy's direction.

"Sure. Go ahead. I'll warn you if there's a quick stop." Brianna sounds cynical, but Freddy doesn't mind that suddenly.

Max pushes himself forward and up and compels his body over the back of the front seat. His head and his shoulders collide with the back seat, but his legs stay up in the air as he struggles to complete his move. Freddy reaches for them and pull them onto her lap, and this causes Max to slip off the back seat and onto the floor. The absurdity of this enterprise sends him, and Freddy, into gales of laughter, the first sound of laughter since they'd gotten the news about his parents' deaths.

He rights himself and finally winds up on the seat next to her. His hair is a mess and his tie is askew. She reaches out a hand to help make him presentable again, smoothing his hair back while he fiddles with his necktie.

"That's better," she says. They smile at one another briefly, the laughter behind them now.

"Thanks." He takes her hand. "Now, what happened?"

Quietly, in a voice too low for Brianna to easily share her words, she tells Max about her encounter with Mikhael. Brianna snaps on the radio, finding a station that plays loud rock music, completely drowning out Freddy's words from the front seat. Freddy initially reacts to this intrusion with anger, but that is quickly assuaged as she understands the other woman's motive: she is giving Freddy the privacy cover she needs.

When she finishes her short tale, Max puts his arm around her shoulders and pulls her close to his side. He whispers to her that things will be all right, that Mikhael is no threat. He says the things she needs a man to say and he says them without urging or cues. He is there for her in her need and she feels grateful. She nestles into his side, her head against his shoulder, looking more fragile and breakable than she ever has at any time in her life.

"What am I doing?" she thinks. "I'm supposed to be comforting him and he's comforting me."

When Brianna stops the car, suddenly, it jars Freddy out of her stagnant reverie.

"Find a place?" Max asks her trying to get through the music, but it drifts away as Brianna turns off the engine. "Find a place?" he asks again.

"Yeah. Looks decent. Let's try it."

Freddy takes a look and has the sudden realization that she has no idea where they might be. It is a park, but she can hear rushing traffic nearby. The cottage they are parked in front of has a neon sign flashing the word "OPEN" on its gambrel roof. There are fewer than half a dozen cars in the lot. The three of them get out of the car and approach the eatery. They are greeted at the door by a diminutive woman who finds them a quiet booth in the rear of the place and leaves to bring them a carafe of wine and a bottle of water.

"Very European," Freddy says. "Where are we?"

"On the Saw Mill Parkway," Brianna says. "I remembered this spot from years ago. Wasn't sure it would still be here, but it is."

"Well, it's perfect, Brie," Max adds.

With the wine in hand, they order dinner and in silence eat it. When

Max goes to the Men's Room, Freddy opens her bag and hands Brianna the passport she's been holding.

"Yeah, thanks," Brianna says.

"You've been a brick about me, really," Freddy says. "Sorry if I was a bit over the top."

"I get it. I do. And I'm leaving tomorrow, back to old Blighty. You'll have him all to yourself, Freddy."

"You don't mind...?"

"I mind a lot, but I'm willing to risk it. He seems to really love you. I don't get it, but maybe I will one day."

"Max is a special man, Brianna. You don't really know him."

"Well, I thought I did. Maybe I will sometime."

"I hope so." Max is back with them then.

"You hope so, what?" he asks Freddy.

"I hope we'll see lots of your sister when we get back to England."

"Back to England?" Max asks. "Who's going back'"

"Brianna is. And we are."

"Brianna is, sure. But why would we go back?"

"We have to go back. My work isn't complete and you. . ."

"I have no work."

"What about Drew, Max?" Brianna asks.

"I'll write to him, explain it all."

"That's not good enough," Brianna says.

"It's what I'm prepared to do. I don't want to go through another of those painful breakups. Paul was enough."

"You can't just walk out that way. We don't do things like that."

"Our family, you mean? Well, sis, we're the family now and we're changing our ways."

"Don't be flippant."

"I'm not. I'm serious. It's over for me. I'm going back to school. I'm going to make something of myself. Freddy is here for me and she'll help me through this."

"Freddy is an outsider, Max. She'll never understand us."

"Freddy gets me."

"Freddy isn't one of us." Brianna is angry and it shows.

"This is my decision, Brie, and I'm sticking with it."

"You're going to sit there and let him do this, aren't you?" Brianna demands of Freddy. "This is what you want? A limp-wristed mind that flits without responsibility from one open relationship to another?"

"Brianna, you don't understand him," Freddy says.

"Oh, no. Don't do that to me. I understand him. He just went from being my brother, my grandmother's favorite, to being a little, unfeeling whore. My blood is boiling now and nothing would make me happier than to never see him again."

"Brie, be sensible, "Max says "Calm down."

"Don't even think that you can talk to me unless you come to your senses and act like a responsible man."

"I've made my decision. It's my decision, all mine, no one else's."

"Well, in a week of disappointments, brother mine, you have provided me with the deepest and most hurtful one of all. Congratulations." She crossed her arms over her chest, pouts, then lets herself relax again. "The car leaves in two minutes. Be in it or find your own way back to the city." She stands up and heads out the door.

"Did she pay the bill?" Max asks Freddy.

"No."

"Well, we better do it and quick," he says waving to the waitress. "I know my sister and she means what she says."

CHAPTER FORTY-FOUR

From The Reader's Digest, April, 1946:

> From Ultimates: "At a dinner in St. Paul, Minn.,
> Mayor John McDonough limited the oratory of each
> speaker – all politicians – to the time he could, or
> would, hold 25 pounds of ice in his bare hands."

We were quiet all the back into the city. Freddy made a few attempts at small talk, but was met by the eerie silence of my sister and the disquieting quiet on my part. There was nothing left for any of us to say, really. I was getting out of what had been my uncomfortable existence and doing it while I still had a chance to undo what my father had done so long ago. It was, really, my own small memorial to the man who had sired me, a return to complacent normalcy.

Brianna drove like a demon, or someone possessed by one. She hunched over the wheel and stared intently at the road. I thought I saw her squinting a few times from my position in the shotgun seat. Once I turned and looked back at Freddy, alone in the rear and realized that she was watching Brie also. I think we were nervous, a bit frightened actually, that she might decide at a certain point to just drive, hell-bent-for-leather, into a tree or a utility pole and kill us both, maybe even herself.

Of course I knew she was happy with the life she led. I knew she adored the man in England with whom she had become connected. We had talked about him, and I'd met him at least a dozen times during the time I was living there with Drew. He was nice, if a bit common, rich if a bit overly stuffy about it. But she was content and he seemed pleased to have her company. She wasn't young anymore, but she looked terrific. At thirty-seven she was just at the edge, a little too much her father's child and not enough our mother's clone. But she handled it well, with good clothes and great hair and a wardrobe that killed. She would easily last in her work for another ten years barring anything that might accidentally age her.

"I'm sorry, Brie," I muttered, almost under my breath. "I just can't keep doing this."

She was silent, still staring hard at the road. My skin goosebumped as I felt her hand suddenly touch mine on the seat. I smiled a tiny smile. She was sending me a message that she didn't want to share with Freddy. I avoided looking back at her, for my sister's sake.

"Max, you're a man. You make your own decisions. You said so," Brianna said.

"Thanks."

"Don't thank me. Don't thank anyone. It's your choice."

"And if I marry?"

"Well, who's to say that's wrong, Max? After all our parents were married."

"That's true."

"And Daddy wasn't a part of all this when they were first together."

"True again."

"But he was happy, don't you think?" Her voice took on a sullen quality.

"I think so. I think he liked who he was, who we all were."

"He did. I think he did."

She went silent again after that as we approached the city lights glowing in the distance. Once we were on the west side of Manhattan, heading down Riverside Drive, she addressed Freddy for the first time.

"Can I drop you, please?" she said.

"I'll go back with you to the apartment, thanks."

"Can I drop you, please?" Brianna repeated.

"Fine," Freddy responded. "You can leave me at 53rd Street and Ninth."

"Why there?" I asked.

"I have to see a man about a dog," she said, sardonically. I didn't like the tone of it. "I'll call you in an hour, Max."

"I'll be home."

"I'll call." Brianna pulled the car up to the northwest corner of that intersection and braked to a sharp stop. Freddy bounced back against the seat. Then, without another word, she opened the door and left the vehicle. Brianna instantly gunned the engine and pulled away from the curb.

More than an hour passed and Freddy hadn't called me, so I tried her number but got nothing, not even the machine. Brianna had gone to bed, leaving me alone to wander through our parents' apartment, the home I'd called my own for so many years. There were things there I couldn't bear to touch just yet, things that had been so personal, so much a part of their lives. I went into the library and perused the book bindings on the shelves, seeking something unique, something I couldn't connect to either of them, or to my life as a youngster. It was hard, but I ultimately found a small collection of poems by Edna St. Vincent Millay. I hadn't read her in years and wasn't sure I'd want to now, but I opened the book and took a look at it and was actually surprised, not once but twice.

The first surprise was the fly-page, that blank page between the cover and the title page on the right hand side of the volume. It bore an inscription, a dedication almost, signed by the author herself and directed at my grandmother.

I hadn't really given Granny Elainie much thought lately. Her name had come up, of course, in my fight with Brianna, but that was all the time I'd spent dwelling on her. How I'd loved her. How she had adored me. The inscription brought her back to me without emotion and without even a sense of loss or absence. And yet, there was something nagging at me when read what Millay had written:

"To Lainie, who knows all there is to know and reveals so very little. With my heart, Edna St. Vincent Millay."

Underneath that inscription, but in the same hand, were these lines, obviously from a poem of hers, "She loves me all that she can, And her ways to my ways resign; But she was not made for any man, And she never will be all mine."

I didn't know the poem, but I thought the writing was beautiful and certainly would describe Elainie's relationship with any woman she knew. I wondered if there had been anything between them, if there had been an affair or a one-night stand or anything. I realized that now, with both mother and grandmother gone, there was no one I could ask. Even Tooie, her friend, might have had an answer, but Tooie was dead now also and I would never find the answer to my new and sudden question.

I opened the book, Second April, and looked for the quote, but this particular poem wasn't among the contents of this particular collection. I did find a poem that I stopped and read all the way through, one that touched me deeply. It was called "Dirge."

"Boys and girls that held her dear,
Do your weeping now;
All you loved of her lies here.

Brought to earth the arrogant brow,
And the withering tongue
Chastened; do your weeping now.

Sing whatever songs are sung,
Wind whatever wreath,
For a playmate perished young,
For a spirits spent in death.

Boys and girls that held her dear,
All you loved of her lies here."

I found myself, at the end of the poem, weeping softly, tears splashing on the page. I closed the book quickly, fearing I'd damage it, smudge the words, dull the sentiments. I put the book down and left the room, then went back and fetched it out again. I went down the long hallway toward my bedroom, carrying it with me and wondering if I should share it with Brianna. I felt a bit foolish that a piece of quiet poetry should get me into such a state, but I realized, instantly on thinking this, that I was in need of release, that nothing so far had given me the right to unleash the emotional burden that my parents' death had put me to. I knocked on Brianna's door.

I heard her moving inside the room, then I heard her voice.
"What?"
"I want to show you something."
"What is it?" Her voice through the door was muted and soft.
"A poem. I just found it. You should read it."
"A poem?" I could hear the disdain in her voice. "Really?"
"Brie, you should read it."

There was silence from the other side of the door. Then she opened it. It was instantly clear to me that she'd been weeping also.

"This may help you," I said, handing her the book. "It helped me."

"What am I looking at here?"

"The poem called 'Dirge', about halfway through."

"Okay. I'll read it. Thanks." She closed the door, keeping me out. I smiled to myself and went on into my room. There was still no call from Freddy. I picked up the phone on my desk and tried her number again, but there was still no answer.

I sat down, took off my shoes and socks, then my necktie. I was sitting on the edge of my old bed with its too soft mattress, wondering about the future. My parents had been tenants in this building for most of my life and I had grown up here. I wasn't going back to Drew, back to England. I was determined to stay in New York and pursue my aborted education, find a career that suited me and establish a real life. I thought about keeping this place. It was large, but I'd need large once I established myself and I thought I could rent out the other three bedrooms for an income while I was back at Columbia. That was a plan, the plan. That was the way to go.

There was a knock on the door and before I could say anything the door opened and Brianna walked in, the Millay book in her hand. She held it out to me. I reached up for it and gave her a nod. She nodded back at me and then turned and walked out of the room, closing the door behind her. I put the book on my night stand and took off my shirt and my pants, leaving me with just my shorts. I check my wristwatch and saw the time, Freddy was almost two hours late calling. I picked up the phone and dialed her number again but there was still no response - no machine, no Freddy. I was beginning to worry.

I picked up the book of poetry and thumbed through it reading poems at random, which is the only way I can read a collection of poems. I liked most of them, but a few seemed a bit arch and over the top to me. Several more affected me instantly and I cried, sometimes before I'd finished the words on the page. This book was certainly having a cathartic effect on me and my sister. It seemed more than ever that I had been fated to find this particular book, to read it and to find that relief in tears I needed.

I waited as long as I could for Freddy to call me, but when four hours were up, and she hadn't checked in with me and wasn't reachable, I redressed myself and set out to find her, find out what was going on with her. I couldn't make myself believe that she was letting Brianna have the final word about us and our friendship, our relationship. That just wasn't like Freddy. She was stronger than that. I knew it. So I set out to find her and determine our next course of action. It turned out to be as dreadful an experience as hearing of my parents' sudden death.

CHAPTER FORTY-FIVE

From The Reader's Digest, April, 1946

> From "Picturesque Speech and Patter: Definition:
> Civil Service: Something you get in restaurants
> between wars."

Where was I hiding when I was learning the new truths of my life? Why wasn't I in class, listening and taking notes? Brianna had gone back to England and I was alone in the apartment, a newly printed crop of schoolbooks on the table waiting to be sorted by color and size. A week had passed without a call from Freddy. Not a word, not a note. She had just stepped out of the rental car and disappeared into the streets of Manhattan. On the third day I went to the police to report her missing.

I'd been by her old apartment and found it occupied by a very nice woman who had heard from Freddy, briefly, when we first got back into the city for the funeral. Freddy had alerted her to the possibility of needing to crash in her own place for a short time, before returning overseas and the woman, her name was Muriel, had agreed to let her stay in the guest room. Her own sublease for the place was up in three months and I think she was angling for a renewal by being so nice. The only problem with her informal charity was that Freddy never collected on it. She had never shown up. That information, and my never having heard from her, is what prompted me to go to the authorities for help.

They took down the information I gave them, her description, her state of mind, her clothing as I remembered it. I told them her things were at my apartment, including her money and jewelry. I explained, partly, the fight she'd had with my sister. I even told them about Mikhael who, for all I knew, was still wanted by someone, somewhere. I had two recent photos of her which I gave them and then, with nothing else to give them, I took myself home to wait for some news.

Four more days went by with nothing reported. I called at the end of the week and was put on the phone with a Captain Jenkins, "Call me Steve" Jenkins.

"Call me Steve," he said.

"Okay, I will, Captain Jenkins. I will when you tell me you've found her."

"Well, finding's a difficult word. You see we could find her somewhere, okay but sullen and not willing to talk much. Or we could find her hurt and in trouble. We could even find her dead, damaged or just depressed and in hiding. . .from you. There's all sorts of findings."

"But you haven't found her, have you?" I asked him.

"No. No, we haven't as yet."

"Is there anything I should do? Anything I can do?"

"I don't think so," Steve said. "But if you do hear from her, or even think you've seen her, like across a street somewhere, you call us and let us pursue it. You don't do anything yourself, see."

"Okay. I understand that."

"Looking through this report I can't help but see you traveled together from London. Is that right?"

"Yes, it is."

"Do you think she'd have gone back there?"

"Well, if she did she would need her passport and her ticket, don't you think so Captain Jenkins. . .?

"Call me Steve."

"They're both here in my apartment along with her cash and her luggage.'

And that tells you...?"

"That she hasn't gone back to England. How could she?"

"I see what you're saying."

"Good."

"Unless she had another passport, of course."

"Steve, why would she have two passports?

"Well, I don't really know. It was just a thought."

"Yeah."

I hung up the phone after agreeing to be in touch with him if I heard anything and he agreed to do the same. I wasn't too sure he'd remember to do such a thing if he did, indeed, learn anything.

I opened one of my books. It was a literature survey text covering the twentieth century, so far, in American literature. The course had started the day before and I had another class to prep for so I thought it would help to read ahead and see what it was I was supposed to learn. It turned out to be poetry, again by Edna St. Vincent Millay, but I already felt I knew what I needed to know, so I closed the book again and decided to take a walk instead.

I changed my shoes, leaving the black and tan leather oxfords for a pair of slip-on tennis shoes. My feet seemed to like the informality now attached to them, for they stepped lighter and quicker to the door. When I opened it, planning to head out to Central Park, a note fell from the outer doorknob to the welcome mat. I was stunned by the sudden, unexpected action and I took a large step backward, leaving the door ajar and the note lying on the mat. Then, recovered, I moved forward and picked it up. I closed the door, then opened it again, took a step into the hallway to see if there was anyone there. The hall was empty.

The note had been folded over four times, making it small and sturdy. I slowly unfolded it, but each flap seemed to open more quickly. Finally I had the full, 8x10 piece of paper in my hands and I read the contents of the strange note.

"Max, Stop searching for her. She has made peace with me and we are married and she will soon be pregnant and we will soon be parents. Call off the search. Call the police and tell them she is fine now, married and happy and living with her husband in a place far enough from here to be safe for her. She wants me to tell you that she is happy, with her husband, and that she will always love you a little bit like she always did, but that she is happy, married and with the man she should be with. You know, Max, that this is the way it was always supposed to be, don't you? I was always the big love and you were always the little love. That is your position in her life, the little love, the late love, the love that goes only so far in her life when the big love, the true love, is hers. Tell the police to stop looking for her she is fine. She sends you her best wishes and her little love, Max. When we have the first baby, she will send you its picture. Thank you for caring for her for me while I was away and for taking care of her things too. I will come for them when I can. Mikhael."

At the bottom of the page, in a different handwriting that I could swear looked like Freddy's handwriting, but couldn't swear was hers, there was a P.S.

"I do love you, Max, but my place is here with Mikhael. Forgive me. Freddy"

There was something so terribly unreal about this letter and its post-script that I wasn't sure what to do about it. I thought I should call the police station again, talk to Steve Jenkins, read him the note, but something about it made me hesitate. Was it too soon, too close to this latest chat with him to call with this revelation? I would have to explain Mikhael and his strange history and I wasn't sure I could do that.

I folded the note back up and put it in my pocket, then I opened the door again, checked the hall for... I wasn't sure what, and headed out for my walk. Every few steps I checked my pocket to be certain the note was still there. Every few blocks I took it out and reread it, just to be sure I hadn't imagined it. There was something so unreal about it.

After an hour I found myself in front of the Police Station. I took a deep breath, checked my pocket again, then went inside. I asked to see Captain Jenkins and was told to take a seat on a bench near the door. I did as I was told. After all, this was a police station and I was who, and what, I was.

Five minutes later I looked up from the magazine I'd found on the bench to see a handsome, young man in a suit and tie approaching. I stood up instantly, knowing this had to be Steve Jenkins. He extended his arm, his hand open and flat, in my direction. I shook his hand and it seemed to linger a second too long.

"Come on in," he said and I recognized the voice instantly.

"I have something to show you," I said as we approached his desk.

"Sure, sure. Sit down."

I did so, taking the note out of my pants pocket as I did. I held it out to him and he took it, touching my fingers again as he removed the note from my hand.

"This was balanced on my apartment doorknob," I said.

"Quite a note," he remarked, not looking up at me. "Quite a note, indeed."

"It is."

"What do you think it means, Max?"

"I think it means she married him and she's fine."

"Do you? Do you really think that?"

"Yes."

"Then why did you come down here and bring in this note for me to see?" Steve asked.

"What do you mean?"

"Well, you could have called, told me you'd heard from her, that she got married and wasn't missing. Instead you brought me the note. Why?"

"I don't know. I suppose I thought you should see it. It's proof. Isn't it?"

"I don't know. Is it?"

"I don't know." I was getting dizzy from this rounded conversation.

"I don't think you do know. I think you're still suspicious. I think you don't believe a word of this note."

"You do?"

"I do."

"What do we do?"

"We don't do anything. I do something."

"What?"

"Well, what's this guy's next move, Max? He wants the luggage, the passport, the money that belongs to his wife, right?"

"Yes."

"So, when he comes to collect all that, someone should be there to greet him, don't you think so?"

"Well, I'll..."

"No. We'll be there, Max. We want proof that nothing bad has happened to your friend. We don't just buy into this story, do we?"

"I guess not."

"You guess right, Max."

"Okay."

Now I was confused. Either the story in the note was true or it wasn't and I was supposing it was, I thought, although now I was suspicious of my own beliefs and motives. Why hadn't I just called him? Why had I shown him the note?

"So, Max, we'll have to place an officer in your apartment to wait for this guy to show."

"Oh, I see."

"It won't be a hardship for you, will it?"

"No. I mean there's plenty of room, rooms."

"Good. We'll set it up and I'll call you when we're ready to proceed."

"Okay."

"We want to meet this guy, Max, and we want to see the girl, don't we? We want to know that she's really all right, not being held against her will."

"Oh, I see. Of course we do."

"That's the ticket." He stood up and held out his hand again. "I'll hold on to this note. It's evidence, you see."

"Yes, all right."

"You're a good man, Max." He shook my hand and flashed a dazzling smile in my direction. "A good man."

I would remember those words and the touch of that hand for a long time to come.

CHAPTER FORTY-SIX

From Brewer's Dictionary of Phrase and Fable:

"Hans von Rippach: a Monsieur Nong-tong-pas - someone asked for who does not exist..."

She hasn't walked far when it hits her, the concept of what she must do. She had seen it, felt it for herself, but she hadn't paid attention. Everything has screamed at her that this was wrong, that this was right, that one way led to Hell and the other to a plain where no one could touch her. She just has not paid attention. She has heeded her heart and not her guts, her loins but not her brains. She has to change it all, while there is still a chance of survival. It will be difficult, she thinks to herself, and she would have to do it oddly, with a twist that can't be undone.

Freddy wanders through the west side of Manhattan, the growing dampness only dimly settling into her clothing and her hair, with this argument raging in her head. Brianna has been right about her. Brianna had seen right through her. Max is a substitute for other things, other people. Max is not the man she should be with at all. Max is a friend, not a mate, a mate in the companionable sense and not a lover, a lover but not a husband. Brianna has been right all along.

She stops at a phone booth, enters the cubicle, its plexiglass structure so marred by weather and graffiti that she can't see through it, and deposits a dime in the slot. When the dial tone returns after the machinery gobbles up her coin, she dials Max's apartment, but on the first ring, she hangs up the receiver. She hasn't thought this through. She has nothing to say to him.

She had promised to phone in an hour and it was past that now. She had promised him. She made a promise. She had to keep a promise. That was her code. It was the way she had always been, had always worked in her life. You promised to do something and you did it. This is different, however. She has nothing to say to him that would make her choice any easier, any more reasonable. She has nothing to say.

She steps back out of the phone booth and feels the first drops of the gentle rain that she had felt gathering around her as she walked the streets. She looks up at the sky, a unique sky available only on the cross streets of Manhattan, perceived through the rising sides of uneven buildings, its darkness a backdrop to the wood, cement and glass of the city. There are no stars visible, no moon. Only the bunched clouds above moving and altering the picture as they do so can be seen. Rain falls on her uplifted face and it feels cool and it refreshes her temporarily.

"Funerals bring out the worst in us," she thinks aloud, "not the best. The worst."

"You said it sister," comes a voice from the stoop in front of which she has stopped for her mini-reverie.

"Sorry'" Freddy says, caught unawares.

"Funerals bring out the worst in us," comes the reply.

"Oh. Yes. Did I actually say that?"

"You sure did."

She looks at the man sitting on the top step. He is nondescript, one of those Manhattan men who lumber through days and linger through the nights. He has no feature on his face that impresses her. His hair is messy. He is wearing a tattered black raincoat.

"At least you're dressed for this weather," she says to him.

"Hans," he says. She doesn't know what he means by that.

"I'm sorry?"

"My name. Hans."

"Oh. You're German?"

"Native New Yorker. German mother, though."

"I'm a native too," Freddy tells him.

"I can tell," he says. "You sound like one."

"I don't think so."

"You do, Lady. What's your name?"

"Freddy," she says simply, then regrets telling him.

"Freddy? That's a boy's name."

"It's an abbreviation." She starts to move off, but he stops her with his next sentence.

"So who died? And why was it so important you talked about it to the curbstones?"

She halts turns and looks at him. "Why is it your concern? Why the interest?"

"You're a different kind of woman. I can see that."

"What does that mean?"

"You have some class. You have some cash. You have an interest in the death of people you're not related to."

"How could you know. . .?"

"You're not in mourning. You're only in confusion. I can read you, Lady. I can read you like poetry in the bathroom. Your feelings would bounce off the tile walls like so much shampoo spilled in the tub. You've got secrets, but you share them with the world. You interest me greatly."

"Well, you don't hold much interest for me," Freddy snaps at him.

"Sure I do. If I didn't you would have kept walking."

She stares at him with a petulant sneer on her lips.

"Oh, that's attractive, all right. And soooo scary too. What are you trying to do? Put a hex on me? You can't. The best have tried, but Hans doesn't receive ill will from the best of them. Why would he do it for you? Freddy?"

"Don't say my name."

"Don't say my name," he echoes her, imitating her. "You make me laugh but you make me cry. You don't know who you are, Lady with boy's name. You don't know who or what you are or what you want. You are pathetic."

"That's enough!" She can feel tears in her eyes and she determines to keep them there, not let them fall, not in front of this arrogant street bum. "I'm out of here, now."

"Go. What's keeping you? Truth too compelling to take a hike?"

"You're an idiot."

"No woman can call me an idiot until after the sex."

"There won't be any sex with you. You can bet good money on that."

"Say my name, then."

"Hans!" She throws it at him with all the arrogance she can muster.

"That said sex to me, Lady."

"You're a total idiot."

"I live here. Second floor. Apartment 23. Just ring the bell when you decide."

He gets up and turns and goes into the vestibule of the building. She is ready to walk away, but she stands and watches him as he moves. In the outer lobby, in front of the inner doors, he turns, unzips his fly and takes out his penis. It is large, thick and a pale pink. He waved it at her and she watches him do it. She wants to throw something at him, but she has nothing in her hand she is willing to part with. Instead she races up the seven steps to the landing, behind which he stands flaunting his member at her.

"You're a gross pig," she shouts at him.

"Yeah. I am. But you came up the stairs anyway, didn't you?"

"I just want to hit you hard," she shouts.

"So hit me, then."

"I. . . I. . ."

"You can't hit me, because you know I understand you and that scares you. You can't hit me because I'm everything you despise. You can't hit because you're coming upstairs with me and you're going to let me fuck your brains out."

He turns and pushes open the inner doors to the hallway of the brownstone. The doors swing back into place and she is alone in the vestibule. She is sweating. She can feel the moisture on her neck and her chest, knows it isn't the gentle rain. There is a slight sense of fear in her heart, fear that everything he has said to her is true, is right. She turns back toward the stoop and the short flight of stairs to the outer world. She takes the first step to her freedom, then reaches back and touches the doors behind her. They aren't locked. Without looking she pushes one of them and it gives, opening the way to that unsought for sanctum. Without turning her face to the inner hallway she steps backward and into it. Her fate is sealed.

Freddy spends four days in his bed, her tears at her own self-explored humiliations are nothing to the laughter engendered in his treatment of her, alternatively gentle and worshipful and at other times dominant and strange. He had tied her to the bed post and threatened to rape her, but not delivered on the threat. He has tormented her until she cried, then loosened her bonds, and held her gently for an hour, kissing her eyelids, her ears, her breasts. She has never known a lover like him and she hates him for that. He is everything that Max could never be with her, everything that Mikhael had attempted to be but hadn't succeeded in becoming.

The morning of the fifth day, she steps out of his bed and into the bathroom. She has eaten little, drunk a hair more. She looks at herself carefully in the tiny shaving mirror that swings out from the wall behind the claw-foot tub. She doesn't like the face that stares back at her. It is old, hideously old although she is only thirty-four, not old, not hideous. There are dark circles under her eyes and her cheeks are puffy. The minor laugh lines around her mouth have deepened into crevices. Her lips are cracked from too much kissing, blistered in one corner, chapped. She has not washed much in this week, not bathed at all. Her hair is disheveled and stringy. She is a mess.

Her dress is on a hanger on a hook. She takes hold of it and slips it over her naked body. It feels strange with no bra, no panties or slip or stockings to keep the suddenly unfamiliar cloth from touching her body. She smoothes it over her breasts and her hips. Then she returns to his one-room apartment.

"What's the dress for?" Hans asks her.

"I'm going now," she replies.

"Like hell you are," he saiys

"No. Really. I am." She steps into her shoes as she says this. "I'll leave you my under-things. I don't need them now."

"You're my whore, you bitch," Hans says simply, but his words sting her deeply as though he has hissed them in her ear as he has so many other things over the past two days and nights.

"No. I'm not. I'm myself again. I'm nobody's property."

"And you think that's enough for you?"

"It is enough for me. Thanks for asking." She picks up her purse and her hat. "I'm going and you can't stop me, Hans. You'll never know how much you gave me."

"I paid you nothing."

"I said gave, not paid." She smiles at him. "You'll never know."

He is sitting naked on the edge of his bed, looking at her. Suddenly the scowl that has seemed almost perpetual broke and he grins at her.

"Good for you, Freddy," he says. "And good for me. I'm Pygmalion."

"He hated all women, didn't he? Until he made one he could count on."

"You got me there. Educated bitch." He smiles again.

"I'm not your Galatea, Hans."

"Get the Hell out of my room. Shit, you didn't even pay for the bed for the four nights you occupied it."

"I think I did."

He smiles at her again. "Yeah, you did." The smile drifts away like smoke from an unpuffed cigarette. "Take care of yourself. Stop talking to the curbstones."

"That's over. Over." She waves at him and he nods to her. She leaves the room and, a bunch of new decisions in her head, she moves out of the life she had been leading, not for two days, but for at least two years. Mikhael and Max are now her past. Her future is uncertain, but it will be all her own.

CHAPTER FORTY-SEVEN

From the Reader's Digest, April, 1946:

> From Hollywood Round-Up: "A motion picture mogul recently bought a ranch and put up palatial stables, barns and chicken houses. 'And are the hens laying?' asked a friend.
>
> 'They are,' said the movie monarch, 'but, of course, in my position they don't have to.'"
>
> Kansas City Record

Mikhael hadn't come for Freddy's things. It had been more than a week since his note and still no sign of him, no sign of her. Steve Jenkins had sent a man over to the apartment and I had moved him into Brianna's room. He'd been there for five days when Captain Jenkins came by himself to check on things.

"Nothing yet," I told him. "But you know that already."

"Yes, we do," he said. I motioned to him to sit down, but he remained standing.

"I have a few additional questions for you, Max, may I call you Max?"

"Sure," I said and I knew what was coming next.

"Good. And, please, call me Steve."

I nodded, knowing I probably wouldn't.

"Go ahead," I said.

"Well, first of all, Max, and this is a big one. . .this Mikhael. . .this husband of hers. . ."

"I don't believe that. I think that's a lie. I almost shouted this.

"Well, let's call him the boyfriend, then, just to keep it kosher, okay? This guy Mikhael...have you seen him lately, anywhere?"

"No. Not for over a year."

"But you'd know him if you saw him again, I suppose."

"We were all kids together," I said softly, "and I'd know him anywhere."

"Good. I may have to ask you to come and take a look at someone... see if you can identify him."

"What does that mean?"

"We'll get to that."

I nodded again, not knowing why I did it.

"Your girlfriend, his girlfriend, whomever. . .still no word from her, I assume?"

"None."

"Any idea where she might have gotten to?"

"I thought she might have gone back to London, actually. Freddy's always been meticulous about finishing whatever she starts to do and her job wasn't completed when we came back to New York."

"Can you check on that yourself?" Steve asked me.

"I haven't done it. It's awkward. I left a. . .situation there and I don't want to reopen that door."

"I see." He took out a small notebook and wrote something down in it. I tried not to strain my neck hoping to catch the turn of his hand, a dotted 'i' or a crossed 't' or any other hint about his comment to himself.

Is there something else?" I asked him.

"Yeah. In a minute, Max." He kept writing. Then he stopped, let his right hand drop to his side while his left held that notebook close to his chest. "Here's the thing, Max," he said, "if she went back to London and you can find that out, you should. It would save the taxpayers a lot of money."

"I understand that," I said.

"Would you make the call, please."

"Well, what if I made the call, but you asked the questions," I suggested.

"I could do that. I would have to say where I was and how I got the number and the person at the other end might want to speak with you, though."

"I couldn't talk to him."

"And why is that?"

"I left in a hurry."

"Did he know the situation?"

I paused before answering. "Some of it," I said guardedly. "He knew my parents had died."

"He wasn't aware of your relationship with the woman."

I was cautious. I think I cast my eyes down for the second it took me to answer. "No."

"And she was his girlfriend at the time?"

"No." I think that sounded more quizical than the first 'no.' "She was working for him. She's an architectural designer."

"Okay. Then the problem is. . . ?"

"Let's just say, Steve, that my friendship with the man was souring."

"Souring." The word sounded odd in his voice.

"Yeah, souring. We weren't the friends we had been."

"Would you care to tell me something more concrete about this friendship, Max?"

"It's not germane," I said quickly.

"This is a police investigation, Max. There's no such thing as not germane."

"Let's make that phone call, Captain Jenkins. Let's do it right now." I was suddenly eager to do this, to have it out and finished, to let Drew know that I wasn't coming back there, ever.

I reached for the telephone and picked it up, removing the receiver and about to dial when the policeman at my side took the instrument from me and hung it back up.

"You don't have to do this, Max. It's done."

"Excuse me?"

"It's done. I already spoke to Mr. Drew Hatton in London. We found his name through the firm your friend works for here in New York. I was surprised when he asked me about you before answering my question about her."

"What did he say, exactly?"

"Oh, interested in him now, are you?" The cop smiled, almost smirked I thought. "Well, let's see. He asked if you were here and how you were.

I thought that was a nice touch. He asked me if you and 'Freddy' were a couple. That made me curious, too. Are you?"

"We have been," I answered cautiously. "But he wouldn't have known about that. We didn't share that with him."

"Why not? Sounds natural to me," he said.

"Yes. Of course it is. Very natural."

"And you've been friends since childhood."

"Yes. Did you ask Drew about her? Was she there? In London?"

He shook his head slowly. I didn't know which question he was answering.

"She's there?" I asked again, hoping for an affirmative answer.

"No. She didn't return to him either."

"What do you mean by that?"

"He wanted to know if you were all right, how you were holding up under the loss of your parents, if he should come over and be with you?"

"He was a good friend to me."

"Was he? Or was he something else?"

"He was a friend."

"Not something closer than a friend?"

"What are you getting at, Captain?" I knew I was sounding strained now. I couldn't help it.

"I have a file in my office, Max, about your parents, your sister, you."

"A file? I don't understand."

"People never get it. They think that as long as they keep clean and quiet that no one pays attention to them and their little dirty business."

"This is...." I got no further with my protest.

"The authorities aren't stupid, Max. So much more is noted than any citizen would ever believe. Your mother, did you know this, was arrested back in 1942. She might not even have told your father about it, but it's true. One of her - let's say clients - filed a complaint about her and she was picked up and taken in for questioning and she spent a night in jail. We had to let her go, it says in the file, because the complaint was dropped. But that opened a file. Do you know what that means in police parlance, Max, to open a file. It means that a person is no longer flying under the radar. It means that new information can be gathered from all sorts of sources and that the file grows and the information is kept."

"What do you know about us? About me?" I asked him.

"What I know is what I read, Max. That's all I know."

"What do you know about me?" I repeated.

"I know you're not like your parents. That's one thing I know. But I know something else about you. I know that we have different religions."

"Excuse me?" Now I was very confused.

"You believe one thing and I believe another, Max. I'm a moral man."

"So am I."

"Are you? Well, your morals and mine are very different, then. I believe that the body is a temple and is sacred and should be reserved for a single form of worship. I believe that to throw yourself at an ever-changing congregation is not a moral way to live."

"You're bizarre, Steve," I said to him.

"I'm bizarre," he said. "I'm normal."

"I'm normal, too," I responded. "I'm so normal it kills me sometimes."

"One man's ways are not anothers."

"Take your phony morality and get out of my apartment," I told him. "My parents were good people. They had a profession and, like it or not, they practiced it in an honorable fashion. They hurt no one. They abused no one. They took advantage of no one and they loved their children. That's the definition of normal, Steve. That's normal."

"Is it."

"My sister is a good woman. My grandmother was a good woman."

"The unmarried one, with the daughter who bore you?"

"My grandmother was a lady, goddammit, and you can't make her anything less than that, no matter how much you try, no matter how often you sneer at her."

"We come from different religions, Max."

"And what does this have to do with the case, anyway? Where's Freddy? Find her. That's your job."

"Max, I still need you down at the station. There's something there you need to see. Later."

He looked at me with a mixture of pity and anger showing on his face. "And if we do, I'll be back," he said. He tore out a piece of paper from his notebook and threw it down onto the floor infront of me. Then he turned and walked out of the room, out of the apartment. I left the paper on the floor for a long time, but when I finally picked it up and read it, it made me cry.

"What's a nice boy like him doing in a place like this?" the note began.

"What's wrong with this world? This picture? What the hell can I do to change it for him? Such a nice kid."

I crumpled the note up in my hand as I stood there, tears rolling down my cheeks. I didn't have an answer for him, and I didn't think he wanted one.

CHAPTER FORTY-EIGHT

From the Readers Digest, April, 1946:

> From Last Whim and Testament: "A Boston bachelor bequeathed his fortune to the three girls who turned down his offer of marriage, because: 'I owe them what peace and happiness I enjoyed.'"

contributed by Charles I. Burgess

Attending to official business in a police station in New York City can be very, very unnerving. At least that was how it made me feel when I got there and when I finally left there, an hour later. I asked at the desk for "Steve", calling him by his official title, "Captain Jenkins." The uniformed woman at the high desk took my name, then gave me an odd look, then told me to have a seat on a bench against the wall and someone would come to get me when everything was ready for me.

"You sound like you've been expecting me," I said to her, "but didn't believe I'd show up."

"You got that right," she replied, emphasizing the word "that."

"What do you mean?" I asked her.

"It's none of my business," she said, gesturing to the bench again. I nodded and went over to it and sat down. I was looking straight at her, hunched over her paperwork and her telephone. She was paying no attention to me, or to the others in this way-station space of wood and linoleum. I hadn't brought anything with me to read and there were no magazines such as you'd find in a doctor's waiting room. I had nothing to do but watch the people around me.

Sitting across the room, at an angle to me, was a woman who was clearly a prostitute, and not one that my family would approve of either. She was wearing net stockings and very high-heeled pumps, a short red leather skirt that, seated, barely kept the view between her legs shaded. She had on a halter-top that was too tight and too small to restrain her breasts and keep them from urging upward so that her nipples were straining against the turned hemline of the material. With a bare midriff, this halter seemed to say "one heavy breath and my tits are yours." Her hair was curly and long and more brass than bronze in color. She wore too much makeup and it was hard to determine her age, but I put it at about 25. She was chewing gum and, if I hadn't seen her type in movies, I wouldn't have believed that anyone could look so obvious and so trashy. She saw me staring at her and she winked at me. I looked away, but I couldn't help wondering if she had been pulled in here for something she'd done, or something that someone imagined she had done, or might do.

On the other side of my bench, where my eyes now strayed, there were two men, one in his late teens and the other, clearly his father, about 40. They were not looking at each other, not really noticing much of what was going on around them. They stared instead, the father at the floor and the son at the clock on the wall opposite us. As I watched them the son suddenly kicked his father in the shins, but the older man never responded. He just kept sitting and staring. I heard a cuckoo clock somewhere chant the hour in a low, moaning voice that seemed to say "coooo koooooo nuts! coooo koooooo nuts!"

I was aware that someone had come over and sat down next to me. I turned to look, hoping it wasn't the prostitute, and found myself staring into the eyes of my missing friend, Freddy. It took me a moment, a weird, short moment, to realize who it was, but when I did it took me even longer to react.

I wanted to instantly grab her, hold her, pull her close to me. I wanted to shout her name out, over and over. I wanted to cry and to laugh. I wanted to slap her silly. All I did was look at her. I think I may have smiled. She did not. Two policemen strolled past, neither one looking at me, at us, at me.

Freddy was playing cat's cradle by herself, changing the shape of the string lines almost without moving and I thought about asking her if she had taken up origami or if she was limiting her finger-art to Marie Antoinette games.

"Where were you?" I whispered to her, not quite the greeting I had anticipated.

"I needed time," Freddy said.

"But where were you?"

"I'll never tell you."

"Was it something so horrible, then?"

"Yes." Her face had not altered in this tiny chat. There was nothing in her mouth's slight turn-down, nothing in her darkening eyes that could tell me anything. Her fingers kept moving, the string turning into phenomenal shapes as I watched.

"I've been frantic," I told her.

"Brianna?" she asked.

"Back in England."

"That's good."

I nodded, but didn't really know why I nodded. Freddy had still not looked me in the eye, her concentration focused on the moving strings for there were now two cat's cradles in the works, simultaneously. I didn't know how this could be happening, but it was.

"Are you married?" I asked her, still whispering.

"What do you think?" she responded.

"It doesn't matter what I think. Are you married to him?"

"Who?"

"Who? Who do you think I mean?"

"I'm not sure anymore. I'm not so sure about many things."

"Mikhael. There. I've said his name. Are you his wife?"

"No. That's not possible."

"I beg your pardon? Not possible?"

"No."

"I don't understand."

"You will, Max," she said and she raised her eyes to look at me but, it seemed, she was looking straight through me, seeing behind me and not me.

"Max," came the voice of Captain "Steve." It cut through me like a lead pipe would if it connected with my guts. I sat looking at the officer at the desk for a moment. Then Captain Jenkins spoke again. "Come with me, please."

I stood up and went to him. He looked much the same as he had earlier in the day, except that here he seemed less friendly, less accusative, more professional.

"And Freddy?" I asked him, not completing the sentence.

"We still don't have a bead on her, I'm afraid."

"But she's...." I turned to where Freddy had been, but she wasn't there any longer. I quickly glanced around the room, but I didn't see her. I gulped, craned to see corners that were slightly darker, tried to spot Freddy in some other part of the waiting room, but she wasn't there. I couldn't have imagined her, I thought. I couldn't have had that conversation with the air, it had to have been with Freddy.

"She's what, Max? Have you heard from her?"

"I thought so.... I... I'm not sure," I said.

"Well, come with me. I have something to show you." He made a gesture in a direction away from the waiting room, and I moved off toward the door he had indicated.

He was right behind me. I could hear his heavy footfalls and smell his Lime cologne. I stopped at the closed door and waited. He reached around me, grabbed the knob and turned it. The door swung open inward and Steve said, "that's how we open doors here at the station. Go on in, please." I did and he followed me in.

It was a spartan space, with a long table and three chairs placed on two sides. Steve indicated the solo chair to me, so I moved to it and sat down. He took one of the others, and we sat there for a few silent minutes while he watched my face and I watched his.

"What did you think of her?" he asked me suddenly.

"Her? Who?"

"The whore. Out there in the waiting room." He smiled broadly. "What did you think of her?"

"You really want to know?"

"Yes."

"Is that why you brought me down here? To get my opinion of a street-walker?"

"No. I'm just curious."

I looked at him trying to understand him and his motives, but there was nothing in his face to even give me a hint of what he was hoping to hear from me.

"Well, I thought that if my grandmother was here she would have had harsh words for that woman. Granny Elainie was pretty outspoken and she didn't believe in the garish or the declassé. I thought if my mother were here she would ignore the woman entirely, not even acknowledge her presence. My mother, whether you believe it or not, was a woman of high principles and while she never did understand me, she would never have allowed me to consort with a woman who made her work such an obvious part of her appearance. For that matter she wouldn't have had much to do with the uniformed lady cop either. Same reasons. I wondered about her reasons for being here and if she would need some help or guidance."

"So you thought a lot of things."

"Yeah. I guess I did."

"You're a smart kid."

"First of all, Steve, I'm not a kid. Secondly, yes, I'm smart."

"Sorry for the first thing."

"I don't understand. Sorry for which first thing? Sorry I'm not a kid? Sorry you called me a kid?"

"Sorry." He didn't elucidate, and I found that fact to be more irritating than being called a kid by him, or by anyone any longer.

"Why am I here, Steve?"

"I want you to try to identify someone for us, Max."

"Well, that's pretty straightforward."

"Yup. I just wanted to prepare you for what you'll see."

"What? Five guys in a lineup and one of them a familiar face?"

"Oh, no. One guy on a marble slab, face-up, or what's left of it."

"What'"

"We think we have your friend Mikhael, Max. We think so, but we're not sure."

"Dead?"

"Oh, yes," Steve said, a frown seemingly holding his face in place, not allowing a smile to grow there in its place, "very dead."

"Where? How?"

"Later on that. I just wanted you to know, in advance, that you're not looking at a pretty picture here. We're hoping you can make the match, but it may not be possible."

"What happened to him? It sounds like his face won't be easy to recognize."

"A lot happens to people, Max, when they die. If they lay around too long, a natural process takes over and ... things happen."

"What happened to him?"

"Come on. Let's go downstairs to the morgue and see if you can recognize this guy."

"I'm not sure..." I started to say, but I caught myself, stood up and followed him out of this private room and back into the general melee of police business. As we passed through the room, I saw that the prostitute was gone. The two men were still sitting where I'd last seen them, and Freddy was nowhere to be found. "I had to have imagined her," I thought. "I wanted to find her so badly, I created her." I turned that over and over in my mind, but couldn't quite make myself believe it.

I followed Steve to an elevator that stood open and waiting. He punched a button and the doors closed and we started to descend. It took a while, although I found out later that we had only gone down two levels. Still, the ride seemed almost interminable. When the door finally reopened and we stepped out I was aware at once of the change in atmosphere. It was cooler here and damper as well. Lights were dimmer. Doors were unmarked except for numbers and Steve consulted a note he was carrying before he moved me toward a specific door, room numer 12. We entered and the atmosphere changed again, altered into something suspect and dangerous.

The room was basically empty except for a large marble table in the center and a wall with six large doors, about four feet square, in it. Each one had a latch and a place to insert a label. I could see that two of them had labels, one green and one pink. Steve pressed a button on the wall next to the door we had entered through and threw me an encouraging smile.

Neither of us spoke while we waited and it wasn't long before an attendant in a white coat, with an electric-colored ID badge came in and joined us. He greeted Steve by name, nodded to me and proceeded across the room where he opened the door with the pink marker label on it. With apparent ease he pulled out a dolly on which lay a body, covered by a sheet. The dolly, supported by heavy metal rods, reached the marble table and the attendant, whose name I never heard, or read, swiveled it around so that it was stretched the length of the high table. Then he shoved the rods back into the cupboard from which they had come and reclosed the door. Nodding to Steve and me one more time, he left the room without a sound.

Steve walked around to the other side of the slab-table that now supported the dead and covered body.

"Here's the way this works, Max," he said. "I'll leave the room and when you're ready, when you're comfortable with it, you pull back the sheet and take as long as you need to look at this man and see if you can identify him. When you're ready...when you're quite finished, you can cover him over again, or not - it's your choice - and just come on out into the hallway. I'll be there, waiting."

I didn't answer him. I just stared at him.

"I can't be here with you. It's not allowed."

Again I just stared at him.

"Are you okay?" he asked me.

"I didn't even have to do this for my parents, you know," I told him.

"Someone did."

"It wasn't me."

"Are you going to be okay?"

I nodded, although I wasn't too sure about that. Steve nodded back at me, walked around the table and pressed my shoulder with his hand as he went on by. I heard him behind me open and then shut the door. I was alone.

There was a light fixture over the table, just the way there often is with a pool table. It shed a fairly bright, though not very bright, light on the still figure of the dead man before me. Most of the rest of the room was shrouded in a dim glow. All concentration was on the body.

I put my hand on the cloth and realized I was trembling a bit. I could see it before I felt it, but my hand was definitely shaking. I steeled myself for whatever it was I was about to look upon and touched the cloth. It had a clammy sense to it, a little bit damp, a little bit cool. I gripped it with my thumb and first finger and slowly moved it downward, across the face and neck and upper chest of the dead man.

There was something very wrong with this man. His face was not immediately apparent. The skin had grown blotchy, discolered with grey and purple spots, almost like the pattern in military pants meant to disguise the wearer in a jungle. I couldn't find his eyes, but I could see the shape of the nose beneath them. His lips were purple and swollen and I couldn't be certain of much. There was no way I could identify this man from his face. No way at all.

The hairline looked like Mikhael's and the hair had gone colorless, a dull gray with flecks of brown. It could have been his hair, but it was messy and disheveled, a look I'd never seen on him. The brow, as discolored as the rest of his face, gave no clue. I felt like crying, but there was something so awful about this man's missing features that I didn't let go and express any grief. In fact, the longer I stood there, the less human this figure became, and certainly the more distant from my life.

I remembered something about Mikhael I had long forgotten, a scar he had on his belly from an accident with his stilts when he was young. I wondered about pulling the cloth down to expose that area of his body, but I was also reluctant. I had seen these identification scenes in movies and no one ever looked at anything other than the face. Still, the face here gave me nothing. There were no distinguishing features or marks that could help me. I decided to go for it. I pulled the cloth off the body in one quick stroke.

It was there. I couldn't have any more doubts about the identity of this man. The long scar across his abdomen, its crazy shape, zigging downward to his pubic hair and back up to his belly button was unmistakeable. And there was his penis, stiff now in death, but so very much his "princely member." I reached out my hand to touch it, but couldn't do it. Instead, still without a tear shed, I turned away and walked to the door. I was about to take the handle and pull it when I felt the urge, the need to see for myself once again that scar, that clear identifier of Mikhael's lifeless body. He had always been without a soul, I said to myself, but there was such life there, so much energy, so much life.

I could see the scar easily now and this time I traced it with my thumb, the light bump that it produced so very much the moon-scar I remembered so very well. I couldn't count the number of times I had carefully licked that scar from one end to the other, tracing its outline with my teeth in a gentle if odd caress. Without another thought I turned, held back the tears that frankly didn't want to fall, and walked out of the room. Steve was there, waiting, as he said he would be.

"Well?"

"It's him."

"You're absolutely sure?"

"Oh, yes. He has a scar on his belly that is unmistakable. I looked for it. It's there."

"You really did know him well."

Without pause I said "Very well. Intimately." I thought Steve flinched once when I said that, but I didn't care.

"We still need to find his wife."

"She's not his wife. I know that for certain."

"How would you know that?"

"I saw her today. She told me."

"You saw her? Where?"

"Here. In the station waiting room. Just before you came to get me."

"Why didn't you say something?"

"I just did. It was. . .odd." I smiled. "By the way, I didn't cover the body. . ."

"Someone else will, Max. About the woman. . .we need to question her."

"Why? She seemed all right. He's dead and can't hurt her anymore. It's over, Steve."

"And it ain't over till the field is plowed, Max. That friend of yours, her husband he claimed in that letter, was murdered. We need to talk to her."

I hadn't even asked about his death. I hadn't thought enough to ask and now I knew that there was something so very wrong about all this that I might even be caught up in the middle of his suspicions. I looked at him, heard the sounds of footsteps behind me and I fainted.

CHAPTER FORTY-NINE

From Brewer s The Dictionary of Phrase and Fable:

> "Loathly Lady: A lady so hideous that no one would
> marry her except Sir Gawain; and immediately after
> the marriage her ugliness, the effect of an enchantment,
> disappeared, and she became a model of beauty. Love
> beautifies."

Where did she go, what did she do? Those two thoughts plague Freddy for
days when she wakes up in the motel on the beach. For that matter where
was she? How had she gotten here? Why?

She sits up, half-dressed, in the badly battered chair by the window of
the small room and watches people at play outside, across the road on the
white sand with little shade. Her head aches severely this time. She can feel
it throb and when she places her hand over the worst of it she can actually
feel that throbbing with her hand. It is as though someone with a large
hammer is trying to batter a hole in her brow, from the inside out.

She sips from the glass of warm water that she'd found on the table.
She imagines it with ice in it, and holds the glass to her forehead hoping it
might ease the pain a bit, but it only makes things worse. She thinks about
ice, looks quickly for an ice bucket but doesn't find one.

If she leans closer to the window and looks down the road she can just
see the sign for this place, a motel on the beach in. . .somewhere. "O'Brien's
Boatel" it reads. A motel for boaters with boats that floated but didn't
sleep passengers. This was a harbor then, she thinks, and not just a beach.
Freddy lets her eyes roam the room again, seeking a phone, or a phone
book or even an ashtray with matches in it. There must be something to

help her memory, jog that sense back into action. There is no phone, no ashtray. "O'Brien's Boatel," she thinks and thinks she says aloud, but it has no resonance this time either.

"I've always been so put together," she thinks. "I've never been like this, ever, not ever." She shakes her head twice, but the pain is too great, so she stops. Pushing herself back up and out of the deeply dented chair, she staggers the three feet to the bed onto which she collapses and instantly falls asleep.

She dreams. She dreams of people whose faces and names don't match up. She thinks she dreams of Max, of Mikhael, of Brianna, but their names were all wrong, confused and distorted. She dreams of men whose faces call up no names but her own. She dreams of other beds, other rooms. She dreams of other things that make no sense, shapes and smells and sounds that bring no answers, no fully-developed concepts. The dreams are never bad, never frightening, but they are incomplete and inconclusive. There are indistinct voices, there are shapes. Once she thinks there is blood, but it becomes mud immediately. She dreams, and sleeps, until it is dark again and when she awakens it is night.

She is very dry, very thirsty. Her clothing is wet and sticky and smells bad. Her headache is gone and she remembers that she is at the O'Brien Boatel, on the beach, somewhere. It makes her smile to remember that much, but for the moment that is all she remembers. Slowly she pulls herself to the edge of the bed and makes herself sit up. Remarkably it feels good to be sitting upright. Her hands cling to the mattress as her feet struggle to settle, toes and heels, on the carpeted floor. There is an odd smell in the room, an odor of illness that hangs there in the air around her. She looks at the uncurtained window, wondering if it would open, if it would allow fresh air in, or stale air out. She decides it might and tries to stand up, to move to it. Her legs are weak, though, and won't instantly support her, so she sits back down on the edge of the bed, breathing hard through her open mouth.

It takes her a few minutes, but she manages, finally, to rise and go to the window where she cranks it open. A burst of clean sea air streams in through the opening and hits her in the face, and across her chest. It feels good and instantly refreshes her, but that new feeling lasts only a moment. Then she is only chilled by the air and that sense of reawakening is lost.

Freddy looks around her, takes in the entire space and finds the door to the bathroom. She staggers to it, enters into the darkness and finds the sink which she holds onto as she turns on the cold water tap. She can hear the water lapping about in the cold bowl. She dips her fingers into the water and slowly brings both hands up to her face, letting the cool water slip down over her skin. The sensation is divine. She feels renewed by the chill of it. As the water drips down her chin, falling onto her breasts, she reaches behind and unzips the skirt she i wearing, letting it fall to the floor around her bare feet. She steps out of it and kicksit aside. Then she proceeds to wash her face, dishing up water in her cupped hands until she can breathe easily again, until her eyes clear and her sight is restored and her head feels pleasant and reliable again. She turns off the tap and, without drying her hands, takes off the rest of her soiled and spoiled clothing.

When she is naked she moves over to the stall shower, turns it on and steps in. Fifteen minutes later she knows who, what, where and why. Then, and only then, does she permit herself to cry.

Her memory of the time with Hans was somewhat vague, veiled as it was with liquor and drugs. Her memory of meeting Mikhael in the park was equally dulled by the experience that followed it. What remained of both of those encounters was a less-than-vague sense that neither had ended satisfactorily. What comes clearer to her, instantly and irrevocably, is the experience that followed. It is that memory which now haunts her waking hours, leaves her so inexpressibly sad.

She feels the need to share her thoughts, but there is really no one in whom she can confide. She is in the O'Brien Boatel, without a car, in the small coastal town of Belfast, Maine. She clearly remembers the bus dropping her off a few blocks away and her walk to the beach at sunset. She has only one small bag with her, a knapsack of sorts, with a few changes of clothing inside, a toothbrush, which she has now used several times in a row as she tried to remove the awful taste of her own drying saliva from her mouth, and a hairbrush. Her wallet is missing along with its combination of cash, credit cards and photographs.

She recalls watching the sunset and the peace that brought to her at the time. She remembers crossing the road and checking into this place, but she remembers little of what happened afterward. She does recall the walk from Hans' apartment to the small apartment she had once shared with Mikhael, wondering if he had kept it, had a lease in his name. She mounted the front stoop and looked at the bells outside the massive wood and glass, both painted green, front door. There was his name, still over the bell to their apartment. She rang the bell, waited for a response, got none, and then, with resignation, she sat down on the top step of the stoop to wait for him. She didn't have too long to wait.

He came out of the green door in a hurry, nearly kicking her in the back, and almost falling over her. He cursed as he caught himself, righting himself, asserting balance over tumbling down the stairs.

"What do you....?" He stopped realizing it was Freddy. "What are you doing here?"

"Waiting for you. I rang the bell but you didn't answer."

"I wasn't expecting any one. You're a surprise, Fredericka."

"May I come up?"

"I am on my way out. To an appointment."

"May I come?"

"It would not interest you, I am afraid."

"How would you know? It's been years since you've seen me. I may have changed."

"You could not change, my darling. You are still this Fredericka I once loved."

"Only once, Mikhael?"

"Well, at least the first time, then, Fredericka."

"That's nice. That's honest at least."

"Was there something you needed?"

"From you, Mikhael, no. But, just a few things. . ."

"Then you must excuse me, please. I have places to go."

"I need my stuff, Mikhael. . ."

He moved around her and headed down the stairs. Freddy stood up and without undue haste followed him down the street. It took her two blocks to realize he was headed for Central Park again. That left her smiling. She was sure she knew where he would be if she lost sight of him. They had always met in a certain spot in the Ramble, a wooded enclave above the Central Park lake. Surely if he was headed in that direction she would find him there.

She turned back to the building, headed up the stairs and discovered that her old key still worked. She let herself into the building and headed upstairs where her key did its magic. She was in their old apartment. On a whim she opened a drawer where she had kept some of her clothing. It was all still there. She did the same with the cupboard they had purchased together and found outfits, no longer fashionable but still hers, hanging there. She noticed a knapsack slung over the back of a chair and she grabbed it, quickly stuffing a few things inside. With her minimal changes of clothing, a toothbrush and a comb, she slammed the door on this part of her life and went back outside.

She thought about Mikhael and knew that he was indeed headed in the very direction she had surmised. She decided to let him go and find him later. This way she would not be hurrying and he would have his tryst and she could surprise them, eliciting a bit of revenge for her mistreatment by him and his callous admission of his lack of love for her.

She thought she had come a long way emotionally twenty minutes later when she stumbled into their tiny glen in the rocks, sheltered by arbor vitae shrubs. She was proud of herself for making the emotional transition. The forgotten darkness of the glen had surprised her as she made the transition from late-day sunlight into eternal twilight. She swung her knapsack of possessions over one shoulder and stooped low to get between two of the bushes without scraping her face or disturbing her hair badly when her foot came up against an unfamiliar object. She pulled it back quickly - an obvious reaction to the unexpected, then slowly moved forward again. As the thick dark green branches parted in front of her and snapped together again behind her head, she saw him. Mikhael was lying on the rocks, not moving.

She gasped. She stood very still, holding her breath. The sharp intake of wind, held for an interminable interval, slowly seeped out of her leaving her deflated. She gasped again, this time unable to hold the breath and as she let it out, her knees crumbled and she fell forward, into the dead body of her almost husband, her former boyfriend, her life-long tormentor. He was lying on his back, looking up at the sky, his eyes wide and clearly horrified. His right hand was over his heart, his elbow crooked. His left hand, holding a long knife was thrown up high above his head, the wrist broken against a shark piece of granite that grew perpendicular to the rock below it. To Freddy's untrained eye it looked as though he had been thrown down abruptly by someone and that he had struck his head on the same hard-edged outcropping and died that way, possibly instantly.

All of this she remembers now in Maine. This entire sequence is now so clear that what happened next seems more like a dream to her.

There had been a sound from behind the bushes. Freddy had been tempted to call out, shout for help, but her knees and her hands were now covered in blood, Mikhael's blood. She struggled to her feet, but never made it to the full upright position of someone standing . Instead, arms came from behind her and held her tightly even as she fought against them. A third hand reached across her face, clamping itself across her mouth and her nose. It held a handkerchief, wet and smelly and in fewer seconds than she realized she had fallen into a stupor, her eyelids heavy and her senses dulled.

Two men turned her over and laid her down across Mikhael's rapidly cooling body. As she lay there she could feel the heat leaving him as his blood thinned and cooled. His body felt so completely unfamiliar to her, yet she knew it was his. Above her, in the vague blindness that the sun on her face now produced, she heard two voices, indistinct and indistinguishable.

"Who...she?" said the first one.

"Dunno...b....sh....in street," said the second. He was lying; she knew it then and she knows it now in memory.

"Foll....th....mug?"

"....thnk s..."

"Frisk....r."

"Yu.....d..t, Jah..."

Freddy felt hands on her hips, her thighs, her legs. Then the same hands, she was sure they were the same hands, on her arms, her armpits, her breasts. They lingered there longer than other places. Then she felt her hair being pulled away from her face.

"N...thi..." said the first man.

"Y...shu...?" asked the second.

"Absolutely," that word was so clear she could hardly believe it.

"O...k....liv... r."

"No. Too dangerous," another phrase that seemed complete somehow. And that voice, that voice she knew.

There were quiet mutterings, then a laugh, then nothing for a while. Finally she felt the two men lift her to her feet.

"Can you walk, honey?" the second voice asked her.

She responded with a sort of grunt, tried to move her legs and found that they would move, almost in a forward fashion.

"Good enough," said the first one. "Let's get her out of here."

Together, one on each side, they moved her forward and she obliged by moving her legs in a sort of rhythmic pattern that felt like walking. She heard one of the men whistle after a while, a sharp, single high-pitched sound followed by the clear scraping of automobile brakes. Then a door was opened and she was put inside the vehicle.

"She has a bus to catch," the first voice said. "Can you get her to Port Authority?"

"Sure thing, but who's paying?" asked a new voice, she presumed was the driver.

"Here. This should cover you with enough left over to get her to the bus."

"She got a ticket?"

"Yeah. The five-forty to Belfast, Maine. It's in her pocket. She may need help getting on board. It was quite a farewell party, you know."

"Yeah, Bub, I can see that."

There was a low murmuring she couldn't hear and then the driver spoke again.

"She's kind of hideous, dirty too."

"You should see her when she's not drinking. Kinda cute, actually," said number two, that voice again ripping through her semi-conscious state.

"Beautiful, more like," said number one.

There was a long silence. She had no memory of what came next, but she knew that someone was looking at her.

"This her luggage?" asked the driver voice.

"No. No, that's mine," said number two. "She's got her knapsack. You okay with this, fella?"

"Yeah, sure. Actually, I've seen worse in my time."

A car door slammed; she heard the engine rev and felt the forward motion of the cab as it sped off into traffic. Until she woke up in the O'Brien Boatel that was all she remembered. That was everything.

Only now she realizes, she remembers one other thing. She remembers what man number two looked like. She had seen him there, holding her things, frowning a bit, but looking right at her. There had been something oddly familiar about the conversation she had partially heard, something oddly familiar. Then, suddenly she knows what she had forgotten until this moment, realizes what she had known all along. She knows that face.

CHAPTER FIFTY

From Brewer's The Dictionary of Phrase and Fable:

"Happy as a clam at high tide: The clam is a bivalve mollusc, dug from its bed of sand only at low tide; at high tide it is quite safe from molestation.

Freddy picks up the telephone receiver half a dozen times before she places the call. She knows it won't be easy, but she has to make what she knows known to others. She also is aware that nobody is going to believe her, not after the past week or however long it has been since she left Max's parents apartment. She listens to the phone ringing four hundred miles away, echoing through the receiver in her hand, pressed against her ear. Part of her wants no one to answer; part of her hopes that Max will take the call.

After the sixth ring she hangs up the phone and sits staring at it, inert and silent, on the bedside table in the tiny cabin room at the Boatel. Finally, aware that she is doing nothing again and feeling, at last, that this is against her nature, she stands up and goes to the window. Pulling back the rough curtain she looks out into the sunny world beyond this dark, spare room. There are people out there. Boats and people. Men are working and somewhere there is singing, light and high but still a masculine voice. It is a song she doesn't know, in a language that sounds vaguely Spanish, slightly French. Her brain tells her it is Portuguese but she doesn't accept that as truth. Not immediately.

"What do I do?" she asks herself out loud. Her voice is raspy, and her throat aches when she speaks. She finds the glass again, downs some more water and tries to lightly gargle with it at the same time. It feels sweet against the strained muscles in her throat, against the too-dry membranes. She asks the question a second time and her voice sounds more natural, freer. The question, though, is still a strain all by itself.

She is still dressed in the rumpled clothes she'd had on when she followed Mikhael into the park, but she is barefoot. She looks around the room but sees no shoes. She lays down on the bed and leans over the edge, pulling up the spread to see if they might be tucked underneath somewhere. They are. She fishes them out, pulls them on her feet and stands up again. Her head is light and she feels dizzy. She needs food and she needs air and light and so many other things as well. One of them is the room key. That is easy. It is on top of the small television set. She pockets it and heads for the door.

Outside, Freddy finds herself confronted by a totally foreign world. The smell of salt-water fish is overwhelming and her stomach rumbles instantly as she inhales the clean smell of clams and lobsters. She realizes something else: she has no idea what time it is, or what day. She looks at her wrist automatically, but there is no watch there. That has been lost, or taken, somehow in all of this madness. Her eyes drift upward to the sky and she can see the sun just descending into the western sky and she knows it is afternoon. She searches the crowd for a newspaper, hoping to see a day or date, but no one here has one. That information will have to wait.

As she walks down the waterfront road, cobblestoned and old-fashioned, past two and three story brick buildings, warehouses mostly, it occurs to her that she could be somewhere no one would ever discover her. That here there is a level of safety and anonymity that she hadn't expected. That makes her smile. Hans could never find her here. Max would never need to know what had happened to her. Mikhael's killers might not even care to look for her here once they realize that she might know too much, have seen and heard too much. For the first time since Brianna attacked her, Freddy feels safe again, in charge again.

She stops at a small roadside stand and orders some fish and eggs which is served to her wrapped in newspaper. She attacks it hungrily, burying her nose in the cone as she devours the delectable local food. When she finishes it, she orders another and goes at it the same way. Then she asks for some coffee and when it is served, bitter with chicory, burning away the last angry, drug-induced phlegm in her throat she sighs with relief at the sensations of new life in her body.

The feeling is a double sense for she understands, almost immediately, that she is pregnant. The odd reality of this new knowledge is both painful and pleasurable. The thought of a child is wonderful, the understanding of its parentage was not. This would have to be either Max's or Hans' baby, the result possibly of that awful recent period of humiliation. She also knows she would never have to make anyone aware of this. She could go forward, never acknowledge the paternity, keep it her dark, devilish secret, and raise the child as hers and hers alone. That was a miracle. Marvelous.

Then the thought of that dream passes into a darker reality. She would be facing this alone. The word "facing" causes her to gasp as the face of the second man, the one who had kindly put her in the cab to the bus station, the man she recognized, came jumping into focus. She remembers her goal of reaching Max, finding the police, reporting Mikhael's death and the name of the man she recognized. She turns and heads back to the Boatel.

Back in her room, she picks up the phone again and places the call to New York City. This time she waits a long while, hoping that Max would answer. The phone rings a dozen times but there is no response. She hangs up again, slowly turns to look at her surroundings, and then she begins to pack the few things that had spilled out of her knapsack. She will find a bus, Freddy thinks, and she will head back home, take the risk, face the music.

The return trip is different from the journey northward. She is awake for most of it, watching the world alter as mile after mile she motors through the towns of coastal Maine, the shopping mall community in New Hampshire, the outskirts of Boston with its oil refineries and finally Boston itself, an amalgam of the old and the new brushing up against one another. Then the long haul on the highways through Rhode Island and Connecticut and finally, just at sunset, the spike spires of New York City rise into view. Knowing her goal is near she is suddenly weary and she falls asleep, not waking up until the driver announces the Port Authority Bus Terminal, the final stop in this daylong trip. Freddy gathers up her few belongings and moved into the aisle, even though the man's voice urges her to remain seated until the bus has come to a full stop at the terminal. This is a minimal risk she is willing to take, one that will prepare her for the worst moments to follow.

In the terminal, she finds a pay phone and once again dials Max's number. This time he answers.

"Max," she says quietly, "it's Freddy."

"My God, Freddy, where are you? We've been looking for you. Mikhael's. . ."

". . .dead, I know. I was there." Max is silent for a moment.

"The police are looking for you. They think you killed him."

"I didn't."

"I know that."

"How? Do you think it's impossible for me to kill that man?"

"Of course I do. Don't be an ass." He laughs and she doesn't like the sound of it. "Where are you?"

"Port Authority."

"Come over. Now. It's safe right now."

"You're sure?" She isn't so sure.

"I am. I promise."

"Are you alone, Max?" she asks him knowing exactly how he'll answer her.

"You know it."

"Do I? Fine. See ya." She hangs up the phone and heads out through the long passageway to Eighth Avenue.

When the bell rings, Max answers quickly.

"Get in here, you," he says, grabbing her arm and pulling her through the narrow slit of a doorway he has opened for her. When it is securely closed behind her, he puts his arms around her and holds her tight in his embrace, his fingers slowly, carefully massaging her back, his cheek pressed against her own. He is warm and he smells good - clean and perfume-free. "God, I was so worried, Freddy."

"I've been. . .places."

"I want to know. . ."

"No, you don't. Not really."

"I do."

"No, Max. Never."

He pulls her into the living room and carefully shoves her down onto the couch. Then he sits down in front of her at the midpoint in the large, overstuffed piece of furniture. He sits there staring at her, waiting for her to say something, so she does.

"You look good, Max. So good."

"I'm the same as I ever was," he replies.

"So very good."

"You know, I dreamt you, Freddy. I was in the police station and I dreamt you were there with me, telling me things."

"Bizarre, boy."

"Exactly. But it was so real. I wanted to know you were all right and so you were."

"Why were you in the police station?"

"Mikhael. They found him. They needed someone to identify him."

"How did he look?" Her curiosity scares her a bit.

"Horrible. Just horrible. But I knew it was him."

"I see." Her voice is so quiet even she can't hear it, a wisp if anything.

"And now you're back and you're all right, Freddy. I have to let them know. The police. They're looking for you all over the place."

"NO!" She stands up quickly, abruptly. "I have to go, if you do that I have to go right away."

"Why? You didn't kill him."

"I didn't. But I was there. I saw it, Max. Those men know me and I know one of them and I can't be a part of this. I have to go."

"It'll be okay, Freddy. You tell the cops what you know and then it's all right again."

"No. You don't get it. This isn't just Mikhael. Or me or you. It's very big and I can't be a part of it again."

"Again?"

"Yes." She nods three times, once slowly then twice very fast. "It's them."

"Who?"

She sits down again slowly, carefully. "I can't tell you. I can't tell anyone."

"Freddy, this is crazy. You have to. Otherwise they'll arrest you."

"Maybe that's the best thing for me, Max. They'll protect me, won't they?"

"I don't know."

"What should I do, Max?" There are tears in her eyes all of a sudden. "Tell me what I should do."

"I'm calling this cop I know, Freddy. He's been on this case since I reported you missing, long before Mikhael's letter and then his body showed up."

"Mikhael's letter?"

"Yeah. He wrote me. He said you were married to him and he'd get your things, but he never showed up." Max gives her a half smile. "Why did you marry him?"

"I didn't. I swear to you I didn't." She thinks about the baby she is carrying.

"Why would he write me then?"

"I don't know, Max. He was crazy."

"But you went to him when you left here."

"No, but I saw him. I saw him twice."

"When'"

"It's a long story, Max and I'm exhausted. Can I just sleep please? Can I?"

Max studies her for a moment. He can see the fatigue sweeping over her, see it plainly. There is something odd about it, he thinks, something different, but he has no idea what it is that has changed her so much.

"Sure. Come down to my room. Lie down and don't worry about anything. I won't betray you."

"Thank you, Max."

She lets him help her up off the sofa and then, her hands in his, he leads her down the corridor to his bedroom. Inside he makes her sit on the bed. Then he kneals down and takes off her shoes, swings her legs up onto the coverlet and pulls down two pillows to place them under her head. She sighs heavily, letting herself be pampered by him.

"You do that so well, Max. You could make a living helping people into bed, you know."

"Yeah," he responds, "it's a family trait, I guess."

She giggles, but it is almost too much of an effort for she is falling asleep as she responds to him. She feels him lean over her, feels his exhalation as he kisses her on the forehead, feels his hand brushing lightly over her hair. Then she is asleep, her breathing easy and regular.

Max closes the door from outside in the hallway. Then he goes swiftly into the kitchen, picks up the telephone receiver from the yellow wall phone unit and telephones "Call me Steve."

CHAPTER FIFTY-ONE

From the Reader's Digest, April, 1946:

From: Collected Letter of John Q. Public:

"Editors of Collier's received a letter from an aspiring contributor: 'I am enclosing another of my masterpieces which I have been sending you since 1930. You never paid me for any of them though I know you took ideas from all of them, even from the ones I never mailed to you. Please attend to this matter as soon as possible.'"

W.D. in Collier's Magazine

I never was so relieved in my life. Freddy was safe, even if she wasn't exactly sane. I sat in the living room for an hour, I think it was an hour but it might have been less. Steve knew she was in my apartment and he didn't seem to care all that much. There was no one else I could call or talk to about all this. So I sat, felt relieved and even napped, I think.

I think. I think I've been saying *that* all too often lately. I think, therefore I am. I am, therefore I think I am. I don't really think. I ramble. It's always been my problem, I realized recently, this tendency to rample on and on about anything, even about nothing, like now, when what I really want to do is focus. But focusing is hard for me now. I've tried to stay focused my whole life but really what I've been doing is running away from focusing, I think. There I go. I *think!* Therefore, I go.

My mind and I fought like this for a while and then the doorbell roused me from my tirade about my inability to do what needed to be done. I went to answer it, expecting Steve and found Steve.

"I knew it," I said.

"Knew what?" he said coming in and closing the apartment door behind him.

"I knew it was you." I shrugged. "I thought it was you and it was you. That's what I do."

"Are you drunk?" He sounded perturbed.

"If only."

"Then what? Stoned? High?"

"Me? Don't be ridiculous."

"What then?"

"Oh, I like the way you turned that around, that phrase. so clever."

"What the hell's going on here, Max?"

"Oh, don't mind me. I'm overtired, I think." I stamped my foot at that, angry that I'd let the old phrase out once again.

"Why don't you sit down, kid, and let me pour you some coffee?"

"You'd have to make some first," I told him. Then I added, "And you'd have to go back out and buy some. . .pre-first."

"All right, that's enough of that." He shoved me down onto the couch and I sprawled there, dopey, stupid. He plopped down next to me, too close to me I thought.

"Hey, move over, cop," I snarled, then I laughed.

"You sure seem drunk, Max. I know drunk when I see it, but you don't smell it."

"I'm not. That's all. I'm just exhausted." Without meaning to do it I leaned over and put my head on his shoulder. To my surprise he didn't lurch away or even move. Instead he patted my cranium with his open hand, gently.

"Yeah, you're tired, all right, old kiddo. Tired of it all."

"I am."

"You've had a hard time. Death all around you, a friend missing, no one to talk to except this old misery man."

"Misery man? Now you sound like a music cue for a blues number," I said.

"Yeah, I know. This is my softer side, Max. People don't get to see it much. I can't let it out."

"Why now, then?" I sat up straight and looked at him, a direct reaction to the awkwardness I'd been feeling in this conversatino.

"I don't know. I feel sorry for you. A kid like you."

"That again? I'm not a kid."

"You are, you know, in spite of your age. You're a kid. You need a daddy." He coughed once, then added, "and a mommy, too."

"My folks are gone, Steve. Everyone I've ever cared about is gone." I expected something to well up inside me, but there was nothing.

"What about your girlfriend?" he asked me. "You called me and said she was here."

"She's here. She's asleep in my room. She's gone, too. Not the same woman I've loved since I was a kid. I *WAS* a kid, you know."

"Yeah, I know." I decided to move a little bit away from him.

"I guess you need to talk to her."

"Yeah. I do."

"Should I wake her up'"

"Would you mind, Max?"

"Yes." I paused and looked at him looking at me. His eyes were shining with some sort of anticipation. "But I will. For you." I stood up and went quickly out of the room and down the hall to my room where I'd left Freddy asleep.

I opened the door slowly letting light pour in through the widening crack but I could see almost immediately that she wasn't there. I reached for the light switch, sure that once I'd illuminated the room there'd be no one there, no evidence of her presence there, that this would turn out to have been another illusion. I went to the bed, expecting nothing but found instead the impression her body had left on the sheet and her head on the pillow. She had been real, but she was gone again.

I looked around the room, looking for a hiding place, but even the closet in this room wouldn't accommodate a person, standing, crouching, there was no way. I tried to understand, thought about the bathroom next door and went there quickly, hoping to find her there, but the door was open and she wasn't inside. I called to Steve without thinking about it - no thinking just doing - and he came on the run.

"I can't find her. She was here and now she's gone."

He rushed into the room and saw what I had seen, saw her impression on the bed, saw it on the pillow. He came out into the hallway and instantly started to open doors and to give each room in the apartment a quick once-over. There was no sign of Freddy.

"What do you think happened here, Max?" he asked me.

"No thinking. No thinking." That word in all its forms just plagued me, ached and pained me. "I have no idea what happened and I can't think about it."

A thought had hit me and I was burying it hard and fast.

"What are you thinking?" he asked me as I pushed past him and went back into my room. This time I started to tear up the bed. Steve came in behind me and grabbed my arms and restrained me, but only for a moment. I think we both spotted it at the same time. The note under the pillow I had just moved.

He dropped my arms, reached around me and picked it up. It had my name on the outside of the single-fold. Slowly Steve handed me the note, then he equally slowly turned me around and easily seated me on the edge of my own bed, her last bed. Freddy's last bed.

"Can you read it, Max? Or would you like me to read it to you?"

I nodded, not understanding which question I was answering. Steve reached down and took the note from my hand and he opened it, read it silently to himself, then slowly nodded. I was crying even before he read the first sentence aloud, for I knew what that nod had to mean.

"Max, you don't need this. Me too. But here's what I know that you need to know. When I left here I met a man and went home with him and he treated me like a sex slave and he raped me and, Max, I liked it. When I left him - days later; I don't even know how much later, how many days and nights I lived with him and his cruelty - I saw Mikhael and followed him but it wasn't any good. I couldn't save him or myself. Two men killed him over drugs. One of them was the man I had just spent all that time with, my hideous love, my tormentor and, when I woke up in Maine, drugged and dazed and so confused about everything, I realized I might be pregnant by this awful man. I should have just ended things then, but I wanted to see you one more time.

I was going to go away, have this baby and forget everything bad that happened to me in my life, but I'm a stilt-walker, Max. I'm not a risk-taker. I only walk a few feet off the ground and only on large, thick, safe stilts. I don't fly planes or water ski in a fur coat. I don't take chances.

This baby is a chance that seems too risky. Look at his parents - a coward and rapist/killer. I can't hurt you any more than I already have. I'm not what you need. Maybe once I was or maybe could have been, but not now. You are too good for me and you always were. You should be doing great things and not suffering the stupidities of your former friends. I know you'll call that cop and he'll take me in for questioning and I'll tell him everything I know and that will kill me, or Hans will kill me. Someone will kill me, Max, and it might as well be me. You don't need this. I'm sorry. I love you. Freddy"

I was still sitting there on the edge of the bed that smelled slightly of the only woman I had ever wanted, ever loved. Steve put the note down next to me and walked as softly as he could to the window seat in my room. I realized the window was open when a gust of air rushed past me. I hadn't noticed that earlier. Some Sherlock Holmes, I thought. I heard Steve gasp. Then I heard nothing more for a while.

He came and sat down next to me and put his arm around my shoulder. His other hand he put over mine and pressed it gently.

"She's down there," he said. "She's lying face down and it looks like she's just sleeping." Down there was the third floor roof over the super market next door. The apartment was only on the eleventh floor so that meant she had fallen only eight stories.

"She could still be alive," I whispered. "It's only eight stories."

"She's dead, Max. I can see that from here."

"Get help!" I shouted. "Don't sit here with me, get help!"

Steve was up like a shot and out into the hallway. I heard him pick up the phone and make the call. I was relieved. At least I think I was. Yes, I was relieved. Some real pain in this world had been eased and now I was truly alone.

CHAPTER FIFTY-TWO

From The Reader's Digest, April, 1946:

> from In Humanity's Name! By Dr. Harlow Shapley
> Astronomer; director of Harvard College
> Observatory
>
> "To forget unpleasant realities, some people lose
> themselves in mystery stories, moving pictures, even
> comic strips. I have found myself using numbers in
> the same way. I turn with relief from headlines about
> starvation in Europe or riots in Palestine to familiar
> digits and symbols; they are impersonal things, that
> do not bleed."

Is time something you count or is it something apart from reality, something that happens on its own and makes little sense relative to your own daily life? I have no sense of how long it was between seeing Freddy's body on the roof down below and my waking up in the morning not screaming. It could have been the next day or the following week or a half a month or more. I just don't know. I paid no attention to the workings of the world. I saw no one, talked to no one. I don't think I went to her funeral - if I did I couldn't recall it. There were no newspapers piled up in a corner of the living room. There was no mail on the hall table. In the fridge there was no milk grown sour or leftovers with mold. It was as empty as my life. Time had ceased to exist for me and the philosophical questions about reality had no resonance.

What I knew was this: I had lost my parents, my lover, my friend and my enemy. I had lost them all together somehow. There was nothing but me and I didn't believe I existed any longer. I couldn't see myself in a mirror. I couldn't feel myself in my clothing. I couldn't find evidence of my being in the daily trod from room to room. I had ceased to be, to belong, to beware, to be anything. For the first time in my twenty-eight years - and somehow that number rang true to me, I had no reason to believe in myself.

It was 1974. Cher was divorcing Sonny. Patty Hearst had been kidnaped by the Symbionese Liberation Army. President Gerald Ford had granted a full, free and absolute pardon to former President Richard Nixon. I knew these things somehow. That was the sum total of my knowledge.

I couldn't look out my windows for fear of what I'd see. I couldn't answer my phone for fear of what I'd hear. I think I watched television: Merv Griffin's talk show and The Mary Tyler Moore Show and Carol Burnett. Nothing real, nothing with news of the day, just comedy and gossip, comedy and gossip. Those were the foods I lived on. I was in mourning like I had never been in mourning before. And I dreamt.

My dreams were the worst of it. They brought back the people I missed the most, even the ones I hated the most. Sometimes at the center of my dreams there would be a light shining, a dimmed bulb under a dark shade, but a light nevertheless and that gave me a false sense of hope. I remember that feeling of hope and of helplessness tied together in a bow around my throat. I wanted to untie the string and to toss it away, but my hands could never find the place where the loops met and the knot constricted. I would wake up coughing and gagging from the sensation and that dim light would be gone again and I would fall back on the damp pillows and lie there staring at the blankness of the ceiling and of the day ahead.

Time, how long, how often, with what frequency...I do not know. Once, in the dream, I reached the lamp and snatched away the shade and in place of a lightbulb I found my grandmother, Granny Elainie. She was sitting there, cross-legged like she sometimes sat when she was alive, her arms across her ample bosom and her hair just a little bit out of place. She smiled at me the she way she always had and made me feel like there was a life buried somewhere inside me. When I woke up that morning things felt a bit different, brighter, more hopeful. I wondered what day it was for the first time in a long time and got out of bed with both feet forward and lightness in my heart. Mourning, such as it was, was over.

It wasn't such a long interval after all, I discovered. A week. That was all. It had been one week since Freddy's funeral, attended by distant cousins, I learned, and a few old friends and colleagues, but no one who loved her. I hadn't been there and I was the only one left who had truly loved that woman. I tried to make myself believe that having loved her once upon a time was enough, but I knew that I was wrong. Freddy hadn't needed the extra burden of my adoration. She was carrying too much on her shoulders without that.

"Call Me Steve" attended. He came to see me and told me about it. He had hoped to find the mysterious *"Hans"* of Freddy's note there, but no one answering the vague description came to see her off. It made me believe that she was right to do what she did. I could comprehend her despair at the loneliness of the life she might have led. . .with or without that man.

I asked myself what Elainie would have done in my place. Would she have showed her face if her lover had leaped to his death from her bedroom window? I think she would have, and I felt ashamed when I thought that, not for her but for myself. I hadn't the courage that woman had possessed.

I thought about Tooie and knew without even asking the question that she would have been there, dressed in violet and spangles and sitting up front. Even Vinnie Compton would have put in an appearance, and it seems he had.

"Get dressed," he said to me when I opened the door. "We're going out."

"I don't go out anymore. I'm not in that business."

"You mind your speech, young fellow," he said to me harshly.

"Mr. Compton, I'm not going anywhere."

"Max, you can't hide in your room like a little boy. You have to face things."

"I've been doing nothing but facing things, thank you. I'm tired of it."

"Max, you've had a bad run of luck, that's all."

"A bad run of luck? Are you crazy? Look at the death toll mounting around me. I'm a disaster area."

"Your old lover died. He probably should have died years earlier - you kept him going. Your parents died - that was a freak accident - nothing to do with you, Max. Your old friend Mikky died, and rightfully as I understand it. He was despicable and he treated you badly. Freddy died - that's a tragedy all right - but what choices she made were her own, not yours. Face it Max. You're not responsible."

"I haven't a friend left in the world, Vinnie. Not one except you."

"I'm unreliable, Max. I'm married. I'm older than even your grandmother. Do you know how old I am?"

I shook my head. I really had no idea and he never looked much different to me than he had when I was a child.

"I was 29, Max, when I met Lainie. You figure it out. Do the numbers."

I tried not to use my fingers to tote up the figures, but I had to resort to at least two or three digits.

"You're 78'" I asked him.

"Seventy- seven, but not for much longer."

"I wouldn't have believed it."

He put his hand on my shoulder and I stood there waiting for the "pass" that never came. Instead he slowly pulled me into a gentle, fatherly embrace and patted the back of my head.

"I hope you've cried, Max. There's nothing wrong with a good cry. Most men do have them, even if they won't admit it. It's a healthy reaction to the bad things."

"I've cried."

"Good. Now put on some nice clothes and let's get some sunlight into you again."

I nodded and went back to my room to find something to wear.

We ended up in Schraffts. I had read that it was finally going to close and Vinnie thought I should have one more ice cream soda before that happened. As we sat there, him drinking tea and me indulging in more ice cream than I really needed, he told me about his afternoon there with my father waiting to meet the woman who would change his world forever. I hadn't known that story. No one had told me.

I told him about Lainie and me and our afternoons here. We both cried a bit, remembering our stories, hearing one another's. When we were done, had said our farewells to the old soda shoppe, we walked across the street to Central Park. We sat on a bench overlooking the small pond at the south end and we talked. We talked about so many things and so many people that at the end of the conversation, as we said goodbye, I felt lighter than I had in a long time.

"I won't be seeing you much more, Max," Vinnie Compton said as he shook my hand warmly.

"What do you mean?" I didn't like the sound of that at all.

"I'm pretty old, Max, and I've seen and done a lot. It's probably that I'm the next one you know who'll be off the map."

"I don't want to think about that," I said.

"Well, I need you to. My wife will be lost without me. At least I think she will. You won't be able to help her, but maybe I can help you both."

"I don't understand."

He took an envelope out of his inner coat pocket and handed it to me.

"You're not to read this unless you hear I've died, Max. Do you understand me'"

"What is it?"

"It's not my will. My lawyer has that. This is a letter I want you to read. It's personal and it's secret. I want you to know some things but not until you need to know them."

"I'm really confused here," I said.

"I know. I'm sorry. You have to promise me you won't read it now."

"What if I don't promise'"

"I'll take it back, Max."

"But I'll get it, somehow, when you've died."

"No. I'll take it back and destroy it. You'll never know what I wanted you to know."

I considered that for a moment, then looked him straight in the eye and put my free hand on his shoulder. Man-to-Man. A gesture of support.

"Whatever you say, Vinnie. I'll do it just like you said."

"Thank you, Max. God bless you."

He released the letter and watched me put it into my own inner jacket pocket. Then he pulled me to him and hugged me hard.

"I've loved you like the son, or grandson, I never had, Max. I know I slipped up once, but that was something else, something I can't really explain. You remind me of Lainie, I guess. You always did."

'You really loved her."

"She made me the man I am," he said, and he straightened up, his back stiffened and he looked even younger than he normally did.

"And I know she loved you. She told me."

There were tears in his eyes as he turned and walked away, down the street toward Sixth Avenue. I watched him for a moment, watched him strong and steady and young again. Then I turned toward Fifth Avenue and started to wend my way home.

The air was brittle suddenly and there was a chill in it. A peculiar dampness that only happens in a big city descended. I could feel it hit my brow, then my cheek, then my hands. Weather, season, whatever it was, it felt refreshing and it opened up my senses. I was hearing noises through the traffic, sounds of children playing, babies cooing in their cribs. I could smell bread baking and the yeasts made my eyes tear. Through the foggy dampness I could see lights in far-off Queens across the East River, more than a mile in the distance. I was experiencing everything at once and it wasn't overwhelming at all. It was liberating.

I started back to the apartment, but knew that wasn't my goal. I was heading off to discover me and who I might become. My history was all behind me. There were no markers set for me, no predetermined destinations. My mother had been wrong about that and so had Brianna. I was young enough to voyage out, discover the new lands within me and explore the world that had been left for me to find.

Small ironies that had always informed my life, oddities that bore no resemblance to logic, were in place around me. I unfurled myself like a tightly wound flag and waved at the future.

✴

EPILOGUE

From The Reader's Digest, April, 1946:

From: Collected Letters of John Q. Public:

"In Hastings, Nebr. the Chamber of Commerce got a
simple, heartwarming request: 'Please send me all the
information you can. Thank you.'"

- Time Magazine

In the spring of the year that followed I went back to school. I was the
oldest one in the place, other than most of the teachers, and I didn't care.
The open pathways across the common areas at Columbia, buildings in the
distance, gave me a thrill every day. I felt at home there, where I had started
twice before to learn life, to earn a place in the future. It was comforting to
find the familiar among the new and the strange. My studies started out to
be general interest, character building things but in short order I discovered
an aptitude for the law. Here was something that had never occurred to me
before, that I might find a place among the adjudicators of my world. There
was a bit of irony in that decision and that decided me once and for all. I
turned my attention to the study of all things legal and not so legal.

One aspect that fascinated me about the law was the inequity of the
process as it affected "working girls." You know, by now, what I mean I
hope. The early acceptance of those engaging in the 'oldest profession'
followed by the wholesale denigration of them as a class had sadly affected
their position in modern-day America. I spent the summer in Europe
where I toured the red-light districts of Amsterdam, Berlin, Prague and

Rome. I went to Paris for a week and met with two women there who had tried to form a guild, an association of prostitutes, but who had come up against a rigid set of restrictions imposed by the current government that prevented them from organizing. I returned to New York without a stop in London. I didn't want to see Drew.

What I had seen and heard and learned on this trip excited me. There was a chance, I thought, to create a new wave of respect for the women, and men, who worked in this way. There was a way to clean-up this profession that had created me and kept my family going. I would endeavor to find it.

Late in September I got word that Vinnie Compton had died. I had almost forgotten that letter he'd entrusted to me the year before at Schraffts. I had been too busy to take notice of it on the mantle in the living room of the apartment. When I placed it there it had been the best place, I thought. I'd be aware of it, have it at hand when I needed it. I'd pretty much forgotten it, half hidden behind the mantle clock and a photo of Freddy and me when we were young.

I fished it out, dust-covered and oddly discolored on one end, on the day of his funeral and pocketed it before I headed out to the funeral parlor. There were lots of people there, young men and boys I'd never seen and, naturally, my imagination dragged me in one direction when the truth lay in another. These were the boys he had worked with, worked for and helped to make a better life for through the St. Jason's home. This was what he had spent himself on, exhausted himself doing. I knew that, on the one hand, but had never really examined it with the other. This was a tribute, this collection of men who all seemed to have their futures firmly in their hands. A flush of pride informed this truth and I was glad that I had come.

His wife Susanne, whom I had never really gotten to know, delivered a simple, soft-spoken eulogy about Vinnie's belief in the people he knew being greater than his belief in himself. There was a disconnect there that felt wrong to me. I wondered how well she really knew him. But then she said something, just at the end of her speech, that changed that perception for me.

"It wasn't that he didn't love all of you," she said, "but that he loved you all too much. His first love, Lainie, and his first wife, Tooie, understood more about him than I ever did when he was alive. They understood his morality and his firm assurance that love could not conquer everything. What his love could conquer for them, for him and for me - and maybe for you as well - was misunderstanding. Vinnie could come to believe in the people he cared about no matter what they believed. He could quietly support, through his love and his willingness to be there when needed, every ideal that was cherished by the people he cared about. He certainly did that for me. Maybe he did that for you as well. If he did, then you'll miss him more in a few months or a few years than you do right now. I know I will."

She sat back down and I waited to see if anyone else would speak. A young man about twenty years old, got up and went to the podium. He cleared his throat a few times, seemed about to cry, then he gripped the lectern with both hands, gripped it so hard you could see the veins in those hands begin to emerge. He nodded to Susanne and then he started to talk about Vinnie in much the same way.

I reached into my pocket and took out Vinnie Compton's letter to me. I quietly, or as quietly as I could, opened the flap and took out the crisply folded piece of paper and read it to myself. I don't make quick decisions, as you know, but this one was instantaneous. When the boy finished I stood up and walked forward, hoping that I wasn't usurping some order of business, but when I reached the front and turned around I saw that I was the only one making this move. I stood behind the podium and smiled at everyone before I spoke.

"Pardon my smile, please," I started, "but I've known Vinnie most of my life and I know that he would be smiling to see so many of you here." There was a titter in the crowd. "Susanne, we've never been very close and that may have been due to my many absences, or to my long-standing devotion to Tooie and to my grandmother. Thank you for your kind words about them."

She smiled up at me and nodded twice. I don't know why, but I stepped out from behind the lectern, moved down the two steps off the platform and went to her. I kneeled down and took her hands in mine and kissed them. She began to cry softly and I quickly returned to the speaker's spot I had just abandoned.

"I'm not good at this," I said next, "but Vinnie would have wanted me to say something and he actually provided me with the script." I held up his letter. "He handed me this about a year ago when he was helping me to get over the immense losses of my parents and my best friends, all of whom died within weeks of one another. I wasn't sure..." I choked back a sob. "I wasn't sure I could live on after all of that, but Vinnie took me in hand, perhaps he's done the same for some of you, I don't know, but he took me in hand and set me on a different road. He showed me the value of not mourning, but of regaling. He taught me the value of an ice cream soda. He taught me that the past is never so far away from us, so to mourn it is only to bury it. He taught me to move forward, not away but forward. He was a special man.

"He handed me this letter which I wasn't to read until he was gone. I just read it, here, a few moments ago and although it is personal and private it seemed to me that to not share it with everyone he card about would be a mistake. May I read it to you?"

There was silence throughout the room. No one moved, no one spoke and I was about to say something else, apologize for my effrontery, sit down and hang my head when a voice piped up from somewhere in the parlor.

"Please read it. This silence is killing me."

I looked around for the source of the voice.

"Who said that?" I asked. " Would you stand up please."

A two-beat pause. No one moved. Then a man, I'd say of twenty-three or four, sitting toward the back of the room slowly, almost reluctantly, stood up. He was holding a hat in one hand, much the way Vinnie used to do when he'd come to visit us. He was wearing a suit that was just a size or two too large, also like Vinnie often would wear. He was tall, taller than me at any rate, and he had light brown hair that was so straight it hung down on both sides of his head and framed his long, sensible face.

"Would you join me up here, please," I asked him. He shook his head. "Please. For Vinnie." He hesitated, then moved out of his row of seats and walked up to where I was standing. I shook his hand and his grip was firm and pleasant, a bit warm but not moist.

"What's your name'" I asked him.

"Freddy," he said. I almost choked, but I restrained myself.

"Well, Freddy," I said, "this letter is for you."

He smiled at me, half turned to the audience, smiled again and blushed. I turned to face him, knowing that my voice would carry well in this space and I read Vinnie Compton's letter looking at a new. . .another Freddy.

"Dear Max, " it began, I added, "Dear Freddy,"

"I won't have many more opportunities to explain life to you or to anyone else for that matter. So, I thought I'd put down these thoughts and let you read them when you no longer had any recourse with me. I learned what love was, and what it could do, when I was younger than you.

I learned that lesson from two extraordinary women - you knew them both and that's a blessing. Let me tell you what they never told me, but showed me. With any luck I've shown some of it to you, but now I'm telling you.

"Being dead, by the way, I cannot help you or Susanne in any other way than this. Share my thoughts with her, won't you'"

I looked over at Susanne who was sitting upright and smiling at me. I knew she was hearing his voice as I read his words and she felt their honesty and their warmth.

"Max, love is not what you give to someone else. That is devotion. Love is what you get from someone else, not as a gift, not as a duty or responsibility. It is something that emanates from the soul. Your soul emanates this force in many directions and so does the soul of anyone else who cares about you. You cannot give away something over which you have no control. All you can do is accept it when it comes your way and know that others are accepting what you are allowing to come from you.

"This may be hard to understand, Max. I know that. It took me a long time to understand it myself. Ironically, my dear boy, understanding it cannot change it. It cannot stop it. It cannot generate it. It can only help you to find ways in which to engage it. I found it in the St. Jason's Home; I found it in Susanne. I always sensed it with you. You will find your way to utilize this gift from God, my boy. You will bring joy to more people than you will sorrow. I think it is rare in this world for the soul's pure love to be exploited for the worst in our natures rather than the good. That was something I learned from Lainie, from your grandmother. If I had known this, or even sensed it when I was younger, my life might have taken a different path, but the path I've been on for so long is not one I have ever regretted. I had the grand good luck to always have Lainie and her children and their children in my life. If that wasn't evidence of the soul's giving nature, than I am a dunderhead.

"I've witnessed for years the greatness of those rays of hope and love that come from within you. You have valiantly fought to subdue them, without even knowing what they were, and you have failed and that failure is the greatest success in the world today. You radiate this soulful power, my dear. You need to know that what you share with me, with all of us really, is this potency for support. Learn to accept it and live with it and you'll go far, find love for yourself and respect and support. I have. You will.

"I wish I had something to leave to you and to Susanne. I have never

347

been wealthy, though I have been what I consider successful. What I can leave to you both, and to anyone else you wish to share this with, is the simplicity of living with the knowledge that you are good. Inside you are good. If I was able to do anything in this world it was to give the boys I helped that belief in themselves. They are good."

I turned away from young Freddy and looked at the assembled friends of Vinnie Compton.

"I'm going to read you that part again," I said. "Inside you are good. If I was able to do anything in this world it was to give the boys I helped that belief in themselves. They are good."

I turned back to Freddy and moved a step in his direction to embrace him. He looked right back at me, never moving, never flinching and he accepted my arms around him and my kiss on his cheek. Then I released him and finished Vinnie's letter.

"There is a world of splendor, Max, that we can only see if we allow ourselves to see it. Find work that enthralls you. Find a partner who engages you in every way, mind, heart, loins. Find the world as it is and leave it a better place. That is what I hope I have done and will do for whatever time I have left to me.

"There are small ironies out there that sometimes make no sense, Max. You start off in one direction but the lane you wander takes a sudden and unexpected turn and you end up somewhere new, or somewhere you've already been and it can be confusing, but if you maintain an open mind you soon realize that you are where you need to be, where you should be. Not a detour, Max, but a road that shifts your world. The irony in this is coming to grips with it instantly. You think you can't, but you can and you must. And at every turn you'll find me, your parents, Lainie, Freddy, even Mikhael. . ."

I turned to the group and explained quickly that this part only dealt with me and my history, then I continued.

". . .everyone you ever knew waiting for you. Those shafts of light never leave you. They are your resources. They are what the simple mind calls love. Never forget to let their love shine through you as well."

I took Freddy's hand and pulled him close to me at the podium.

"That's his letter to me, his legacy to us," I said. "I wish I'd spent more time with him, gotten to really know him when that was possible, but he still gave me more of himself than I probably deserved when I was a kid. For now, there's nothing else for me to say. Thank you for letting me read his words to you all."

I squeezed young Freddy's hand and let him go.

"There's only one more thing I want to say, Vinnie." I was beginning to smile uncontrollably and I didn't even try to wipe it off my face. I turned from his coffin to face the congregation. "Knowing this man changed my life in more ways than you might believe. If that is true for all of you, and I must suppose it is or you wouldn't all be here right now, then we need to go out of this room and take on the world as we see fit. We need to hearken to his words about love and find someone to give love to, not selfishly but because we must."

I went my way to my seat and he went the opposite way to his own.

Two days later, while working at my desk in the living room, creating a paper that would outline the first American Union for Working-Girls and Boys, with legal protections and health-care rights, my doorbell rang. It was an oddly persistent ring, three long pulses followed by a pause and then two more. I wasn't expecting anyone, but I shoved my feet back into my shoes which were under the desk, and I headed out to answer the door.

As I put my hand on the doorknob I simply knew who would be on the other side. My second Freddy. Somehow, in my soul, I just knew it.

END

About the Author

J. Peter Bergman is a New York City native, educated in city schools and colleges. For a decade he worked for the Rodgers and Hammerstein Archives of Recorded Sound at the Performing Arts Research Center, New York Public Library at Lincoln Center. His first book, The Films of Jeanette MacDonald and Nelson Eddy, written in collaboration with Eleanor Knowles Dugan and John Cocchi was published during that time. He also served on a Congressional Commission to create a White House Record Library, produced a series of Ethnic Arts Festivals at Lincoln Center and hosted an eight year series of lectures on theater and music at Lincoln Center.

His book of short fiction, Counterpoints, was published in 1999 and won a 2002 award from the Friends of Charles Dickens. A chapbook of poetry was published in 2001. A graduate of Queens College with additional studies at NYU, Juilliard School of Music, and The New School, he has worked as a journalist for CBS Newsfeed, the television news syndicate of CBS-TV, for a variety of newspapers and magazines including Encore, Playbill, New York Times, Gay News-London, Edge, The Advocate, The Chatham Courier, The Independent, and The Berkshire Eagle among others.

Currently the Executive Director of The Edna St. Vincent Millay Society at Steepletop in Austerlitz, NY, he has been a free-lance writer and publicist in the arts for the Herman Melville museum Arrowhead, for Sheeptacular Pittsfield (he was, unofficially, the "flock flack"), for Art of the Game (Baseball Art public art project in Berkshire County, MA), and for many individuals in the dance and music world. A former cruise ship booking agent, he also operated his own music management company, Berkshire Concert Artists, after an apprenticeship with Thea Dispeker in New York. He has worked as an actor, director, and playwright in New York, California and the Berkshires. This is his first published novel.